Wet Wings

Wet Wings

The Wrath of Real Love

Joseph B.T. Mosata

PARTRIDGE

To order additional copies of this book, contact
Toll Free 0800 990 914 (South Africa)
+44 20 3014 3997 (outside South Africa)
orders.africa@partridgepublishing.com

www.partridgepublishing.com/africa

Contents

I often wondered what I could've done to align our

stars perfectly on a beautiful night, Terrence.

There I was, bruiting around with an open, bleeding

wound of which no one else could see except for you.

Through my depressive state of emergency consisting of long thoughts,

I wandered through my dreams in search of faulty glitches I'd

implanted into my soul, of the passion we could have had and

The false projections I'd painted onto my heart of

Our love stitched from threads of peace and harmony.

I discovered how special I was for having a patient

heart and repeatedly trying to reach out,

Calling out your name from the top of a steep hill,

Waking up in the middle of the night alone,

Yelling out for your attention, and at the end of my rippling

echoes washing over my ears and over my soul,

I realised how lonely I'd become, and through that loneliness,

this novel was born and, with it, came peace and harmony,

I finally understood the wrath of real love.

I was able to liberate myself from the darkest hour

eclipsing into my existence, to grow, to understand what

true love meant and what I needed from it . . .

Chapter One

Thought Rails

On this specific day, everything appeared differently indeed. The cool air worming through a small slit-opened window made it almost impossible to breathe whilst Quinton stumbled over one of his opened luggage bags. He squinted through his reality right as bright rays of morning sunlight glazed through the maroon curtains, appearing brighter than usual. It left him completely baffled as he attempted to recover from a hangover. Everything around him looked awfully pale and confusing, leading his mind into oblivion right as he opened his heavy, baggy eyes widely again. The day was indifferent from any other, but something was different within him and it was presently in his brown eyes, but he couldn't quite see the pain plastered over his brut face, even after looking at a lengthy wall mirror beside his double-sided bed. It was slightly cold despite the fact that it was a midseason summer morning.

The wood pigeons and house sparrows he loved so much weren't there to chirp by his wooden window frame as they usually did every morning, nor did his phone alert him of any notifications, which was quite bizarre because he was economically relevant to his nightlife. His old grey alarm clock beside his bed did not go off, and yet it ticked loudly in between his throbbing headache. His heartbeat was extremely loud, and it sounded as vibrant as an African drum right as he got back onto his bed. It was quite evident that his day was indeed going to be a very unpredictable, and he definitely knew that he wasn't prepared for its challenges. He stood up straight with a glimpse of hope, praying that the grey tiled floor wouldn't be as cold as the first time, but he was wrong. Matter of fact, the floor screamed of chills creeping up all the way to his spinal cord, almost paralysing his heart back into a greater depression. The matter at hand gazed his mind into confusion, and the numb feeling on his feet made it almost unbearable to walk for a while. Regardless of that, he stepped into the glass shower booth within the next room, which was positioned along the hollow passage. He felt differently about the outside world—a dreadful foreign place he'd once dismissed, for he wasn't able to trust anyone anymore.

After showering, Quinton went to his wardrobe to find clothing suitable for the day, but couldn't find anything acceptable for his dull mood. He could only find was his skinny-fitted black jeans, a black silk shirt, and a tightly fitted grey designer blazer he'd worn once to an event that he was once invited to by an old flame. It was mournful and sadistic as he wore his semiformal clothing. He tightened his black high-top sneaker laces, bended his light brown crocodile watch straps around his left wrist to compliment the colour of his smooth skin. He took a few seconds to gather his thoughts by his maroon apartment door and wore a pair of black shades to darken his vision. It seemed as though the clothes he wore ironically suited his foul mood for the morning. As Quinton opened the door and revealed himself to the outside world, the bright sun absorbed onto his clothing, and he felt unfairly treated by Mother Nature. The wind brushed against his face, and for a while, it became extremely hard for him to grasp for closure through the mildly polluted air in the atmosphere.

The rain had precipitated from the evening before, the same way his eyes had leaked drastically from what he'd been through in the past.

However, the weather was cooler than usual as he stepped onto the side path, allowing a whizz of wondering whispers into his mind that morning whilst walking passed Old John by the wet left sidewalk. Old John smiled and waved, but Quinton remained hostile towards the old homeless man. Quinton reeled his mind back into that exact memory of the first time he moved into the apartment block and greeted John for the first time on the sidewalk. They'd merged a strong questionable friendship that nobody else understood, and yet on this particular day, Quinton walked past John as if he didn't know him. John's rehearsed story of a college dropout who'd failed to progress on in life seemed to have wracked a nerve within Quinton's body on this very morning. He looked downwards onto John and suddenly found the old man's reasons to be unwarranted. John being homeless must have been because he'd once lost everything from a gambling problem, Quinton assumed.

The young man's strides grew longer, and he appeared to be unkind and unforgiving towards the old man as he walked. Finding the old homeless man to be very repulsive on this very morning, he, therefore, didn't greet back. Old John did not resent Quinton for doing so, but instead found it within his aged heart to forgive another human being for being inhuman and insensitive.

Old John's unwritten history was unquoted amongst others around him, which definitely made him an outcast and a stranger to the world from his birth, orphaned after his mother passed away in a correctional system. The words to his story were remarkably heart filling and yet unnoticed by everyone who'd walked past his rotting corpse. He sat quietly on the street corner with a summarised idea of why Quinton behaved so unkind towards him.

The mournful sight of a young man wearing black reminded him of a story so familiar to him. Quinton's mournful material covering his body winded John's clock back to the time of his youth, and he relived his memories. It had been a memorable occasion on a hot day in the summer of his youth during the cold war. John had fallen in love with a beautiful woman who'd travelled to England on a quest for work and other pleasurable things. John's foster care family was moulded from a background of Catholic authority and would never permit him to be with an Indian woman who worshipped another higher power. He didn't know much of Yumna's religious beliefs, but his heart was melted by her unquestionable beauty. She wasn't tall at all, to say the least, but she walked tall with her head lifted up high with excitement. Her beautifully light-toned skin swept him from his feet as he watched her step off the train within the platform—a train which had railed all the way from heaven and landed with an angel from another world.

John worked as a shoe polisher, always rubbing a nickel and dime to make ends meet. He wasn't from a privileged background nor was he educated, but he was a king within his empire state of mind. He knew his big heart had so much more to offer to the world.

Yumna's beautiful strong black hair moved to the air blowing from the train on the right railway, and John completely forgot that he was shining another man's shoe as he watched the love of his life carry her luggage away from the train with her right hand. She walked past him without even noticing his existence, and he was smitten by her appearance. She was wearing a long silky dress, designed from Indian fabric, and her small palm shoes gave her an elegant look.

With all hope gone, John believed that he wasn't worthy of Yumna's attention, thus didn't bother to chaperone her away from the gross smell of industrial fumes. His hands shimmered black from the shoe polish, and he smelt slightly posh yet wretched from the cheap cologne he'd nicked a while back. Sweat dripped from his forehead as he brushed his blond hair away from his eyes. He knew that he was in love, but the thought of her supposed middle class structure rattled his shanty heart as he kept polishing away.

The sun had faded into the night, and John had completely forgotten about the beautiful Indian woman that he'd seen early. To him, she was just a moving mirage, and maybe that was it—the heat had gripped on to his weakness for beautiful Indian women whilst at his weakest, he thought. He stood by the street in his torn shoes after he'd washed his dirty hands, and as he looked to the left side, he saw her again. It seemed as if she was waiting for someone as she remained seated on a brown bench, impatiently looking at her bronze watch whilst holding a written letter in the same hand. Her long black hair moved towards the opposite direction every single time she turned her head to look around. Her heart was steadily beating, and John didn't like the sight of her beautiful facial presence evaporating to disappointment. Therefore, he slowly moved towards her and hoped that she wouldn't make assumptions about him based on his clothing.

'Hey, miss, are you okay?' he asked in a gentle manner and hoped for a response.

She looked up and her light, round brown eyes gazed against his ocean-blue eyes. He believed she was his fate as her beautiful heart acknowledged his profound courage. Her eyes drew him one step closer as he waited for a reply, waiting for love to blossom inside of his dark world.

'Hello!' she responded with a foreign accent, but her vowels weren't as clear, which brought greater joy into John's heart because it's all he'd ever wanted—someone from another world.

She smiled, and he absolutely drowned in love as she spoke. Her teeth were white and straight, aligned by her beautiful pink lips curving around her small mouth. She mentioned the letter within her hand and explained that she needed some help finding a certain place because it seemed as though her aunt had forgotten about her. John turned chivalrous and gentlelike as he picked up her light luggage and addressed forward. He knew of this place scripted within the letter and hoped that he'd get to know Yumna better whilst walking beside her. She did not hesitate to follow.

Her story was different, and that kept him interested. She was the youngest out of all six siblings, who were all married back India. Out of all her siblings, she was the only one who was smart enough to study ahead of the rest instead of settling into routine like her father had hoped. Her father was a respected member of a tiny remote village in the depths of the grandiose mountains within the Indian Himalayas, a very dominantly strict figure within their household. His hopes were to have his only daughter married to any man with power, but deep down inside Yumna's heart, she wanted to travel instead of being chained away from the wonders of the world. She told John that she'd ran away from her village because she wasn't in love with the man that she was supposed to marry. It all felt like a business transaction to her. Thus, she followed her heart to a different location with a reference from her distant aunt. She knew that she would have a better chance of happiness in England despite the fact that she was friendless and lost.

'Will you be my friend?' she asked,

'Sure, I will be your friend. I've had a short supply of friends these days!' John mentioned as he showed Yumna the location from the letter.

She smiled because running away from her poverty-stricken village was a blessing. She'd disobeyed the elderly members in her community, yet she'd never been happier.

An older woman by the name of Avani rushed out of the household in a hurry but sensed relief as she saw Yumna outside her yard. The house was built from maroon bricks with an English brick bond. It was normal to the average citizen, but to John and Yumna, it looked luxuriously beautiful and a soundly place to mould a new foundation of love and have children. It glowed bright to them as they stood still next to one another, wondering what else to say to each other.

The older plumy woman, Avani, was Yumna's aunt who'd left India with her husband in their early twenties to start a life of their own. She spoke to her niece in a foreign language as she hugged and kissed Yumna continuously on her cheeks. They cheered as they walked towards the front yard, but as Yumna reached the front doorstep, she realised that she was leaving something behind—something very important, someone she'd immediately felt drawn too—as she blinked whilst turning around. She looked back at John as his heart shattered a little.

'Thanks!' she shouted then rushed back to give him an old rupee coin, perking his cheek with love. 'Thank you so much. I know it's not what you expected, but this coin will represent hope. Remember me whenever you look at it!' she yelled whilst running back to her aunt.

The light brown door closed, and John walked away quietly. He didn't wanted her foreign money but wanted her rare love instead and therefore took in every single word that she'd said and allowed her voice to repeat aloud within his mind again and again. His mind remained fixated on her beauty and her powerful presence whilst walking back to his wretched home, wondering if it was a wise idea to publicise what he'd just encountered to his foster clan, or wondered if it was wise to conceal the secret and keep it sealed within his heart. One thing was certain. John had fallen in love with Yumna! He knew his heart was spoken for more and more as he disappeared into the darkness of his poverty.

However, months dreaded by slowly as summer wore off its pleasance. The smell of train smoke and black polish depressed John as it sunk into him that he'd missed his opportunity of luck. He didn't want to go unnoticed anymore. He'd hoped that he would run into Yumna as days went, but fate wasn't on his side as he'd believed and therefore took it upon himself to make changes that Friday afternoon. He had managed to scrape off enough money to buy decent clothes and to take Yumna out somewhere expensive.

His greased blond hair waved backwards gave him a clean look from afar but tapped into his lack of finances by anyone who'd walk past him and whiffed his transparent poverty. Nevertheless, he felt dapper and ambitious. He felt like a Jay Gatsby type with his black tuxedo and polished black shoes, a charismatic young fellow with his heart on his sleeve. The only colourful aspect on him where the tulip flowers that he'd purchased from the local florist by a flea market.

He had to defeat all odds and find triumph. Positivity relished his heart towards hope. He believed that Yumna would love his choice of flowers, and he stood by the maroon bricked house, waiting to knock on the door whilst tiny drops of sweat raced down his pale face. He stood by the light brown door and prayed for success.

Her new home glowed in happiness as he stood there, listening to numerous people laughing inside. The living room was warmed up with chattering from the women within it. He knew that his next moment would change the course of his life, if he were to ever knock on that light brown door. The idea of beautiful mixed-race children running around in the green village sides where he'd always imagined settling brought a smile to his face as he knocked on the door twice, waiting then knocking twice again. An avalanche of laughter within the house slowly settled down, and footsteps crept closer towards the door. He brushed his blond hair backwards with his right palm and waited for an introduction at the doorstep.

Avani opened the door and greeted him politely.

'Please, please come in!' she said, and as John entered, he noticed a crowd of people in the living room drinking tea from anticlike cups, eating vegan sandwiches whilst waiting for a grand dinner to be serviced.

He stood by the arched entrance but felt a wrecking ball of hostility knock against his face from every single person within the living room. It had occurred to him that he had interrupted a family gathering, and on his right peripheral vision, he could see the wondrous works of a God he'd never known. The love of his life—Yumna. His heart throbbed intensely fast as he smiled for the first time and showed his crooked teeth, which immediately advocated for judgement from those staring at him. Her tulip flowers in his left hand stated the obvious. However, he couldn't care less, for his appearance brought happiness to Yumna. She smiled gracefully at him, but within seconds, her gorgeous brown eyes leaked of a sadistic future and cloaked her true happiness, right as a tear fell from her right eye.

It was slightly later that John found out that his blossoming flower, Yumna, would be married soon. The thought of it crushed him, for he'd never felt this way about anybody except her. He glommed and mopped around in the background, hoping that she'd explain her reasons for getting married after successfully running away. And as she spoke, every single word entering through his ears deepened his wounds even more. It had been an arrangement married, forced by her father who'd also travelled from India with the supposed eligible bachelor and others who were in support of the arranged marriage.

Yumna whispered to John in the hallway in hopes that he would say something meaningful back or maybe runaway with her. She had also fallen for him too. The signs were visibly shown, and only Avani and her husband, Iyal, knew of the attraction blossoming in the hallway.

John and Yumna had planned to run away in secret after their conversation.

The full moon shone brightly over the cloudy sky that evening whilst John stood by the nearest corner, patiently waiting for his beloved with high hopes. They did not know that Iyal knew of their plan, for he'd heard everything earlier whilst everyone else was chatting away in the living room.

It was quiet, and the streetlights shined brightly onto the wet roads. John seemed slightly weary but remained positive and patient by the street corner, hoping for the best, but Yumna never appeared. He wandered up and down the street as hours passed, passing underneath the streetlights with high hopes, but he did not know that Iyal had revealed their plans to Yumna's father. Her father was outraged by that thought as he realised that he would lose his only daughter to a British man. He wasn't liberal nor did he tolerate interracial relations clustered with different religions and therefore knotted his daughter's wrists with a thick rope by her bedside and clogged her mouth with a white towel. Yumna screamed to the top of her lungs, but nobody could hear anything. Her tears raced down her face slowly as she struggled and screamed out for John. However, he could not hear anything from the street corner. To him, it seemed as if she had decided to enter into a marriage of convenience.

He was later arrested after Yumna's relatives had called the police. The officers said he looked overly ambitious as if he was man about to pull off a con or some sort. His charge—idling afterhours.

Yumna wept to sleep that evening and hoped that John would forgive her for not being able to break free from family bondage. She looked at her father as he spoke, but none of his words sunk through into her ears.

After a long weekend of incarceration, that Monday morning, a warm breeze had settled in, and as the sun rose above the grey clouds, almost creating an oven as the heat baked everyone underneath, John was released from the local precinct. He ran back to Avani's house with hopes of interrupting everything but arrived to a quiet house. The light brown door was awkwardly open, and without knocking, he rushed in, shouting out for Yumna. Her name echoed through the hallway, but nobody responded. Avani was seated on a living room chair filled with guilt, weeping for her part in destroying her niece's happiness because she'd alerted Iyal. She saw the pain that she'd inflicted onto Yumna when her niece left for their trip to the coast of South Africa with the rest of her family. Avani and Iyal did not realise that the pain they caused would ripple for eternity, causing an unstable future which would lead to a horrific and catastrophic present for John.

Both lovers' hearts sunk into black waste, and as days passed, they each turned dark within their souls. Yumna looked at her bruised wrists as the ship left the harbour. The sound of seagulls and ship horns rattled her mind, and she knew that she would never be able to see John again. She immediately realised that she was in love with him because he was chivalrous and gentle towards her unlike the ruthless men she'd been used too.

Soon after, John's heart remained rattled for life. His heart searched for love in other places, but he never once stopped being optimistic about seeing Yumna again.

Long years dreaded passed, and his heart turned into stone, leaving his handsome face dry and aged with wrinkles. His body shrunk and he became weaker. Nobody could bring him happiness like Yumna did with just one smile. It became clear that he had found endless love, which had left him depressed and unwilling to work for a living. Therefore, John sat by the same corner from when he first spoken to Yumna, subconsciously waiting for hope to return into his life.

As Quinton Barker walked past homeless John, the story that had just projected within John's mind uprooted an old stigma of sadness within his heart, but regardless of that, he smiled like an old fool prepared to perform a trick then wiped sweat from his forehead and picked up an old rupee coin he'd received from Yumna when they'd first met to remind him of how beautiful the world used to be when he was young and ambitious. He immediately tossed it into the air and waited for an answer, a confirmation of some sort, a way to bring him peace as it landed on the head side. He looked up and prayed that he'd get to see Yumna one last time before passing away or dying from kidney failure. He knew that he was drunk in love for eternity, and seeing Yumna would bring him the closure he needed to move forward.

Quinton Barker walked passed numerous stores on his left side after by passing ol' homeless John. He thought about the irrelevance of a newspaper to him and wondered why people liked reading about bad news, as he called it. 'The world will never be at peace because nobody knows how to love purely without expecting anything from anyone,' he said out loud, wondering why hippies pretended like everything was okay whilst they inhaled their mind-controlling substances. The concept of peace dwelled within his mind, and peace signs took his mind back to an event he'd been to a while ago and how everyone there would pretend to care about humanity and the wars occurring around instead of actually standing up and making a real difference.

One thing was clear to Quinton as he walked—all those thoughts within his mind were irrelevant to what had happened to him awhile back. A part of him had completely lost interest with anybody that he knew. He tried the usual approach to his day by checking out beautiful girls that walked past him and yet none of them were remotely attractive at that moment.

Within minutes of walking past other human conventions and old establishments, Quinton entered the Grey Bird Café. The place as amazingly decorated with paintings and pictures of events before his time—a picture of Marilyn Monroe with her stunning smile and her glowing blond hair. She seemed like such a charismatic soul, and Quinton fell in love with that picture every time he walked past it. He glanced at Marilyn's well-shaped legs and yet felt indifferent. The cafeteria had another enlarged painting of a diverse group of people, dancing to what looked like jazz music because of the instruments in the background. They were dressed in tuxedos and long dresses, projecting a time from the prohibition era in New York City. The painting added vintage to the cafeteria, and the walls were covered in dark polished wooden planks, which merely gave the place a warm vibe. Quinton sat outside and ordered a cup of medium roast coffee and two chocolate chip muffins. After doing so, he witnessed a moment so genuine to him. It was beautiful to witness old love. This moment deflated his sourness for a while. It was a real-life clip projecting onto his frame of an old interracial couple. They walked past him on the sidewalk whilst holding hands tightly. They had nothing but time on their hands, and their love was completely mesmerizing to watch. The blue exhausted veins on their forearms said all, for they were very happy to have each other in this lifetime. They waved at Quinton, who'd been momentarily caught up with what he'd just seen. And as he smiled, he realized the vulnerability behind within him and therefore dismissed his own happiness and remained brut whilst indulging on what he'd ordered.

His old alarm clock by his bedside clocked within his mind as he stood up and left money on the table. He felt like he was running out of time, and his breaths grew shorter as he rushed towards the underground train station. The normal occurrence to his day seemed boring and outwearing. He wanted to be away from everything that he knew. The atmosphere around him was always negatively charged, and the idea of leaving to another place grew fondly within his heart.

His clogged mind slowly started to clear as the train moved away. He knew that he couldn't run away from his problems, but having his current state paused seemed so ideal to him. It was awfully strangle how eminently weightless and pure he felt to the idea of peace. This was the first time he'd been able to think clearly in a while and not worry about his next lecture nor about everything else weighing him down. He needed to recuperate from his cloudy thoughts and mingle with current events—to eat good food, to drink expensive alcohol, to dance with beautiful shallow women he had no intention to care about, and to made even make love to one of them.

The next city appeared different and tame to a rowdy city person. It was awfully quiet in between trains stopping and going, yet the silence itself brought a smile to Quinton's face as he walked up the stairs and onto the sidewalk. People walked past him, and it felt refreshing to be a stranger. Moving black cabs steamed for kilometres, and he hailed one. He did not know of his final destination, but he was momentarily set on finding peace within his heart and thus questioned the cab driver on current events.

'There is a music and carnival festival going on!' the cab driver mentioned and turned his steering wheel towards the right. 'It consists of famous bands, magical acts, and solo shows all in one,' the cab driver said, indicating right towards the second lane.

'Take me there, please,' Quinton mentioned and sat back to observe the new scenery.

Quinton arrived by the entrance of the musical festival by a large park, glancing at green leaves which had plucked off from trees, painting a vivid picture in his mind. Event organisers handed out booklets whilst he waited in line for a ticket, and as he entered, the sounds of guitars and piano notes lured him away from all his problems. It felt intriguing to commence in different activities. Therefore, he moved closer towards the music festival and found himself seated by a pub stand, drinking a mixture of vodka and Sprite. He removed his grey blazer and rolled up his slight shirt after untucking it.

Waves of fresh air brushed over his soul, and the soothing touch of nature endorsed him with peace. He looked towards the western section of the festival and felt his heart throbbing loudly to the sight of this specific red-and-white striped tent, one he hadn't noticed before, almost as if it had just magically appeared from nowhere. The sun was setting over that specific structure, glazing before his brown eyes. There were so many other tents pitched around, but they appeared indifferent from that particular tent. He felt emotionally consumed by its beauty and completely compelled by its appearance. He stood up and moved closer with curiosity, slowly skipping over pitched tent ropes and ending up by an open flap entrance. The other flap was tied up, merely welcoming his heart towards a feeling he'd never felt before. It was exciting and dangerous at the same time.

Quinton entered cautiously and called out, 'Hello!' but nobody responded to his calling. Something magical had drawn him to this specific tent, and it was clear that he wasn't leaving until he'd satisfied his curiosity. The sound of piano notes arose as his call echo cleared in the distance. He stood still within the empty tent but noticed a smaller open flap located on the far left side of the tent. The floor felt slightly slippery from the dry thatched grass as he walked slowly towards the soft voice humming in between the piano key notes. It all felt sweet and cunning. Quinton called out again but only heard the piano sounds responding to him as he opened the smaller red flap with his left hand and entered into a smaller joint tent filled with a lot of stacked carnival fences and dusty furniture. He moved past a row of dark brown wardrobes and stacked dark wooden chairs until he could see a lamp lighting the edge a black piano. Its structure stretched out for a while as he moved away from the last dark wardrobe and closer towards the light to see clearly. So many shadows glazed over him as he moved closer whilst calling out, 'Hello, anybody there?'

His questioning initially made him feel stupid because he could hear a soft voice wailing sweetly to his ears. Finally, he could see everything. It all looked so beautiful—a picture-perfect moment drawn into an endless frame of generations to come.

There she was, gently pressing her fingers onto the piano keys, smiling as the sweet notes gushed into her ears. Quinton stood before fate, not that he knew it at the time. Her back remained fixed towards him as he moved slowly. She did not responded to him, but that did not discourage him at all. He noticed a print of red stick marks on the brim of an empty wine glass on top of the black piano and an opened bottle of red wine pitched right beside it.

She turned around whilst seated on a rotating black stool, and the visual before him stunned him remarkably. He smiled from infatuation and from the sound of her sweet voice as she spoke.

'Hey!' she said.

'H-he-hey!' he stuttered, stepping closer whilst the universe electrocuted every single fibre within his body.

He could not figure out who she was, but her beautiful face heisted his heart away. She looked famous. Important. A star shining brightly. Her green eyes drew Quinton closer, and he could almost see an endless possibility of real love. She had a unique smile. A dimple on both cheeks which made her look heaven sent. He did not know who she was, but her kindness appealed to him more than anything he'd ever experienced before in his entire life, which led him one step closer to the black piano.

'Would you like something to drink?' she asked and smiled, waiting for a response only to be greeted by awkwardness. 'I think we have some beers somewhere! I will go and check okay!' she said as she stood up from her wooden black stool and searched for beers inside the nearest box fridge connected to an electrical cable stretched out to another tent.

Quinton noticed multiple crumbled tissues on the dry thatched grass floor right next to her stool and wondered why misery was clouding her heart into darkness. She rushed back towards him with cold beer in her hand and twisted its cap with her right hand.

'Here you go!' she whispered and giggled as Quinton took a small sip from the green bottle and placed it next to the empty wine glass.

Quinton remained speechless as she sat down again and pressed onto the piano keys slowly.

'Should I play you a song? Maybe a commercial song you've heard on radio before?' she asked and played one of the many songs she'd fallen in love with whilst touring with other artists that one trip in Europe.

'I have a show later!' she mentioned and paused. 'I'm actually so nervous and drained to be honest!'

'Oh, really! I couldn't tell!' said Quinton as he took another sip from his beer. 'You seem so calm and collected! Almost as if a cool breeze has just blew in an angel's feather. You seem so light and pure to the finest touch,' he mentioned and made her blush.

'Courtesy of the wine!' she stated and looked up at Quinton whilst pressing onto the piano keys. 'Who are you?' she asked. 'Your face is so handsome and must be warm to the finest touch!' she mentioned and mumbled to the piano notes wailing into their ears.

She felt drawn to a stranger and found herself weirdly interesting through her dehydration from consuming booze, and weirdly enough, she was clumsy yet composed as the same time. Quinton introduced himself, and as he shook her soft right hand, a flashback from a week ago projected within his mind. He pulled back and felt bizarrely confused and lost like little lamb looking for its mother.

'Are you okay?' she asked and frowned, wondering if he'd notice how sadistic she was at that moment. 'Did I do something wrong?' she asked, pulling her hands away to guard herself from being hurt by a stranger.

'No, no, no. It's nothing!' he said as she stood up and dusted off her shimmering dress with both hands.

She picked up her wine bottle and her wine glass, strolled towards bundles of dry thatched grass to find comfort away from her music, and sat onto the closest one covered with red cotton blanket.

'I wonder,' she said and dwelled on a thought, 'I wonder what tomorrow holds for all of us!'

'What do you mean?' he asked and took another sip,

'Well, I wonder what will happen tomorrow!' she whispered. 'It seems like we have no control over destiny no matter how much we try to wield everything!'

It felt like time finally stopped for a while, allowing the two to arrange their hearts accordingly, allowing them to fall in love. Quinton moved closer towards the mysterious lady before his dazed eyes and saw a glitch of the future—there she was dancing beside him, holding his hands tightly on their wedding day. It all felt real as he blinked back to reality and observed her decor. She was dressed in a long white gown and wore white short heels. Her make-up sparkled a little on her silky caramel skin. She was definitely mixed race, and her green eyes looked so compellingly beautiful. Her natural hair was brunette and curly, almost like a thatched mystical bush covering her ears.

'Do you believe in love?' she asked.

'I'm not so sure!' he responded without contemplating on the question.

'Well, you should!' she said and carried on talking. 'It's a beautiful feeling. It's our paradox of war and peace. It's one for the ages of our time in this world. It's all you need in this world!' She smiled.

'Do you believe in fate?' Quinton asked and wondered if she would unveil her real name afterwards.

'It depends!' she said. 'It's depends on one's path, I think!' she stated and poured red wine into a wine glass.

Quinton took a large sip of his beer as he sat down next to the mysterious lady. Her persona was sweet and different, for she wasn't shy nor was she uptight. She gladly welcomed him into her personal space. They sat closely to each other, and she leaned sideways onto his right shoulder, metaphorically leaning for guidance.

'I want to be normal again!' she whispered. 'I am drowning in this pool of fame!'

Quinton's ears collected every single word coming out of her mouth, and he felt closely related to her struggle. Her British accent sounded so profoundly sweet to his ears, and he listened carefully as she spoke. He wasn't a good listener at all, but for the first time ever, he listened to a stranger uncloak their hidden background. She sat closely and leaned onto his shoulder, and as she did so, he gently kissed her forehead. It felt right to do so.

'Thank you!' she whispered again. 'That feels so good and genuine!'

Quinton felt another electrocuting feeling astonish him as they glanced around and observed all the objects piled and packed in front of them. There was a half-painted canvas right next to the first dusty wardrobe. It was tilted sideways and appeared to be unfinished towards the right side of it with pencil linings sketched beautifully, and regardless of its transparent procrastination, it seemed like it had a story to tell.

'I drew that awhile back!' she said as she tilted her head clockwise. 'I haven't finished it!'

'What is it?' Quinton asked as he also tilted his head clockwise and smelt the compelling smell of her perfume through his sensitive nostrils.

'Not so sure yet, but you can have it for now,' she said. 'That way, it forces me to find you so that I can actually finish it one day, and when that happens, we will both know what real love feels like! I promise.'

She looked at her silver watch as the hands of time took her away from their comfortable. 'I'm going to leave now!' she said as her supposed manager entered from the darkness. 'Please do not go anywhere. I will be back!' she said standing up. She picked up the long dangling piece of white cloth at the end of her dress and walked into the darkness.

The night turned long. Quinton looked at his brown watch repeatedly whilst lying there like a sick patient waiting for aid from his cloaked past. He knew that he had to return to his reality and face his problems. The idea of love was unscripted to his life at that moment, and yet he remained puzzled as he stood before that unfinished painting, waiting for a sign or some sort. He walked around and discovered a lot of objects within the tent, but none of them explained who the mystery lady was. She was as miraculous as an angel, landing onto the plains of miserable existence. He could hear her singing in the background, and her voice rippled away his fears of finding peace within someone else and loving again.

A decision was to be made at that moment as he looked at his watch again. He realised that he needed to get onto the last train of the evening, or he would be homeless for the next twelve hours, which seemed like a plan until he remembered that he hadn't fed his goldfish. A part of him wondered if this mysterious lady was worth it because essentially everything about her felt right, but the timing was all wrong. His mind became polluted again, and a dark cloud hanged over his head as he left the red-and-white striped tent with the unfinished painting underneath his right arm. He left his grey blazer by her wine glass with his email address within the left chest pocket, with hopes that she would find it and maybe even keep herself warm with his blazer, then looked back at the tent whilst she sang loudly in the background. The little ounce of peace stored within his heart dried up as he walked away, and funny enough, the tent disappeared into nothing but a dream as he glanced back.

There he was in his averagely sized apartment after a long eventful day, making a light meal in the kitchen and contemplating about the woman he'd met earlier. He sliced the loaf of white bread, and as he looked at the sharp knife, he could hear the piano notes playing again along with the mysterious lady's soft voice relishing his heart towards a place of no return.

Quick flashes of the artistic lady played within his mind as he closed his brown eyes. Her beautifully textured skin and perfectly aligned white teeth left him dreamy until he accidentally nipped his index finger. He was definitely infatuated by what he'd heard and seen. Her deep dimples deepened his mind's state, and he was temporarily lost in a flustered mirage of love and lust at the same time. He laid his head onto a pillow in his bedroom, and minutes passed as he wondered if the lady he'd met earlier had found his details.

He unlocked his phone and viewed a new message. He'd had hopes, praying for it to be the mysterious lady he'd met, but he was wrong. Matter of fact, the message he'd just received was awkward and yet conducive. It was Quinton's past. A girl he'd met at the Grey Bird Café two months ago. Quinton read the message and remembered that she was the reason he'd woken up rattled in the morning. He kept replaying those visuals of her inside his head as he closed his brown eyes, railing back to that exact moment where his ex-girlfriend, Calista, deceived him. He recollected her dashingly beautiful thin black eyebrows. These memories infected a greater pain in his heart.

Calista seemed perfect and very capable of maintaining a good relationship especially because she was so down to earth. They'd shared an intimate moment together, and that thought made Quinton uneasy because he wasn't sure if he was in love or in lust with Calista. He had unresolved issues, and that was something he'd have to work on if he wanted to be happy again. His brown eyes became heavy as he lay onto his bed after having his light meal. He hoped for signs within his oncoming dreams or at least hoped that he'd remember what he'd dreamed of as he shut his eyes and rotted back into the past.

His dream pattern winded back to the previous months before and felt like he'd not had an ounce of sleep as he slumbered through his memory lane, diving back to his last relationship. Everything unveiled, and he could feel every sense, almost as if he was back to the beginning of the moment he welcomed Calista through his apartment front door. She smiled but seemed highly emotional, for she wasn't happy at all because she was nostalgic for love. Her brown eyes were moist from sobbing, for she was upset for some reason.

'Please come in!' Quinton suggested as he blinked continuously.

His invitation was ambiguous because he indirectly welcomed her into his heart regardless of his trust issues. His mind was inflated with decadent pride, but he was also tired of being alone through the long nights. Therefore, he allowed his heart to feel something. She was also drawn to their previous encounters, momentarily lost within a ruze.

They weren't certain of what they were doing, but it felt right to be with each other. She turned to him as he sat closely and looked into her beautiful brown eyes without saying a word. His heart had lost every piece of purity to precious relationships. Thus, he wondered if he would be able to survive the next wave of love or drown in it. She parked her pink lips onto his lips slowly for a while, and they closed their eyes with a bit of uncertainty. Her senses recollected as she pulled back, hoping that he would say something more assuring, but he remained speechless.

'I think I should go!' she said and stood up in a rush.

'I'm sorry, I shouldn't have come here!'

'No, wait!' he said without thinking, and at that moment, he realised that his heart was bonded to hers as she slowly turned around.

'Do you want me to stay? Because I can stay if you want me to!' she asked and gave the most adorable puppy eyes any woman could ever give.

He did not say anything, and a few seconds passed as he moved closer whilst his eyes remained fixed on to hers. His words came crippled all the way from his heart, and it took a long time for him to swallow his pride.

'I . . . I wa-want you to stay,' he stuttered as he realized that he was indeed infatuated, and there it was—a feeling he'd tried to avoid because of its worldly romantic projections, its heartbreaks, its imperfections which left people desiccated whilst seeking for attention to be shielded from being terribly vulnerable.

Despite his thoughts on romance and love, he felt lucky and blessed to be with someone like her. She gently shut the door and held on to his left hand, leading him towards the bedroom. Quinton had embraced the goodness of it all into his heart, and that moment itself changed his perspective. He was almost driven to believe that Calista was his goddess because he'd began to worship her body like a foolish man would do.

She was just as rare and majestic as a great white moose snickering within the great plains of his green pasture of a reality. It wasn't long before Quinton's memory lane turned towards recent events. He could hear the sound of piano notes rushing through his ears again and again whilst dwelling on the memory of the musical festival, and at the same time the pain that Calista had caused lingered at the back of his mind like an anchor dragging his sinking ship down. The sounds of bands playing and people clapping in the background of his mind gradually took his heart away from his body whilst his mind relived the moment when Calista would come over to his apartment. The laughter and tickling. The wine and the food. The music and atmospheric dream of an endless love. He was darkened by confusion as his mystery lady's lingering scent whiffed through his nostrils and over his memories, washing away memories of his pain caused by Calista. He couldn't quite ignore his bizarre train of thought, along with its surreal moment cloaking his mind away from a pleasant reality. He opened his eyes and fixed them towards the window and wondered if he was infinitivally infatuated with the mysterious woman he'd met earlier or just missed Calista because he undoubtedly loved drowning in the pleasure of her love.

Slowly but surely, he shut his heavy eyes again and slumbered between reality and his imagination, hoping to rail into a beautiful dream of some sort, a moment unhinged from wealth or status, one scattered out on to a priceless frame to take him away from his pain and towards the plain fields of peace. Nevertheless, his imagination danced away in the personification of his mysterious beautiful woman. He took a glimpse of the fire burning inside her green eyes as she gestured for him to follow her away from reality. She projected a vivid canvas within as he drifted away from the world he was accustomed to and felt drawn to his dream. She consumed his heart as followed his imagination and landed elsewhere.

Chapter Two

Accepted Illusions

Quinton woke up inside of his dream, within his peaceful state of mind and felt calm and collected from the earthly components magically floating within. He believed the beauty behind every dream isn't the path that reveals itself to a person. Rather, it's the remarkable positive feeling that a person always gets when they wake up from that dream. It's the significant beautiful confusion of the dream that makes the mind so special and the inspiration he'd always get whilst sleeping, along with its sense of spiritual essence he'd always get whilst seeking for a higher power to answer back to him. It's the abstract structure within his mind that made his imagination so pleasant to drift into. At times, it's unbelievable what a person's mind can think of when it is assigned to work with their heart—like two magnates positioned perfectly to each other. It was incredible what music, speech, a sense of smell, and the fruitful sight of beauty could create whenever one was dreaming or reliving through a pleasant memory.

Quinton walked through the rain within a dark clustered forest of thick trunks of aged trees with endless carved-out names of people who'd hurt him before. He could smell the sweetness of nature through his sensitive nostrils as raindrops washed over his broad face. His short black hair felt extremely soft and smooth as he brushed it backwards. There was a sense of relief flourishing within his heart as his inner pain from his recent heartbreak evaporated into nothing but clarity and peace. The smell of wet spring roses still lingered. Its fragrance also saturated his fingertips. Essentially, it made him appreciate his growth as person and admire the sweetness of pollen.

He could hear piano keys playing in the background as he kept walking over many of the exposed tree roots along his way. His moment had created entitlement. He kept on walking, not that he knew where he was going nor where he was, but walking away from his issues brought closure. It was ironic because Quinton felt like he'd been casted into the *Wizard of Oz* Broadway show whereby he felt like the Tin Man who'd finally realised that he had a heart—a big one to be specific. Quinton was drawn to that moment as if it were his last, and the moment itself didn't want for it all to end. However, everything changed with a blink of an eye.

The wind grew stronger and the clouds darkened. Rain poured and wore down Quinton's body. He immediately realised that the moment was upset and confused, wrapped with vulnerability because it had allowed Quinton to enter into its world.

The clingy moment asked, 'Will you stay with me forever?'

Quinton didn't respond but dwelled within his heart. He couldn't stay forever. Everything looked pleasing and beautiful to the common naked eye, but Quinton couldn't settle into a moment and become average.

Without reasonable doubt, the moment grew into rage and impatience. Its branches grew longer and started to cover up the night sky into utter darkness. The wind pushed Quinton and threw him in all directions until he tripped over an exposed tree root and fell all the way back to where he'd first began.

'I haven't been honest with you, my love!' Quinton yelled and frowned at his sprained right ankle. 'I understand that you trusted me, but I do not want to be a part of a moment. I don't want to dream anymore but want to live more than anything!'

Quinton understood what he'd done wrong. He'd tried to keep the truth buried deep down inside his heart, that his true love was reality because reality didn't just give a moment but gave him a life and he wanted to live more than anything.

After discovering the purpose of his dream, his peaceful state of mind turned the table upside down, and his past slid onto his timeframe and backtracked to the memory when his second semester was almost at its end. His heart was cracking all over again from a woman's deception. He relived every second of that memory when he was on his way to Calista's apartment on their anniversary. The day where he'd purchased roses, chocolates, and the likes of romantic gifts to shower his so-called beloved with heavy clouds of love. He remembered her deceit, the way she laughed and his heart breaking as he found her cheating with another man. Her laughter stated the obvious, which kept Quinton indecisive, hoping that it was all in his imagination. He stood by the passage and looked at the reflection on the mirror on the wall, of two shadows merging into one. The image was heartbreaking and unpleasant, and it was quite evident that she'd hit where it hurt and it was ironic too, to say the least, because he's done the exact same hideous thing to somebody else years before. Karma was a bitch.

There wasn't much to do as Quinton gently placed his romantic gifts aside and walked away from a heartbreak, essentially attempting to forget about what he'd witnessed. It wasn't as scripted as he'd always thought it would be where he'd find himself covered in rag and ready to paint a bedroom red with another man's blood. He couldn't be violent nor allow anything to get the best him regardless of the situation. There was a moment were darkness appeared within his soul and where demons came out to play. Tears leaked from his eyes as he walked away. He knew he'd never see her again, not only because her apartment was miles away from his, but also because the graphical display ensured that he would never open up again. He became sceptical, undoubtedly aware of anything which could hurt him again.

And whilst stumbling away through the polluted air filled with a wreck of disgrace, he recollected her every touch and felt a deep hatred boil in his mind. His feelings washed over his body, and he felt as dead and rotten as a corpse.

It all began to make sense whilst another reality clip played within his mind. He felt a tide of clarity wash over his heart as these memories projected through his sleep. His mind was running through this other occasion, and every dark grey second drove him into depression.

The moment had occurred to Quinton to checkout of the heartbreak hotel after a while, and to a certain extent, he began to enjoy the little declining pain that usually streamed through his broken heart. It had started to define who he was, and everything that was remotely soft with regard to love made him want to vomit. He was repulsed by love, and it was very ironic how he was back to square one and boxed up at the same time. It made him grow estranged to the possibility to being in love again. His faith was destroyed by the acts of one human being.

He'd spend his late evenings declining texts from other girls, smoking Camel Lights cigarettes, and indirectly visualising what had happened at his ex-girlfriend's apartment. The more he kept contemplating of his past, the more its legibility drove him from goodness, and he began to associate himself with bad people. The retro hipster lifestyle became apparent to him, and he wore black consistently to mourn the metaphoric death of his old self, he'd say. He believed the old him was weak and stupid for falling in love. Therefore, burial was a definite move to make.

However, his body still needed affection regardless of how much he tried to deny it a woman's touch. A spontaneous moment occurred a few weeks after the semester ended. He'd allowed himself to be dragged into an intimate ruze on a windy afternoon. The sky had dangled its heavy dark clouds. He'd received a message from a beautiful liberal girl he'd met at the Grey Bird Café on one of his very first weeks of attending lectures. Her name was Sarah Dove. He'd met her whilst exploring the city with a group of international students. She had these blue eyes that seemed welcoming and a body which could make any single man dive into his deepest desires.

Quinton finally wanted to dive into his darkest desires as he replied back and showered, preparing himself for an evening with the girl he couldn't quite shake away from his troubled mind.

He walked into her apartment that late afternoon to a surprisingly gentle atmosphere. Everything was different and amazing. He felt like he'd stepped into a different world as she closed the door behind him. The lighting was low, the curtains were closed, and the appearance of the lava lamp on the study table painted an illuminating picture.

Quinton could smell cigarettes. He immediately knew that he was in trouble as soon as he saw her walking from her bedroom in a silky red night gown. She wasn't shy about what she wanted, and he felt his heart throbbing extremely fast as she entered into his sphere. Sarah took a sip from her glass and handed it to Quinton. The liquid was crystal clear, but Quinton could smell the infamous Polish vodka that everyone drank on campus. The bottle wasn't expensive at all, and it was the most affordable bottle anyone could get their hands on from the local student liquor store.

Quinton sat on her couch, and after hours of conversation and drinking, they made love just as he'd scripted within his mind. It at was what he'd hope for in the beginning and afterwards. He dwelled within his own thoughts whilst she whispered sweet nothings into his ear.

'You were amazing,' she whispered into Quinton's left ear, and he knew the rest of the dialog, so he wasn't amused by the truth or tarnished by her little white lies.

He looked at his sporty orange watch and realised that he'd spent too much dwelling and hovering around a person he was beginning to open up to, and quickly, he got dressed and parked his longing lips onto hers. They closed the act with a long kiss, and something about that kiss gave them an understanding—they were lovers carved out from the same rock. A piece of his heart left his body as he walked out and never returned, and with final details emerging from the darkness, he finally understood why he'd woken up in rut before meeting his fate at the music and carnival festival, or so he believed. His heart was confused from the pained he'd experienced before.

Hours lapsed over into a cold morning as Quinton woke up during twilight and finally understood why he'd woken up with mixed emotions from the previous morning like a bipolar patient. It had made him act out of character. However, he couldn't quite help but wonder who he'd met that the festival hours before as he bruited on his bed and looked at all the irrelevant missed calls on his phone.

A few international students stayed with their host families a few days later after the semester had ended, but Quinton felt different as usual. He wanted to live more than anything and wanted to see the world, to travel to different parts of the globe and explore to the smallest towns. He'd thought about going back home, but that reminded him of the corporate lifestyle that he wasn't apparently not suited for. He imagined visuals of fat overly ambitious men gathering around boardroom tables and how they would make selfish decisions to profit off other people's pain. Quinton thought about his father who led some of these profitable ventures with his high achievements hanging in his big office, and despite these thoughts, Quinton wasn't allowed to complain because it was the way that the world was made, and it was what got his university tuition paid to begin with.

The semester had ended on a graceful note, allowing Quinton to dwell on the idea of travelling to Little Venice in Colmar, France, for the summer. He had high hopes to encounter something different, another amusing adventure or some sort. His excitement was mainly justified from the festival event he'd attended.

It was a coincidental miracle the minute he received an email from his mysterious lady the day before his departure. Her name, Juliana Rose. A beautiful rose with sharp thorns. An independent musical artist travelling freely across the globe to catch fuelling inspirations to drive her music to a different level of success. She'd parted ways with her record label simply because they didn't have her best interests at heart anymore. They'd had become commercialised. It was a coincidence that she was also travelling to French on the same day, ironically at the same time, on the same flight. It was fate. They believed it to be as they exchanged details and spoke to each other with excitement, laughing and bonding over the phone. They sounded like little children excited on a scavenger hunt. Maybe they were looking for love or more pain and heartache.

'A handsome, dreamy African man,' Juliana said to herself as her heart throbbed faster after dropping her wireless home phone within her the bedroom.

She shut her wondrous green eyes whilst seated by a large corner window in her bedroom, praying for hope and peace, clutching on to her large red pillow with both arms. Her corner was piled with different-sized pillows in her bedroom of peace and tranquillity. It was her serenity away from the world. Juliana couldn't quite shake Quinton out of her mind and remembered the beating sound of his heart. She wanted to see what magic it possessed whilst chatting with him on her phone, which sparked her beautiful smile within the darkness. She'd pleaded to follow him to his final destination because she wanted to be with him forever. A part of her believed in following her heart wholeheartedly without doubting its ability to make proper decisions.

'Go to bed, Juliana. I don't want you to miss your flight in the morning now!' Teresa, her grandmother, said and closed Juliana's cream-white bedroom door completely.

Juliana's bedroom was enormously large with a spare room for her artwork. The walls were painted cream white, which was her seasonal colour at the moment. Despite the darkness, the light walls enhanced a sense of peace into Juliana's heart every single time she'd sit by the windows in the corner, looking at the dark empty sky from time to time whilst contemplating real love.

The new lovers finally met at the Heathrow International Airport, and Quinton immediately realised that he was attracted to mixed-race women or at least women who appeared different from what he was used to, with a complex of different heritage and a sprinkle of uniqueness to overtop their dramatic personalities. It was fatal preference maybe given the fact that not so long ago, he'd made love to Sarah.

However, there was something different about Juliana Rose. It was right there in her eyes as he observed how beautiful she was from a distance. He walked towards his fate with a smile plastered over his face whilst his insides cracked from a tremor of sadness building up within.

'Never run away from me ever again!' Juliana said as she hugged Quinton at the terminal.

They smiled at each other at that very moment, and everything felt weightless whilst they waited to board, listening to Juliana's playlist through her earphones and some of her new songs she'd just recorded a week ago.

Their chemistry was astounding. There were sparks of love which had lit a flame within their hearts as they arrived at their final destination. Juliana made an irrational decision to cancel her accommodation and follow her heart.

The sun was setting over the romantic town, and the enchanted bit of sunshine deflected a wondrous glow from all the shimmering townhouse roof tiles. It lit a fire in Quinton's heart as he looked into Juliana Rose's eyes. He knew he was about to fall in love. The atmosphere raised a glare from their eyes as they discovered the land of lovers, or at least they thought it was. They observed other couples holding hands and making out passionately under street lamps. There were so many people of different origins walking along the streets and into different restaurants.

It seemed as if it had rained a lot before they'd land. The cobbled street pavements remained wet from the rain as people walked, and the fresh air whiffing through the window was moist. There were pieces of litter there and there, but somehow the imperfections of the place made the experience perfect. It kept the fire within their hearts burning bright.

'I absolutely love this town!' Juliana whispered and grew nostalgic, slowly parking her soft lips onto his soft lips, and just like that, his past evaporated into nothing.

Quinton had booked a week before and paid for hotel room on the day they arrived. The hotel was an old yet modernised French quarter rooms with wonderful crushed rock plastering on parts of the walls, along with shisho trees waving to the direction of the wind and light wires wrapped around all the dark wooden balcony rails. The lighting decorations were remarkable and endorsed the hotel with a sense of romance. It threw Quinton and Juliana off guard as they entered their bedroom. It was warm, spacious, and homey. It came with a complimentary wine bottle. Quinton poured himself and Juliana a glass of wine before looking over the lovely town from the open balcony door. The town light settling lit up Quinton's mind as he sipped from his glass and he fell in love with the scenery.

Quinton switched on the television to international news channels whilst Juliana went into the shower booth to refresh herself. There was a documentary on about modern-day slavery and how poverty led the youth into human trafficking and modern-day slavery. Images of children from third-world countries working for free under humid conditions flooded his mind. He pictured those children being recruited for a civil war they didn't want to be in, and he thought of the young girls that were forced to work as sex workers in compound brothels in other countries.

As an African, Quinton drifted into a different spectrum where he felt an obligation to making a difference in areas that needed change. He questioned himself as he sat on the comfortable bed and drank from his wine glass. The money he had wouldn't make a difference, and it would never be enough. Questions rose up inside his head, and he began to question himself, thus wondering why he felt responsible to taking action. What would he say? What curriculum vitae would be required for him to be political? Did he want to be a politician?

At the rate that he was going, the opposition would have enough information to shut down his whole operation before he even got started. His images on social media portrayed an individual that knew nothing of the struggle that less-privileged people went through. He'd always thought of himself as a narcissist, but were those thoughts helping him realize that he could actually be more or add more to the world? It was definitely present in his face that the life he was leading was inquisitive, but he liked it that way.

Quinton noticed that Juliana's light-toned skin looked as incredible as the caramel that he desired so much. Her skin was exquisite, and she had small freckles on her shoulders. Her scent kept Quinton wanting more of her, and every time Juliana spoke, Quinton fell away from his high horse and drowned in love. He was in love with her British accent, and she was falling in love with his charismatic persona.

She thanked Quinton for that moment as they both drank from their glasses. She began to feel safe around him and started to trust him. Quinton had an album that he'd purchased from the festival. The song made them feeling extremely nostalgic and warm inside. And as the song reached its climax, she sat behind him after lighting a cigarette. She blew rings of smoke over his head. She began to love the fact that he allowed himself to connect or interact with her on an emotional level. Juliana would say that moments like these reminded her that the world still had its good attributes and that being in love made it wonderful to live in. She would blow rings of smoke towards the opened sliding door as they sat close by, and Quinton would sit there wondering what ran through her head as she laid her head onto his back.

They became accustomed to the lifestyle in Little Venice. The walk paths during the weekends were full of people selling antiques and old books that dated back to the times of World War II. Some of these books were poetry books which were filled with sad themes of death and prostitutes selling their love for a better high off addictive substances. It seemed as if the people there loved to feel something even if the feeling was unpleasant.

Quinton had met a new friend whilst he was there in the city looking for medicine for Juliana because she had fallen sick that morning. Quinton and his new friend, Levi, bonded over Mexican Corona beers at an old vintage restaurant, which played mellow jazz sounds in the background. It was known for its trumpet displays, loud evening live music, and it endurance of entertaining people, allowing its customers to smoke inside despite the fact that it was prohibited to do so.

Levi was African too like Quinton, but the difference between the two of them was that Quinton was from the southern part of the continent and the gentleman was from the north-eastern side of the continent. Unlike Quinton, the gentleman wasn't in France by choice but by convenience. He had left his home town because of better job opportunities in Venice, Colmar, but despite this, he disliked being in a foreign place because he didn't feel like he belonged and felt discriminated by some of the locals there. He felt the racial atmosphere every time he used the public transportation system. He would sometimes imagine that the couples behind him in the bus were dismissive about something else besides him, but Quinton chose not to see the negatives in the world. He would walk through life like a donkey with its blinds on and, most of the time like Juliana, believe that the world still had its good attributes. Nevertheless, Quinton understood Levi fully. Therefore, the revelation that adorned them at that moment made it clear that life would always have its ups and downs.

Quinton walked back after realizing he'd started to miss Juliana and her beautiful smile. He entered the bedroom and found her coiled up inside a blanket on the bed. She was watching channels that were in French, and they both stared at the screen as if they understood the language. Everything about that moment made Quinton crave her soft lips even more. He eventually kissed her lips, and the touch whisked away her doubts about him. She stared at the screen again and laughed out loud. Quinton knew at that moment that his heart was in the right place as he smiled to her laughter. He adored her giggle, and her heart wasn't as fickle anymore. Some would find the ability of loving another person to be weak, but Quinton always found it to be the strongest quality a person can ever have. He believed that it was what made humans different from other primates. Thus, he allowed himself to care even more. She began to love him for that ability, and he could see it in her eyes whenever they looked at each other. She smiled so eagerly because she felt safe around him and thanked him for not trying to blatantly use her for any publicity.

A few days passed, and they made their way to the country vineyards with the accommodating transportation from the hotel after Juliana had fully recovered from her fever. The place was lovely. The purple and green grape plants lined their way for hectares, and it was refreshing for the couple to be in a different place. They loved to be surrounded by nature and its fresh air. The local villagers working on vineyards waved at the vehicle that Juliana and Quinton were in after the driver hooted alongside the farmer's section. The location smelt of fresh paint, and the walls were white everywhere. They got to the reception, and on the left, Quinton could see a locked outlet store that had a lot of things and a passage on the right that led to a lot of doors. He finally began to appreciate the work that his parents had put in for him to be able to visit such places instead of taking them for granted.

Juliana ran on the soft grass on an empty field as time passed, and in the meantime, Quinton sat on the picnic blanket next to the steep embankment, taking the moment in, watching his lover laugh whilst drunk off the wine that they'd had. She ran and cartwheeled in her white summer dress. She tripped and laughed whilst Quinton refilled their glasses with white wine. He took a few pictures of that moment from his phone to post them into Instagram when they got back to the hotel.

'You two married?' Pete the waiter asked in a French accent as he brought Quinton two slices of vanilla cake.

Pete was the short skinny waiter on duty at the vineyard restaurant.

'No, not at all,' Quinton replied.

'You have a happy girlfriend, hey!' Pete stated as he glanced at her.

Quinton laughed out loud and smiled.

'No, mate, she is just a good friend of mine, hey,' Quinton said. 'But she is amazing.'

'I can tell. May love bring happiness into your world,' Pete replied and walked away.

Juliana made her way back towards Quinton, and she seemed very happy. Quinton was momentarily happy to have her express herself in a childish manner. She sat by his side after grabbing her wine glass.

'I think I saw a white rabbit by the bush,' she said. 'I'm not sure though.' She giggled. 'Must be the wine,' she mentioned whilst breathing heavily.

'Come closer, Julie,' he said and waited for her to gain composure.

She kissed his left shoulder before pressing her lean chin onto it. 'I'm enjoying myself,' she said.

'I'm glad you are my lover,' he replied and kissed her lips.

Her sweet taste of saliva and the bitterness of the white wine on her tongue fermented into his mouth as they kissed. Quinton exhaled the fresh air slowly and smiled as he looked up into the empty blue clear sky whilst Juliana attempted to press his body onto the ground. However, he resisted due to the lack of privacy around.

'We must head back to the hotel soon, babe,' he whispered.

She hummed to acknowledge his request. 'We must definitely head back to our apartment right now,' she replied and moaned after Quinton placed his right hand underneath her summer dress.

He nodded and kissed her lips once more before standing up. 'Come!' Quinton said.

She stood up and walked alongside him to sign out of the reception and head back to their hotel.

Quinton opened the hotel room door after struggling for a while because of his low tolerance. He couldn't get the card into the slot, and Juliana wasn't helping at all, with her hands scratching against his abs with her sky blue nails. The fact that he was struggling to place the card into the slot made him feel less confident, and he began to wonder if he was ready for what was about to happen next.

The dusk sun had set in the background at that very moment. She stood there for a while, well fitted into a perfect canvas.

He slowly looked into her green eyes as he made love to his beautiful muse. Her round eyes widened in shock to the wide of his love. The moment was intense as his nerves recollected the feeling of her warmth. She began to take deeper breathes. He kissed her wet lips, and it was evident that she longed for his long love.

'Don't get off,' he whispered after a while of lovemaking to his queen.

They remained glued against the wall, and he parked his lips onto hers, kissing her passionately as if the world was about to end.

Their moment portrayed the first essential steps of their love. He looked into her eyes at that moment, and they knew that nothing was ever going to be the same again.

By the end of second week after Juliana had performed at a radio studio, the lovers made their way to South Africa where Juliana's parents had decided to settle down and retire. The trip wasn't long as Quinton had remembered. Matter of fact, he was preoccupied by his lover that time went by so quickly. They got to the international airport at 20:30, and it was extremely cold. Winter had just arrived on the streets of Johannesburg. The wind had creeping chills, but nevertheless, it was Juliana and Quinton's favourite season.

This was the first time that Quinton would meet Juliana's parents, and he was a bit nervous. Juliana had described them as beautifully liberal whilst they were travelling on the plane, and from Juliana's description of things, she said that her mother, Marissa Rose, was Zulu. She also stated to him that her father, Andrew Rose, was British. Her parents had met in London when Marissa was part of the exchange student program and Andrew was finishing of his medicine degree.

As Juliana and Quinton walked through the terminal in Johannesburg, Quinton remembered the times when he came from his home country of Botswana for every term to attend his high school institution in Pretoria. He remembered how privileged he felt with his private school boy blazer on and started to recall how small-minded he was and how self-entitled he felt to the wealth that he hadn't earned.

Juliana's parents were so happy to see them as they walked into the arrival section. Marissa hugged Quinton tightly as if though she knew him. They resided in their yard in Bryanston, Johannesburg. The yard was huge and the driveway was long with mini street lamps on the sides. Their yard looked like a safe haven. It was quiet, and all Quinton could hear were car movements passing by from the freeway in the nearby distance.

Quinton went straight to bed that evening and had a dream that he woke up on an island. On this island, he saw a flock of angels gathered by a cliff as they were crying out loud. There were images of people placing memorial flowers by that cliff as the world mourned for those that had disappeared alongside the famous airplane. He tried to move closer to see what the angels were looking at to find himself zoomed into the cold streets of Johannesburg at night where he was walking behind a toddler in rags and a dirty blanket. The toddler led Quinton to a blind old woman in a dirty alley around the corner. A voice said to him, *'The old woman under that torn blanket could either just be someone in need of help from you, or it could either be the devil pretending to be homeless and waiting for you to come closer to him so that he can put an end to you.'*

And as Quinton moved closer, he was sceptical about what he was about to discover. Nevertheless, he offered to help the old woman. The two beggars didn't understand his language nor did he understand them, but after offering his hand towards the two, they all had an understanding that they were all people. They all understood that the world could be bad and still be good in its weird ways. This must have been a test of faith from God and to find out if Quinton's heart was a pure as he believed it to be.

He woke up confused in the early hours of the morning to find Juliana right next to him. He guessed that she came in whilst he was sleeping to avoid parental confrontation, but everything felt surreal for him at that moment regarding his dream. He went downstairs to make himself a cup of coffee and found Andrew getting ready to go work out. From what Quinton got from Juliana, Andrew was always highly motivated. He was always on time and didn't believe in doing things halfway.

'Morning, want to join me for a run around the estate?' Andrew asked.

'No, I'm okay,' Quinton replied as he thought about all the cigarettes he'd smoked over the last year.

'You know, Juliana seems happy. It wasn't always the case with her being in London and being away from us!' he said as kneeled down and tied his shoelaces.

'Just wanted to let you know that we thank you for being there for her as she pursues her music career!' he said and dwelled by the refrigerator,

'You are welcome!' said Quinton and wondered if he'd used the right words.

'Well, I'm off now. Have a great morning!' Andrew mentioned and walked away towards the main entrance.

'You too, sir, have a wonder run!' Quinton responded.

The conversation went by so quickly, and Quinton began to wonder if it was all happening too quickly, this thing that he had with her and yet it still remained unofficial. They both had commitment and trust issues. Juliana liked the fact that their relationship didn't have a title because then that laid the pressure off a lot of things that couples went through. Quinton went back straight upstairs with both cups of coffee and placed them both by the bedside. He noticed that Juliana was still sleeping, and he joined her. She wrapped her warm body around him and laid her head onto his chest.

The coffee smell must have woken her up. Her nose was pink that morning from the chill as she looked up at him. Moments like these get intensified by the stimulation that occurred whenever they both had the time to merge. She played with her fingers, giggled out loud, and made her fingers gallop on his chest. Juliana's mother was in the next room, and Quinton had enormous respect for Marissa and therefore behaved like a gentleman. That was the toughest decision Quinton had ever made that morning, but Juliana found his strength incredibly attractive and admirable. She took off to the shower and invited Quinton to join her a few minutes later.

The shower room was extremely steamy from the entrance. It was peaceful as he walked in, and it sounded as if it was raining. The light setting was low, and all he could see was her and her beautifully dipped caramel skin tone. Her hair was wet and loosened by the water from the shower. Moments like these kept the magic alive. At times as a man in the twenty-first century, Quinton found those moments to be extremely clingy. However, Juliana found it to be romantic. She was a hopeless romantic, and it made Quinton reconsider to care about her more then she'd ever know. He wasn't one to invest on something that would end up failing, and he believed that their love would never fail. Their hearts were gambling and winning whilst their minds were losing badly. Their vulnerability made her feel alive. She would express to him of the way his hands felt finest to the touch.

'Whenever you touch my back, I get goosebumps, my blood rises, and all of a sudden, I get vibrations on my knees,' she would whisper to him.

She would hold on to his other hand every time as she expressed herself.

The sun was coming up, and it was still cold outside. Everything started to feel busy again as the dogs started barking as the garden service van arrived. It all reminded him why he liked South Africa at this time of year because of the little morning frost melting from the grass. He liked the thick fresh air that hovered around the sloppy city every morning.

The next Sunday, Quinton felt the urge to head back to his home country of Botswana as a part of him began to feel homesick. It was the sight of Juliana and her parents that made Quinton feel nostalgic at times. It had been at least two years since he'd been back to the land of cattle trading and big diamonds. From what he'd heard from everyone, the city Gaborone was growing exceptionally well despite the South African problems that Botswana also had such as the major power cuts and a lack of good water distribution.

They all sat on camp chairs around the fire with Juliana's parents and Marissa, Rose's older sister who came along with her family to reintroduce them. Juliana always acted as if she had amnesia when it came to meeting people she didn't feel close too. That's what Juliana and Quinton had in common. They believed that not only blood was the secret bond that connected relatives together but also the little efforts of calling once in a while or helping out wherever help was needed. They all sat there and Quinton wondered if it was the best time to tell Juliana that he wanted to head home soon. He wondered if she would want to come with him. He wondered if he was ready to let her go for a while. They'd both grown attached to one another, but this decision had its ability to end the fragile relationship that they had. Quinton knew that deep down in his heart as he sat there.

Juliana sat by Quinton's side whilst talking to her relative, Samantha, who studied business administration.

Minutes passed.

Juliana looked at Quinton.

'You have been quiet for a while now. Out with it!' she commanded as Quinton sat there with his eyes zoned into the burning firewood.

He felt troubled yet didn't want to talk about it at that moment. He yawned and acted as though hadn't didn't hear a single word that Juliana said. A few hours passed and Quinton sat there, listening to everyone share their stories about the experiences that they'd had. Slowly but surely, the number of people decreased until only Juliana and Quinton remained cuddled in a blanket. The heat from the fire gave that moment significance, and such moments were to be cherished for life. He began to feel his heart beating extremely loud as if it was about to burst out of his chest. They both looked into the dark sky, and there were no stars to be seen.

'Sometimes I sit next to you, and I don't even feel your presence,' she said as she kept her focus on the sky.

'What does that even mean? I've been right here,' he replied and frowned a little.

'Yeah, I know, but you've been so quiet, so I'm going to ask, is it me?' she said.

'No, not at all, I've been thinking about going home,' he replied.

'You must miss your family, huh?' she asked.

'Yeah, just a little bit. I think I just have to go and see them. Even for a few days you know!' he replied.

'I understand,' she stated.

After a long pause, she continued, 'I'm going to miss you then. Do promise to come back to me, okay?'

There was a paused as Quinton looked into the sky with a bit of uncertainty. He knew that they all had to return to the university for another semester. Thus, he wondered if he'd leave with her or alone.

'I was kind of hoping that you would want to come with me for a little bit,' he said and waited for her to reply, but she just sat there.

'So that you can see where I'm from, you know!' he added.

'I don't know if I can. I wanted to spend more time with my parents before heading back, and to be honest, what we have here seems a bit farfetched. I love the way you treat me and touch me. The way you put your hand in between my hair, the way you kiss me and hold me tightly when it's cold, but I can't go with you,' she said.

At that moment, Quinton felt like he'd overcompensated for that relationship without any insurance of knowing if it was ever going to work. Juliana appeared to be very selfish and conceded to only which appealed to her own needs and wants.

Quinton never found it useful to argue with someone when their emotions are heightened because then foul things could be said instead of the conversation being euphemistic or productive. He stood up and walked towards the main house. Juliana sat there as though she hadn't said anything wrong.

Quinton made his way into Andrew's house and thought about Juliana's words as they sunk into his head. He felt that maybe he was overreacting by walking away. The reason why he had asked Juliana to go with him to Botswana was because he wanted to see if Juliana would be able to fit into his world like he did in hers. The relationship itself was fragile, and anything negative could set it off.

Quinton entered the shower booth and hoped that this wasn't the end of their relationship. To his surprise, Juliana joined him, but it wasn't as romantic this time. She looked into his eyes as the water streamed downwards, and she hoped for a kiss, but Quinton was done hoping that she would change her selfish ways.

'Why do you have to complicate things? We were just fine!' she said, trying to keep her voice down.

He highlighted 'were' on his mind and wondered if she now thought of them as part of the past. He wouldn't be surprised of Juliana's recent attitude because he expected the worst from anyone but hoped for the best nevertheless because he loved her. Quinton did not say anything back, and she knew that it was a sign that he wasn't in the mood to discuss anything. She walked away and out the door without speaking to Quinton, and that moment, her silence pierced Quinton as he entered the bedroom. This was one of those disagreements that could ruin everything. Their ignorance could easily wreck their whole ship. He lay there thinking about the lessons he was learning. Inevitably guys like Quinton were born to be heartless towards such vulnerabilities that most women like Juliana presented, but there he was thinking about the future that he wanted for the both of them. Her precious soul had an impact to alter his golden path towards success, but at the same time, Quinton wasn't one to give up being himself for someone else. He would not allow himself to be belittled by another human. His guardian angels that flew behind him always remained positive towards such altercations that came towards him, and the more he thought about them, the more he started to feel obligated into persuading Juliana that coming with him would be better for the both of them. They were both liberal, but their cultures were different, and his only hope was that she understood his world.

He switched on the lamp on the left side of the bed after some time. It was late, and all he could hear were sirens from what could have been ambulances or police vehicles. He lay there quietly as the door opened and knew it was Juliana.

'May I come in?' she asked.

'Yeah, sure!' he replied.

She came hesitantly and asked, 'May I join you in bed, love?'

A part of him was hesitant, but he allowed her into his bed anyway. She had these forgivable puppy-dog eyes and the most sincere face whenever she felt bad about what she'd said or done.

'I'm scared that you will realize that I'm not worth your time, babe, that you deserve someone better,' she said as she put her hand over his chest. She overcompensated for times like these with tears that didn't make sense.

'I will come with you,' she whispered as they both looked into the painting hanging across the room which was a picture of what looked like the perfect description of the Industrial Revolution with men painted in black dust. They are leaving a coal distributing factory and tired from a day's work from the looks of things.

'Are you sure?' he asked, hoping that her answer would be more assuring.

'Yes, it's scary, you know!' she said.

'What is?' he asked as his lips gently touched her forehead.

'Us, this thing we have. I feel connected to you and find it hard to be away from you now,' she said as she placed her right hand onto his chest.

'I feel the same way. I'm honestly naïve to what we have because it seems unrealistic! We have been travelling together. We made love in Little Venice. We've seen places together. We are in bed in your parents' house in Johannesburg, and somehow it feels just right. So what happens after the trip back home?' he replied and asked.

'Baby steps, love, you worry too much! We will figure it all out,' she said.

Quinton always seem to worry about things that he had no complete control over, but maybe this was a good thing and maybe this is exactly what he needed—a sense of surprise to keep his life interesting. From what he'd heard from people, love had its own course and that he shouldn't try predict the outcome.

Time passed that night as Quinton lay there with Juliana by his side. His mind always fascinated him as he zoned out. It was incredible how gifted he was with his imagination. The painting he looked at of the men leaving that factory had its own significance and showed him the hardships that were endured in the past. He'd always wondered what his purpose was on this world. Life itself was unbearable at times when he thought of those in townships around the Johannesburg City and the daily decisions that the people there had to make for their own survival. These thoughts made him wonder if his obligation was to help out people because he essentially felt like that's what he owed the world.

Chapter Three

Homebound

A few days passed by, and Quinton felt it was about time he introduced his nation to Juliana Rose for the first time ever. It was a windy day in the suburbs. Andrew drove the couple to the airport. They were a bit behind schedule because of Juliana's organizational skills—she was slow and indecisive when it came to packing necessities and luxury items. Quinton played music on his phone, and they plugged the earpieces into their ears. Juliana loved moments like these, where she would look at the street lights as they drove past them and wrapped her arms around Quinton's left arm. The one thing about being in love was that their senses become amplified and everything he could smell went into recognition. The coco butter lotion that Juliana liked to apply to her hands took him places as he kissed her hand. He closed his eyes as he did so and felt like nobody else was with them. He felt like they were in a parallel universe that had a population of two people drifting towards a place of war and peace at the same time. The rush of love adorned the both of them as they silently kissed in the back seat.

Quinton started to feel like his reason for living was to love Juliana, and she felt the same way.

They sat down at the boarding gate, and Quinton started to reflect back on his life. He understood that at times people all lose their ability to love another person because they'd all get so hurt and wounded badly, but this was one of those moments when a person's heart could restore itself and mend to love again. They were in sync, and everything was telepathic at times. She would sometimes finish off Quinton's sentences, and they both craved the same types of food. Juliana loved romantic theatricals and movies. She would cry when watching romantic movies.

In the cold world that they lived in, Quinton believed that finding a woman with love as her strongest quality can only lead a man to be stronger. He felt invincible, untouchable and annoyingly cocky about their love.

Their flight to Gaborone didn't take long, and they were close to landing that evening when they both glanced out the window lit up to a pleasant sight of a growing city. Everything about the city looked different from the sky. The city had more lights lit up than before. It felt good to be back home, and everything was better for Quinton because Juliana was with him. She was nervous, but she smiled anyway after they'd landed. She walked by him and held on to his hand tightly as they made their way through the terminal. It was crispy cold that evening, and Quinton couldn't wait to be home. His country was different and unique in its own way. He felt cleansed as he entered back into his domain.

He was greeted by a mild aged woman who'd noticed that Quinton's passport had the country's logo on it. He felt welcomed to the woman who greeted him in Setswana and smiled. *Dumelang* were her exact words, a general greeting term within the country.

Quinton's mother was there to pick them up, and she was amazed to see the beauty that Quinton saw in Juliana. His mother, too, hugged Juliana like Juliana was one of her own. They'd entered Quinton's yard, which was located just outside the city by a lonely hill. The yard wasn't as big as Andrew's yard, but the household was massive. Quinton's oldest sister was married with her second child on the way. His younger sister had just been accepted to a private school in South Africa, and that made him miss them even more. The house was empty without his sisters, but at least Juliana was around to keep him company. Quinton's father was mostly found in his office afterhours, driving his whiskey, at times getting up to mischief with his mistress over the phone. Marcus Barker enjoyed drowning himself at his office afterhours instead of coming to his beautiful wife. Quinton's mother, Beth, loved Quinton regardless of his unpredictable behaviour. Everything looked the same for Quinton, except for the British pug that resided in his home. He absolutely hated it because British pugs always had a lot of energy. Despite his recent hatred for the adorably ugly pug, Juliana absolutely loved it.

Days passed and winter rallied through the streets without sympathy, but the lovers were prepared. They liked to wear black in the winter to help absorb the heat from the sun, which seemed like a smart idea until it got hot during the long dry afternoons. They spent most of their days together whilst Quinton's parents were on their business trip in South Africa. What was first just a sceptical thought about Juliana going to Botswana slowly started to faded away as she enjoyed being at his home. Despite her different roots and having an English accent, she began to find comfort in Quinton's world. She began to fit in it, and Quinton began to love her even more for feeling that way. He expressed his affection towards her and that he loved her, which was definitely a courageous statement that he'd ever made to her.

On Thursday, they drove into the city to stock up the house with groceries and for her to see what his city looked like during the night. She was an admirer of city lights, and her face lit up whenever they were around them. Every time Quinton's parents were away, they would check up on him via landline at home every night, but as he got back home that evening and found no voice mails or messages recorded on the home phone, he wondered if his parents were settled. It was very different occurrence, but Quinton dismissed it because Juliana had taken up most of his time.

A few days later, Quinton's uncle came over to check up on him. Steve met Juliana, but his beliefs were different and cultural. He didn't like her at all the moment he saw. He went through his whole life, believing that a black man belonged to his own race and that all African-descent people were only blessed by their ancestors if they were all united again. His own beliefs were probably the reason why his ex-wife left him in the first place. He would say to Quinton, 'You must not fall in love with a woman of another race' every single time during Quinton's youth. Despite his poisonous advice, Quinton grew up to be very liberal and kind, unhinged from the hatred within his uncle. Steve walked through life believing that he was chosen to lead the people of the nation into an unknown salvation. His so-called realistic advice were his own dismiss. He was a man of many foes, he was alone, and Quinton could see it in his eyes whenever Steve spoke. Steve reminded Quinton of a child that grew up orphaned and abused, but nevertheless Quinton's uncle was wealthy from hitching his wagon on to Quinton's father's success.

Uncle Steve wanted to be a king when the country ran on a democratic system. At times, Quinton would read a lot of people's tweets and thus believed that there were too many philosophers in the world that hardly anyone got anything done, and that was his uncle.

'Inevitably your words should come with leadership,' Quinton would say to people, and he knew that his uncle didn't possess that quality.

Juliana made her way up the stairs whilst Quinton was in the living room with his uncle. His uncle's breath reeked of indirect hate, and his words drained the soul from Quinton who sat there paying special detail to his uncle's face. Quinton yawned a lot throughout and made hints that his uncle wasn't welcome anymore. His uncle had had a lot of alcohol to drink that evening. Therefore, Quinton dismissed everything that his uncle said. He didn't take anything to heart and remained primarily focused on Juliana's well-being.

He made his way up the wooden paved stairs to see if she was okay. He remembered that his parents would never permit him to be in the same bedroom as her, but they weren't there that evening. It had been awhile since they'd connected properly with her being in a new environment. There she was in bed with her hair unclipped. She didn't look too happy about Quinton's uncle and his presence, but regardless of that, she wanted to be with Quinton. He lay on the bed, and she held on to his body so tightly. She looked absolutely beautiful without any make-up on, and at times, Quinton was amazed that he was with her. He was amazed that she was in bed with him and that she loved him. She wondered whether their love would last if they interacted more with other people, but he had no doubt about their bond. They were very special to each other. He wanted to let her know how special she was to him, but his words would never be enough.

All the worries in the world disappeared when he kissed her soft lips. Nothing else mattered to him but Juliana. They would look into each other's eyes, and she would smile at him because she knew that she'd steal his heart away. She was glad that Quinton was gentle towards her, and she allowed herself to be vulnerable towards him. Juliana found peace within the relationship that she had with Quinton whilst the world was at war with itself. She wasn't afraid to open up to Quinton anymore, and he listened to her speak even when she didn't make much sense. He allowed himself to be a book of secrets to her, and she would write anything important on him. He became her safe haven, and their love wasn't something that anyone came across in the twenty-first century. This type of love required them both to be brave towards anything because anything was unpredictable, and that was what made them grow intimately fond with each other. Such moments withdrew them from the world and secluded them on a different plain field covered with red pedals.

They were drawn to every colossal moment. Every touch. Every kiss.

The guest room was warm, and they lay alongside each other and made passionate love for a while. His love for her was so strong within, which initially kept her paralysed. Tears of love streamed from her green eyes, and she gripped on to Quinton's left hand. She'd never ever felt love so consuming, and it was emotionally pleasant for her. Neither one of them moved after a while. They lay there, connected and vulnerability nostalgic. Her green eyes glowed, and they sparkled with life as he looked into them. He didn't want to be anywhere else. He felt attached, and he couldn't even explain the feelings that were gushing from his heart.

They closed their eyes to the magical atmosphere. Juliana didn't know that she would ever feel this way for somebody from another origin. She didn't understand why this love was consuming her deeply. Not once did she let go of his left hand, and not once did he take his right hand off her left chest. The moment was beautiful as two humans performed the act of love and connected deeply.

However, Juliana's parents wanted her back in Johannesburg for the last bit of the holiday that they had. Quinton avoided the reality of it until the last night when he found Juliana miserable in the guest room, halfway through one of their last dinners. She was close to weeping, and all Quinton wanted to do was make the last night special for her. Maybe the dinner and the candles were a bit too much and maybe the indie genre wasn't such a good choice. Time stood still as he stood there, watching Juliana weep and long for his arms to wrap around her body.

'This is your fault!' she said as she sobbed. 'You just . . . just had to bring me along, and I don't want to leave now,' she stuttered a little.

Love was confusing, and they were just as confused. He wondered if she was blaming him because she loved him so much and indirectly thanking him for opening her up to a world of sparks and flames, or if she was distorted because he had enviably invaded the space in her heart. He wasn't happy that she had to leave either. He felt like she was being taken away from him, and he felt hopeless because there was nothing he could do about it. He wondered if he was going to lose her to the world for it was a cruel place.

Juliana was notably safer around Quinton. Her giggles replayed inside of his head as he stood there, thinking of the time they were at the countryside in France. He remembered the way she ran across the empty fields so eagerly and happy to be part of an adventure whilst they were drunk on white wine. She was so happy, and he felt horrible to see tears drop from her eyes. He pulled her closer and hugged her. Quinton could feel her beautiful heart aching at that moment. Her heart was beating so slowly. They didn't pack her clothes that night, but both got into bed to keep warm. They started reflecting on the times they shared together, the times when the weather was good and when the birds came out in the morning to sing. Their hearts were impatient and didn't want to understand that life had to go on. They had to understand that they weren't going to wake up next to each other for a while. He believed that she would be okay, but the sound in her voice stated otherwise because she love being with him dearly. The universe had started acting defectively towards them, and slowly but surely they started too accepted. They fell asleep hoping that this wouldn't be the last time they shared such moments together.

Taking Juliana to the airport was one of the most agitating moments for Quinton, with her being quiet throughout the whole trip to the airport. She smiled at him as he drove but remained vague. Quinton could see the tears that dangled on her eyelids, but they tried to avoid the void that they were both beginning to feel. They sat at a restaurant, and no words were spoken nor were any emotions shared. All he could hear in between small chats around were the sounds of airplane engines and the intercom updates.

Juliana sat there with her face masked to the menu, and she pretended to be preoccupied. Quinton could see through her curly hair dangling over her head. She was staring into his eyes, wondering what she'd say to make him smile. He pulled her chair close as they sat by, observing all airplanes landing onto different landing strips. Quinton pulled the chair closer, and he kissed her as if they were never going to see each other ever again. Tears came down her eyes as she closed them, and he could feel the tears wet his cheeks. His lover was compassionate, good-hearted, and a bit theatrical at times, but that's what he loved about her. She gave their moments life. He was going to miss the intimate connection that they shared and the way she would scream out his name as if she had just remembered who he was whilst they were making love.

Quinton thought of the love and remembered what his friend said to him once, that having sex is like gluing two pieces of paper together, and the more you keep having sex with that person, the more you get attached to them. He then added on to say that 'Once you try and pull the two pieces of paper apart, the separating of the two papers will result in them tearing up unevenly, with one piece ripping out another.' His friend's words spiralled on within his mind that parts from the first paper would be glued onto the second paper, and Quinton wondered at times if that was happening to him. Was he losing a bit of himself every time he had sex with someone? Was he going to end up not being able to identify his sexual desires to his future wife in-depth because he would have already been used up? He had all those thoughts after making out with his beautiful lover.

She sat there waiting patiently for her food and trying to smile again. Quinton found peace when he was with her. He wasn't angry, nor was he impatient. He had nothing but time when he was with her. Being alone was their worst enemy, and he had to be brave for the both of them. He had to have composure and be strong for her as he watched her get through the immigration gates. She hugged him tightly. She wasn't as tall as Quinton was, but she walked tall in her black heels and walked with purpose. She disappeared into the distance, and Quinton's heart drifted into the distance with her. He would never be able to hold on to the additional time that he wanted to share with her, and saying goodbye for a little while was inevitable.

Days went by without Juliana and Quinton speaking constructively over the phone. Quinton had a week left until he'd return to London to complete his course, and it was starting to get cold in Botswana with the rain dropping randomly in the humid weather. He sat on his bed that evening. He began to pray to God for forgiveness, for his love towards Juliana was not affirmative towards his faith mainly because of their lust. Quinton was a child when it came to his faith with God, and like his earthly father, he hoped God would forgive him. Quinton hoped that he would be understood even when he would misbehave at times, and he prayed the Lord would give him comfort through the pain that he was beginning to feel.

Quinton began to miss Juliana waking up by his side. They texted each other afterhours, and it was evident that she missed him too. She said that this was becoming the coldest winter and that Quinton's absence made her nights unbearable. All those memories of them together took up space in his memory bank, and they played inside his head that evening. Her perfume scent lay permanently on his pillows, and the more he could recall her scent, the more he began to miss parking his lips onto hers. Quinton couldn't bring myself to understand the magnitude of the love that he had for her. He wasn't merely alive but could see his future turn brighter. The more he thought about Juliana, the more his arteries would expand wider and allow more blood to enter into the rest of his body. Every breath Quinton took was a gift, and he was presently blessed to have such an amazing life and to be grateful for Juliana Rose.

A few nights before Quinton's departure, his closest friend of nine years came over to pick him up for a night out. The sun had disappeared over the hills, and the sky was orange. This was the first time that Quinton had ever gone out that month after being apart from Juliana. He felt that a night off from being alone at home would ease the tension that he had. It was an average week night in the Diamond City. Quinton realized that reuniting with his old friends would help bring some sort of happiness into his life, and his closest friend, Benjamin, was a good lad that lived life curiously, bending a few rules. Benjamin was always humble for the opportunities that he got through the same private high school education that he and Quinton went to. The remarkable common denominator that he and Quinton had was that they were short tempered towards other human beings that walked around the city as though they were above everyone else. The two friends didn't tolerate bullshit from anybody, but regardless of their low tolerance, they did understand that people were different and that they weren't always going to see eye to eye with most of the people out there. Benjamin came from a long line of rich farmers, who'd capitalized off the food industry and the deeply entrenched poverty of the country by paying workers below minimum wage.

Quinton and Benjamin went to the restaurant, which was located by the only dam. The place was dark in certain areas and bright at the main pub area. Quinton met a lot of old friends that he used to hang out with, but he wasn't particularly interested in rekindling old friendships. As the hours passed and the waters caused a cool breeze to brush onto the landscape, Quinton found himself completely caught off guard by an unfamiliar scent. The smell of a sweet scent whiffed into his nose, and he was slightly infatuated. He noticed a beautiful white girl, brunette with a pointy cute nose. He was sceptical of her

51

because he didn't believe she was interested in him, nor did his heart want anyone else. His heart was manufactured to gamble, so he didn't trust its judgement. He'd felt alone and the alcohol had poisoned his soul. His mind was marinated in lust, yet his heart belonged to Juliana Rose. It had been at least two days since Juliana and Quinton spoke. He remembered a saying that a lot of men who spend their whole lives searching for love from women lacked an emotional support system from their fathers whilst they were younger, and he knew this must have been a physiological barrier he needed to break out of. He didn't want to let the devil enter and fester the relationship he had with Juliana. He allowed himself to let go of any recent attachments that he had for the brunette with the cute pointy nose.

The night was at an end, and they had to get back home. Benjamin drove onto the main road to head to Quinton's house on the other side of the city, but none of them knew that Benjamin was as drunk as a clumsy pirate. Quinton guessed that they'd missed each other to the point where they celebrated and forgot that someone of them had to drive back home. Quinton and Benjamin subconsciously believed that rules were meant to be broken from time to time, and maybe that's what came into play that night. They, at times, liked to disobey and pretend that they were above the law. The music was loud, and Elaine, Benjamin's girlfriend, was texting away in the passenger seat. Quinton sat in the back seat smoking cigarettes and contemplating Juliana Rose whilst Benjamin was in the driver's seat with his seatbelt on, but he lacked focus. He kept zoning out into the street lights and a moment that could have been avoided if they'd stopped at the red traffic lights instead of turning happened.

It felt like Quinton had slept forever with his body aching on a hospital stretcher. He blinked and his vision was blurry, for he couldn't see properly. He felt drowsy and sedated from injections. Everything appeared brighter. Sleep was the cousin of death, and she too was deceiving with the dreams that she helped sell to people. Quinton was almost sold to death, for death was the highest bidder that early morning. He woke up that morning and couldn't remember what he'd dreamed of, nor did he know what had happened to him. He'd woken up to excruciating pain on his lower back and had a mild concussion. The news changed his attitude toward life.

Devastating headlines were on his social media timeline, and he realized that his best friend of nine years, Benjamin, had died alongside his girlfriend of two years. Quinton realized that they would never awake ever again. They were permanently dreaming, and their hearts stopped beating. Their souls lingered by the bed in his imagination as he lay there in shock, thinking of how to process this information. Their two souls hovered by his side as the angel of death's dark horse kicked the intensive care unit door open. He lay there facing the ceiling with his eyes closed. It all felt real to him as the room became windy, and he imagined images of the angel gravitating Benjamin and Elaine's souls into his dark bag. Their souls were gone within a flash, and it got extremely quiet.

All Quinton could hear was the heart monitor on the left side of his bed. It was so quiet that his mental state clouded into darkness and he began to hear voices crying extremely louder. He'd never heard something so terrifyingly loud that his head began to ache. His imagination was dark with vastness, and he started to see black crows flying around him whilst his body remained on the hospital stretcher. He imagined his soul surrounded by loud screams, and he viewed his body on a dry thatched field. He tried to open his eyes again, but the truth of his best friend's death was too unbearable.

Quinton didn't eat much whilst he was under intensive care, and his parents came to visit every day. Melinda, his oldest sister, came once that week with her new beautiful family. Quinton wasn't particularly intrigued to have a lot of visitors view him in such a compromising position. The scans came back after a few days, reporting a mild damage to the head. The doctors explained carefully the side effects of having a minor injury to the head. He entered a new league of devastation and depression as he thought of recent events. The thought of maybe overdosing to reduce the pain and maybe passing on occurred to him. He felt that he had died inside, but his human instinct to survive wouldn't allow him to commit.

Quinton's expectations for Juliana to be by his bedside after the times that they shared left him vulnerably sad. He was alone on the hospital bed, and at times he zoned out into the window by side of wall whilst the small television screen was on. It came to his attention that he'd missed his departure date, but he didn't care much about that because two people that he knew were deceased. Their bodies were cold and beginning to deteriorate. He wondered what he would say to their parents if questions were asked. It was already bad enough that the police who came in between visiting hours asked him questions he had no answers to. He could not remember what happened at those traffic lights, and the more he tried to remember, the more the thought of the accident itself led him to heavy headaches.

His days at that hospital were days of reflection, and it became official afterwards—his dark thoughts consumed him and all negatively impacting events that had occurred throughout his whole life gathered into one motion and it had begun to define him. Quinton clinched for intimate love, but his mind was slowly but surely becoming cold to the feeling, and he began to think that maybe caring for people was the reason he felt so down. He believed that if didn't care for Benjamin and Elaine, then he wouldn't feel sensitively weak. He felt impacted by their death so much to the point where he believed that he had to reinvent himself to gain strength, and he realized that he'd himself to care so much for the world yet got nothing back. That realization flicked his whole persona, and he discovered that he'd invested a lot into developing emotions that were useless and depressing. All he wanted was love. Instead, he got nothing back from the world but pain and pills. His dark thoughts kept him quiet, and he wallowed in sorrow.

He didn't speak much whilst his family was around, yet he pretended to smile in happiness whilst they all spoke amongst themselves. The reality of his roots were projected as he witnessed his grandmother from his father's side holding her rosary and her Bible in her hand. He looked at her as she prayed in Setswana with her members from the nearest Lutheran church. After being alive for more than two decades, Quinton still didn't understand the real concept of faith as he watched the church members singing softly.

Late hours consisted of loud screams from the accident, and at times, Quinton felt like an abandoned child as he lay on the stretcher crying. His bruises started to heal with time, and the amount of visitors increased as days grew closer to Benjamin and Elaine's funeral. He never heard once from Juliana that week, and that bruised his ego. He kept looking at his phone and wondered if she'd call him. His ears craved her voice and her voice only. Quinton imaged that she must have been so distorted to the point of depression, yet a part of him realized and saw it as evidential that everyone's lives were graveling well without his effort. Metaphorically speaking, his heart was on surgery, and it was opened up to bleed. He began to feel stranded and lost in the world and in his own imagination.

Quinton missed both Benjamin and Elaine's funeral out of respect for their families because he was embarrassed and carried the blame on his shoulders. He wondered why he'd survived out of all three. An admission of guilt trailed onto Quinton's conscience. He thought of praying but felt conflicted with that act because he knew that he was a sinner at heart. It all left him confused to the reason why people asked for forgiveness but carried on sinning against God. He felt unworthy of forgiveness.

He was sent home as time passed and found himself being nursed from his massive bedroom with a king-size bed. The repulsion he felt made him question everything and started questioning why he was so privileged when a lot of people in the country weren't. His recovery was speedy.

He'd look for signs all around and thought deeply whilst weighing his sins. He looked into the mirror in the bathroom, and he saw nothing impressive. The ideal man that he wanted to be wasn't remotely close to the figure reflected right before him. He envisioned his whole future slipping away right before his heavy eyes as he came to an understanding that he had to change his weak ways. He knew that only he had the power to the change the outcome as he thought about therapy.

Essentially, he had trust issues and couldn't find it in myself to trust a stranger with any information. The only person he thought he could trust was Juliana, but she was a new heartbreak song. Quinton had honoured a young woman that didn't seem to be loyal to him, and at times, his family looked at him with pity. He noticed that they all wanted to say something to him about her, but they never eventually came around to doing it. The looks of pity left him in pain as he scrolled through all the pictures of her on his phone. Tears raced from his face, but he never once showed a sign of emotional pain to his family.

Winter took its toll mid-June within the country, and Quinton found himself working as a manager at his father's distribution company after he'd recovered therapeutically from the accident. His state of mind completely changed after realizing the value of money, and his self-esteem lifted to the idea of real wealth. On random occasions, he made and laughed at jokes that the colleagues made—a casual additional commentary to the mediocre conversations that other workers had. The events that occurred before June that year were mentally inflicting misery, and he loved its company. The emotions that came with the high were incredible to him because he liked the dark attachment.

Quinton became damaged goods and proclaimed as written off to a lot of young women around the city. Physically, his body was golden, but his heart was in need of service, and that sad quality began to attract young ladies that felt compelled to repair broken men. He wasn't ready to play a monogamy game or childish games, and at times he only craved the love that he used to get from Juliana. Her beautiful green eyes kept him compelled. Quinton relapsed when it came to the thought of her, and from time to time, he would see her in every tall beautiful mixed-race curly-haired girl that walked the earth. All he had were images of her in his mind. Those thoughts were beginning to disappear from his memory, and he felt like he was losing his old self. He remembered that his distant friends would advise that, 'The only way to get over someone was to get on top of somebody else'.

His old friends positioned themselves by calls and text messages, advising him to forget about Juliana Rose. The love that he had for Juliana was consuming, and he was a wrecked ship that was sinking from an ideal false love. At times, a bit of him began to miss events that had not even occurred yet because he truly thought that they were forever. The future that he saw once slowly turned from a beautiful picture into a vague memory and reminded him not to ever let anything temper with his feelings.

Days passed, and he had to open his eyes to see that the world was a cold place when you opened yourself up to people that had no intention of staying. A lot of money had gone into preparing Quinton for life, but he wasn't taught of the side effects of having feelings, and that initially depressed him. The nights in the country were cold, but something about the crispy chills toughened up Quinton. He started to appreciate the tough love that he'd gotten, and the emotions that had come through his heartbreak brought a whole new perspective to understanding women. Quinton was being bred, and his heart was being manufactured into steel. He became avoidant to the bullshit that the world dished out to him, and he was stronger, more ruthless without care. The thought of his siblings was only a reminder that not all females were bad, and initially that reminder chaperoned his heart the right way.

The idea of making a lot money kept Quinton essentially focused and distracted from his previous heartbreak. Quinton's father started to feel proud to see his son taking initiative and being responsible. By the end of that month, Quinton started taking trips with the truck drivers that drove the company truck carriers into South Africa. It was always refreshing to be in different places, especially after the year that Quinton had had.

He felt peace for the first time that month as he lit a cigarette whilst the distributing loaders started packing the commodities into the trucks. It was evident that music was a way for him to escape the world that he was in even if it was for a little while. As days passed, he grew accustomed and compassionate for materialistic things. He was drawn to making a name for himself because he, too, wanted to drive expensive cars and fill his longing void with money.

Quinton spent every minute in Botswana dedicated towards making money. He wanted everything about him to glow and to sparkle brightly in anyone's eye. The desire for beautiful women soon made him selfish and slightly possessive. He relished in love without care and dove in and took no responsibility for his actions.

Weeks passed, and a lot people began to dislike him because he'd become slightly deceitful. He was blind to humanity and had lost all faith in other people. The idea of maintaining multimillions sunk his soul as he terrorized people and tried to fight through most arguments with people. His monsters had a foothold in his life, and he began to hear the whispers of evil from his back whilst he walked around. He felt the claws of a dragon scratching against his back from time to time.

Months later, Quinton moved out to live on his own, and thoughts of going back to school rapidly depreciated with time. He'd taken Smuggles with him because it reminded him of Juliana. He had everything he wanted, with medium investments bringing back money into his accounts at a consistent pace. His life became a soundtrack themed with laughter hinged with sadness. His recent twenties were golden ages, painting everyone false. Everyone around him spoke senselessly of hot sex, false feelings, speculating dreams to each other, and those that claimed to be relevant towards Quinton became irrelevant as time entered into a new era.

Bank statements weren't misleading, plasma screens became wider, and the women became more scornful. Quinton was very aware of the dark side he was living in, yet he lusted in it. Every moment that legs were dripping were a mental tick for Quinton that the world he lived in was cruel place. There he was in a world where most wishes came with clauses, where marriage seemed to be a business transaction, and where love was a dream sold through romantic Sunday movies. There was nothing pure about anyone he knew. They were all the same to him, and he viewed them as dolls that were controlled by the element of money. Imminently they loved to use each other repeatedly and backstabbed each other for profitable amusement.

Quinton's apartment had turned into a circle. It was the funniest place to be, but also quite sadistic. His soul had a dark hole within itself as the weeks went on, the emptiness he felt were moments of him intoxicated in the bathroom. He knew that none of the numbers that he could call from his phone could heal the fatal inner wounds that he had. The blind truth was that he needed Juliana's affection, but he didn't want to dwell on that thought because it seemed to leave him in pain.

Chapter Four

<hr />

Dwelling by the Black Window Paint

The year came to a near end, allowing the Barkers to vacate towards the east coast of South Africa, Plettenberg Bay to be precise, for some peace and quiet away from the world of business and other controversial issues spiralling around their name. Quinton stayed behind for overtime work and be became a workaholic. He drowned himself in paperwork and started to guzzle down his father's alcohol supply. It wasn't evident to anybody that worked under Quinton's supervision that he was self-destructing. He was a ticking time bomb that had an unpredictable clock. The workers that worked under his management received bonuses around the Christmas interval.

He spent his worthless time in his office one quiet Thursday afternoon and felt an empty sense of accomplishment. He wanted to feel proud for the work that he'd put in, but he felt a self-loathing feeling that gripped his damaged heart. The feeling of being alone was quite painful to him as he walked around the office block. He'd always thought that success meant well-tailored suits, fast cars, beautiful women, and trips overseas for the summer, but this lifestyle wasn't for him. Well, at least his perception of it wasn't for him. He felt extremely close to crashing and burning merely because Juliana's acts had dented something within him. Something within him was seriously damaged as a tear dropped from his eye. He stood there quietly by the window, staring into the distance and hoping that he'd hear from her again one day.

The moments that Quinton and Juliana had shared together led him into behaving like an absolutely prick. He blamed her for the way that he'd been acting, and that blame bred a monster within him.

The festive season came to the country. Shopping malls were closed for the holiday season, and the streets of the Diamond City were vacant as most of its people vacationed in their tribal lands to reunite with their extended families. It was a windy afternoon, a few days after Christmas, when Quinton was relaxed on his couch, adding his opinions to people's philosophies on Twitter, and immediately, he dozed off into a dream so peaceful. His body and soul embarked on a spiritual journey into his imagination. Quinton's mind set, and he gravitated into a different world. His eyes were closed shut, and he dreamed away like an exhausted child who had just come home after a long day of playing hide-and-seek with his friends. Quinton knew that he was losing touch of reality at times and his imagination was getting the best of him, yet his dream set was the only place where he'd found an understanding of peaceful prosperity.

In this dream, he walked out of a dark room and saw numerous people fighting for a big golden coin that was placed in the middle of that dusty field. The men were soldiers from different nationalities, and they were all fighting for that one coin. He moved closer to see what the coin looked like, but it was bright and the sun deflected the light into his eyes so he became blind for a while. The men pushed him around, and he felt defenceless to react back. Shots were being fired, and his African body got pierced by their bullets. To him, the pain of the bullets replicated the pain that third worlds endured. He lay there on that field and felt weak. Quinton turned his head to face the room that he came from, yet he saw nothing but an angel in beautiful white cloth. Her bright shine represented the hope that Quinton once had, and that shine didn't go away as he lay there quietly. The soldiers kept fighting away like controlled figures, and none of them knew why they were fighting. He turned his head to look at the golden coin again, and there were more coins stacked on top of each other this time as blood flowed from him. Paralyzed and fragile was the state that Quinton lay in as he tried to move his arms. He was helpless as a lot of bodies dropped next to him, and at that moment, he looked into a soldier's eye as the solider lay there in pain. The soldier's eyes visualized it all as Quinton zoned into them. Quinton felt like he was staring at projected pictures of a man that was once happy until he was recruited from a poverty-stricken area. Quinton viewed images of the soldier's life and saw children cry whilst being ripped from the same soldier's arms. Quinton saw the fear in those eyes as the soldier passed into the afterlife. The fear of dying on that field scared Quinton as tears leaked from his eyes.

The soldier's fear, which is also known as (f)alse (e)vidence (a)ppearing (r)eal, became real to him. The last image painted the view of the soldier's previous struggle, and Quinton witnessed the tough upbringing that the solider endured and the wrinkles on his face which represented the stress of having to grow up at an early age to provide for his family because he had no father. The solider felt robbed from his family. He felt robbed from his small dose of happiness, and tears dropped from his eyes to the ground as the dust covered his face, which represented the struggle of all humans that had no ability to make decisions for peace in their violent regions.

Quinton looked up, and the pain from the bullet wounds started to go away as the angel came close to him. She was beautiful, and her shine radiated purity around her, for her heart was kind as she touched his wounded chest. Quinton began to heal as he lay there, and his senses came back. He wasn't stuck on that field anymore, and for the first time in that dream, he could breathe properly. The subject of wealth in his dream and the money that he supposedly longed for on earth was what inflicted pain on the world. Therefore, Quinton had to make a decision as he looked at the blood flowing close to the field. Was he was going to base his life on inflicting pain to the world by obtaining money or focus his efforts on changing the world?

Quinton woke up relieved the next day to his phone ringing. The angel in his dream must have been a coincidental miracle because as soon as he answered the phone, the voice that came out of the earpiece revived him. Her pronunciation of the English vowels was beautiful. The softness of her tone was pleasant to Quinton's ears. He awoke fully as he realized the familiar voice that his heart so longed for. Quinton's heart fell into a stream of content as he got up from the couch. He took in a breath of fresh air, and the feeling of his lungs expanding drastically gave him composure as he listened to her speak softly.

'So I was kind of hoping that I would surprise you,' Juliana said.

The pause was intensely dramatic as he sat there quietly.

'And just end up at your house last night, but my flight got cancelled from Johannesburg. I only managed to arrive in Gaborone this morning,' she added.

He couldn't believe it, but it was Juliana, and her voice compelled him every single time. He thought he would never hear from her again and was shocked. A lot of questions were pending within his mind, but he remained speechless and craved her affection.

'May you please come and see me?' she asked.

'Of course,' he replied.

'Thank you. I do hope to see you soon. I will email you the location, baby,' she said.

A moment of realization took its toll as she called him baby.

'Do not call me that. You don't deserve to,' he said as he made his way to the balcony. He was slightly hesitant to agree to her request but had missed her so much, yet he couldn't allow her to think that he still cared so much. 'I have things to do. I will see if I make it later,' he added.

'Please don't be harsh towards me, please!' she pleaded.

Quinton dropped the call and realized that he'd just lied to her. He had nothing but time because it was a festive holiday. This was the first festive holiday that he'd spent by himself, and heaven had just opened its doors again for him. Slowly but surely, his face lit up to the sound of her voice. Quinton's intention was to treat her as though she were disposable, but a part of him knew that he was still in love with her even after all those long dreadful months.

He lay on his bed, trying to process the phone call and trying to understand her request. Quinton immediately got up to get ready for the most agitating day of his youthful life. He entered into a deeper mindset as he started to wonder how the night would go. Visuals of her face had faded from Quinton's memory, but he knew deep down inside that Juliana was the most beautiful lady he'd ever laid his brown eyes on. His heart throbbed faster at the thought of her, and he knew that he was in trouble again. He couldn't deny it and thought that he would be upset to hear from her again, but it was quite the opposite in fact. He smiled and walked around his apartment whilst Smuggles kept nibbling on the wretched pillow. Hours started to clock down into the early night as Quinton got ready to meet up with Juliana. The memories of her running and hopping across the green fields in France projected in his head as he wore his loafers. Her beautiful smile enchanted his wild soul, and her laughter began to tame his mind as he started to remember his lover. His eyes weren't sore anymore as he closed his eyes to visualize her looks. His mind was murky and clouded, for he couldn't picture her properly.

Email from Juliana:

May you please come and get me from Room 338, Arabella Hotel, the receptionist knows so just verify by using your name downstairs

Quinton read the email continuously throughout the hours but never replied. A sense of dominance prevailed in Quinton's mindset throughout the months, and he'd adapted to the cruelty that the world had offered him. Quinton could recall that Juliana feared the dominance that other men had over their women, and she despised it at the same time. The reason she was so in love with Quinton was because he wasn't possessive nor was he controlling. She'd believed in the past that too many dominant personalities in the same room could lead to an unnecessary war, and Quinton knew that she'd hate what he'd become. Regardless of Quinton's epiphany, he hoped that they wouldn't be too different from each other after all the time they spent away from each other. Quinton knew that they were at war, for the love that they had for each other left them bleeding because their own ambitions made their hearts casualties. As he thought of her, he remembered that he loved by a code of loyalty and honour, a code that Juliana had broken months ago, but Quinton found himself yet so forgiving towards her. The thought of Juliana's hand touching him rose up all of hidden feelings that he'd buried away a long time ago, but he still couldn't believe that the simplistic things in his life could be altered by the touch of Juliana's hand. He remembered the sweet scent of the Dior perfume she wore. The feeling of the way he felt months ago triggered his senses again. His heart started beating faster as he felt the symptoms of love again.

He wore a white shirt and white jeans for the evening and a golden watch on his left wrist. He wore his white suede loafers on his feet before leaving his apartment. He drove onto the main road slowly, and as he was driving, thoughts of standing her up knocked on his door of opportunity, yet he missed her so much that he railed into forgiveness. Those thoughts floated out the open tinted window, along with the smoke of the burning cigarette. His nerves breached his head and caused a mild headache. He swallowed his pride and the excessive saliva that kept excreting inside his mouth.

The hotel entrance was incredibly amazing as he entered through the sliding doors and waited by the reception to verify his identity.

He looked at the room card that he'd been given at the reception, and every started to go into account as he smelt the fine wood in the elevator. The elevator was covered in shining brown wood and a mirror. The attached carpet seemed soft as Quinton stood on it, and after a few seconds, Quinton stepped out onto a different floor. He looked into the distance and started walking past every number until he stood in front of room number 338. He stood there looking at the door and wondered what would happen once he entered. It seemed dramatic as he moved his hand towards the card slot. He was extremely nervous yet bound to that very moment. That moment had the influence to change everything, and he wondered as he still stood by the door. It all felt slow to him as he heard the loud beat of his heart, throbbing dramatically in his chest. He thought of a lot of things at that moment, like would the pain go away if he lay next to her? Would he genuinely smile again if he allowed himself to connect with her emotionally? Would his nerves disappear? Would his guilt of breaking other girls' hearts disappear? What was he looking for? Would the past that he had with Juliana be healthy for him now?

He stood next to the door and looked the room number whilst his hands became sweaty. The room card began to slip from his grip as he kept his eyes fixed onto the door. His cologne scent became amplified as he started to heat up from the pressure. He looked towards the card slot as he slowly inserted the card into the door. The green light went on, and he opened the door slowly.

The room was dark and candles were lit everywhere. The smell of the vanilla herbal sticks that she loved so much floated into his nostrils as he stood there. There she was, looking into the distance by the window and wearing a silky white nightgown. The city was beautiful, but nothing could ever compare to the beauty that stood before him. Juliana didn't look back as he closed the door and walked towards her slowly. Her hair matched her skin tone as he noticed the glow from her body whilst standing behind her. Her hair was different this time around. It was long and straight. No words were shared at that moment, and all he could hear was her heavy breathing as she stood there. She was so nervous and scared of turning around to face him.

Quinton heard Juliana's heart beating faster as she stood there, impatiently waiting for him. A moment of significance adorned them. She felt so alive. She turned her neck towards him, and their lips merged in passion. Both their hearts throbbed. Juliana jumped onto Quinton's lean body. He threw her onto the bed and made love to her.

'I missed you so much,' she whispered in between her kisses.

'I missed you too,' he whispered back to her with his eyes closed.

Quinton got back onto the bed. They looked at each other with so much fire in their eyes.

'I love you so much,' she said, but he wasn't really ready to start hearing those words yet. He pretended like he didn't hear her words. Her tone turned her extremely vulnerable, and Quinton realized that

Juliana wasn't just any woman he'd been with. She was extremely emotional after confessing her love for Quinton again, and he kissed her gently.

They were intimate lovers of the nights, and everything felt so right to them. These moments created a spark, and she looked into his eyes again like he was he the only one alive.

She was apologetic for being absent as she lay there by Quinton and felt absolutely horrible for not being able to be with him after the accident. She just kept speaking, but he wondered why she'd taken so long to return to him! He found it affirmative for a young man like himself to be attached so deeply at an early age and found himself to be very controversial at that moment as he thought of his latest encounters with other women. He was in love with one person throughout this entire time regardless of how he behaved.

Quinton and Juliana were prisoners of the sheets, and they were serving time for being in love, which was a cruel punishment for their hearts but they deserved it nevertheless. The wine overflowed as the night went on, and their laughter grew intensely after all was forgiven. They lay on the bed covered in white sheets whilst their legs were intertwined and time moved slowly for a while. Their love painted a perfect mess, and the mess in the room described their relationship because nothing was in the right place, but they were happy regardless. It was quite evident that Quinton wasn't leaving room 338 that evening, for their hearts were at home and their minds were marinated in lust.

Quinton got up from the bed and headed for the shower to wash his guilt. Juliana joined him after a while.

The moment prevailed marvellously as they stepped out and tripped off the shower step. They fell onto the floor and laughed at the clumsiness that had occurred. She crawled onto the carpet on her way to the bedroom, and Quinton followed her, gentling wrestling and kissing her passionately. She laughed out loud as he lay there smiling, glancing at the fire she had in her eyes. She was so alive, and momentarily, Quinton figured out that he was still a romantic, and that's what she loved. Juliana stated that to him right after they kissed.

Quinton knew that nobody could ever fill that void that Juliana felt except for him. She'd spent her days in the United Kingdom. They felt controlled by a higher power of some sort, and they couldn't explain it even when they tried. Metaphorically, the two were bleeding through their hearts because they felt too weak to move or do anything. They were vulnerable.

The freedom of being young and unengaged to the world had set a platform of excitement for them. They got back onto the bed as she giggled and smiled. The smile that emerged from her face lit the fireworks within her lover, and his heart burned in love as the veins on his neck enlarged from his heavy breathing.

He thought of the daily images that that wandered into his mind which featured a broken world of people starving and dying because they had no aid. Quinton realized at that moment that he only thought of saving the world when he was with Juliana, and for some reason, she brought peace alongside her every time. He began to feel as if Juliana was his muse because was his inspiration to being better overall.

They got back onto the bed and dialled down towards resting. Juliana slept by Quinton so peaceful with her legs wrapped around him. She was so beautiful when she slept, with her light-skinned cheeks turning pinkish from the cold breeze. He lay there stroking Juliana's hair as he watched the see-through curtains move because of the cool breeze that had entered through the balcony sliding door. It was absolutely quiet, and all he could hear was cars moving and a helicopter hovering in the near distance for a while. Everything was weightless as he kissed her forehead, and it all started to click inside his head that Juliana didn't know of his recent behaviour. She didn't know that he was wrecked, unstable and vindictive, after being hurt. Juliana didn't know of the adapting that Quinton had gone through whilst she was away. Quinton appreciated this night as he cuddled and placed his warms arms around her. Everything changed as he lay by her quietly. He didn't want moments like this to end, and he pleaded with himself at that moment to chase her heart until the end of time.

Juliana woke up and looked up into Quinton's eyes. She wasn't surprised that he was awake.

'Are you okay?' she asked as she looked up.

She was so beautiful, and at that moment, Quinton appreciated her parents' liberal interracial love. He appreciated the genetics which moulded her soft face and the gentle growth that she had gone through her whole life with both her parents supporting her. Juliana understood love and its magnitude.

'I'm okay. Are you okay?' he asked her as he kissed her lips.

'I'm okay,' she said.

'What I did was wrong,' she whispered after a few seconds.

'What did you do wrong, love?' he asked and acted none phased by her past efforts in testing the depth of their love.

'I should have been there for you after your accident, but I panicked,' she said and sniffed.

Quinton lay there quietly and tried not to think of the death of Benjamin and Elaine. Juliana didn't know the pain that lingered in Quinton every day since. She thought that Quinton had recovered well. Juliana started to notice that Quinton wasn't open as he used to be because a lot of words were held back in reservation in Quinton's part. A part of Quinton implicated Juliana for a crime regarding his changes throughout the months, but deep down inside, Quinton's own jury blamed him for the occurrence of the accident. He carried that blame forever, and it damaged him permanently, but he wasn't ready to open up to her about that event.

'It's okay,' he said. 'I'm alive and we are together again.'

He looked up at the ceiling as Juliana switched the side lamp on. She stumbled towards the balcony entrance to smoke a cigarette. They were drunk, and Quinton noticed that Juliana's words slurred when she tried to speak. He made his way to her and held on to her for a while.

The city lights were so beautiful to them as they exhaled the smoke towards the cool breeze. The ash from their burning cigarettes floated away into thin air, and they stood there kissing. The lightning across the city landscape painted a beautiful picture of twinkling stars. Juliana always called them earthly stars because of their unpredictable scattering over the Diamond City. A helicopter hovered in the near distance again, and Juliana wished for nothing but the best for the Diamond City as she stated the significance of the flickering and moving light. She said that the light from it reminded her of a shooting star as she kept smoking her cigarette. Juliana looked at Quinton with her beautiful green eyes as he yawned. Her attention was deposited towards Quinton, and she asked to be held.

Juliana took Quinton's hand after a while, and she led him to the shower again. The vanilla essence sticks still burned in the room, and it smelt amazing.

The lovers made their way to bed and slept whilst the heater was on.

Quinton woke up in the afternoon to a spectacular lunch on a tray. The lunch consisted of a juicy steak that had soup on it, a healthy salad that consisted of tomatoes, green lettuce, cooked onions, salad dressing, and French toast that had garlic spread onto it. Juliana woke up Quinton properly with a few kisses and a song playing out of the surround system. She danced with her salsa moves and swerved her body everywhere with her white nightgown, creating an exotic atmosphere. Her laugh was amazing as she danced away in joy. There was a cool breeze swinging though the curtains as Quinton sat on the bed, eating and moving his head to the rhythm of the song.

Somewhere in between that moment of her dancing and her continuous laughter, Quinton noticed a remarkable quality within her that made him fall in love with her all over again as he felt everything move in slow motion. He sat up straight and looked at her smile. She tripped whilst dancing, and they both laughed because she was incredibly clumsy. They felt like they'd woken up drunk because their love was still so intoxicating. Quinton got dressed before joining Juliana and they danced away for a while.

The sun lapped towards the western world as Quinton looked at the time on his watch. It was getting late. For the first time ever, they understood that all things had to come to an end as they felt their happiness perish away into the darkness. He had to leave for a while, and she knew that too. The moment had a dramatic flair to it as he finally put his shirt back on with half the buttons missing. She laughed as she realised that she was to blame for his buttonless shirt. She held on to

Quinton's hand and kissed his lips so passionately to the point where he started to grasp for air.

'Come back to me,' she commanded. Juliana looked into Quinton's baggy eyes after commanding so. Her warm tears streamed from her eyes and onto their cheeks as they kissed again. 'Promise me,' she said.

'I promise I will come back to you,' he replied.

Quinton left room 338 that evening because he remembered that he'd not fed Smuggles. He never understood why his dog had so much energy and wondered if God had installed a battery into its body. He watched it run around the lounge area as he entered his apartment. Quinton wanted to bring Juliana back the apartment but had to have boundaries with her and tried to remain doubtful towards her. He sat on his couch, checked the local and international news channels. He scrolled on to the catch-up section and paid less attention to the screen as seconds passed. He felt empty within as the episode played. Therefore, he diverted his attention to his social accounts, checking the latest news feeds on his Facebook profile and viewing pictures of other beautiful girls on his Instagram and yet couldn't get Juliana out of his mind. His feelings for her ran so deep, and those feelings were immeasurable. It drove him wild to be in his apartment alone. Thus, he changed into comfortable loose clothing and fed Smuggles.

Following his heart, he drove back to Juliana, playing indie and alternative music on radio. One song by Bastille caught his attention whilst steering onto the highway. A song called 'Oblivion' played sweetly. Essentially nothing else mattered but being with Juliana, he thought whilst he drove his heart back to the Arabella Hotel. He made it off the highway and back onto double lanes, passing red traffic lights on his way back to the hotel parking lot.

The same receptionist from the night before gradually handed him the room card to room number 338. It was an intense few minutes as he stood in the elevator and zoned out into his own reflection on the wide mirror. He walked extremely fast towards the room without hesitation.

Quinton opened the door, and Juliana ran towards him without doubt. She jumped onto him happily and hugged him tightly. Quinton walked inside the room with her body attached onto him and kicked the door shut with his left leg. Juliana didn't move her body whilst he walked towards the bed. She kissed his lips as he placed her body onto the bed, and tears dropped from her eyes as joy gushed into her heart.

Room 338 in the Arabella Hotel became their sanctuary and safe haven away from the world. This was the only place where they both wanted to be in the world. Their love brought peace into their lives.

'I missed you so much,' Quinton whispered.

'I missed you so much, baby. I didn't even want to leave this room,' she said as she lay beside him. She giggled as Quinton tickled her. 'Stop it,' she said as she laughed out loud. 'I'm going to scream if you don't stop,' she said, and she laughed out loud again.

Quinton looked into her green eyes and wiped the tears from her cheeks with his hands.

'Kiss me please?' she asked, and Quinton graced his lips onto her beautiful lips. Her tongue wormed its way into his mouth as they kissed. They were lost lovers, yet they understood that as long as they were together, everything would have direction.

Juliana didn't want to leave that room, and she was very fragile to any other suggestions. She was very selfish with Quinton and wanted him to lie with her until the clock hands clocked into the late hours of the night. Quinton felt like a married man with a beautiful mistress. He was secretive about her and her beauty, unwilling to show the world just how sacred her love really was. Juliana was someone Quinton held so close to his heart.

'Are you coming back with me after the New Year, love?' she asked as she stroked the facial black hair on his cheeks.

Juliana never could resist placing her hand onto Quinton's cheeks whenever they spoke on the bed.

'Not so sure. Do you want me to?' he asked.

'It would nice to have you back. I missed you every day, you know,' she said.

Quinton hadn't thought much about school lately, but enrolment was in late February. His family was back from the coast of South Africa, and he remembered of the evening soirée that his parents always liked to host on New Year's Eve. Not a lot people had the courage to state that the evening soirée was just an excuse for wealthy people to come together and weigh each other's annual profits under one roof.

The evening event looked marvellous with luxurious cars, expensive beverages, beautiful women dressed in evening gowns, and valet parking. Quinton had always wanted to go when he was younger but was not allowed to. He enjoyed evenings like those—an evening of tuxedos, young fit women in tight dresses. He knew his beloved Juliana would fit in very well because she was classy and elegant. Quinton asked her out to the evening soirée, and she wasn't hesitant at all because she enjoyed such decadent classy events. She'd also wanted to meet the people in the city but never got the chance to. Juliana fitted well in her society back in London. Thus, she wondered if the ladies in Gaborone would welcome her into their society.

Quinton immediately realized that his family wasn't too fond of Juliana anymore after the accident. They believed that she wasn't worth his attention because she didn't make an effort to see him after his accident. Quinton remembered that his father sat him down at the warehouse office on random occasions and how his father would hand him a glass of brandy after a long day's work. The elderly men in the family that worked for Marcus would join Quinton and Marcus to discuss the perks of life and the pleasures of it. Marcus always thought that he knew everything about women, and at times, Quinton would zone out into Marcus' words whilst his father spoke. Quinton's mind would click, and he'd wonder why he was even in his father's office. His father was a workaholic that forgot how beautiful his wife was. These were trends that Quinton witnessed growing up. His parents didn't fight any more like they used to when he was a child, but instead they just ignored each other as much as they could. Quinton wondered if it was all the money that caused the conflict in the beginning or just difference taking its toll.

He looked at Juliana again as she wondered what was running through his mind whilst Quinton thought of his parents. She began to notice the unpleasant quietness that came from him after a while. She resented herself and blamed herself for his barriers being so tall. An expression of sadness and concern revealed itself from Juliana's mouth as she spoke. She couldn't break the tight barriers that Quinton had up, and she became agitated as Quinton replied vaguely to most of her questions. Quinton noticed that Juliana was much more grateful towards the future and smiled happily towards him as she spoke. Her new attitudes melted Quinton's heart away and knew that he was drawn to her personality more than anything. Despite Juliana having such an exquisite body, Quinton was attracted mainly to her kindness and her soft heart.

Juliana's personality somehow reminded Quinton of Marilyn Monroe as he remembered the painting hanging on the walls at the Grey Bird Café. Both she and Juliana replicated a beautiful light flower. Juliana's flower grew in the wild, and Quinton loved the way her face blossomed ever since time he came to collect her pollen. He started having premature thoughts of wanting her to be a queen in his castle.

The night was dark and the clouds had turned dark grey. The power had gone off on the outskirts of the Diamond City as Quinton walked towards the balcony. Juliana followed him a few minutes later. Everything seemed to see peaceful until Quinton confessed of his recent acts. Juliana seemed highly shocked at the revelation, and she immediately removed her hand from Quinton's shoulders. She looked at him as he tried to explain the reason why he felt compelled into acting that way. Juliana felt repulsed by his actions and didn't want to understand. An immediate instinct gripped her heart, and she slapped Quinton across the face. Her nails scratched his left cheek, and his bruised cheek turned slightly red. He remained shocked after she did so, and she walked away from him as he pleaded to her. The atmosphere completely changed, and Juliana raged as she threw the empty wine bottle towards his direction and missed his face by an inch. Its shattering impact affected Quinton in more ways than anticipated.

'Do not come near me!' she shouted. 'You disgust me!'

Her words left him broken as he grabbed his slippers and walked towards the door. Quinton looked back, and Juliana started crying. Her tears leaked from her eyes as she grabbed on to the nearest light object to throw at him. He wanted to comfort her, but he'd been the one that caused her to cry. The empty wine glass smashed next to Quinton's face as he closed his eyes and ducked it. Juliana kept crying as Quinton closed the door. He stood there afterwards, listening to her cry, and he didn't move. Quinton felt so shameful, and this was the first time he'd ever seen that side of Juliana. It scared him and he was extremely puzzled. He sat outside her door and hoped that she would forgive him for being so reckless.

Time passed and so did a lot people, coming back to their rooms. Quinton looked at his Blackberry, and it started to grow quiet. It turned cold as he slept by her door.

Juliana lay on the bed in the dark but couldn't avoid the shadow that covered the light from underneath the door. She tried to rest her eyes yet felt extremely bad for overreacting in that manner. As two hours passed into a new morning, Juliana switched on the lights to avoid, stepping onto the broken glass by the door. As she opened the door and found a cleaner's trolley filled with white towels, she looked at the domestic worker that told her that a tall young male had just woken up and walked away. Juliana ran towards the elevator lobby but noticed that the door had just closed. She pressed the numeral buttons continuously and hoped that Quinton hadn't left yet. The elevator door opened after she'd entered from the top storey and rushed towards the reception.

'Hey, Tracy, do you know where he went?' Juliana asked the receptionist.

'I didn't see him leave,' she replied.

'Are you sure?' Juliana asked and looked around.

She knew that it was extremely hard for Quinton to trust anybody; therefore, she didn't stop looking until she found him by the hotel restaurant. Quinton sat there, eating quietly and looking around the scenery. He noticed Juliana walk towards him slowly, but he didn't speak to her. She sat by him quietly and asked him to return upstairs.

'I'm sorry too. I shouldn't have acted that way towards you, baby!' she said and picked up a potato chip from Quinton's plate. He didn't say anything back but quietly paid for his meal.

'You threw glass at me' he said.

'I know. I'm so sorry,' she pleaded.

He walked up the stairs as Juliana walked behind him. 'Go on the elevator,' Quinton stated. 'Would like to be alone for a bit.'

'Promise to come up. Can't sleep without you, babe,' Juliana whispered.

Quinton entered Juliana's hotel room but didn't say anything. He got into bed with her yet didn't want to touch her. He wondered why she'd acted so cold towards him and allowed him to sleep outside her door. 'Surely she knew!' he thought to himself as he shut his eyes. Juliana was very persistent and indeed placed her arm around him minutes later.

Everything seemed normal again as Quinton woke up in the late morning. He looked at Juliana as she looked at the city. He slightly distorted as he remembered their fight from the night before. Juliana faced him and walked towards the bed slowly.

'I promise I won't act that way ever again,' she said.

Quinton tried to view all angles on how to proceed yet also knew that he couldn't be mad at her forever. 'It's okay!' he said.

They pretended to be two complete strangers in the same room. Their moments were highly sensitive, and words had to be chosen carefully when they spoke to each other. Quinton wanted to leave, but his heart was resistant towards that motive. He sat on the bed whilst she lay next to him, and they watched the television quietly like an old couple that had nothing else to say to each other. 'You must deprive yourself from the things that you have so that you learn to deserve them again' were the words that replayed inside Quinton's mind as he stood up.

'Don't leave!' she said.

'I have a better idea. Let's go out,' Quinton said as he realized that the family evening soirée was the next day.

They left the room that morning, and they were still so quiet towards each other. No jokes were shared, and no comments were made as he opened the passenger door for her. He remained gentle towards her, and that made her felt extremely guilty and ashamed for slapping him. Quinton drove towards a shopping mall, and they entered into the public world without holding hands. They walked separately, and

Quinton noticed other voile men looking at Juliana as she moved alongside him.

The retail store by the furniture store sold beautiful evening wear for adults. Juliana picked a beautiful delicate blue dress and a pair of dark blue heels. She looked absolutely amazing in the blue dress as she tried it on. The assistants at the store complimented her repeatedly as she turned her body towards him.

'What do you think?' she asked. 'Be honest!'

'You look beautiful,' Quinton stated as he picked out his dark blue tuxedo with a dark blue bow tie. They walked out the store, and suddenly, they spoke to each other again.

Juliana kissed him as he opened the car door for her again. She smiled and entered a deeper train of thought whilst Quinton drove her back to the hotel. He didn't assort her upwards yet got out of the car and kissed her before leaving.

Quinton entered his apartment and went back to bed. He closed his heavy eyes and dreamed away peacefully whilst Smuggles ripped up the smallest pillow on the floor.

Juliana became the dreamer of his dreams as he slept on his bed alone. Everything was peaceful and felt like he hadn't slept at all as Juliana woke him up within the dream. She smiled so eagerly as she took Quinton's hand to touch her pulsating stomach.

'Can you feel that?' she asked in excitement.

Quinton could feel a kick from a foetus, and they both laughed in amusement.

'Can you feel it?' she asked again with a smile on her face.

'I can feel it!' he replied, but the feeling of it became scary as the atmosphere within his dream turned grey and there was no colour at all.

His dream turned into black and white. The scenery changed, and they stood by a deserted farm that had burnt-out wild grass. Juliana wept because Quinton didn't want to touch her belly again. The foetus kicked again as Juliana looked at Quinton. Her eyes became slightly baggy, and her glowing face turned pale. They held each other's hands tightly as the rain began to pour on to them. Their clothes became wet and heavy as they ran to find shelter. Quinton stood and held on to

Juliana's body whilst they stood under a well-branched tree. The wind blew scrapped items towards their direction, and Quinton shielded Juliana from harm's way. He looked at her face, and it began to turn cold and a disease of sadness grew from her face. Her tears froze; they turned into glass and shattered as they hit the ground. The shattered glass pricked into Quinton's feet, and blood dripped from underneath. The pain was illusively bearable as he tried to move. A baby grew inside of her, and that baby wasn't part of their plan yet. It was surprising how they'd committed adultery through their affirmative love, and yet God still gave them a gift to bear, a gift that they didn't deserve. The foetus kicked repeatedly as Quinton looked at her stomach, and she started screaming because she was in pain. Quinton felt that pain too as she gripped his hand tightly and her nails pierced into his skin. Her scream grew louder as he laid her onto the hay, close to the horses' stables. They were in an abandoned old barnyard, and Juliana's scream grew even louder inside of Quinton's head.

He woke up paranoid and sweating excessively to his phone ringing repeatedly. The caller identification was unknown, but Quinton answered anyway.

'Baby, please come back!' she said. 'I had a bad dream.' Juliana's voice sounded bleak and worrying. She sniffed and sounded like she was crying.

'What is wrong, love?' Quinton asked. 'What was the dream about?'

Juliana started to cry through the phone, yet she couldn't remember what she'd dreamed about. Her body crumpled up as she kept crying in the hotel room. Quinton knew that their dreams must have been different but alike at the same time. She didn't remember what her dream was about, and she was in shocked. Quinton was surprised of the coincidence, but he didn't say anything to her about his dream. 'I'm sorry,' he whispered through his phone, which felt like the right thing to say. Quinton didn't want her to cry yet felt like he'd caused her pain.

The moment was soppy and soft as she laid her head onto the pillow and watched the television in her hotel room whilst speaking to Quinton on the phone. She laughed out loud as Quinton spoke and made jokes. He started to miss her as he spoke to her through the phone.

Juliana responded to Quinton's words, and at that moment, Quinton pictured her face and imaged her smiling. She had these thin eyebrows that complemented her beautiful eyes and one dimple on each cheek which made Quinton adore her presence even more. The dream he'd had about her kept him on edge. They weren't stupid because they used protection. He hung up the phone and slept after realizing the exhaustion of being in love with Juliana.

The hours clocked down as Quinton showered and wore his navy blue tuxedo afterwards, anticipating the night out with his beloved. He imaged how the night would go as he faced the mirror and fixed his navy blue bow tie. His body was scented with cologne and looked extremely handsome for the occasion at hand.

His watch ticked as he drove to the Arabella Hotel, and he found Juliana waiting for him by the reception entrance with the beautiful receptionist Tracy. Juliana stood up and walked as Quinton entered through the sliding doors. He stopped walking as he discovered Juliana's body moving towards him slowly. The skin on her arms glowed, and she smiled gracefully. She held on to Quinton's hand, and they walked away towards the parking lot. Juliana's perfume was incredible as Quinton leaned over to kiss her.

They found themselves to be guests at Quinton's family home, and the valet service took his car away after he'd guided Juliana out the car. They stood in line and listened to people around them gossip.

The Barker household looked beautiful with all the decorations that were hanging around the chandeliers and all the wall lights. The lighting arranged was lower than usual. The three-meter Christmas tree remained decorated in festive designs, and the house was full of guests. Quinton noticed family members from different parts of the country and others from South Africa. Quinton and Juliana shook a lot of people's hands and made their way through the crowd of a hundred-plus people. Quinton could hear the whispers in between, people talking about him as he walked through with Juliana, and their words were hurtful.

'Look at him trying to look fancy with his father's money,' they said.

'Oh, whoa, he reminds me of Steve.'

'Where did he find that girl?'

'His accent is different. Therefore, he believes that he is better.'

And as Quinton reached the wooden stairs, his mother, Beth, greeted them politely. 'Didn't know Juliana was back,' she said. 'Welcome back, love.'

'Thank you so much, feels good to be back,' Juliana replied.

'Well, I will see you guys soon, must meet Dorothy. She still owes me a favour,' Beth said as she walked away.

Quinton took two champagne glasses filled with Moët champagne and gave the other to Juliana.

'Cheers, baby,' he said as they toasted to a new year.

They kissed by the stairs and a lot of people witnessed it and addressed the matter at hand. One thing was certain—Quinton and Juliana did not care about sideline opinions, nor did they care about babysitting other people's feelings towards their relationship. They night clocked up and the alcohol consumed featured its side effects as voices grew louder. Quinton understood at that moment that a lot of people around that room were just a bunch of nobodies that pretended like they knew everything. He saw that a lot people making noise to try remain relevant, and those that revealed themselves to be opinionated actually knew nothing of actual current events. A lot of people in that room were too busy making noise throughout their lives to actually make something out of themselves, but what they didn't realize was that at times it was best to keep quiet and actually listen. Quinton walked past a lot high-profiled people who'd make underlying jabs towards each other.

Juliana remained with bunch of socialite girls that were so stuck up and boring. Quinton walked upstairs and found his father, Marcus, puffing a Cuban cigar by the balcony with Benjamin's father. They turned around and faced Quinton as they spoke. Quinton shook James' hand, and he felt the tension in the air. They carried on speaking and discussing the way forward next year, and as they spoke, Quinton noticed the blueprints of a building structure on Marcus' table that was yet to be built. It had fifty storeys and looked extremely long. It seemed like Marcus and James were discussing the next level of wealthy until they were interrupted by Quinton's uncle, Steve. Steve was the family black sheep. He was just different and a well-known underachiever who blamed everybody but himself for not being able to progress in life. The family fuck-up as Marcus would say.

Steve smiled at Quinton, but a feeling of darkness hovered over the two as Steve shook Quinton's hand. The feeling of it was despicably cold. Quinton didn't speak much as the three of them pretended like they liked having Steve around. One of Steve's escorts called out for him in the passage, and he left. She poked her head in and waved at all of them, but neither Marcus, James, nor Quinton greeted her back. Steve's date for the night seemed like a lady that was interested in the next best man. She didn't seem loyal whatsoever, and everyone around knew that.

Quinton stood by the pillar on the first floor and looked down at everybody. The atmosphere was extremely different as he watched people pretending to like each other. Those that had ended up in headlines were smiling at each other and shaking each other's hands, making jokes, and laughing out loud. Some of them engaged in political conversation yet knew so little about politics. Quinton always found himself amazed by the arrogance of some men that discussed leadership and yet had never actually led anybody. He stood there, looking down and wondering how some of them could actually call themselves men when they knew nothing about taking care if their own families. Some of the women were dressed appropriately and looked beautiful, yet the rest of them came in short dresses, and their body languages screamed of desperation. They were seekers for attention and mostly because some of them lacked the attention of good father figures whilst growing up. He noticed the big-ego women with their three-dimensional foreheads, and at that moment, Quinton remembered that women that showed a lot of skin made it too easy, and he loathed how easy they were.

Quinton smiled as he realized that Juliana who was covered up well, and that excited him even more as he realized that he would get to undo her clothing well into the new year. The hour before midnight revealed a lot of people making rookie errors around each other. Half the congregation in the household was drunk, and everyone started acting inappropriately.

The Barker household remained extremely loud, and people were dancing around the pool area. Quinton's mother, Beth, was nowhere to be found, and frankly, she never liked to be surrounded by a bunch of false people. She spent most of time in church and only showed up to these events for Marcus because only he liked the whole 'perfect family perception'. Quinton and his father liked the idea of presenting the image of a strong household no matter where they were.

Thirty minutes were left. Quinton took Juliana's hand. They walked upstairs and stood by the main balcony. It all felt to intriguing for Juliana as she smiled and waved at her 'new' friends who'd adored her for her elegant style. She was happy to have been with Quinton at that moment.

The New Year's Eve countdown started until the last second of the previous year wound down slowly and the fireworks exploded in the air. The fireworks caused sparks everywhere, and the sky was painted beautifully as Quinton placed his hands gently onto Juliana's neck and kissed her passionately. He placed his right hand onto her waist and brought her closer. The moment was magical as they looked towards the sky and viewed the fireworks crack open the dark sky. Fireworks went off in the distant city, and it looked wonderful from their view.

Chapter Five

Juliana's Rose

The stars were aligned for the first time in a long time. The two lovers entered into a new year with nothing but delight and peace. Quinton had expressed his excitement about looking for a place in the world where he and his lover belonged, a place where their love would flourish. He'd replied to the admissions office at his university in the United Kingdom, letting them know that he will be returning in February to complete his course work for another year. Juliana had taken up residence at Quinton's apartment and his pug, Smuggles, absolutely loved her presence. She felt so responsible for it, and she treated it like a small child. Quinton would notice Juliana speaking to it at times whenever he was in another room, which sounded ridiculous, but her presence was felt by their hearts, and that presence gave Quinton's home a lovely atmosphere.

She lay on his bed that Wednesday evening, a few days after the New Year, and she must have ovulated a few days before, which was a good sign that the dream that Quinton had about her being pregnant amounted to nothing but a thought. Quinton looked at her as she lay there on his cream white duvets reading an article on her tablet. She took a glance at Quinton as he stood by the bedroom door for a while then moved forward to please his beautiful lover. Within seconds, he did so.

'You are wild,' she whispered right as she opened her eyes.

'And you're so beautiful,' he replied as she blushed, trying to catch her breath.

'We are not done yet!' she yelled.

'Oh, but I'm over it,' Quinton mentioned and got up to find his cell phone.

She lay there, acting distorted and saddened by his sudden change in interest whilst he made his way to the kitchen. He made two glasses that consisted of vodka and Sprite. Smuggles began to bark as it heard Juliana's vocals arising to a justified orgasm. Smuggles seemed to be more concerned about her than Quinton was. It kept barking at the bedroom door. Quinton found the situation funny because Smuggles must have thought that its new mother was in danger, yet little did it know of the actions that occurred behind that door. He made his way back to the bedroom and found a picture-perfect moment of Juliana Rose lying there. He walked towards her and gave her a drink. They took a large sip from their glasses and carried on making love. The wind blew through the curtains. Everything felt weightless and slow.

He was addicted to her. Those were feelings that he held from her for his own good. The wind inside his mind blew everything into smithereens. Nothing else mattered whilst they were connected.

Quinton loved his patriotism of a zebra and loved to compare it to Juliana Rose because she was the final sculpture moulded from the love of a black mother and a white father. Her heart represented unity. It made Quinton feel like he belonged. He felt like he finally had a purpose, which was to love and hold her body tightly until the end of time. She was his blind spot. He was beyond the blink of return, unable to see past her green eyes. Her curves flooded his heart with lust. The moonlight, which had emerged from the flickering curtain made her skin glow brighter. She almost appeared fictional, like a character drawn out of a romance novel or drawn onto a canvas.

Juliana Rose became the producer and director of Quinton Barker's dreams. She was the endless sip of wine, mysteriously intoxicating her lover to be in love for eternity. She knew it. He knew it, and there was nothing he could do about it but to allow the wrath of her love to dominate his heart.

'The beauty of human nature,' Quinton would say to himself whenever he looked at Juliana or even at the mere thought of his dreams of her lying on his bed.

He understood what Juliana had scarified. He understood the magnitude of her love and also understood that she'd given him everything, including her mind, body, and soul. Quinton respected her for that and respected the sculpture that lay before his eyes. He was grateful for these moments and didn't take any of them for granted. His mind manifested, and for the first time in a very long time, his life was fully erected to the gifts of pleasure.

He fell asleep moments later and woke up a few hours after into the wee hours of a chilly morning. Smuggles was groaning and ripping its maroon sleeping pillow apart in the living room. The breeze outside blew in through the balcony sliding door. Quinton remembered he'd forgotten to shut it. Therefore, he stood up and made his way towards his living room. He walked through the sliding door and threw the curtains out of his way. The sound of chimes rattled by the balcony. Quinton whiffed a sense of freshness as the wind blew past his face. He stood by the balcony, looking at the world, and at that moment, he saw something so differently amusing or deceiving, to say the least. Quinton saw a visual like no other, and the moonlight shined on the city, and everything was visible as the street lights shone brighter. He looked down at the city, and all the negative connotations that seemed to be leased into most of the people's mindset disappeared, especially from his mind. Quinton looked at the Diamond City and saw a nation that was at peace.

The tree branches waved frequently as angels hovered over the rooftops of many homes. Quinton looked down at particular figure that climbed up the apartment block. It didn't seem remotely holy to him as he witnessed it draw itself closer to him. The lean figure climbed over his balcony and stood right before him in a hunched-back position. He covered his nose because it reeked of trash and other foul smells. Quinton was extremely puzzled because he didn't know what it was. It flicked dust towards Quinton's face. However, he shut his heavy eyes as the dirt touched his face. It walked past and entered Quinton's apartment. Its feet pressed onto the wooden floor as Quinton unintentionally followed it. It started levitating past furniture whilst Smuggles remained snuggled on the kitchen floor, unaware of the dark magic in the apartment. Quinton looked back as his feet moved forward. He saw angels flying over the building rooftops, but this hunched-back figure in his apartment didn't look like a soul that radiated peace. It seemed angry at the world and probably had a vendetta to handle.

'You shouldn't be awake!' it said.

Quinton stood shocked and gasped for fresh air.

'You must go back to bed,' it commanded.

A lot of questions were to be addressed, but Quinton didn't even know where to begin. 'Who are you? Why can't I see your face? You sound familiar? Who are you?' he asked as it turned its body towards his bedroom.

'You shouldn't be awake!' it said. 'I am the dark angel, here to take her away.'

The apartment block shook tragically. The items in Quinton's apartment trembled as he tried to keep balanced. The place shook in tremor, maybe a movement of two tectonic plates underneath the city. The dirty monster flew through the bedroom door, and Quinton remained puzzled as he wondered how it flew through the door without opening it. The dirty monster stroked Juliana's head with its left hand. Quinton remained quiet and still, unable to move farther to prevent it from touching the love of his life. His feet were magically glued to the wooden floor, his flesh almost merging into the wooden boards.

'I am here to take her away,' it said and grinned.

'You will not have her. She is the love of my life,' Quinton mentioned and attempted to scream but found his mouth muted.

'She has to come with me,' it said as it touched Juliana's forehead.

Quinton started to move close to the bed as Juliana turned to face the opposite side of the bed whilst sleeping.

'Don't take her away from me please,' Quinton pleaded within his heart.

'There is nothing I can do. I follow orders,' it stated and stood up whilst looking at his lover.

Quinton had promised he wouldn't let anybody or anything break the bond that he had with Juliana but, at the same time, felt completely powerless to do anything about the event occurring before his heavy eyes.

'You can't take her away from me, not in this lifetime,' Quinton muttered.

'But this is an order I must follow! She must come with me,' it said as its wretched wings began to rise.

'Don't do this to me,' he pleaded as tears dropped from his cool face.

'You must understand that you are made for great things. I am an angel, and you must believe this,' it said.

The so-called dark monster stated this information, but Quinton didn't want to believe it. It didn't make any sense, for he felt that he was being lied too. He stood still and began to feel pain on his chest. It felt like a dagger piercing into his chest, and he started to scream out in tears. The dream seemed remarkably real as he screamed aloud and woke up.

The wind blew through the open sliding door, and the curtains levitated for a while. It felt like spirits had just rushed out in the nick of time. Juliana switched the lights on with the tablet application and rushed back towards the bed whilst panicking.

The apartment block was shaking, and the atmosphere was scary to them both as they held on to each other. The lights flickered and the power went off. Quinton looked around, but the so-called angel wasn't there anymore and he'd just woken up from a nightmare which was aligned with current events. The epiphany of the nightmare drove Quinton wild when he found out that the city had a major tremor experience. That was something that has never occurred within the region, and nobody would be ready for the effects if a natural disaster were to happen.

Quinton made his way to the balcony that morning after remembering the sweet melodies that came from the chimes outside.

The wind blew consistently towards the balcony, and the sounds of the chimes made the most pleasant sounds to Quinton's ears. He felt better yet still so confused and uneasy about his morning. Juliana was making pancakes and bacon for breakfast as Quinton entered the kitchen area. The kitchen had a pleasant smell to it, and her singing was beautiful to his ears. She sang as Quinton sat by the corner kitchen chair, watching her flip the pancakes on the pan. She sang loudly as she turned around and poured mango juice into Quinton's marble glass. Quinton adored her cute, beautiful pointy nose that had turned pink from the cool breeze that morning. She sat on his lap and French kissed him adorably.

'Morning, my lover,' she said.

'Morning, baby!' he replied and kissed her whilst he stroked her lower left jawline with his right hand.

Her essence liaised his heart and mind with lust. Therefore, he found himself completely infatuated with her very presence. They were adorned by each other's kindness and love. An idea clicked inside Quinton's mind as he picked up the dairy whipped cream can that was on the kitchen counter next to them and pressed the nozzle into Juliana's mouth. Juliana licked the opening of the cylinder can as the cream came out onto her tongue.

A certain nerve twitched within Quinton's body as Juliana swallowed the cream. She smiled deliberately. A discovery was made as Quinton noticed a beautiful small mark on her left shoulder mixed up with the scattered freckles. He expressed his hatred for the nightgown she woke and preferred it off, unlacing his strings apart, whilst the bacon fried into a crisp on the stir fry pan.

Quinton looked at his lover whilst she ran away to the end of the passage and into the bedroom. After Juliana's disappearance, Quinton looked at the framed mirror at the end of the hall and the moment that played of Juliana joy jogging with Smuggles into the bedroom tracked backwards. He looked pale and flustered as Juliana's perception came back to him. Juliana's laughter alliterated and hurt his ear drums as the joyful sounds echoed and rippled back from the walls. Quinton lost all his sense as it became quiet.

He fell onto the wooden floor as he lost his composure and his head smashed onto the floor. He couldn't control himself as he blinked continuously. He couldn't hear anything but could see Juliana herself rushing back towards him. The last thing Quinton could remember at that moment was Smuggles' thin legs pressing onto his chest and Juliana panicking over the phone. Slowly but surely he closed his eyes into a heavy daze and was temporally blacked out.

A moment of exhaustion, one without pain, projected into Quinton's night as he woke up and sat up straight. Juliana was sleeping peacefully on the couch. Her body remained coiled and wrapped up in a red blanket. Quinton seemed fragilely soft and drained. He picked up the writing board with the patient information attached to it. No immediate attention was paid to the details on the clipboard as Quinton looked around. Their friction caused Juliana to wake up. She stood up in her cream white pyjamas and walked towards Quinton in her white bunny slippers.

'Lie down. I want to join you!' she said in a calm state.

'How did I end up here, babe?' he asked and leaned backwards.

'I called the ambulance when you fell to the ground! I rushed towards you after I realized that you weren't coming to the bedroom,' she explained as she joined him and covered them both with a red blanket. 'I am worried about you,' she said as she looked up and stroked his eyebrows with her right hand.

'Am I going to be okay?' Quinton asked as she looked towards the window.

'I hope so,' she stated sadly as she sniffed. 'Because I don't want to lose you,' she added.

'What is wrong with me?' he asked her as she held his left hand.

'Nothing major, I hope! The doctors tested your blood levels twice, and the results were different. You temperature kept changing constantly. They gave your results to your mother after I called her off your phone!' Juliana explained. 'You didn't seem too surprise that you'd blacked out, Quinton!' she mentioned and looked up towards Quinton as his eyes remained glued to the sun setting in the distance.

'It's close to 8:00 p.m., baby,' Juliana said.

'So I have been out for the whole day?' he asked.

'Yep, the doctor had to sedate you with some medication,' she said.

'You have been under a lot of stress, haven't you?' she asked.

Quinton's head began to throb, and he lost complete focus as Juliana spoke. His mind wandered, and he thought that he had leukaemia because his late grandfather who'd started the family company in the late '80s had it. Quinton thought of the disease because it could be inherited and drew up a theory that it must have been recessive with his father and dominant with him.

Quinton and Juliana remained utterly quiet and looking at the window. It was extremely quiet except for the heart monitor that had a consistent beep to it. It was very terrifying as Quinton thought about the beeping sound and knowing that one day that sound of his heart pulse could stop. The sounds of a wagon or a supposed trolley moved in the distance in the hallway, but nobody spoke. Quinton felt completely paranoid as he remembered the dream that he'd had the night before regarding the demon's intentions on taking Juliana away. That scary feeling lapsed as he held onto Juliana tightly. The trolley moved away as Quinton kissed Juliana's forehead, and Juliana couldn't understand his sudden care. She appreciated it nevertheless and kissed his warm hands as they looked out the window again.

A mellow song began to play inside his head as he watched the wind blowing havoc outside. The thorn trees in the parking lot waved, and empty dirty plastic bags floated vaguely in the air. He lay quietly and thought momentarily of the world he lived in and found himself lost. He didn't feel like he belonged around such heated conditions. Quinton had adapted to a lifestyle that was intensely entertaining, and the lifestyle in the Diamond City was pleasant yet slower than his norm.

Quinton felt like he was losing his mind at times, but imminently his mind was a gift of extravagance and maturely seeded wisdom. They both realised at that moment that one of them had to give up their ideology of happiness so that the other can be happier. Quinton felt obligated to his world, and Juliana was in love with her world just as much as she was in love with Quinton himself, yet neither of them had the courage to speak to each other about it cohesively. They knew that the subject itself rattled their relationship, and they felt that their relationship had suffered enough. Quinton realised that he was intensely drawn to Juliana's heart. Thus, he broke down his barriers and allowed himself to accept that he would be returning to London.

He closed his eyes and could recall his childhood days and his visitations to the home villages of Botswana, the memories of traditional dishes and the deep-rooted Setswana language being spoken whilst he listened as a skinny boy in khaki clothes. Those memories took him back to the days when his grandparents were alive. Quinton's grandfather was a pastor in a Lutheran church, and his grandmother was a member of his church. They'd all walk to the Lutheran church and sing hymn in Setswana. Quinton would sit quietly like a mute with pride whilst the service processed. His grandmother would sing to him as he sat there quietly, listening to the congregation sing songs that he didn't know. The church was built so poorly, and the candle wax droppings were presently showing on the old wooden tables. Quinton had always found himself lost in translation as the congregation sang so loudly and read the scriptures from their Setswana Bibles. He could speak the language but could never read it properly, and that was one of his weaknesses.

The conversations that he'd have with his grandparents always brought a smile to his face as thought of his graceful grandmother. Elizabeth was peaceful in her white summer dresses.

Quinton remembered their old '70s photo album. The photos within were blurry, classy, and printed in black and white. Their household had antiques, and his grandmother's cup collection was in the cabinet closest to their fireplace.

Prince would at times teach Quinton how to milk a cow, but Quinton was never too fond of such lessons. He'd always felt punished and abandoned by his parents when they'd leave without him. As time entered into an era, Quinton grew up in the developing city and realised that some of the local people there liked to pretend as if they couldn't speak their own languages. It occurred to him on hospital stretcher that a lot of people in Africa liked to pretend like their own languages were a sign of struggle and that their own real traditional identity were a certain dismissal to real wealth.

Quinton remained glue to Juliana as he could recall the amount of times he would go out in his teen years whilst on holiday from South Africa and how most of the local girls would blatantly change their accents whenever they spoke. Those girls would try to accommodate their own insecurities with false media knowledge to try to fit into the bullshit mediocre world. At that moment, Quinton tried to find his true identity and wondered what his role was in all this. He felt like a hypocrite because he couldn't speak his own language fluently anymore and struggled to pronounce some of the words. Quinton had an excellent English accent that buzzed through everyone's ear drums and left a lot local people wondering where he was from, from time to time. Everything cultural seemed to make a stigma in his mind as he wondered why he'd shut out that part of his life. His lifestyle and his selection of people were diverse and liberal. The choices that he'd made until this very day were rooted from beauty, but something ugly gripped his heart as he realised that his motives towards those choices weren't pure.

'What are you thinking of, baby?' Juliana asked as she woke up to Quinton's leg movement.

He remained quiet and kept his eyes blankly concentrated towards the window, gazing at the sun as it disappeared and watching as the city lights glowed brighter. Heavy rain drops fell from the sky as Quinton looked at the window. They washed off the dust on the plain see-through windows.

Juliana smiled. 'Look, baby, it's raining,' she said with her sweet flawless British accent.

The moment was beautiful as she placed her head and listened to his chest to feel his heartbeat. Quinton hadn't taught Juliana anything remarkable about his culture, yet she'd learned a lot things by observing and listening. Juliana didn't prejudge anyone's background, their culture, their ethnicity, their sexuality, nor were her motives premeditated from other peoples' judgement. Her actions were pure, and her heart was undeniably beautiful.

They lay on their sides as the rain fell harshly into the dry city. The wind blew the throne tree branches in different directions as the security guards ran to find shelter elsewhere. A long hour passed as Juliana looked at the raindrops falling, and her mind ransacked itself as she thought about her home. Her facial expression changed drastically, and she appeared to be extremely sad. She wallowed in vastness at the rainy weather and thought about the wet streets in London. She missed being back there, and that saddened them both as Quinton realized what she was thinking of.

'You must miss home?' he asked and leaned slightly forward to kiss the top part of her head.

'I do, so much, but I won't leave you again,' she said.

'You won't have to. I'm coming back with you,' he responded a few seconds later.

'Promise me. Pinkie promise me!' she commanded for his assurance.

She spoke as he zoned to the raindrops sliding down the window. He remembered his father, Marcus, talking to him when she was a child about appreciating rain because it didn't come too often. Quinton remembered Marcus expressing the dark drought days in the late '80s and how a lot farmers loaded their cattle in the humid conditions. An image of cattle corpses rotting on empty fields painted itself into Quinton's mind as he tried to picture the drought's effects. A lot of people in the country then must have lost a lot of bargaining chips to their local butcheries. Quinton imagined people dying because of the devastating heated conditions in the past, and at that moment, Quinton closed his eyes and thanked God for the rain outside the hospital window. He closed his eyes with gratitude and appreciated Juliana's good heart. Quinton paid his respects to those that had sacrificed their time into ensuring that Botswana gained its independence in 1966, those that had fought not only in South Africa but elsewhere too so that he could love another person from a different race without harsh judgement or get punished brutally for it.

Chapter Six

Lessons Learned

The month of February had arrived. There were decisions to be made. Quinton had expressed his desires to go back to school. He'd enjoyed the beautiful company that surrounded him in January with his closest family around the city. They were all happy to see him before he had to leave. His distant uncle Jerry who'd retired from investment banking from Rustenburg, South Africa, sat Quinton down on a special occasion at one of his extravagant properties in Gaborone City. Jerry gave him advice about the concept of understanding the way of life.

'You have to understand yourself before you try and understand the world!' he would say after taking a sip from his beer from his brewery in the North-West province of South Africa.

Jerry seemed as if he had it all figured out, and he didn't need to be influenced by other people. He was a true man of God and a leader of extraordinary virtue. His words were maturely precharged as he spoke whilst staring into the distance. Quinton sat on the camp chair in the garden and tried to under his uncle's life story whilst the meat cooked on the braai-stand. Uncle Jerry had a beautiful family with his admirable wife. His older daughter had studied and graduated from a South African university on the eastern coast of their country. Jerry's middle child was also a privileged scorn who'd studied sports medicine at a private university in the mountains of Cape Town and lived the most liberal free-spirited life ever. Paul was his name. He absolutely had a weak spot for beautiful brunettes that participated in sporting events. Quinton thought about Paul's lifestyle and wondered if it was a good idea to give Paul a call before he left for the United Kingdom. Jerry also had a beautiful younger daughter who was current finishing off her matric year back in Rustenburg, South Africa.

Jerry kept on talking to Quinton as Quinton zoned out and thought about how humble they all were for everything they had. Jerry's children were so grateful for the life they lived and appreciated each other's well-being. Quinton noticed that Juliana bonded with his extended family as he flipped the meat on the stand. Juliana smiled pleasantly as she picked up the salad dish that she made in the heated kitchen, walked, and placed it on the dining table. She wiped the sweat from her forehead with her right hand, and the sight of her making an effort to fit in was heartfelt towards Quinton. The women in Quinton's family absolutely loved her. They laughed out loud like a gang of high school girls as they gossiped about life. Quinton heard that regular big-built aunt that loved to voice out her option to the whole world advising Quinton to marry Juliana and not to waste time. The slightly appreciated embarrassment Quinton felt, and the expectations that the aunt had for the both of them were overwhelming.

Quinton's relatives taught Juliana a lot of Setswana traditional dishes to make for him overseas, and he just remained mesmerised at Juliana's ability to adapt to his world. He was a love-struck idiot that couldn't pay attention nor concentrate on anybody that spoke to him whilst he was looking at Juliana. The sun set beautifully behind the south side of the city hill, and everything turned to musk.

Juliana sat on Quinton's lap hours later. They leaned back on the camp chair next to the small campfire that Jerry had made before Jerry made his way to communicate with Marcus who liked excluding himself from everybody. Quinton watched the both of them puff out cigars and talk about boring politics. He looked at the campfire, and lust flowed into his bloodstream.

'I don't want to give you a heart attack now, granddad,' she whispered.

Quinton felt utterly embarrassed and could see that she was extremely flattered.

They arrived back the apartment block parking space and sat joyfully in a metallic red Jeep whilst the engine idled. The beautiful melodies of indie music came out the surround system whilst they spoke. They reminisced about the events that occurred at his uncle's house, and neither one of them wanted to get out of the car because of the heavy dust winds. Empty black plastic bags hovered around, and dried-out leaves moved in a confused manner whilst they circled around the parking lot, and on the far corner by the wall light, Quinton saw a security guard covering his face with his black scarf as the wind blew towards him. Complete sadness hovered over Quinton, but he realized that he couldn't do anything about the situation that the security guard was in.

Quinton closed his eyes as they rotated their seats backwards until they could see the Milky Way through the panoramic sunroof. The trillions of stars shining above painted an image of peace, and the sight of it was wondrous to Quinton's wide eyes. His brown eyes glowed, and he felt better after viewing the stars. Juliana opened a bit of the tinted window to smoke a Dunhill Light cigarette, and she ached the cigarette into a cup holder. Quinton didn't seem to mind it at all because he smoked too, yet he had no recollection of why he did so. In the beginning, it seemed extremely cool because he was in high school and felt the peer pressure from other students. He looked at the smoke, and he immediately realized that he had no reason to smoke now. He was caught in a conflict as he felt his lungs twitch. Juliana finished off her half of the cigarette, and she gave the last bit to him. He inhaled it extremely slowly as he laid his head and nerves began to rush. He felt extremely lightheaded as he exhaled out the smoke.

'Quinton!' she said. 'Are you ready to leave home with me?' she asked.

It was quiet as the songs shuffled and Quinton lay quietly after Juliana questioned him.

'My mind will forever wander here and to the dry landscapes of this country, but my heart belongs to you, so I'm guessing that I will have to be ready nevertheless,' he replied.

Juliana reached out her left hand and stroked the black facial hairs on his lean cheeks as he looked up at the sky. She leaned over and kissed him.

'I know it's hard, but this decision has to be yours. You don't have to worry about what I want,' she whispered and looked into his brown eyes.

'Where will my heart be if it's not with yours? I felt an emptiness when you weren't around,' he responded. 'You must understand what I am giving up.'

She nodded slowly to signal understanding. Quinton hoped that those words would sink into her mind and that she would remember this dialog forevermore.

'This moment is perfect, Quinton,' she sighed.

'You are perfect,' he interrupted, which was a lie because nobody is perfect.

Her dimples deepened into her cheeks as she blushed. He cared for her enough to spoil her regularly. Therefore, he walked to the passenger door, picked her up, and took her upstairs. Smuggles barked in excitement as it saw Juliana cuddled onto his body. Quinton felt incredibly envious as his own dog kept chanting for Juliana's arrival.

'Hello, my baby' she said to Smuggles as Quinton carried her to the bedroom.

She seemed so exhausted from cooking with Quinton's extended family. He gently placed her on the bedspread layer. She lay there as he removed her Tom's designer shoes from her feet and later removed her clothes.

Quinton stood up in front of the mirror and understood that he had to respect her wishes. He was always such a gentleman towards her and thus picked her up and placed her into the Modero Duo Island bath. Juliana sat quietly as Quinton squeezed the soapy water from the blue sponge onto her upper back. The sponge dripped onto the freckle spots on her shoulders and washed away the little dirt off of her back.

A peek on her lips seemed suited for the moment as Quinton kissed Juliana whilst her eyes were closed. He instilled discipline into himself as he washed Juliana's body. He behaved like an absolute gentleman and gently placed his wet hands onto her shoulder. Her muscles were so tense as Quinton rubbed and massaged them gently.

He grazed the heavy sponge onto her pink knees, and the water dripped downwards into the bath. She seemed extremely sad as she leaned forward and folded her arms on to her knees.

'I miss home,' she said. 'I miss the regular rain and fresh green grass in the countryside.'

She exhaled out as Quinton squeezed out water onto the backside of her beautifully shaped head. Her hair became wet and silky as she bowed down into the water to wet her face. Juliana sat there orderly, and her quietness made that moment so intense. Quinton's heartbeat persisted to be irregular for a few seconds as he sat on the edge, wondering what ran through her mind.

Juliana went straight to bed.

Juliana was the architect to Quinton's reality and a persuasive seller to his expensive twenty-first-century dreams. Her laughter alliterated inside his head as he sat on the suede couch by the lamp shade on the corner of his bedroom. He watched her sleep peacefully. A lot of people would find that extremely weird, yet they both found that romantic because their hearts were stapled to the dramatic arts.

Quinton stood up to feed Smuggles in the living room, but it was sleeping too. Quinton sat on an Aquarius outdoor chair by the balcony with a glass of brandy and Coca-Cola. The smell of brandy and Coca-Cola combined with the burning Camel cigarette smell and created a luxurious atmosphere.

Quinton wondered who'd call him at such a time as his phone rang repeatedly. A voice mail message alerted, and he played it out loud. The message was so racially condescending and negative. Quinton felt disrespected by the caller's tone. Quinton wasn't raised to acknowledge a person by their skin tone or disapprove of people because of their origin and thus felt vaguely sorry for people that felt that way. The caller was one of Quinton's pawns on his chessboard before Juliana made her return to the Diamond City. He'd always known that his demons would come back to haunt him after sometime, but regardless of that, he didn't care much because he'd been honest with the one person that mattered the most. Inertly, Quinton felt like an absolute coward for using all those girls for his own pleasures and throwing them away. He'd set his sights on being a stable character in Juliana's fairy tale because that's what mattered to him most—Juliana's happiness.

Quinton tweeted away after being dismissive towards the voice mail message. He followed verified American celebrities and wondered about the balance of fame and the fortune. It always seemed to him that those that possessed the stardom quality were often pawns on a larger chess set. It seemed that a lot of celebrities persisted to be actors in order to remain as relevant factors, like a massive cover-up for most politicians to keep the world glued to the screen of entertainment whilst they plotted to take over the world. The world was so clueless to the undertaking, and Quinton noticed that he was right when he realized that the local television broadcasting station was owned initially by the government. The people in the country would never see the news without it being biased at times, and a lot of controversially linked topics were censored to the public because there was only one television station. These trendy thoughts raised up a lot questions in his mind as he realized that democracy was also just an exaggerated system to keep a lot of people blind from the truth. People would vote for their leaders without looking at the blunt bigger picture. It was also understandable to Quinton that initially most politicians supposedly entered into their parties in the beginning to help bring about change until they reach a certain an optical barrier that would change their whole perception of life. Their words of wisdom and persuasion quickly turn into empty whispers that vanish into thin air as time goes. The forever-growing inflation rate would impact the way most of them make their decisions, and corruption would become the rooted core in their domain.

The world wasn't fair, and Quinton knew that fact, and for some reason, that very fact kept him up late at night. Quinton looked at the beautiful city from the balcony as he stood up to pour himself another glass of brandy and Coca-Cola. He immediately realised that he'd left the front door open widely and thus ran to the bedroom to check on Juliana. His heart settled as he discovered her sleeping peacefully underneath a clean set of black duvets. Quinton didn't understand his paranoia, but he was glad to be that way because that element itself kept him aware of most things.

A thought blossomed into Quinton's jungle of wonders as he switched off the bathroom light and kissed Juliana on her right cheek. He realised that God had brought her into his life for a reason and that her genuine love tamed him. He wasn't fighting for an existence anymore, nor was he angry towards the world. Her peace made him feel like her infamous love would run through his beating heart for the next ten thousand years.

He looked at her before leaving the room as the cool breeze blew through the bedroom and the moon glaring from outside shone brightly onto her beautiful face. Quinton absolutely hated British pugs, but he had growing a slight attachment for Smuggles as he walked passed it in the living room. It snored like a dwarf, and at first, that sound was annoying to Quinton until he adapted to its character.

A significant moment lapsed on to Quinton by the balcony as he witnessed a rare star flying across the sky and dashing underneath the Milky Way. He took a sip from his glass and made a wish, a wish for wisdom and love because his dreams were aligned with those abstracted feelings. The cigarette burned like his heart did, and that immediate sight dazed his mind to Juliana's smile and soft laughter. Every breath he'd ever taken until that moment had destined him to love, and he was filled with gratitude and appreciation. Quinton pleaded a legion to the thousands stars that lingered in the open space as they sparked. He smiled and pleaded for an endless love for Juliana to the sky. The last liquids of the mixed alcohol burned his insides, and he felt completely rejuvenated to that feeling. A sense of relief loosened up his nerves as he made his way through the narrow passage to lie next to his beautiful lover.

'I missed you!' Juliana whispered as Quinton held on to her body tightly after brushing his teeth and switching off the lights.

She turned and faced the balcony entrance again as Quinton placed his left arm underneath her left arm. The air was fresh and felt moist to Quinton's skin as he kissed Juliana's left shoulder. He watched the curtains flicker in different directions, and his eyes became impeccably heavy as he prayed silently for forgiveness and understanding. He felt that Juliana's love was the only way he can coexist without being at fault with the world.

A week later, on a warm early evening, Juliana and Quinton started packing for their departure to London. Quinton packed all four seasonal clothing layers for the unpredictable weather that adjourned the wet streets of London. Beth Barker came over that afternoon to say goodbye to her only son and his lover. She seemed saddened by Quinton's long-awaited departure. Quinton kept his head up at all times when she was around and didn't want her to see his sadness and thus spent most of his time in the bedroom whilst Juliana bonded casually with Beth.

Juliana seemed happy to be leaving, and Quinton couldn't blame her for her excitement. He understood her feelings, and he'd probably felt the same way if he was visiting a foreign land too. Quinton felt like he was leaving everything behind despite the fact that all his clothes were packed into branded luxurious suitcases. A feeling of absolute rare sadness tortured his heart as he finished packing. He felt robbed of his comfort, but it was quite understandable to Juliana as she noticed Quinton's slightly mournful face.

Beth left after a while and seemed humbled with the situation at hand. The clocked winded slowly into the dark twilight hours of the night, and Quinton stood quiet by the balcony and felt his happiness withdraw from the heart of the Diamond City. His cheap cigar scent burned and smelled like dried-out banana leaves, and that thought itself drove his mind to the hideous images of the deep jungles in the middle of Africa where it occurred to him that the various items that he was smoking was the result of the extortion. Quinton's mind gravitated to images of children being exploited to work for little pay in the humid villages of Central Africa. Those children must have been forced into a life of harsh treatment and abuse. The men conducting those lower-valued ventures must have been men of hardship, and as Quinton realized that fact, he understood that the world was indeed a cruel place, a world of cowardly practices filled with souls that gravitated towards capitalizing off the weak and vulnerable. The cigar smell tormented his weak heart, and he threw the burning bud to the thin air. The cigar kept burning as it dropped onto the green grass, and its red burn went off to the wet moistness.

Bags were plunged and fully packed to the hilt in the heights of Quinton's bedroom. The wardrobe had been cleaned out, and Quinton's ideal home was ready to be leased. The water in the shower booth rained, and it was quiet for a while as Quinton cleaned the living room. Boxes were stuffed full in the nearest corner.

'My baby!' Juliana said as she caught Quinton's divided attention. 'Join me!' She reached out her right hand towards him and led him into the bedroom. Her hand was wet from the shower, and Quinton held on to it tightly. They entered the shower booth and made love.

They washed off and walked out onto the cold tiles and straight into bedroom. Tiny drops of water splashed onto the wooden floor as she dried her hair. Juliana found her pair of blue knickers with a small red ribbon on the waistline to wear. She looked at Quinton as she put them on, and the light from the wall lamp exaggerated her green eyes. Her eyes had sparks of emerald within them, and they glossed like marble. She entered the bed and lay by him.

'I love you,' she said.

'I love you too!' he said as Juliana slept. He parked his lips onto her right cheek, and her dimple showed as she smiled to the warm feeling of his fine touch.

The morning dawned with a bright shine from the warm sun.

'Morning, baby,' Quinton said and kissed Juliana's lips.

'We must get ready to go. I don't want us to be late, Quinton.' She nodded happily.

She was so alive, and that moment was an immediate heart-throb for him. He preferred her to be happy even if it meant that he remained cohesive throughout their arguments. One hour passed into the midmorning as his oldest sister came to fetch Smuggles and to collect the apartment keys. She drove them to the airport around midday through the Diamond City. The wind blew heavy dust through the central city lunch traffic. Juliana didn't say much yet placed her head onto Quinton's chest whilst Melinda drove.

'You guys didn't forget your passports, right?' Melinda asked. 'Because I'm not driving through that traffic again.'

'That won't be necessary. We have them,' Quinton said and looked at Juliana for assurance. She nodded and faced the window.

'This is a beautiful nation. It's going to grow well,' Juliana stated as she looked at the development buildings through the back window.

'Melinda, I promise to take care of him, okay!' she said as she looked at Melinda through the rear-view mirror.

'I know you will. Keep safe! Both of you,' Melinda replied as she parked the car by the empty airport parking lot.

She left in a hurry because she had to return to her office for a meeting with her senior directors. Quinton understood the responsibilities of those in the working class and thus held no grudges towards Melinda.

Quinton and Juliana boarded a flight from Gaborone, Botswana, to Johannesburg, South Africa. He'd always had an uneasy feeling about getting onto planes regardless of the amount of air mileage he had. Quinton hated flying, but it all felt better this time around because he was with Juliana. He gripped Juliana's hand tightly as the plane took off the ground and the take-off shook the plane intensely. He shut his eyes as the plane shook, and he inhaled slowly whilst his heart throbbed extremely fast.

Peace was stored within him again as the turbulence settled. It's was a terrifying feeling to know that any moment could be his last, that none of them were invincible, and that death was inevitable at any moment. Quinton promised himself to live more once they reached their final destination.

They landed safely at the O. R. Tambo Airport in Johannesburg, South Africa, within a short hour after their departure from Gaborone, Botswana, and the atmosphere at the airport was congested. The air within the terminal clogged his mind and barricaded his happiness as they walked. Juliana's parents found them checking into the airline by the international departure section, and they also seemed saddened by their daughter's departure. Quinton understood their pain because he too felt it before when he dropped Juliana off the year before. They found their way through the crowded booking gates to a good restaurant lounge. The restaurant was amazingly designed, luxurious, and classy. The walls were dime blue, and the waitresses were dressed in dark blue dresses. Juliana sat by Quinton's right side on the oval couch and started smoking her cigarettes as they ordered beverages.

'Cheers, baby,' he said.

'Cheers to you too, my handsome lover,' she replied and she took a sip.

The first order turned into a second and into a third. They laughed and shared admirable words with each other. The whispers and soft words entered each other's ears. The whole world was busy moving along, yet they remained seated quietly and smiling at each other. They were in a completely different world, a world of their own, and the drinking loosened up their nerves whilst they spoke. They were close to the brink of turning drunk as they ordered another round of drinks. Juliana's cheeks started to turn pink and so did her adorable small ears. She smiled and spoke to Quinton, but he wasn't listening at that moment. Her mouth moved, and he was sure that words came out, but to him, everything was quietly brilliant to him. She spoke as he kept his eyes focused on her beautiful smile. The dimples deepened into her cheeks as she spoke, and her teeth were amazing.

'You are looking at me as if I'm a happy meal, Quinton. Stop it,' she said as she blushed.

She loved the way he paid attention to every detail on her face. It was smothering at times, yet regardless of that, it was still flattering to be adored in that manner. Quinton smiled back and felt intensely infatuated.

'Should we order another round?' he asked in a soft tone.

'Yeah sure! Why not?' she whispered back as she grazed his hand. 'You know, I am glad I'm with you,' she stated as she frowned and a tear dropped onto the table. 'I love you,' she added.

'I love you too,' he replied. 'Smile, baby, no more tears.'

The waitress brought another round of Mexican Corona beers, and Quinton was honestly surprised that Juliana was consuming them. She hated the taste of beer and anything bitter.

The bill was paid within minutes after they were done drinking, and they proceeded towards the final booking gates. Quinton was leaving Africa again, but this time it was different. He'd grown to love his own continent like never before and would miss the bright summer mornings, the quiet bushes, the wild animals, and the friendliness of the people. A moment of anxiety and depression drilled onto his face as the sun set its sights to the western world. They stepped onto the departure bus as the wind blew towards them, and Quinton knew that he was leaving Africa in more ways than one. He felt alone even though Juliana had her arms around him tightly.

The bus doors opened up.

'Hold my hand' she said. 'It gets better. I promise.'

Quinton stepped out onto the concrete paving close to the plane, and he couldn't hear anything. The moment was silent again as he stepped onto the flight as Juliana's hand gripped his. Change adorned him, and a deep sadness lingered onto him as he buckled himself tightly onto the seat. He began to hear different songs of different genres playing inside his head again. The retro lifestyle flashed into his mind, and the different United Kingdom accents that he'd heard over the period that he was there felt normal to his ears again.

A difference started to emerge within him and he felt bleak and thus closed his eyes. His heartbeat sounded loud inside his chest, a sound of African drums beating loudly to the sights of war as his body felt disturbed. He found himself within a dream at that moment. His soul left his body as the body remained rested on the seat. Quinton's soul stood up slowly and gravitated forward. He felt a cool breeze smack him and cripple his movement. The world was discovered through a different eye whilst his body remained glued temporarily to the seat. He opened the curtain that divided the business class section that they were in to the economy class. As he did so, the scenery changed completely as he stepped onto thatched green grass with his bare feet. The place was so different and unrealistic to him. Tall well-branched brown trees surrounded him as he walked gently on the soft grass. The sky was vivid from the small openings amongst the branched leaves, and birds chirped loudly from all different angles. The forest was peaceful and beautiful. There were rocks by the path that Quinton walked on. He was surprised to see a view so rare to him projected itself so brightly. He late grandparents from his childhood were seated close to the waterfall. They were wearing white clothing, and they seemed at peace. The water streamed along the wet dark rocks, and his grandparents had their feet dipped into the shallow edge of the water.

'Come closer, son,' Prince commanded. 'You seem stressed! What is wrong?'

'Prince, he is so tall now,' Elizabeth stated as she smiled.

Quinton noticed their wrinkles continuously disappear as he took a step closer towards them. They appeared younger and happier. Their beautiful light black skin glowed on their bodies. Prince had his gold watch on his left wrist and had his white linen pants soaked into the water where his feet resided. Elizabeth had a sparkling diamond necklace that she wore on her neck, and she wore a remarkable white dress.

'Talk to us,' Prince said.

Quinton smiled at the beautiful, pleasant sight of them, and happiness flourished into his soul as he sat in between them.

'I feel lost, hey. I'm beginning to wonder where my place is in this world of ours,' he said, and whilst doing so, a horse appeared on the opposite side of the bay. It drank from the streaming water and wiggled its tail.

'You see that horse, Quinton,' Prince said. 'It's lost in the wild just like you. Pay attention to its details.'

Quinton looked closely and noticed the light brown fur on it. He noticed the light hair on its neck, and at that moment, he saw a white line marking on its leg, the same scar Juliana had on her left thigh.

'What is this all supposed to mean?' Quinton asked.

'What do you think it means?' Elizabeth questioned back as she smiled with grace.

'I don't know! You are the ones wearing the material that angels wear!' Quinton said, and they all laughed.

'She is loyal to you, son,' Prince stated. 'She too doesn't know where she belongs in the world.'

Quinton sat there looking at the ripples that they were all making with their feet.

'She belongs to you, my son' Prince added. 'You must treat her with respect. She's not as much mature as you yet, but she will grow into someone marvellous, and she will age with grace!'

'She will love you regardless,' Elizabeth added. 'I know this because even through death, I still look at your grandfather the way that she looks at you.'

Quinton looked back at the horse as it drank from the stream, and all these signs were confusing. He began to have trust issues towards the supposed angel that came into his dreams weeks before. Quinton sat on that rock quietly for a while and didn't flinch. Quinton had missed his grandparents so much that it always occurred to him that they know exactly what to say and when to appear. A writer by the name of Christopher Poindexter once said, 'I loved her not for the way she danced with angels, but for the way the sound of her name silenced my demons.' That quote ran through Quinton's mind, and for the first time after, he was sure of his fate with Juliana. He found peace within himself whenever he said her name out loud.

Quinton woke up to the cooling air in the airplane with a slight head rush from the Mexican Corona beers that they had at the O. R Tambo Airport. He looked at Juliana who was reading a romance novel whilst covered in a blanket that the air hostess had provided.

'We are almost there, baby' Juliana said. 'Share your dream with me please.' She glanced at him with those adorable green eyes.

'Nope,' he said and smiled.

It wasn't long before the plane landed. Quinton and Juliana walked out onto the tube connection from the plane into the airport in London. He understood the dream he had and appreciated the vague wisdom. It was always good to dream about people that had an impact in his life whilst he was away in la-la land.

Chapter Seven

Breaking Hearts

Juliana's apartment was extremely cold and hallow. They entered through the front door, and it was completely dark. Everything seemed to have been in place as Juliana switched on the lights and the heater. Her place was decorated in art and other artefacts. There was a black guitar and a few notebooks on the low glass table. The place started to warm up to Quinton as he walked onto the carpet in her bedroom. His lover was generous enough to make them both a cup of hot chocolate whilst they waited for the living room to heat up. They were pretty exhausted after cuddling on the couch and drinking a few more cups of hot chocolate.

'Join me in bed, baby!' she said.

'Okay, my love!' he replied.

The hot chocolate settled into his stomach as they entered underneath the blankets. It was extremely cold, and Juliana remained clinched on to Quinton's body for a while. Her warmth kept him comfortable, and he rested his eyes that evening in peace.

Weeks had passed into a new month, and everything was going well. Quinton had moved into a new apartment from his previous one with help of his university friends. His apartment had more space in the living room and a bigger bedroom. The location was farther from the university, but that made it better because that gave him time to focus on schoolwork and avoid any unnecessary temptations. The only downside to his new location was that he was farther from Juliana and that kept him unsettled. She sent more of her days in the recording studio downtown and used Quinton's love as a muse and an instrument to make more music.

They felt strained by the little distance.

The cold weather seemed to be wearing off into summer as nights became warmer. Quinton sat by three windows that were in a row in the living room that evening, tweeting away on his study chair and listening to local bands when Juliana knocked on his front door. He opened the door, and she started crying. She collapsed to the floor by the entrance and cried out loud. He kneeled to the floor to hold her.

'What's worry, baby?' he asked.

He was highly concerned and very confused. She muttered in between her words, and he couldn't understand what had her feeling this way. His heart sunk low as he felt her depressing tears stream down his arms. She kept crying as he picked her up into the apartment and tucked her into his warm bed. Quinton gave her some water to reduce the oncoming headache, but she didn't drink from the glass and couldn't stop crying. Something was wrong, and the atmosphere immediately altered his mood. She cried herself to sleep, and after that moment lapsed, Quinton gently removed her shoes off her feet. Her phone rang on the table in the living room as Quinton switched off his laptop. It was a South African code number, but he didn't answer it because it might have been have her parents. It rang again and again until the battery alerted a low battery notification.

Quinton joined her in bed a few hours after finishing off an assignment and charging both their mobile phones. He cuddled her body so tightly, and she started to cry again.

'My father is dead,' she whispered.

It all started to make sense why she was so upset. Quinton wanted to comfort her more than anything after she told him the bad news, but she didn't want him anywhere near her.

'Please go away,' she said indecisively.

Her words pierced into his stomach like dagger, and at that moment, he was lost in direction. He didn't know what to do, nor did he know what to say to her. He was speechless, unsure of what to do in his position.

'Come here,' he said and tried to hug her tightly.

She broke down in tears underneath his blankets. Her blue veins cropped out on her forehead as she frowned, resting on his chest as he lay by.

He contemplated the pain that she felt and began to feel a bit of it too as he thought of her sudden sadness. Her heart ached badly as she slept that night, knowing that she would never be with her father again.

Her phone rang in the early hours of the morning, and she picked it up whilst he slept by her warm body. The mildly positive energy that she possessed disappeared after that phone call, and her cold temperature crept into the apartment that morning, leaving Quinton's body devastated.

'Okay, I understand,' she said. 'Okay.'

She wept quietly again after dropping her cell phone then stood up with great difficulty. There was no life in her, and her demons had stolen her happiness away. Quinton felt like he was losing her at that point as she point blankly dismissed him when he tried to join her in the shower.

'I just want to be alone,' she said.

He accepted but quickly got fed up because he wasn't her punching bag. Quinton made her breakfast that morning regardless of her actions and lit a cigarette by the window in the living room. His feet pressed onto the old red wall-to-wall carpet in the living room, and the comfort from it gave him a sense of understanding that Juliana was in pain.

She didn't eat the breakfast that he'd made for her after she entered into the living room. She just sat there on the couch, looking at the Coldplay wall poster and her mind zoned out into it. Quinton immediately realized that he'd never once sang to her and thus tried to do so. His voice was horrible, and yet he kept singing as her eyes turned red whilst she wept. Her pointy nose was pinkish, and she looked miserable. None of the songs that Quinton knew and sang to her could bring her father back to her. Her happiness was enslaved, and her sadness whipped her back senselessly. She sniffed as the tears flowed from her eyes, and her dimple smile that Quinton adored mostly on her face vanished. He didn't leave her alone that day nor any other day. He cried with her too. He knew that if he cried, she would stop crying, and it worked mostly, yet he still felt helpless. She didn't want him anywhere near her, but regardless of that, he held on to her slim body tightly as she cried on his bedroom. She was so exhausted from all the pain, and Quinton stayed up late, stroking her hair whilst she sniffed and cried.

'It hurts,' she said. She touched her left chest firmly with both hands. Her cheeks were as pink as her palms as she glanced. He noticed how stained they were. She wept and felt her knees weakening whilst she clamped on to him.

'I don't know what's wrong with me' she stated.

He picked her up so gently and remained kind. 'He was your father' he replied. 'You don't have to be like this. Let me be there for you'

She nodded whilst her head remained glued onto his chest.

'Come to bed, baby,' he said.

Juliana slept so peacefully for the first time in ages. Her mother called whilst she was asleep. Quinton picked up.

'Julie love,' she said.

'No, it's Quinton. Juliana is sleeping,' he replied. 'So sorry to hear about Andrew, Marissa!'

Marissa sniffed for a while, and Quinton respected her enough to keep quiet whilst she had her moment on the phone. 'It was a carjacking,' she mentioned and sobbed through her words.

Quinton remained shocked at the revelation of the news as the information entered his ears. 'Andrew didn't deserve to die, nor did his family deserve to lose him so suddenly,' Quinton thought to himself. 'I am so sorry to hear that,' Quinton replied.

'We will be in England on Monday with his body for his burial.' she said. 'Keep Juliana safe for me, okay?'

'Yes, ma'am, I will keep her safe,' he replied.

Quinton opened the fridge after the phone call and opened a beer bottle, wondering how he'd feel if he was to ever lose his father. A negative energy hovered over his apartment, and he did not know how to get rid of it. He hoped that Juliana wouldn't do anything drastic when he wasn't looking because she seemed highly suicidal and vulnerable. She didn't care about anything, and Quinton feared for the outcome.

Slowly but surely within a few days, she started to gain composure, and her friends would visit her whilst Quinton was away. His apartment became a mess, and so was the relationship they were in.

It was a Friday evening, and Quinton entered his apartment to a moment that changed everything. The study table was a mess. Quinton's beautiful angel was a mess. She was intoxicated yet tried to stand up to hide in shame. A blonde girl walked into the living room from the passage.

'Oh, hey, you must be Quinton,' the girl said and sniffed. 'Whoa, you are cuter then she described you,' she interrupted with a cocky smile.

'And who are you?' Quinton asked as Juliana fell back onto the couch.

'Oh, I'm Charlotte,' she mentioned and picked up her underwear. 'Relax, she is okay.'

Juliana was highly inebriated on the couch for a while, and Quinton wondered how he'd wrapped his mind around that exact moment, for it had never happened before. He picked up his girlfriend and chivalrously tucked her into bed within his bedroom then made his way back and dismissed everyone from the apartment.

He wondered if he was being selfish for not understanding what was happening in his apartment. Quinton wanted nothing but the best for Juliana, yet she seemed to view him as an obstacle, getting in her way. Whilst cleaning up that evening, he discovered used condoms underneath the couch, which was a shocking revelation. Quinton sat by the wall, disgusted by what he'd seen underneath the couch. He couldn't wrap his head around the event that could have taken place in the apartment. The blue suede couch had love stains on it, and that broke his heart into a million pieces.

111

Quinton did not move from that very spot. Instead he lit a cigarette and drifted into his imagination to try and conclude a story for himself. The devil had made his presence felt in the apartment, and Juliana had allowed the beast into their lives. Everything seemed wrecked as he shut his eyes. He could hear loud laughs inside his head, and his happiness diminished into none.

It was awfully quiet. The last bit of hope whizzed into the darkness as he imagined the worst scenario. He just shut his eyes to a world of pain, and his heart absorbed the darkness that came with it. He lay quietly in tragic pain, lying on the carpet still like a paraplegic, unable to pray that evening.

Two startling hours passed into a new morning as Quinton thought of the events that had occurred since Andrew's death, and he realized that death had a ripple effect on their relationship. Juliana was so different from the girl that he'd fell in love with, and the spark that she had in her eyes disappeared into the darkness.

The street light memories that had shone brightly within her eyes suddenly deflected from within, and everything switched off completely. Quinton sat on the chair by the bedside and switched on the side lamp. He looked at Juliana Rose whilst she was sleeping, and he stroked her hair softly.

A tear dropped from his eyes as negative thoughts streamed within. He didn't want to be with her when she was like that, and it was heartbreaking for him to see what she was becoming right in front of his eyes. Her face didn't glow anymore, and the texture on her beautiful skin started to dry. Quinton still loved her purely regardless of her actions. A part of him believed that she would never sleep with anyone else or allow anyone to touch her the same way he did, but as he thought of the used condom underneath the couch, it all cast monsters onto their lives. Her shoulders were bruised, and he noticed bite marks on her neck which highly upset him as he sat there by the bed. He remembered that she didn't like to be bitten by anybody because she hated pain, and that thought demoralized him as he felt the pain inside his gut, the same bites feeding off of his pain.

Those thoughts buried his mind into a deep dark grave, and his heart sunk into all-time low as he felt himself drowning in pain. He couldn't breathe properly and felt an oncoming anxiety settling in very quickly as his mind became dazed and his body dried in exhaustion. Quinton walked to the kitchen to drink some water but felt an immediate craving for something stronger. Therefore, he opened a vodka bottle and poured some of it into his coffee mug whilst making some strong coffee out of the coffee machine. He was repulsed by the stains on the blue suede couch and kept drinking his own version of Irish coffee.

It was extremely late, but Quinton remained by the heater, drinking by himself and nursing his broken heart. He repeatedly tried not to think of the worst scenario, and his face turned mildly sour as he found himself mesmerized by the drama. The only option was to sleep by himself. Therefore, he fetched his blanket and slept on the cold carpet floor.

Quinton opened his eyes widely hours later and felt like he'd never slept. He hoped that the previous night was a nightmare and that everything was back to normal. His head pounded, and he felt highly dehydrated. Everything was completely different as he stood up. He didn't feel peace within his heart anymore and felt merely vindictive towards the whole saga.

Juliana had woken up before him and cleaned up the mess in the living room. She knew what she'd done but hoped that he wouldn't read too much into the situation. Quinton walked towards the bedroom, and they collided at the door as he closed his eyes to the brightness in the bedroom. They bumped into each other, and it was awkward.

It was quiet.

They were speechless.

Quinton seemed extremely exhausted. He didn't want to bring up the issue at hand and hoped that she'd be honest. She felt incredibly guilty and sickened by what she'd done. Juliana entered the bathroom and cleaned herself up quietly. They felt like two strangers and tried to avoid each other as much as possible. The conversation was highly inevitable, but neither one of them wanted to address because they feared the outcome. The negative energy in that apartment drained them both as they tried to avoid each other, yet fate itself had a way of bringing them back into the living room after they were done pretending that everything was okay.

Juliana entered the living room and stood by the door frame quietly. She tried to speak, but nothing came out her mouth as she opened it. Her facial expression projected shock, and it was obvious to Quinton that she'd betrayed him. He sat on the study chair quietly, hoping that she would say something completely different to what was already obvious to him.

A knock on the door interrupted the awaited conversation, and Juliana opened it to find her uncle Luke. Luke entered and greeted politely, but a cloud of misery was hovering behind him. He walked inside confidently and spoke to Quinton as he waited for Juliana to pick up her bags. Luke had taken leave from his advertising agency in the heart of London so that he could organize his oldest brother's funeral without feeling fully obligated to the world. He was a responsible man and definite replica of Andrew Rose. Luke was a younger version of Andrew and possibly a doppelganger because they looked terrifyingly alike. He didn't speak much whilst picking up Juliana, and they both left Quinton's apartment in a hurry.

Juliana looked at Quinton as she walked out, and he knew the truth at that moment. It was abstractly written on her face as she covered her face with a black hoodie. She'd allowed the devil inside, and demons were dancing on her shoulders as she closed the door. Quinton felt utterly betrayed. He still needed answers but would have to wait. His legs stiffened from the cold air coming off the third window, yet he sat quietly and contemplated the busy week of tests coming ahead. He wondered how he'd complete the following week after what had just happened, but a part of him had already been through a situation like this.

The name 'Calista' rang a bell within his mind as he lit a cigarette by the window. Quinton realised that he was indeed too good-hearted to be with just anybody of the normal crowd, and he'd hoped that Juliana knew that part. He never once stated that fact to her because stating it before had resulted to Calista breaking his heart. A cloud of smoke hovered over his head as he exhaled and felt his heart burning into ashes.

So many thoughts dwelled within him for days to come. Saturday evening was one of them. It was pitch dark outside, but the lights closest to the student square sparked the atmosphere, and it seemed joyful outside. Quinton never left his apartment once that evening. He was brut and unhappy. He was lost in a world of whispers and lies. His three closest friends came out to visit after rumours had spread around campus. Their names were Cindy, Anthony, and Layla. Cindy was so beautiful with her genuine smile and was definitely a pleasant sight for Quinton's sore eyes. She was short and had naturally long black hair. She aspired to be a model but remained forever sceptical because of her height difference to others every single time an opportunity presented itself. She studied law from the same university and definitely liked Quinton just as much as the next girl because of his incredible quality of being a gentleman. Cindy always stated to Layla how she could do a better job at taking care of Quinton than Juliana and always seemed envious of the relationship that Juliana had with Quinton.

Anthony was his father's successor. Therefore, he and Quinton had a lot in common. He was born in South Africa where his parents resided. Anthony's parents were Americans with new money and thus decided to move South Africa in the mid-'90s after the first democratic elections. They believed that they would strike gold but instead ended up buying out a lot mineral quarries to have a consistent return on their investments. Anthony was young man that lived his life carelessly and used young women. Quinton could never understand how someone so graceful like Layla would end up with Anthony. Their chemistry wasn't exactly romantic, yet she loved him even though he cheated on her consistently. Quinton knew of Anthony's acts but never judged him once because he believed that God was the only one to judge everyone's sins.

It was extremely rare for Quinton to witness someone so pure and greet him politely, and it was heart throbbing as Layla touched him. She looked exquisite every single time, and her brunette hair painted a picture so beautiful. Her Persian roots enhanced her beautiful glow. It was quite evident that she deserved someone better than Anthony.

They all entered into Quinton's apartment and found comfort in the living room. The food from the local restaurants smelt so good, and

Quinton's apartment had life inside it again. Layla spoke, and her words were always so positive. She was close friends with Juliana, and it was understandable why! They were brunette, liberal, and kind.

'Quinton, you know!' Cindy said. 'I'm sure everything has been blown way out of proportion, right?'

'Well, I don't know to be honest!' Quinton replied.

'So who was the guy? Anthony asked.

'I don't know. Hey, I got back and found my apartment in a mess and there was a girl. Charlotte is her name,' Quinton stated.

'Oh, I know Charlotte. She is bad news, hey,' Layla said. 'Trust me, she doesn't have anyone's best interest!'

The apartment was clouded with smoke, and something about their presence only made Quinton more and more into himself. He became so distant and missed Juliana. His friends spoke and laughed, but none of their voices sounded like Juliana's.

'So what now, Quinton?' Cindy asked.

'I don't know!' he replied and noticed Cindy's cleavage trying to bust through her top.

'I'm sure you will be okay, right? Cindy asked.

'I love her, but I can't be with the person that was here this morning. She seemed so different,' Quinton replied as he carried on smoking his cigarette. He noticed Cindy frown to his obvious statement.

'On the bright side, we bought you plenty of hot wings to eat!' Layla said and smiled.

Something was so pleasant about looking into Layla's brown eyes. Her smile invited purity and grace. She, too, was an angel that walked the earth. Quinton believed that she was locked out of heaven or supposedly sent down to earth to help bring about peace. Everything about Layla painted an image of what heaven looked like. Quinton immediately blinked and closed his eyes to imagine it all. Layla's smile and peaceful tone touched his soul. She was vividly unreal to him, and something about her voice invited angels into the picture. Quinton opened his eyes and felt pleasant again. Happiness whizzed into his apartment as he stood up and picked up the plates on the table.

Anthony didn't say much as he noticed a change in Quinton's facial expression. They all laughed as Anthony made his hilarious jokes whilst Quinton washed the dishes in the kitchen.

'Stop! Come here,' Cindy commanded. 'You need a proper hug'

'I know,' Quinton replied. He hugged her body so tightly. His tense nerves rested as she hugged him tightly as well.

'Take it one day at a time,' she mentioned. 'Call me whenever'

Quinton nodded as the information swamped into his ears.

'Oh, wow, Quinton, you seem to have moved on so quickly, hey!' Layla interrupted as she entered the kitchen.

'No, it's not what it looks like!' Quinton replied as he looked at Layla.

He couldn't tell if she was being sarcastic as she smiled.

'I'm playing!' Layla said.

Quinton immediately walked out of the small kitchen to avoid the elephant in the room because Layla knew Juliana personally. Therefore, it was in Quinton's interest to avoid any contact with Cindy. Quinton was still growing up and learning to discipline his untamed heart. He noticed Anthony smiling whilst texting in the living room.

'Whoa, who is that?' Quinton asked.

'Oh, nothing,' he replied. 'So Cindy, huh?'

'It hasn't even been one day, mate,' Quinton replied. 'Juliana and I must talk first!'

'I get it,' Anthony said.

Cindy and Layla walked out with the dessert, and it looked delicious. Quinton ate the malva pudding and custard. It melted inside his mouth. He didn't understand his sudden urge for lust. His body was working against his heart, and he felt animalistic, to say the least. The indecisive feeling of wanting to heal alone or healing within another being brought greater confusion. His mind wanted the clarified truth, but his heart couldn't bear to carry the bad news. He was devastated as they all sat on the carpet floor, chatting and listening to music whilst they all bonded over some cheap boxed wine, and after a few hours, they left him alone on his apartment.

His heavy eyes shut off to the tuneful sounds of Coldplay's latest album. The moment was magical as he imagined a different world, a world where everyone was wearing white clothing in a peaceful environment. The field was wide and prosperous with a green grass layout.

Quinton imagined himself to have been surrounded by everybody he'd ever known, and the guitar strings from the living room gave that moment an impact as he lay quietly on his bed. Children ran around with colourful balloons, and their laughter was incredible in his imagination. The older generations sat by closely and talked to each other pleasantly. Quinton sat by himself within the crowd and the children's laughter alliterated louder as he zoned out into a black box. The laughter grew intensely louder until a climax was reached. Everything stopped, and it was dead quiet.

The music in the living room had stopped playing, and his mind was back on earth. All he could hear was his heart beating slowly as he fell into a deep sleep.

Monday was the same day that Andrew Rose's body arrived at the Heathrow Airport. Quinton remained supportive and wore black that afternoon to mourn on behalf of Juliana. Anthony came to pick up him in an old second-hand Volkswagen Beetle. The red car was an old-school vehicle yet functioned very well.

Quinton felt insecure and unsure about himself because of the heartbreak he was going through. Anthony spoke, but his words meant nothing, for Quinton had zoned out towards the traffic ahead. He wasn't ready to see her, nor was he ready to face the reality of her deceit.

Quinton and Anthony made their way to the beautiful suburbs, and everything was quiet in between the sprinklers hissing. They drove past a lot of luxurious cars and people wearing black. The residence was huge and landscaped with short green grass. The white tent covered the view of the house, and it was highly impossible for Quinton to see what Juliana's childhood home looked like. He was admirably astonished by the number of people that came to the memorial service as he sat at the back of the congregation, noticing a diverse group of people that walked different paths in life.

Marissa Rose, Juliana's mother, sat at the front with the preachers of the local churches from the surrounding suburb area. Misery basked within her heart and she was quiet. Quinton noticed Juliana handing out programs to of people outside the tent. Juliana looked so beautiful and natural with make-up for the first time since Andrew died. She wore a black dress, amazing black scurf on her neck, extraordinary flat shoes that made her looked merely adorably. It was heart throbbing and tragically beautiful for Quinton to be so selfish. He noticed her cheeks look pinkish from her mark up. His heart beat so fast that it almost tried to escape from his chest as he discovered her beauty once more. Quinton's eyes peeled as he watched Juliana greet people and smile as if everything was fine. She didn't look towards his direction, and he was gladly swooped that she didn't do so. It felt right for him to be separated from her, but the distance itself began to desiccate his heart.

'Yep, she is beautiful, bro,' Anthony said.

'Yeah, I know,' Quinton replied as he watched Juliana sit by her mother.

He noticed an empty seat next to Juliana and wondered if he should sit by her side. Juliana's relatives and distant relatives were all seated in the row behind, and as Quinton assessed the situation, Anthony looked at him.

'It's all in your eyes. You do not want to lose her,' he said. 'Go comfort her, mate!'

A notification beeped on Quinton's Blackberry, and it was a message from Juliana.

I know you hate me, but I need you. I really do.

I have a seat saved for you.

Quinton read the message over and over again whilst Anthony smiled confidently to his advice.

'Trust me, bro!' he whispered. 'Just go and take it one step at a time.'

'Just take it one step at a time' were the words that lingered inside his mind as he swallowed his pride and walked towards the front.

Tears began to flow down Juliana's cheeks. She was so tired of pretending to be strong by herself and therefore allowed herself to rest her pride as she wept. Juliana placed her arms around Quinton's body as the numerous people stood up to speak about her father. She smiled at a few times at the jokes that were made throughout the service yet remained sad as the preachers spoke.

Juliana remained seated throughout the memorial service and seemed like she'd come to terms with her father's death. Quinton felt Juliana's hands clinch on to his body so tightly, and the feeling of it made him loath himself for attending. He wanted to run away from his own presence and hide, but the moment was real. It wasn't fiction nor was it scripted. He didn't understand how to cooperate because he'd never been through something like that before. Her heart was longing for his love, but his love was vacant. All he felt was pain. He felt disrespected and used by her more than ever.

The service ended, and people cleaned out to prepare for the funeral the next day. A moment that was so long awaited presented itself as the two meet in a thatched maze garden. There was a small fountain of two toddler sculptures close to the dark wooden bench. The toddler statues held clay buckets with water overflowing out of them onto a clay base that recycled the water. Juliana sat on the wooden bench by the fountain parallel to the small street lamp, and Quinton finally entered the hidden garden. It was awfully quiet, and they were hidden from the world like they'd hoped to be. The trees had covered the naked sky, and the small cricket sounds stopped as he stepped towards the light. The path was paved with grey cemented foot designs, and Quinton started to feel trapped. He sat right next to her.

The pause was dramatic, and despair clocked into their lives as they sat still. Their hearts were beating so loud, yet neither of them was in sync with each other. Juliana couldn't grip on to her courage and face him. There they were again, yet neither one of them knew what to say. Quinton pleaded to God at that moment that she'd say something reassuring, and Juliana hoped that he'd understand the words that were about to come out of her mouth.

Luckily, Anthony found them after searching everywhere. He interrupted them. Quinton stood up, and no words were shared between him and Juliana. He looked back and wondered what ran through her mind that evening. He wondered what made her break her vows to him.

They were initially wedded to each other unlawfully, and as Juliana realized that, an emotion of guilt washed into her soul. She felt ashamed and filthy, but regardless of this, she looked up at Quinton whilst seated. The emerald spark in her green eyes began to shine at him again, and he knew that that he was still in love with her. A part of him was disgusted by her actions, yet every inch of his body wanted to turn back so that he could kiss her again. A part of him wanted to park his lips onto her and forget that another man had ruined everything. She was broken to him, and he wondered how he'd fix something like this. His thoughts paused and he stopped. The crickets began to sound as he waited for her to say something, but she never said anything. She never said a word, and all he could hear was the different beat from her desperate heart. Her heart throbbed so loud and became a seeker for his attention, yet it never quite realized the tension that it was causing between the two. Quinton moved forward and vanished into darkness whilst she sat there quietly and water dripped from the fountain.

No words were expressed as Anthony drove Quinton back to his apartment. Quinton zoned into the reviled street lights and his heart took caution. The traffic lights turned green, and his mind turned red. He was on a lot of pain but couldn't bring himself to deal with it. A feeling of uncertainty overwhelmed him as he felt a deep-rooted pain from being hurt by so many people in the world. That pain reached the core of his heart, and he was angry because all those girls that he'd ever loved deceived him and hurt him blatantly. He grew sick and felt his insides trying to escape.

Anthony noticed a pale look on Quinton's face. Therefore, he stopped the car by the bus stop. A flood of vomit erupted out of Quinton's mouth as he opened the passenger door. He felt stabbed in the back and felt utterly sick. Juliana had destroyed the last bit of faith within him. He lost hope as vomit came out of his mouth and a headache flashed his thoughts of love. His head throbbed to the beat of his heart, and he felt lost as he took a seat by the bench.

Anthony lit two cigarettes and handed another to Quinton. They smoked and spoke. Anthony tried to vacate Quinton's thoughts to another place, but his words weren't persuasive enough. Quinton's mind was destructive and bombs exploded within him. It was so loud inside his head, and he felt nothing but anger growing like a cancer so deep within his bones. The stars that lingered in the dark sky weren't there anymore. It was pitch black and disturbing inside his heart.

The streets were wet from the rain forecast as Anthony drove slowly. Quinton did not say a word throughout the whole trip, and he entered his dark apartment to a cool breeze. The lights were off, and it was cold. He sat by the window frame and smoked another cigarette. It occurred to him that he was addicted to nicotine again as he inhaled the smoke deeply. The smoke wavered out the window, and a scene compelled him to glance towards the bottom. A young lady in her late thirties walked out of a store with a few grocery bags in her hands. She looked sadistically aged with her back aching as she opened the trunk of her car and placed the bags inside. Something about that moment made Quinton feel incredibly nostalgic as the lady ran across the street happily and hugged a man. The individual himself seemed so happy, and it looked like they were reuniting after a very long time. They looked like old lovers of the night. The two of them spoke as Quinton watched them, and before he knew it, the couple kissed underneath the street lamp. It was incredibly beautiful and romantic. The lady took a few breaths, and their atmosphere was clouded by the steam for a few seconds.

Quinton flicked his cigarette out the window whilst the two strangers kept kissing under the street lamp. He felt merely envious because he initially loved such moments. He walked into his bedroom to a calm atmosphere as the music played softly through the speakers. It was quiet and cool. The lava lamp shined in blue and green whilst the rest of the bedroom remained in darkness. It was so peaceful and relaxing to be alone until someone knocked gently on the front door.

Quinton remembered that Layla had promised to visit him again. Thus, his reaction to the stranger to the door was joyful until he opened the door slowly. Juliana stood before him and seemed so remorseful. His pulse rate increased drastically as he opened the door wider. She tilted her head slightly to her right whilst she looked at him. Her body was incredibly long and beautiful. Quinton was immediately robbed of his temporary happiness as he moved out the way and gestured a sign for her to enter. Juliana walked inside but didn't sit anywhere. She felt out of place and thus stood still in the living room as Quinton closed the door. She looked around and noticed a home she once knew, but it was different now. Juliana didn't feel welcome anymore and thus decided that it was best she stated the truth to him.

'You—' Quinton shouted but was interrupted.

'I'm so sorry!' Juliana shouted. 'I'm so sorry, baby.'

She tried to move closer to him, but he stepped backwards. Quinton felt highly repulsed and indecisive. It wasn't in his nature to be harsh, but it definitely felt appropriate.

'I did sex with someone else,' she said.

The truth punched and damaged his insides. An internal pain left him completely speechless as he felt a cramp on his diaphragm. His assumption was correct, but he'd hoped for a lie. Juliana remained apologetic and sincere throughout as tension grew inside the living room. Quinton felt his heart rust and his mind grew ruthless towards her betrayal. He immediately lost composure, and he flipped the study table upside down. The long glass by the window frame earned its own air mileage as Quinton picked it up and threw it towards her direction. It flew past her and smashed into the kitchen door frame. It shattered into a dozen pieces, and everything about those pieces represented his heartbreak. She stood frightened and scared as she shook, and with immediate effect, a stream of tears raced down his face.

'Quinton, please stop!' she shouted. 'You are scaring me!' Her eyes poured down tears of sorrow and pain. She knew that she'd become the architect of his engraved pain.

Quinton stood before his lover, panting and unhinged from his reality, driven drunk with rage. However, he didn't place a hand on Juliana. It reminded him of his father and how domestically violent he'd been in the past.

Juliana was scared and terrified and unable to explain. She was speechless a second.

'Quinton!' she shouted. 'Please don't end our relationship.'

123

'Just go,' he whispered as he realized that he was way over his head. Quinton had completely lost touch of reality, and he was being reckless. Another tear dropped from his left eyelid as she turned slowly and moved towards the door.

She stopped by the door frame and took a deep breath. Quinton felt the beginning of another depressing chapter write itself into his memoir as the door closed. An epiphany rang into his mind as he lay on the bed. He started to believe that human beings were dark and twisted because their true nature knew no bounds and they were faithless without religion. Quinton felt a deep-rooted sadness from his body again as he closed his baggy eyes. Hope evaporated from his soul. His pure heart rested in excruciating pain, and darkness hovered around that evening.

Chapter Eight

Lost in the World

The weather turned windy after a while. Days grew cold and slow. Quinton spent most of the time in his bedroom, catching up with family over the phone and chatting with his old-time friends from his home country. However, at times, he'd spend it with his college friends within his living room. Quinton believed that having a lot of people around would close up the loneliness that he felt inside. He always knew as he zoned out to the back of his mind that he wasn't as happy as he claimed to be. Everything spiraled around him, and he was stuck in the middle of the effects of a heart break. He was easily peer-pressured like a high school boy, wild, unhinged with horniness on a prom night.

Quinton relapsed on numerous occasions, and he found himself calling Juliana, but she never once answered his calls. He started to lose weight, and Layla stopped visiting after some time. She couldn't bear to witness what Quinton was becoming, and it was heartbreaking for her to see him in so much pain. Quinton's face turned pale and dry. His soul was temporarily sucked out of his body, and he became a walking corpse. His eyes turned ruby red, and his glowing face perished into dust. He was just human, and nothing about him was significantly special anymore.

He'd struggled to make it past the passage after vomiting in the bathroom. He would lay there with a blurred vision of his reality. His heavy ruby eyes remained strained even more. He'd feel his body quiver from his stomach grumbling from the hunger.

Quinton drifted into a nightmare of darkness gripping his throbbing heart. He felt his body being dragged through the dirt by the same hideous, barbaric brute figure that stood right next to him in his apartment back in his home country. It was dragging him through the mud. Quinton's ankles were chained, and he couldn't break away. He tried to twist himself free but found himself caught within the heavy mud. The moment consisted of an endless struggle as he tried to gasp for air, but the savage roared and slapped his face back into the mud. All he could hear in between the swaths and the footsteps were owls hooting from dried-out dead branches. The surface dried out, and his skin began to peel from the gravel surface. He began to scream for help, but there was nobody there to listen or help him out of his situation. His back peeled and bled onto the rough surface. His ankles were bruised in chain marks, and the metal chain began to burn into his skin as they moved closer to the dark tunnel. Quinton cried out so loud and desperately sought for immediate attention. He could see his life heading towards darkness as he screamed out so loud, so loud that his own voice awoke him from his darkest sleep to the crispy fresh smell of bacon strips in the kitchen.

The atmosphere was completely different to the nightmare he'd had. Purity radiated a positive energy from the living room, and he was amused by it. The positive energy basked into a sceptical thought inside his mind as it phased him that maybe he was still dreaming. He took a moment to grasp the reality as he heard feminine voices, a pleasant feeling into his heart. The feeling that he'd gotten was completely different from what he became accustomed to. There were beautiful flowers growing inside his jungle, and every untamed animal within his wild imagination disappeared into nothing as he walked into the passage. He stopped for a while as his heart sensed peace. There were beautiful angels, ones who'd had flocked into his living room. They spoke and sounded familiar. The apartment wasn't dirty anymore, and every bottle that he remembered seeing hours before had been thrown away into the trash.

Quinton smiled as he noticed Layla and her cousin, Maria, sitting on the couch and chatting about the most irrelevant topics. They smiled back at him and greeted politely. It was amazing how certain individuals can alter the destiny of another person's path for the day with just a genuine smile or an act. His vivid eyes loved the sight of the beautiful tulip flowers that had planted themselves in the living room, and the jungle looked pure and beautiful. Quinton could smell a compelling scent of his significant lover. He could smell her essence through the scent of the egg and the burning bacon in the kitchen. Her essence was the smell he could never forget even if he tried. Quinton knew this familiar smell.

There was a heaven scent of an angel with white wings, hovering around in the kitchen. It was a smell of recognition, an essence of love. Quinton stood quietly as Layla and Maria gazed at him. Neither one of them said anything to him as he tried to guess. They smiled and acted unshaped by his suspension. A few steps towards the kitchen door and every turned slow for him. He started to breath properly for the first time, and the nicotine addiction that he'd had evaporated from his itching body. The cravings of it vanished, and he didn't feel any twitches inside his chest. He blinked a lot as he looked at the carpet whilst walking on it. He made an entrance through the kitchen door and felt a heat wave brush onto him gracefully. The pain from his strained eyes disappeared after he blinked again, and he looked at Juliana Rose.

'I have made you something to eat,' she said and smiled nervously.

She was slightly intimidated and scared because of what she'd done. Nevertheless, she kept speaking to him but didn't realize that he's completely had zoned out into a picture-perfect moment. She picked up the red plate that had French toast slices, bacon strips, and cooked tomatoes. She smiled sincerely, and Quinton was infatuated by her beauty even more. Her beauty made him lose focus on reality. It felt like the first time he'd ever laid his eyes onto her beauty. Quinton stood frozen and speechless. His headache vanished, and all he felt was his heart throbbing extremely fast from the visual that projected towards him.

A healing spirit beamed inside his soul again. He felt his pulse rate ripple in his ears, and as her lips moved up and down, he noticed her dimples deepen into her cheeks. She turned towards the kitchen counter again and moved her fingers to point at the brown muffins by the window frame. Quinton saw a beautiful gold ring on her small index finger, and her nails were painted light blue. Her skin tone looked light caramel from the lightning outside the window. Quinton looked as she grasped and noticed sweat drops emerge from her neck. She was as nervous as he was yet acted calm. Juliana was down to earth and humbled by the past.

Quinton did not listen whilst Juliana spoke. Quinton walked towards her and held on to her tightly, clutching on to his world.

'Well, I think my work here is done!' Layla shouted as she got up and walked out the door with cousin.

'I'm on my way to find Anthony!' Layla said. 'He hasn't replied to my messages! Quinton, have you seen him?' she interrupted.

'No, I haven't, hey!' Quinton responded.

Layla would be as heartbroken as Quinton was if she knew the truth about Anthony's indiscretions. He kept the truth to deeply hidden within his loin but regretted it because Layla deserved nothing but the truth. Layla closed the front door.

It was so quiet in between the heavy breathing and the lovemaking.

Quinton rinsed the soupy fork from the sink after they'd cleaned themselves up, and he ate the meal that Juliana had made for him with gratitude and modesty. It had been awhile since he'd had a meal that was made out of love.

'Try the muffins,' she suggested and offered.

And indeed, he tried out the light brown muffins that had cooled off by the wooden window frame. A piece of harmony entered into his mouth, and the taste of it washed away the horrible nicotine taste on his tongue. He was grateful and finished eating everything he'd been offered.

Hours passed.

Juliana slept on Quinton's bed like a sick patient seeking medicine for her heart. It started to get cold as the wind grew ruthlessly cold; therefore, Quinton closed the bedroom window. Confidence rose within him again as he shaved his facial hair in the bathroom. His face radiated energy of happiness, and positivity arose within his mind again. Quinton's heart pumped out particles of peace, and those particles diluted into the rest of his body.

Quinton remembered the dream that he'd had, and he knew that the battle for his freedom wasn't over. He closed his eyes, and a bright light tall figure walked through the closed front door like a ghost. This figure was different from the hunched-back savage figure.

Quinton started to see clearly.

His subconscious controlled him, and he started to see the evil monsters which had opened a door of terror in his life. He started to see the angels that tried to keep him away from harm's way, and every decision he'd ever made was based spiritually. His body remained unconsciously glued to the carpet floor as the light figure reached out towards him.

'Hold my hand!' she said.

He held on to the light long soft hand and followed his guardian angel through the closed front door. There was a moment of confusion as he stepped through the closed white door. They entered into a different world.

A world painted in black and white.

A world deprived of beautiful bright colours, and the view devastated his imagination.

Colour vacated his eyes, and an absolutely exonerating feeling touch his soul. He struggled to breathe properly as the air became denser, and they kept walking through a path of grey grass until they reached the top hill. Visuals of the desert ruptured his eyes as they stepped onto big circular rocks. A defining moment lapsed onto him as he saw ancient moulded clay huts. They looked downwards and saw a community of people dancing away and chanting traditionally. Their feet stomped the ground, and they embraced their culture with drum beats. It was impossible for Quinton to describe their origin because they were so far away. Their skin was grey and pale, yet despite that, they were so alive. Quinton and the tall angel walked down the sloping hill and passed through thatched wheatgrass.

The community of people kept chanting away, and they didn't notice Quinton's existence. They kept dancing, singing, pleading to their ancestors for rain. They stomped the ground so hard with their bare feet, and the dust covered the atmosphere. Quinton walked past the clay huts with thatched roofs, and he saw an old tree by the edge of the hill. It was completely dead, and its roots were peeking from the dry ground. The tree was personified within Quinton's imagination, and its roots looked like they'd turned into stone whilst struggling for water. The texture of the branch painted sadness and sorrow. His mouth became dry from the dehydrating conditions, and he started to crave water too. Quinton stood right underneath the massive dead tree and faced the people back at the tribal area. They kept dancing to the sound of their drums and praying to their God for rain. Their cries grew louder as Quinton touched the dried-out texture on the tree. He felt his soul levitate from within him and his mind became clear.

Wisdom floated into his ears, and knowledge equipped his mind sorely. A clarified feeling galloped into his heart as he watched the tribe dancing. The rainy clouds lured by them poured heavily onto the community. The wind rushed towards Quinton, and the rain splashed onto him as the people of the community chanted away for the vivid raindrops. The children rejoiced and danced away too as it rained heavily. None of them ran away to find shelter. They embraced the drops of rain and allowed the wetness to wash away the struggle on their faces. Quinton smiled at the filling happiness as he watched them from a distance. At that moment, he learned to appreciate the serenity of the people back in the desert of Botswana, and he appreciated the different yet amazing scenery that floated into his wondrous mind.

He had an understanding that he was part of the detail in the picture.

Quinton felt very fortunate enough to be on the other side of the world, where it rained a lot. He appreciated the significant pleasure of the dream and of the people smiling through their adversities. It brought peace to him. The smell of moist air gravitated and entered his nostrils. His body became cleansed from the bad evils and every pain within him perished. It rained heavily, and his body temperature changed. He felt cold as the angel spoke in her soft voice. Quinton couldn't pay any attention to her words because his body began to quiver even more. He looked up as her soft face was detailed for the first time. She was remarkable and replicated Layla in every way possible. She muttered, but Quinton couldn't hear anything. Her words turned into sounds of sirens and a beeping heart monitor. The siren sound grew impeccably loud inside of his head. He opened his eyes and blinked continuously at a slow pace, but he couldn't see anything. The angel had disappeared from his sight, and everything was blurry as minutes clocked away.

Quinton felt like he was turning blind. Everything paused, and he felt a cold chill creep into his spine. The medical equipment beeped sounds that monitored his pulse rate, and the sounds gushed through his ears as he closed his eyes again. Quinton felt a soft hand touch his right hand, the feeling of warmth being frequently rubbed onto his hand. He felt the symptoms of an oncoming fever creep into his body, and his temperature changed drastically to surrounding conditions.

It was so quiet and cold.

Quinton opened his eyes once more and noticed an old woman in nursing clothing, writing on a notepad and monitoring him. It sounded like she was mumbling. Her mouth moved, but he couldn't hear properly. He closed his heavy brown eyes again and hoped for the truth because he was initially lost between his reality and his nightmares.

Quinton opened his eyes to darkness. He stood still in front of a big gate. He noticed bright lights on the hinges of the thick dark walls, and his heart began to pound faster as the metal gates opened up after a few seconds. Quinton walked slowly towards an eighteenth-century Italian castle ahead of him. The green grass on the road sides looked wet, and the red roses planted alongside were so beautiful. It was so quiet, and all he could hear were his own feet stepping onto the gravel ground as he moved towards the castle. The castle was surrounded by long thick trees, and he noticed a dark green texture on the leaves as he moved closer to the castle. Quinton noticed a large pathway leading to two huge garage doors on the left of the castle and a prevailing lavish arched entrance squeezed in between the castle and the garage doors. As he kept walking towards the arched entrance, he noticed the light from the inside gushing through red curtains and through the arched windows.

The visual brought warmth to his heart. He discovered carved writing on the grey wall as he stood underneath the arched entrance. The writing—'loyalty and honour'—was carved deeply into the wall, and Quinton felt a sense of entitlement as he entered the castle domain. He stepped onto red-painted bricks on the floor, and a German shepherd ran towards him without any aggression. It wiggled its tail as it came closer, and its joy astonished Quinton as it sniffed his legs. A little girl in a white dress ran towards Quinton happily from the back door entrance and giggled. It was flattering and pleasing to see such a delicate creature touch him. He didn't understand the moment at first, but it felt right for him to pick up the little girl and hug her tightly. Quinton noticed the dimples on the little girl's face as she smiled at him. Her voice and laughter was so peaceful and soundly. He noticed a beautiful woman standing by the back door entrance on the left side of the castle. Big potted plants were placed on each side of the door, and the moment was extraordinary as Quinton stared blankly at the mysterious woman by the entrance. She wasn't Juliana Rose, and Quinton felt completely confused as the woman greeted. The little girl on Quinton's arms dangled her feet and waved at the beautiful woman. Bright lights on the wall flickered brightly as he made his way towards the beautiful woman by the entrance.

She grabbed on to his left hand and led him inside the castle. Quinton saw pictures of moments that had happened to him, but he couldn't recall any of those moments as he walked past all pictures on the walls. He was completely baffled by the photos on the frames and wondered if he was living a different life. Quinton felt the soft texture on a red Persian carpet with his feet as they all entered a massive living room. The fire within the fireplace burned the dead wood, and its light shone brightly into the dark living room. It looked elegantly classy and royal. The little girl yawned and wrapped her small arms around Quinton's neck as he looked around the living room. Quinton saw pictures of his family members and a lot of pictures of him with the beautiful woman next to him. This moment must have been a déjà vu for him because he'd been through it all before, yet he wasn't sure when.

'Let's put her to bed, love!' the woman said.

Quinton took the moment in slowly as everything played itself correctly. The woman placed her right arm around him as they walked upstairs on a staircase made out of dark brown wood. The wood was polished, and the scenery was beautiful. Quinton felt like a king in his own domain. They entered the little girl's bedroom, and her bedroom walls were amazingly artistic. There were a lot of cartoon drawings on the walls next to the single bed. The woman took the little girl into her hands and tucked her inside the duvet. Their beautiful little girl slept so peacefully.

'Good night, Arabella,' the woman whispered as she stood up.

Quinton remained distilled by the peace as he closed the door and walked downstairs with the woman.

'Quinton, we haven't met yet, so I'm shocked that you are here so soon!' she said and sat by the fireplace. 'Quinton, you are not supposed to here so soon,' she said. 'It's too soon!'

'What's too soon?' Quinton asked. 'Why shouldn't I be here?'

'You being here!' she replied. 'You haven't matured yet!'

Her vagueness made him zone out into the burning wood, and he watched the wood as it broke off separately.

'You must head back, baby!' she commanded. 'In order for you to have this, you must grow!' She placed her hand on to his chest and kissed his left cheek softly. 'Go back, my lover. I will be waiting for you!' she said, and a light shone bright at the large window on the right side.

It started to shine even brighter as Quinton closed his eyes and woke up in the hospital bed, wondering why there were so many supernatural elements spiralling within him, and also wondered why those elements had invested so much time in him. It left him weary and uncertain of all of things. One factor remained, Juliana had the ability to alter his dreams because she was the most important person in his life, or so he believed at the time.

It was a public holiday, and everybody was in a tangibly good mood. Quinton had come to terms with his medical condition. His family expressed concerns for his well-being, and it felt right to return to his home country.

He finally made it to Gaborone after a trip from the United Kingdom, and everyone was so happy to see him smiling gracefully. Beth expressed great care for her son, Quinton, and she was definitely in disagreement for him to return to the United Kingdom because of his condition.

Quinton sat in his bedroom after he arrived in the family household. The memories of his childhood were printed onto an old dusty photo album by the shelf, and he picked it up to look at the photos of his old friends. He remembered the small house that he grew up in, and the noisy neighbourhood in western region of Gaborone. Thoughts wandered, and he remembered how difficult it was for Marcus to maintain expenses when Beth was pregnant with her third child on the way. It was extremely difficult for Melinda and Quinton to coexist with their parents because their parents argued all the time. Most of his dreams would turn into nightmares because he was haunted by his father's aggressiveness, and that initially scarred him for life. Quinton's youngest sister, Kimberly, was an amazing blessing because when she was born, a lot of focus was given to her by her parents, which made them argue less.

Quinton entered his bed that evening and prayed for the first time that month. He felt blessed to be in a good home and to be safely away from the wretched world. He couldn't imagine having other parents than Marcus and Beth. Quinton understood that his family wasn't perfect, but that initially made it perfect for him.

Quinton woke up late in the morning to visit his mother at her law firm. He drove carefully through the lunch traffic. He expected a difference to impeach his soul as he looked at a lot of people in their cars yet felt nothing. Nobody seemed to be happy. Everyone seemed to be overly focused on the stress and the difficulties in their lives. The traffic lights remained red, and it was amazingly rare to ever witness someone shouting whilst they were on the phone, but Quinton witnessed it, and the man shouting started coughing. At any moment, that man could have easily had a heartache and died in his car, Quinton thought to himself. The traffic lights turned green, and Quinton wondered if he was going to be part of a system whereby an electronic device would have is dictation over his happiness.

'Where is the human race actually racing to?' he asked himself out loud as he noticed the driver on the left lane speeding ahead and indirectly challenging him as the traffic started to clear out.

Quinton drove into the business buildings at that moment; he saw his whole future suppress his eyes. Sadness adorned him, and every time he began to feel this way, it made him miss Juliana even more. Quinton was human with a human heart, begging to God for mercy and perseverance. He got a warm welcoming from all the assistants at Beth's law firm, and they seemed overly friendly as Quinton entered into their division. There were a few new diverse faces in the firm's associate group, and the atmosphere bloated with false characters all around. Beth always seemed stressed and agitated in her office which inevitably was the price of owning a leading law firm.

She spoke constructively to Quinton about his well-being, and they expressed vulnerable emotions to each other. Beth was definitely in the core of Quinton's gentle ability, and he never wanted to let her down when it came to being chivalrous.

As Quinton drove away after lunch and wandered off to the quiet suburb areas of Gaborone to bond with another friend, he realised that he was starting to miss Juliana Rose even more. William's household was peaceful and quiet. The grass was definitely greener, and Quinton felt a sense of comfort. He turned into William's driveway and found local students relaxing by the patio. The scenery was beautiful, and Quinton noticed the same chimes that he'd back at his old apartment dangling by the entrance. The house looked beautiful in white paint. It had a pleasant smell of lavender. The company within seemed happy. William's house was undeniably the best place to be if you were looking to interact with beautiful, attractive young girls who modelled for local agencies. William absolutely loved African women with African curves. He originated from the sloping hills of Cape Town and liked the scenery in Gaborone. William's excuse for moving to Gaborone was based on the fact that he'd fallen in love with a Motswana girl. He was a liberal hippy and a person with a great sense of humour.

'Come in!' he said. 'What brings you by, Quinton?' he asked.

'Just wanted to greet everyone, and I know how you always have girls around, so . . .' Quinton responded, and they both laughed out loud.

Quinton knew that he was treading on thin ice as he picked up the vodka bottle and mixed its liquor with the cranberry juice bottle. William's fridge was filled with beverages and bulks of meat. At that point, Quinton immediately realised that festivities were upon his clock as more people arrived and entered William's household. The realisation that he was part of a generation that took things for granted hit him, and that thought sickened him. It seemed so easy to live and to be careless until everything starts to crumble into pieces.

Quinton looked at everyone as they entered, and he greeted politely. He knew a lot of faces amongst the crowd, and the afternoon commenced with a joyous occasion, with overfriendly women. Most of those had spouses in other locations, but Quinton wasn't one to judge. He sat by the couch in the living room and watched everybody celebrating absolutely nothing. The flirtations and mingling astonished Quinton as he watched a lot of those young women show signs of disloyalty. It was shocking how a lot of people of his generation could stoop so low. It remained him of his ex, Calista, and the events of her betraying him. Quinton drank more and was accommodated by a younger lady by the name Emily to the kitchen.

It was inevitable for him to fall in lust at any given moment. He looked into her brown eyes as she spoke about her life story. She was younger and shorter than Quinton yet persisted to act older. Her skin was beautiful and lightly black. Emily had an accent of South Africa, a privileged girl. It amused Quinton even more as he allowed himself to connect with Emily on a friendly level.

Hours passed and people left as the night turned dark. It poured down heavily. Quinton was all alone with Emily, and her smile had sold his heart to the highest bidder, lust. A fatal attraction grew between them, and they felt like they were lovers from a previous life. They connected, and a deep unspoken truth had brought them closer, the pain that lingered within. The reality was that Emily was heartbroken and Quinton was utterly lonely and willingly ready to accommodate any affection from anybody attractive. Emily's broken heart caused her to behave in a despicable manner, and she knew that she was acting disorderly, but regardless of her weak heart, her acts began to define her in the long term.

'Come with me!' she whispered.

Quinton stood up and watched as she walked away slowly. He followed and wondered how she knew her way around William's household. It rose up a lot of questions within his mind. They both entered a study room, and the breeze was cool. It had begun to drizzle. The wind brushed in from the open wooden-framed window. Emily switched on the bright lights, and Quinton discovered a completely different world of art and design. He saw canvas stacked on the side of the wall and paint brushes piled in a see-through vase with dirty water. The walls were covered in artistic wallpaper made by William himself. The wall lights gave the room a warm feeling, and Emily walked around, looking at every painting on the wall. She stopped for a while and stood before a massive painting framed in dark brown wood.

'It's beautiful, don't you think?' she asked.

'It's incredible, I like it!' he stated.

It was painting with the Drakensburg Mountains in South Africa in the background and an empty wild field filled with thatched light brown grass with two little children playing in the distance. The painting itself came to life as Quinton looked into its details. He wandered into the artistic work and felt like he was part of the painting. In his mind, the wind blew and painted dried leaves onto the path and onto the thatched grass in different directions. He could hear the children speaking Zulu. They played and sang songs. The reddish maroon colour over the mountains visualised the sun setting, and Quinton imagined those little children running back to their mothers by the streaming waterfall in the right side of the painting.

'It's so beautiful!' Quinton stated as he faced Emily.

She held his right hand with both hands, and he discovered that her story was slightly more detailed then she'd described. She was extremely profound and beautiful yet treated herself like a trumpet.

Emily sat gently on the wide dark wooden table and slid her blue Tom's shoes off onto the light wooden floor with a small carpet. Their intentions weren't pure, and they knew that they were using each other for comfort. Her void was definitely filled to the bream, and she smiled after it all.

'Don't leave, yeah!' she commanded after everything they'd done.

'I won't!' Quinton replied as he watched Emily disappear into the passage.

He cleaned himself up before walking out. Quinton washed his hands in the bathroom sink and made his way towards the dark living room. Music played in the background as Quinton sat next to Emily again. It felt right for him. He looked at the sliding door on the left side of the living room, and he saw rain pouring down even more than before.

It was so amusingly different for him to be with a stranger after the relationship he'd had with Juliana Rose. Emily placed her head onto Quinton's chest, and the feeling of a stranger adoring him was conveniently rare. He felt the difference of Emily's long black hair on his chest as he compared the feeling of it with Juliana's hair. They spoke and interacted like old friends, which seemed very bizarre as thoughts of Juliana railed past from time to time.

Quinton began to understand Emily in every single way, and she began to feel loved by him, yet she knew that he wasn't hers to begin with. Emily touched Quinton's chest, and he appreciated her touch because he'd not felt affection in a while.

'It feels right!' he said to himself and kissed her forehead.

Hours clocked away and it was getting late. William had locked the doors, and the music was turned low, yet neither Quinton nor Emily wanted to leave. They stood up and walked into the spare bedroom. Vulnerable, they lay next to each other quietly in condolence and sadness, comforting each other with laughter. Emily closed her eyes and dreamed away as Quinton zoned away into a distant vague memories within his mind.

It's become easier for Quinton Barker to move around the Diamond City as the months passed. He started working out at the local gym in the central business division area, and his confidence arose to an all-time high. He was healthier and fitter. His face glowed, and his smile captured the hearts of many. He remained highly cautious of his retro lifestyle yet distanced himself from drinking excessively. He'd made it compulsory for himself to attend monthly medical check-ups and ate healthy luxurious foods. Having regular encounters with Emily awoke his heart to the possibilities of a free-spirited life, and the ideal thought of attachment grew vague to him. He'd entered into a world of vainness. It occurred to him that he wasn't attracted to Emily emotionally. He was in a relationship of convenience and status.

Over the past weeks, Emily returned to Johannesburg, South Africa, for her second semester, and that gradually had Quinton contemplating his past with Juliana Rose, moments that portrayed romance, and as he kept having those flashbacks, they slowly turned murky. His memories of love turned blurry, and he couldn't ever see himself being in love with anyone else.

Chapter Nine

Unveiling Secrets

Friday drifted in slowly on the last laziest week of the month, and Quinton had taken an initiative to visit his father, Marcus, at the family warehouse office block. Quinton wasn't working for Marcus anymore but spent more of his afternoons learning how to evaluate company chart sheets. It was midday, and the sun shined brightly onto the city. The heat caused a humid atmosphere throughout the region. It was a drought, and the dry air had an impacted Quinton's nerves. He swamped into Marcus' office in the late afternoon, and his head was aching badly, but regardless of that, he greeted his ageing father and bonded over a glass of whiskey on the rocks. Marcus' office was on the second storey of the office block, and it had a clear view of the entire city. The landscape of the city was flat, and the wide window from office gave a view of a lot warehouse rooftops and office parks. It was incredibly hot outside, but something about it outside made the moment seem memorable as Quinton noticed the mirages fickle over the rooftops. The Diamond City seemed spectacular in its own way, and Quinton felt that it was one of the safest cities that he'd ever been, but maybe this was because the population wasn't enough to cause indecent havoc.

It was so quiet, and all he could hear were telephones ringing from other rooms. Quinton looked at Marcus and noticed a few grey hairs establishing themselves on his head as he spoke. Marcus' hairline was beginning to recede, and wrinkles aligned themselves on his forehead. His father seemed highly exhausted, and Quinton started to see his father becoming really fragile right before his eyes. The ambition of wanting to be highly successful had its ability to make a man wrinkle quickly, and it was very evident on Marcus.

Quinton noticed a lot of formal family photos on his father's office and one in particular, a photo of Beth in a beautiful evening dress. She looked so beautiful and remained forever young. Marcus stated his undying commitment towards Beth as Quinton placed the photo back onto the table and stood still, railing through his memories of the past only to hear Steve speaking aggressively on the phone outside the door. His uncle's hostile attitude drove Quinton to the brink of madness. It seemed a bit coincident for a few seconds as Quinton looked downwards at the back parking lot and noticed a truck driver on his cell phone whilst the truck idled. Steve hung up his cell phone, and so did the truck driver.

The truck drove off onto the road with its cargo at the same time as Steve made his way towards the wooden staircase. Quinton always knew that his uncle wanted to take over the family business for himself, yet Marcus remained so clueless to his brother's ambition because he loved his sibling so much. Marcus always turned a blind eye to Steve's activities and pretended like his brother was heaven sent. Everyone in the family business knew that Steve was the black sheep of the family. His ways were sowed differently, and his methods were dictatorial. Quinton knew better than to ignore the obvious signs and therefore left his father's office whilst Marcus was on the telephone.

It seemed strange that the cargo truck was leaving so late in the afternoon, and Quinton hoped that he was just being paranoid towards the issue at hand. He followed the cargo truck as it drove onto the

A1 road towards the Pioneer Border. Four, five minutes passed, and the cargo truck indicated to the right at a four-way cross instead of heading straight. Everything became bizarrely ranged as the truck started speeding ahead and turned into a shady area. The farm belonged to a few unknown individuals. Two men opened a metal gate for the truck driver, and the cargo truck entered a bushy scenery. It passed large rocks and disappeared into the dusty road ahead. Everything about that moment was proverbially suspicious, and Quinton wondered what Steve was up to with his disloyal truck driver.

He parked his car by the nearest pub and blended with the locals. The sun began to set over the rocky hills as the cargo passed by the local pub and indicated towards the A1 road again. Quinton made a decision to let the truck wander off and tried to call his father, but Marcus didn't answer.

It occurred to Quinton that Marcus was becoming thick and naïve to Steve's wrongdoings, and these doings had an impact on the company, a company that Quinton would inherit one day. He knew that his own father still viewed him as young, overly ambitious, and immature to handle and maintain the millions that were in the company account. Marcus' cell phone went straight to voicemail as Quinton tried to call it again, and he sat there with a beverage in his hand. He had completely forgotten that he'd given up drinking so that his life can be receipted easily. A local soccer match was on the television screen, but Quinton wasn't focused on the unclear screen. He kept his focus on the audience as he ordered another round for himself. The irony of southern comfort whiskey marinated his liver as he found comfort by the bar counter for a while, right before departing back to the city.

An uneasy feeling crawled onto Quinton's skin as he entered his homestead and noticed his uncle's grey car on the driveway. Quinton entered the house and heard laughter from his father's study on the far left side of the passage. He finally understood why his father was preoccupied and never answered his phone earlier. Marcus was under the spell of his wizard brother, and he didn't know anything of current events. The smell of whiskey and burning Cuban cigars waivered through the passage, and that irritated Beth more than anything. She'd always disappear into wondrous sectors of the house whenever Steve came by. Quinton finally understood why nobody in his family disliked Steve. Everyone seemed to keep him at arm's length for good reason.

Quinton entered his father's study and greeted both of them politely but never found comfort around them. He entered his bedroom after speaking to his mother, unlocking his phone to staggering messages from Juliana Rose. She was having withdrawal symptoms like he did. It was quite evident that they weren't doing well without each other despite the fact that Quinton was having sex, trying to fill a void that only Juliana Rose could fill.

He read the message whilst Juliana's giggle recurred inside of his head. The giggles and laughter haunted his thoughts, and he saw within his mind a flash of Juliana's beautiful face. He started to feel Juliana's warm body pressed onto him whilst his eyes were closed, and he slept peacefully to that feeling.

Birds chirped outside his window in the morning, and the sprinklers sounded full. The sun shined brightly through his windows, and everything seemed so colourful. The tree branches waved, and the green texture on the leaves gave Quinton a peaceful feeling. It was evidently a public holiday on joyful Monday morning, and the neighbours next door were relaxed and cheery. The atmosphere was different to an everyday existence. Quinton stood up by his youngest sister's balcony, and an interracial couple played childishly around their yard next door. The husband sprayed water onto his wife, and she ran away from him. He laughed, and it seemed ideal to just watch love flourish so beautifully. That image itself brought a vintage memoir in Quinton as it reminded him of Juliana's persona. The happiness and the graceful aspect hovered around their backyard, which inevitably brought a pinch of sadness towards Quinton as he became slightly envious of their love. The couple waved as they realised that they were being watched by Quinton. Thus, he waved back. He walked back into his bedroom after switching on the shower taps, music playing softly in the background from his speakers as he entered the shower.

Those words came out of the speakers as the water rained all over his body. He closed his eyes and started to reflect back to a memory that he held so dearly, a memory that defined his heart. The water poured all over his body, and its warmth took him back to the day when Juliana wanted to kiss him whilst it rained. The memory remained so cliché to him, but it was also a milestone to the love they had for each other. He closed his brown eyes tightly and saw Juliana's face right next to his face. Her eyes glowed of green sparkling emerald, and her smile was so radiant. Her teeth were perfectly shaped and blindly white. The dimples on her cheeks deepened as she smiled, and her skin remained so beautifully moist from the raindrops. Quinton was in a completely different hemisphere whilst his eyes were closed, and he could feel her lips touch his wet lips. Something about this memory renounced his soulful feelings for Juliana Rose, and he was merely lost between their heartfelt world and the world of reality. Sadness remained a seed in their garden as he opened his eyes again.

The shower booth remained steamy, and at that moment, he felt synchronised to Juliana. He could hear the sound of her heart beating and could feel her soft hands on his back as he closed his eyes again. It was completely dark within his mind, and Juliana had disappeared away from him. He was becoming oblivious, and his thoughts were delusional. A feeling of betrayal floated into his heart as he looked around for her within their world. Quinton walked within his darkness and tripped over a rock. He fell onto the soft surface, and his toes were bruised just as equally as his ego. He called out for her name, but nobody answered. Something throbbed faster within the rock as he crouched beside it. It was impossible to lift, yet he tried nevertheless until it magically lifted itself. It deteriorated and broke into a dozen pieces. Quinton noticed a bright shine flickering brighter than anything he'd ever seen. It throbbed extremely fast and loud within his mind. He stood still in wonder, and it magically levitated it upwards towards his hands. Its bright wings spread, and they flapped extremely fast as he saw it at close range. It mended his heart and landed onto his dirty hands.

Juliana Rose ran from the darkness.

'Do not be afraid. I was hiding it!' she said.

'Were you hiding it from me?' Quinton asked.

'Yes, please do not take it with you!' she pleaded. 'Leave it here before you open your eyes!'

Quinton looked at his heart and wondered why she'd tried to hide it away. It belonged to him, and he needed it back.

'We won't have anything left if you take it back, my love!' she stated. Tears fell from her face as she looked downwards. Her face remained tragically beautiful as tears streamed downward her face. Her eyes still glowed of green emerald, and Quinton's bright heart shone brightly onto her face as she looked at him again.

'No, no, don't cry, Julie!' Quinton pleaded. 'We will meet again one day!'

Quinton held on to his heart and leaned forward to kiss Juliana on her wet lips. He opened his eyes once more, and his reality astonished him. He was surrounded by steam, and he was all alone.

His heart had clarification for the first time that month as he stepped out of the shower and walked into his bedroom. The steam from the bathroom door started to waiver away, and he was finally confident, for he'd seen Juliana again.

He felt weightless as growth relished his heart, but something so foul interrupted his peace minutes after dressed up as he heard a lot of loud voices echo through thick passage walls. So much commotion and feet movement sounds thumped through the household. There were so many police officers seated around the dining room table, files scattered around the table whilst an officer explained their investigation.

Quinton prepared for the worst as he left his household to the family warehouse office block. An atmosphere of noise winced towards the front entrance as Quinton entered the ground floor. A dozen people were in the office rooms trying to multitask. Telephones rang, and it was extremely rare for the office to be so busy on a public holiday. No one seemed to have any answers, but Quinton understood that his uncle was behind it all. Quinton walked upstairs and found his uncle's office completely empty and vacant. A part of him knew that Steve's methods were treacherous and his motives were false. A chill crept into Quinton's body as he looked at the distant view of the Diamond City. The sun shined brightly onto the metal rooftops of many warehouses, and everything seemed normal. The office phones kept ringing, and Quinton felt completely helpless because he had no answers whatsoever.

He drove back home whilst everyone in the office was busy with the paperwork. He was curios and concerned, but at least, his father was back home again as he noticed Marcus' coupé. The house was quiet, and poverty had uprooted itself into their household. The devil had entered their lives, and she was prepared to destroy everything that they'd ever worked for. Quinton entered his father's study, and it was completely dark from the curtains. The sun shined on different slit edges, and the whiskey smell was apparent to Quinton's nose. Marcus was completely quiet whilst he had an American bourbon from his glass. The shine on the silver ring on his left index finger reflected into Quinton's eyes as he moved closer towards his father.

'Come in, son,' Marcus said as he exhaled.

'What's going on?' Quinton asked as he sat slowly on the second black leather chair.

'The police have evidence on a lot of things, my son!' Marcus responded. 'A lot of evidence on tax evasion, embezzlement, drug trafficking, and it looks like I partook in everything because I signed most the cheques!' Marcus stated. 'I trusted your uncle, and he had implicated me in his wrongdoings with my company,' Marcus whispered.

His father's words gushed into his ears, and the premature plans that he had completely disappeared from his mind. An unanticipated moment flared as Marcus stood up and threw his glass into the wooden plastered wall. The glass shattered, and the whiskey splashed onto the wood floor. The liquor streamed downwards onto the wooden floor and settled into a puddle.

'I must go and sleep now!' Marcus said.

Marcus patted Quinton's shoulder as he walked past, and Quinton closed his eyes as his father passed him. Quinton could see evil spirits plumage through the wooden walls and floated away with Marcus as he stumbled into the passage. Darkness had found a way into Marcus' heart, and the same taunting horrors of darkness floated back into Quinton's veins as he sat still by the dark wooden table. They were filled with anger. A rage of terror flowed through their long veins, and that anger was beginning to define them.

Beth never came home that evening but instead spent the whole night praying at her local church.

Quinton lay on his bed and immediately realised that he was using his faith to bypass his wrongdoings. He wasn't a good Christian, and it was quite evident that his lifestyle was way too mediocre from his own humble beginnings. All he knew was that he had a good heart which at times, seemed extremely fickle. His behaviour was indeed questionable, and he realised that he had unnecessary emotions that made him create mistakes. He needed to grow up and assist his father in the greatest battle that the family was in. Marcus had become old and unfit, which made him weaker than he used to be when he started working in the early '90s. That feeling of becoming responsible suppressed Quinton as he closed his eyes, and he knew that he'd have to sacrifice his time for the good of the family. He realised the damage that Steve had caused, and that thought adorned a miserable spectrum into Quinton's heart. The idea of loving Juliana Rose slowly started to vanish from his mind, and he lost all hope. He knew that he'd never be able to see her again if his family ended up bankrupt. Juliana Rose was definitely becoming a dream to him, and his dream depressed him because his reality cleared up the misty ideology of happiness.

Quinton's mind spiralled as different thoughts consumed him and all the words that he'd heard throughout the whole day came and rushed into his mind at once. His mind was loudly filled with voices and whispers. Quinton felt dazed, and the words that he'd never said nibbled at his heart. 'Do not depend too much on anyone in this world because even your own shadow leaves you when you are in the darkness' were the words, and Quinton felt completely alone in the darkness.

The house was haunted with saddening regret as the dusky cool weather approached the early morning. Quinton felt like he'd not had an ounce of sleep. It was cold and quiet within the Barker household as the clock punched towards five o'clock in the morning. The sprinklers had set themselves off in the garden, and the sun started to musk over the Diamond City. An abstract dagger stabbed him in the stomach, and he felt pain within as he wondered what events would occur in the morning. He couldn't remember the last time he'd had a decent dream that didn't relate to Juliana or anything negative. Exhaustion flowed through his windpipe as he inhaled the cool air and he didn't want to get up. He felt like he was living in a nightmare because everything was so intense and unpredictably dark. His mind started to drift away to a miraculous dream that he'd had about the castle and the beautiful woman that was patiently waiting for him.

A feeling of misery approached him as his room turned brighter whilst the curtains remained closed. He started to brut and sulk over his reality, yet everything about this morning felt indifferent. Quinton stood up after a moment of struggle and walked through the dark passage slowly. The house was completely dark, and no domestic workers came to clean up the Barker household during that period.

Their smartphone tablet on a three-legged table within the passage alerted him of the events that had occurred from the day before. A lot of front pages had headed the title 'Barker Enterprise Crumbling with Drugs' mentioned his father's name on different paragraphs, implicating him for Steve's crimes against the republic.

His chest twitched as he picked up the last cigarette that he'd saved for a moment like the one he was in. He was enslaved by the nicotine, lighting his cigarette within his room. His eyes zoomed into the ceiling whilst he was on his bed. Slowly but surely his imagination ran wild, and his eyes widened into a different dimension as the white ceiling opened up right before his brown eyes. His imagination opened up his vision, and everything started to make sense as the dimension reflected to the nightmares that he'd had awhile back. He realised that the hunched-back brute, savage figure that kept harassing him was a monster that was sent to destroy his existence on this earth. The incident within his dream which was aligned with the one from his reality was all a vortex and an opening for demons to enter the normal world to cause havoc. The devil herself had entered Quinton's life and had managed to cause utter grief. Andrew Rose was a given example of the treacherous acts committed by those monsters because he was killed violently and his death caused the end of the relationship that Quinton had with Juliana Rose.

'The power of two is better than one' were the words that replayed inside his mind as he remembered the loyalty that Juliana had once pleaded to him. Quinton and Juliana had always felt connected to each other on a spiritual plane because they knew that they were abstractly wedded to each other. Quinton felt his bond grow stronger for Juliana. He felt calm, and his peace was once restored because he'd imaged seeing Juliana again. She was the only person that had an ability to keep him going even when everything seemed impossible.

A song played out of the speakers and Quinton sang it as it played smoothly. The guitar string sounds gave Quinton a moment of relief, and he felt like he had entered his own heaven, a safe place where only Juliana came to see him, and seeing her smile amongst the white clouds within his mind gave him hopes that he would get to eventually get to see her again. His soul was warmed with grace, and gratitude took its toll in his life as he appreciated the wonders of his imagination. He rested his heavy eyes and pretended that he wasn't stuck in the real world. Angels danced around with Juliana on the clouds, and they all laughed out loud in happiness as Juliana smiled and waved at Quinton politely. Juliana called out his name, and her tone was coherently soft. The sound of his name was delightful and miraculous to his ears, for it brought him inner peace as he blacked out to visuals of her smile.

His dream pattern was delusional and consistently led him to the brink of craziness, but luckily his latest dream was interrupted by a disturbing knock on the front door. The police officers gathered at the Barker front door with a court order for Marcus' arrest on various charges. Beth was horrified about the accusations, and watching her husband in metal cuffs brought tears to her eyes. Quinton remained shaken and spooked by the terrible miscalculation because he knew the truth about the incident. He wondered if his words would be able to exonerate his father from facing time in prison.

The police did not take long, and within minutes, Marcus was gone with the wind, and their household was quiet again. The morning grew into a dark windy day, and the city was covered the city with dark grey clouds. It drizzled throughout the late morning, and everything seemed so slowly scripted in sadness. The atmosphere painted a vivid perception of Steve's dirty deeds. At that moment, Quinton started to understand that a lot of people were just a bunch of frogs who were merely loyal to a certain pond until it dries up. Nobody related to them had bothered to contact him and to ask about his well-being. A lot of his friends that he'd celebrated occasional events with never called, and it appeared that his pleasant reality had turned into a fully fleshed nightmare. The harshness dished out by the world remained raw. Quinton's self-preservation loathed, and misery fluctuated onto his face as he washed his body inside the shower booth.

An alert message on Quinton's online social media account went unnoticed for a while as he researched travelling packages on travelling websites. He wanted to run away from his problems in hopes that they would vanish away from his doorway. Another message notified, and his attention was finally undivided towards his account.

Juliana had been online for a while.

'May I call you?' she asked via message.

'Yeah, sure!' Quinton replied.

He immediately turned off his webcam because he knew that he would be drawn back to her heart fully if he looked into her green eyes again. Juliana's face was breathtaking and heart throbbing. The dial tone commenced, and Quinton answered for a while.

Her voice caught his attention, and he was definitely drawn back to her sweet tone. Quinton wasn't reluctant to her at all as she spoke and he realised the characteristic that Juliana shared with Beth. Their souls purified Quinton's heart, and he felt loved even through his darkest moments.

'Quinton,' she said, 'you aren't listening?' she asked.

'I am!' he replied. 'I am!'

Juliana giggled after being assured of her lover's attention. The moment was merely a cliché as Quinton switched on his webcam to a visual so stunning. She was definitely the star in his dawned night, and her beauty drew him closer to the screen. The dimples within her cheeks deepened as she spoke, and Quinton felt completely mesmerized by the glow on her face. Juliana was had make-up on, and her skin tone was incredibly light. Quinton was lost in between worlds as she started to recall a time when he poked her cheeks and the very spots turn pinkish after a while. His face remained goofed and plumped by her beauty until she asked a dreadful question.

'You haven't been with anybody else, right?' she asked.

The dramatic pause itself painted guilt onto Quinton's face as he looked into Juliana's eyes. He pleaded to be honest to her and thus told her the truth and truth broke her heart. The relationship they had for each other was complicated and undeniably elusive. It was indescribable, and they both knew that they we spoken for by each other.

'I have. I will not lie to you!' he responded, and it was quiet.

The webcam was a dimensional window into their worlds, and both sides were extremely quiet. The sun shined brightly behind Juliana's window, and her room was smartly dressed. The walls were painted cream white, and her wardrobe frame was dark wooden and polished. She seemed healthy and happier until she looked towards the laptop camera and started to cry. Tears streamed downwards from her eyes, and she wiped them off immediately as she realised that her guard was down.

'How are we ever going to fix us when you make it so impossible?' she asked.

That was the hardest question anybody had ever asked Quinton, and he sat still, wondering if he should tell her about the latest sage within his life.

'I'm so sorry!' he replied as he looked up in embarrassment.

'Saying sorry won't fix anything. You can't go around behaving that way!' she shouted.

The fire in her eyes burned so brightly, and the passion she had for him remained extraordinary. She was filled with absolute rage and was upset because Quinton was being used up by those who had no understanding of who he really was. Juliana found him repulsive for a few seconds and ended the online call.

'I'm booking a flight some time next week to be with you again,' came a message from Juliana Rose to his phone, and he responded with gratitude and respect. His heart pumped off guilt, and he felt disgusted in himself because he'd upset the one person that mattered to him most.

The day passed, and darkness consumed Quinton again as he remained in his dark room and played his guitar in hopes that everything would turn out better again, but nothing unveiled differently in his heart. His life as he knew it was about to change into a different path, but all he wanted was Juliana Rose back in his life. He had thoughts of buying her a wedding ring and asking her to marry him whilst he tuned his guitar strings.

The thought of his father being prosecuted remained at the back of his mind, and he tried to avoid thinking about the events that were occurring around him. Their family bank accounts were frozen, and the enterprise itself was under investigation. It was a dreadful beginning, and the public tabloids criticized Marcus' intelligence with regard to his decision making. An article had a drawing of a donkey with its blinds on with the name 'Marcus' on its stomach. The world began to disrespect a business icon, and there was nothing that Quinton could do to save his family's reputation from being destroyed in the dirt. Competitors plotted behind closed doors and began to take over as Quinton witnessed the company stock prices plunge into the sewerage. The charts declined, and everything was below zero. It was evident that everything was about to change, and the golden path that he used to walk would soon turn into a pavement cropped with thorns.

The Barkers wouldn't be able to walk on that golden path anymore because their value would decline to less shiny things. Beth and her family would soon enter into a world of earthy possessions and sentimental belongings because it would be all that matters to them. They would soon start to see that most of the materialistic things they have lead bad people into their lives. Thus, a decision would have to be made.

Within a few days, Beth took out a bank loan and bonded the family homestead to it. She knew of the consequence, but it was the only option because all their bank accounts were frozen, excluding Quinton's mild investments. She felt another spiritual plain unbalance her home as everything turned sideways, yet she never once turned her back on God. They started to live off only necessities, and luxurious things were set aside. The expensive cars that guzzled petrol were parked away neatly into the garage, and they practiced on pivoting to their basic needs, coming to terms with the fact that resources are limited and capitalizing on them to maximize beneficial satisfactory came into practice as they started to cut down on a lot of spending. Beth cancelled all her spa sessions because other women started to gossip about her and her family behind her back, and Quinton stopped visiting the local gym because everyone there loved to see him sweat to the world's harshness.

Everything turned difficult throughout the days, and smiles turned into frowns. Nobody was happy with the realistic circumstance, but they lived in avoidance and pretended that everything was okay. They started to understand that nothing was as important as the bond of family after cancelling Steve from the family tree. He was nowhere to be seen, and agents stated that he'd aborted the continent to the northern hemisphere.

Chapter Ten

The Love of His Weary Life

The wind blew terror over this city on a particular Wednesday, and its waves harassed every single weak object standing in its way. The streets were glutted in dust and pollution. The air was flogged in smoke from the industrial factories that brewed booze. An unpleasant feeling gripped Quinton's heart as he drove onto the freeway to head to the international airport on the mute sided areas. He'd not spoken to Juliana Rose constructively since their last Skype session, and he wondered what events were going to manifest into their lives this time around. It was getting dark as the sun dawned away from the Diamond City, and a million thoughts spiralled inside his mind as he drove through the single lanes.

The street lights began to shine brightly onto the tarred surface as he drove underneath them, with the intention of arriving quickly to the busy airport. Quinton's life had become uneasy after his wretched uncle had stolen their family fortune, and he wondered how maintaining the family business would go because he was Marcus' successor. The future had already been planned for him, and everything was already scripted right before his eyes. Quinton initially grew tired of forever growing trends, for he couldn't keep up with increasing prices, the growing inflation rate, and the tax payments that kept a lot of people from growing rich. Quinton felt like he was part of a derogatory system that kept people miserable and angry. The subject based in money became a sensitive topic to him, and he wondered if Juliana Rose would still be interested in being with him without his wealth. He had grown to be insecure throughout that week. Thus, a lot of negative thoughts ran through him. Quinton deemed in positivity as he drove towards the airport and realised that his lover was coming back to him. The green bushes waved wild in the surrounding undeveloped properties by the road side. Wild winds showed aggression towards the suburb areas, and pedestrians on the sidewalks ran away into public transportation circuits to hide from the ruthless weather.

The international airport was mildly busy, but the parking lot remained partly empty as Quinton parked closest to the rental service cars. His thoughts harassed his mind, and a mild headache approached him as he walked through the dusty parking lot with his red scarf wrapped around his neck. He squinted his brown eyes as he walked by the rental cars, and he could smell wet cement on the small renovated section of the airport. The sky blue tiles gave a welcoming feeling to international visitors, and the lighting within shined brightly throughout the international terminal. A restaurant on the corner of the waiting area seemed relevant to Quinton as he walked towards it and sat quietly. He ordered a chicken tramezzini, Greek salad, and a glass of white wine then waited patiently whilst looking at the spectacular view of the countryside from the glass wall.

Dark clouds gathered in the sky, and signs of rain prevailed from the lightning strike casting in distant lands. Juliana Rose's flight was delayed due to the heavy rains in Johannesburg, South Africa. Thus, their reunion was strained for a while merely because of nature's act. Quinton had noticed that the hostile weather flourished into the atmosphere as he was preparing to leave his house and was a bit too coincidental as signs accumulated inside of his head that the universe was acting defensively towards them reuniting. The meal was indulgent, and he drank from his bitter white wine slowly whilst lightning strikes lit up areas in the distance and those visuals filled up his mind as every flash recorded an image.

Quinton's love ran deeply for Juliana as he stood up from a distance and watched her walk through the arrival sliding doors slowly. Her long straight natural brunette hair waved slowly towards the opposite direction that she was facing. She was directing the luggage trolley towards his direction, but she didn't notice his existence for a while until she looked up properly. Juliana smiled, and Quinton immediately smiled back. He felt her beauty grace his heart with wonders, and abstracted stardust was flicked into his brown eyes by the universe. Her sculpture mesmerised him as she dwelled slowly, and the moment was incredibly sweet as he felt her warmth as she hugged him. He couldn't quite figure it out why his heart was racing so fast, but he knew that it was love.

A moment appeared to be slow, yet they knew of its certainty. Her soft, smooth right cheek brushed against his cleanly shaven right cheek, and their lips merged whilst their eyes remained closed. Their world of wonders opened up inside their minds, and their scenery was synchronised. They were in a different world, and their world was peaceful. The birds chirped and the bees buzzed through the greenly textured leaves. It was quiet as their tongues wrestled, and their world sparked in brightness. The sun shined brightly inside their minds whilst their eyes were, closed and their hearts drummed loudly in the background. Juliana's perfume pitched a white flag into Quinton's imagination, and he was lost to the warm touch of her lips. She pulled back and smiled, but Quinton stood blindly quiet. Thus, she parked her soft lips into his warm lips again. The feeling of her lips brought wondrous magic into his reality, and he completely forgot that the world wasn't in his favour anymore. He felt lucky because she was back in his life, and nothing else mattered at that moment.

It began to rain drastically outside in the parking lot, and heavy rain drops splashed onto the tarred roads. Juliana sat in the luggage trolley and remained wrapped around Quinton as he pushed the trolley towards the parking lot. It kept raining heavily as he pushed the trolley and their clothes were soaking wet, but they didn't care. Everything seemed slow and normal to them as they reached the car, placed the luggage in the trunk, entered through the front doors, and made out for a bit.

His phone rang inside his dark blue jean pocket, and he remembered an errand he had to run before heading back home.

'I haven't forgotten!' he answered. 'Leaving the airport right now, Mom!'

'What's wrong, honey? Juliana asked.

'Nothing, babe, we must head back home in a bit!' Quinton stated and kissed Juliana's lips slowly.

She scooted back into the passenger seat and smiled as she pulled her natural brunette hair backwards. Quinton leaned into her and kissed her soft lips again. He immediately brushed her brownish eyebrows into shape with his thumbs, and his gentle hands remained glued to her jawline. It was so passionate and slow.

'We must go now,' he said and reversed.

'Drive slowly, baby. It's raining badly!' she said as she indicated the single lanes that paved all the way back to the centre of the Diamond City.

The evening traffic had emptied out, and the roads were dangerously wet. Quinton drove slowly and stopped at the red traffic lights to kiss his lover again because he couldn't think of anything else but making love to her. The rain had stopped, and the air vaccinating through the sunroof was freshly moist. Juliana spoke, and Quinton listened to her express herself. He was lost inside a different dimension whilst she spoke, and her British accent sounded amazing to his ears. Her words were fluently scripted and wonderfully spoken.

He entered an empty parking lot by a shopping complex. The scenery was completely different to what he was used to. The wheels drove onto cracked beer bottles, and the small green pieces shattered into dozen more pieces as Quinton parked his car next to a dodgy pub. Juliana was curious but never once asked him what they were doing there. A knock on the driver's window spooked Juliana as a man in a black leather jacket stood outside. The introduction between Quinton and the investigator was satisfactory. A heavy brown envelope was handed over discretely and sealed in confidence, but no words were shared about the envelope. It was mildly dramatic, and the investigator never said anything after. There was an ongoing investigation by the government, and words were very fragile throughout those days. Therefore, Quinton remained discrete about everything.

Quinton drove home quietly, and Juliana sat by his side, listening to music from the surround system. She held on to his left hand, and her hand rubbed frequently around his left thumb. Quinton kissed Juliana on her soft lips every chance he got whenever the traffic lights turned red. A CD played inside the surround system, and Juliana sang most of the songs because she was indeed infatuated with soothing songs.

Quinton entered the family yard, and everything seemed normal to Juliana because she didn't know of the headline news. Her heart was content in joy because she was back.

'I love you so much,' she said and kissed him on his gentle lips.

The feeling of those words lurching into his ears brought an expected smile to his face.

'Come, my mother is inside!' he said. 'We must go greet her!'

Quinton chaperoned Juliana through the front door, and her face blossomed beautifully to the warmth inside the house. Smuggles greeted her at the front the door. Melinda had dropped it off whilst Quinton was away. Beth hugged Juliana tightly whilst Quinton headed back to fetch Juliana's luggage. The endless possibilities of sleeping next to Juliana adorned Quinton's imagination as he thought of the love he would be receiving.

Two long hours passed into the dark night as Juliana made her way to Quinton's youngest sister's bedroom. Beth had covered the double-sized bed with cream white sheets, a soft silky duvet, and two pillows that were covered in cream white material. She smiled as she opened the bathroom door and realised that the bathroom connected to Quinton's bedroom. Quinton's bedroom was darkly harnessed, and he loved it that way. It described his personality and his outlook on his life.

The water in the shower booth rained, and it was quiet as Quinton undressed himself. A knock on the door interrupted their scene, and Juliana rushed towards the bathroom and closed the door gently.

'Son, I'm heading to South Africa tomorrow morning!' Beth said. 'I'm sure the both of you will behave, right?' she asked.

'Yes, Mom, we will behave!' Quinton replied as he looked into the mirror whilst his mother remained on the other side of the door.

Quinton showered beside his lover, and they wore comfortable clothes minutes after, brushing their teeth together within the bathroom then snuggled next to each other, drifting off into sleep.

The sprinklers went on in the garden, and the crispy chill in the morning woke them up. They parted ways to different bedrooms. Juliana closed her eyes in exhaustion. She seemed so tired and fragile. Quinton sat on his bed and played the latest indie music that had been released that week. He was relieved that Juliana was right by his side because she was safely protected. She was his little angel that needed to be guided away from harm's and kept away from any demons that had any evil intentions towards them both. Beth knocked on the door and entered.

'I'm leaving, okay? Will call you when I get to Johannesburg!' she said and left with the heavy envelop in her right hand.

Quinton looked into his mother's eyes and noticed she was slowly becoming as devious as Marcus when it came to secrecy and plotting. Her words turned into fragile whispers gushing through winds, and her movement during the day prevailed into questioning. Quinton and his mother were both starting to adapt to a world of uncertainty, and their outlook on everything astonished them with paranoia. Beth became less trusting, and her motives became vindictive towards the whole saga. It wasn't in her nature to be deceiving and deceitful, but something about her husband being in a prison cell made her question her morals.

Quinton chaperoned his mother to her car and watched her leave through the front gates. He wondered what she was up to but also knew at the back of his mind that it was in his best interest not to question his parents' motives. The gates closed, and slowly his curiosity whizzed away with the warm breeze. His thoughts regarding his inner pain rested from his vivid imagination, and he understood that decisions had to made in order for his family to survive.

He entered his bedroom and wore a black track suit and strapped his black trainer shoes tightly. His heart was adorned by misery, and his mind was clouded by anger. He kissed Juliana on his way out, leaving her to sleep peacefully like an angel who'd found refuge in a new safe haven. Quinton knew that he couldn't run away from his problems but started running on the tarred road in hopes that everything would become better. His energy was momentarily low, yet he proceeded anyway.

He jogged past his neighbours' households. Everything railing through his mind came into prospective as he ran underneath the long-branched trees on the side of the wide road. The beaches covered up the sky, and he glanced up to a wonderful sight of dried leaves falling off the branches and drifting away into a foreign place. Quinton understood that the leaves were no longer strong enough to hold on, that the tree of life was letting them go and allowing them to be cast to cruelty. It remained Quinton that the reality of life was woundingly cruel. Everyone would soon grow up and would be cast into a world of cruelty. The world was dry, and yet the warm sweat dripping from his head reminded him of the struggle endured. It was an unending battle of pain and sadness wielded to those that were not strong enough to hold on.

The universe sprinkled dust to those that weren't covered in finances, and their eyes merely turn into a yellow root. Their yellow eyes told a scripted story of hollowness and sadness within Quinton's mind as he ran past the thick-branched trees. The quote 'there is always light at the end of the tunnel' swamped into his mind as the light torched onto his face. It felt so warm as he took the time to sit by an embankment. The fields were green in a pasture on the side that he resided, and yet people's lands remained so dry in poverty. He felt that Africa was robbed from its blessings.

'We are all just people!' he thought to himself as clips of people infected by the HIV and the other epidemics projected inside his mind.

People's lives were stored in expiry shelves, and there was nothing he could do about it. He momentarily felt a surreal bask of guilt and wondered when people in the third-world continent would ever get to find a peaceful prosperity. Luxurious cars passed him by as he walked on the bricked path on the side of the road, and he entered his home to refresh.

He entered a warm bath and dwelled inside it for a while whilst Juliana was still sleeping underneath the duvet. The sun shone brightly into the bathroom, and the metallic maroon tiles looked lavish. The water remained warm as he lay quietly, wondering why his mind took him to a place he didn't want to see. His thoughts scraped away every joyful feeling, and he was troubled with problems that weren't his to begin with.

'Hey, sweetheart!' Juliana whispered. 'May I join you?' she asked.

'Yes, please come in!' Quinton replied.

The water rippled as she entered. Everything negatively connected to pain disappeared from his mind every single time she was around. Her pinkish lips remained glued on to the back of his neck, and her love relinquished his pain for a while.

'You haven't slept, have you?' Juliana asked.

'I haven't!' Quinton replied and felt her silky hair brush against his shoulders.

Her caramel skin gushed in beauty and glowed brightly from the sunlight. She looked into his brown eyes for a while whilst making love, allowing her heart to feed off the moment, and he glanced at his lover, taking in every second as if it were his last.

Chapter Eleven

Drifting into a Different Spectrum

The feeling of love had begun to sicken Quinton because he'd felt utterly exposed to being heartbroken again. He felt exhausted and unwilling to open up to Juliana. His family and their secrets had changed him. He'd withdrawn from his reality, mostly living within his imagination of a better life. Juliana tried to avoid her lover's cold shoulder, noticing strange characteristics such as Quinton being annoyingly quiet at times. She'd wear his T-shirts and loose track suit pants and lie beside him on his bed, trying to understand his sudden withdrawn personality.

On this specific evening, she was right there beside him with her head planted on his chest, stroking his soft hair on his arms with her left hand. A premonition flashed within her mind as she slept. She could hear and envision a baby girl—sounds of giggles and joyful harmony with an allure of mellow chimes moving to the warm breeze. The little girl was so beautiful and had remarkable distinctive features like Juliana, and the child's laughter grew louder as Juliana dove into a deeper sleep, one she embraced with joy.

She was led into a world of mystical magic with a landscape of an enchanted forest. She'd landed onto soft green grass in her natural form. The sky was adversely covered in small white puffy clouds, and the atmosphere was approaching the early hours of dawn. The green grass was softly paved, and there were large red roses growing in parallel form of that path leading towards the tree house village farther down on the slope. One of them sneezed, and a sprinkle of yellow pollen sprayed onto the green grass.

It was amusingly beautiful as Juliana walked through the path and glanced at the pollen sprinkles sinking into the grass, uprooting more roses a few minutes later. A group of people emerged from the darkness of the woods, staring as they kneeled and embraced their mother home. Juliana was surrounded by people of different colours in their natural form, covered with magical leaves around their private areas. Their backs were attached to different types of wings, with shining silver metal feathers on the tips. Juliana walked lightly and stood close to the nearest crowd of youthful women who seemed overly focused towards their men who were building a new construction of thick tree houses.

'Hey!' Juliana said and asked. 'Where am I?'

There was a young woman in particular that stood as tall as Juliana. She turned around and kneeled with the rest of her clan. Her maroon wings melded with her back, disappearing into thin air. She had the same eyes which shimmered beautifully in green.

'Hey, I'm Willow!' she mentioned as she stood up again. 'Welcome home, Mother. This is your world!'

'We . . . we . . . we are in my world?' Juliana stuttered, muttering whilst asking, unsure of her child's words.

'Yes, we are in your world,' Willow replied, 'the world that you and Father have built together!'

It was miraculously insane yet so pleasing for Juliana to hear something so different. Willow's smile brought happiness into Juliana's heart. She felt one with her people as they gathered around her. There were more men constructing more tree houses and others flocking away from their unfinished houses to gather around. Their faces lit up with happiness as they all greeted her.

'Willow, why is everyone surrounding me? You called me mother?' Juliana whispered whilst asking.

'We are all you children!' Willow mentioned.

Juliana looked around, noticing only a dozen people wrapped in their own wings as the cool breeze blew past.

'We knew that we would all meet you one day!' Willow mentioned as her mother began to sob from mixed emotions.

The masses gathered and flocked from the bushy tree benches. It was getting dark, and the birds within the tree branches stopped chirping. They lit up brightly, and their nests shone in different colours. Their glow resembled lamps as they shut their eyes. Juliana's world of wonders magically enhanced her visions, and she could see within the dark, almost as if it was normal. Willow walked alongside her mother and led her mother up a flight of wooden stairs which magically appeared out of nowhere. The staircase had a wooden railing wrapped with thin golden chins, railing all the way up, connecting to the rest of all the balconies.

There were red chimes hanging on the edges of all the dangling branches, and their whispered sound filled melodies in Juliana's ears as she walked upwards and discovered a communal place. The tree houses were stacked on top of each other, and the atmosphere was so alive. There were restaurants, general stores, clothing stores selling clothing made from magically melded tree leaves, bars, and a bank guarded by huge guards. The tree house village possessed a remarkable energy that embraced a powerful atmosphere of peace and purity. The main area was lit in yellow bright birds as street lamps.

Willow grabbed Juliana's left hand and led her into an amphitheatre, where they village council held a meeting with representatives from different regions of the village. The amphitheatre was carved hollow and had wooden chairs glistening from the magical glare of moonlight kissing the hollow space.

Juliana sat quietly and observed whispering and gossiping. She noticed a cloud lowering down from the light above. The was a baby girl floating within covered with sheet of grey melded leaves. The cloud popped, and the baby landed gently into her arms.

'Willow, that baby is so beautiful,' Juliana said.

'Her name is Arabella. It means 'beauty' in the Arabic language. Ever since she was born into this world, it has been raining more often, and she is our hope!' Willow said.

The little baby girl was so beautiful. She had no wings. She was a miracle and a gift from the creator himself. Arabella opened her eyes as Juliana leaned over and touched her youngest daughter's tiny little fingers. Her eyes were as greenly emerald as her mother's, and she was absolutely adorable in every single way possible. She was the spitting image of her mother, and as she closed her mouth after yawning, her dimples deepened into her small cheeks. Juliana smiled and rejoiced with the crowd of people in the amphitheatre once she felt certain that Arabella was hers.

Arabella's weight rested gradually on Juliana's arms for a while, and the people around went on with their business, and everything went back to normal. Juliana walked around the wooden complex with Willow by her side whilst she focused on her unborn child. She has undoubtedly fallen in love with Arabella, and sense of peace radiated from her unborn child as she walked around, acknowledging the world what she and her lover had created throughout the duration of the time that they were together. It was strangely organised, and everything was accommodated for lifestyle. The wooden pavement stretched out through the complex. Most of the stores were built in sections and veiled opening alleys that led to balconies at the edge. Juliana noticed that her world was demurely enduring in a crafted circuit of trade. There was existent life inside this world, and she wanted to be a part of it all. She greeted everyone passing by. They all went on about their lives.

The upper tree house section was filled with families gathered inside their houses, and the elderly men told stories to the children whilst the younger children sat closely and listened. The young men were gathered with their women in a hallway, interacting and bonding.

Arabella awoke again whilst carried by her mother. She seemed snuggled warmly and coiled up in a large silky feather. Juliana couldn't wait to show Quinton what she'd discovered. Her heart was impeccably drawn to this mystical world, and she didn't want to wake up to her reality.

'Willow! Where does Arabella sleep?' Juliana asked. Then she looked back and noticed Willow yelling towards the men guarding the tree house, sounding paranoid and worried. She rushed towards Juliana to guide her to safety before darkness could consume them.

Everyone in the tree house village shut their wooden windows and their dark wooden doors to the deafening silence of horror lurking within the darkness. Dark clouds had begun to spiral over the tree house village, and it turned cold, low in temperature until snowflakes started to fall. A crackling sound prevailed over the complex section from heavy paw steps, and everyone, including Juliana, quivered to the terror sniffing through the wooden floors.

The sleeping birds within the nests awoke, and the street lighting went off. It was completely dark within the complex as the winds grew wild and blew havoc through the empty alleys. The red chimes on the weak branches astounded and grew louder with the harsh winds whilst the fireflies vanished away into darkness. A feeling of fear manifested inside the hearts of many hiding within the tree houses.

Juliana clutched Arabella tightly inside a tree house with Willow, who'd kept her eye peeled through a small hole, guarding the wooden door. Willow peeped through the smallest hole in between the wooden wall again and witnessed a horror like no other.

The clouds descended from the sky and hovered over the tree branches and turned into a pack of mystical dark grey wolves, drooling lava from their mouths. A terrifying feeling gripped Juliana's big heart, and she felt afraid for her children. The wolves terrorised the complex block and ripped apart the displayed decorations. A fire sparked from the trail of lava dripping from their mouths as they sniffed through the holes in the wooden walls. They sniffed their way towards the upper tree house village in search of Arabella. The cold wind blew a grey mist through a wide balcony, and the mist turned into a horse. It snickered through alleys and galloped, fully forming solid, emerging from the darkness with bright lava burning within its eyes as it searched thoroughly. It searched thoroughly within its knight rider whipped its left limb.

The darkness had risen in Juliana's world, and everyone inside was scared of challenging it. The misty wolves tore everything in their path and went around through the communal area, sniffing for Arabella's scent in the amphitheatre. The men found the courage within their hearts and left their households with long spears in their hands to protect their safe haven, but they weren't strong enough to defeat the mist creatures. A lot of them fought within the amphitheatre but were butchered. Their feathers were scattered onto the blooded wooden floors. A lot of them bled to death whilst they helplessly watched the misty wolves ripping through their communal area of trade.

The misty horse galloped through the closest alley where Juliana, Arabella, and Willow had hidden. Willow could hear the horse bray and snicker. She knew that it was looking for Juliana's unborn baby. She glanced into Juliana's green eyes and made a very important decision to protect her little sister from being taken away by the darkness. She turned brave and grabbed a large white feather that had Arabella's scent and placed a pillow inside of it. The misty horse moved closer, and it was quiet within the scenery as its metal shoes knocked on to the dark wooden door. It sniffed on the dark wooden door. The room became extremely cold, and Juliana clenched Arabella tightly to prevent the cold from gripping Arabella's tiny body. They remained hidden in a corner, obstructed by a large wooden cabinet whilst Willow braced herself.

The moon shined through the slit opening of the wooden window frame, and it shined brightly onto Willow's brown eyes which resembled Quinton's in every single way possible. She remained by the entrance and held on to the white feathered pillow tightly. A pinch of golden sparkling powder poured out the bag and was heaped into a small hill by the floor whilst Willow peeped through the wooden openings. The misted horse hauled backwards and kicked down the dark wooden door. Juliana looked at Willow by the corner, and she knew that the chances of her seeing Willow again were very slim to none. A moment of silence occurred. The misted wolves gathered around the entrance, clustering on alleyways and sniffing out for Arabella.

The golden sparking powder contained of a magical spell that muted the senses and blinded everything in its path. Willow placed her right hand into the powder bag and fiddled with the golden sparkle while looking for the courage to lead the dark creatures into a wild goose chase.

The moment turned slow as Willow threw the powder onto the dark grey misty horse's lava eyes, blinding it along with its dark knight rider. She kicked the nearest wolf by the entrance, and her wings sprinkled the golden sparkle towards the other wolves, then she flew through the alley and fled the scene. The rest of the misty creatures followed her and howled through the dark sky, except of the last one.

It remained by the alley balcony and turned back. Its sense remained strangely attached to the room that Willow had come out from. Its silver paws moved closer and closer towards the door and grunted continuously until it sniffed at the front door. Juliana looked at it from the corner of the cabinet and hoped that it wouldn't come closer. Arabella sneezed, which immediately raised its attention towards the closet door. Juliana was unequipped and unready to fight a dark mystical creature. It entered through the open door and crouched towards Juliana, and just she watched it, hoping that its attention would waiver away from them. Arabella sneezed again, and her sneeze alerted the misty wolf. It aggressively bit on to Juliana right leg, and she started to scream out in pain as it dragged her out of the room and into the alley.

'Help!' Juliana screamed out. 'Quinton!'

Her right thigh grated on to the wooden floor, and blood dripped onto her right leg whilst she kicked the wolf with her left leg. Arabella began to cry out loud to Juliana smacking the wolf's head.

Luckily, just as they reached the balcony, a bleeding man on the floor around the corner stuck a long wooden spear into the misty wolf's stomach. Its grunts turned into loud howl through the grey sky, and the moon light shined onto the village again after the darkness vanished into the distance.

Blood dripped from the edge of the balcony, and the courageous man that had stuffed a wooden spear into the misty beast bled out minutes later after a lot of the women came out of their tree houses with wooden pitchforks and golden powder in their bags.

The wind blew through the leaves and through the alleys. The women cried through the communal area as they walked past their dead men. Juliana struggled to walk from her wound. Her baby remained snuggled underneath her arms as she limped through complex and saw pools of thick blood everywhere. Feathers were plastered onto the wooden floor with blood throughout the tree village. Some of those that fought were young, but most of them were elderly men.

Juliana climbed up a steep wooden staircase with Arabella in her arms. She made her way up to the upper section of the tree houses, and it appeared to be darker and darker as she rose up another level. The wooden was designed more elegant, much cleaner and quieter. The alleys were bigger, and the wooden floor was smooth and polished. However, there were a few scratch marks on the planked walls and on the wooden floors, yet regardless of that, the place still looked beautiful. Her subconscious world remained flawless despite recent events. She looked over by the wooden balcony and glanced down as the women mopped up the pools of blood from the floors.

'Come, your house awaits you, Mother!' a young girl mentioned, sobbing, leading the way. 'We hope you like it!'

Juliana followed the young girl into a staircase that spiralled up through a thick branch with light burners hanging inside the hollow passage. The green leaves attached to the weak branches moved in a mysterious motion, waving directly at Juliana as she walked upwards with Arabella sleeping peacefully. Her warmth brought Juliana great joy, yet Juliana remained highly concerned about her child's well-being and thus held on to her tightly.

The entrance door to Juliana's tree house was painted in sky blue, and the door was thick. It took a lot of strength out of the young girl as she pushed the door open, and the entrance room was hallow in light brown and had lanterns hanging from the branches above. Dark wooden blocks levitated and aligned themselves all the way upwards to another door. Juliana turned back and watched as the front door magically shut itself and melded into trunk.

'Larissa, please hold onto Arabella for a bit!' Juliana said.

'You know who I am?' Larissa asked,

'Of course I do. You are also my daughter, darling!' Juliana replied and smiled. She'd realized that her knowledge of her world was finally unveiling before her eyes, and she knew everything about her home.

The birds landed back into their nests and lit up bright yellow right as the weather changed. Clouds vanished, and the moon shone brightly again. The cool breeze swept through the trunk hollow and glided underneath her magically hanging threaded feather curtains.

'Do you like it? Larissa asked.

'I absolutely love it!' Juliana stated.

Arabella awoke and started weeping,

'I think she is hungry!' Larissa said and passed Arabella back to Juliana.

'There, my baby, there you go!' Juliana whispered and stroked the little black hairs on her baby's head whilst breastfeeding. 'Larissa, where is my bedroom, love?' Juliana asked.

'Upstairs, Mother!' Juliana replied.

'Will send for some of the men to come and guard your door for the night' Larissa mentioned then left Juliana by the entrance door.

Juliana stepped onto one of the many round wooden blocks with hopes that she wouldn't fall off, but the opposite happened. Her weight settled on to the wooden blocks, and they remained steadily balanced. The wooden blocks magically levitated up and turned into a flight of stairs, which she used to enter into the bedroom door above. The moonlight shined brightly through the bedroom window, and everything was illuminated inside. There light burning flared ghost pinkies dancing onto the red chimes mellowed tunes playing from outside.

'I wonder where your father is,' Juliana said as she walked towards a large wooden frame bed and tucked her baby underneath a layer of a soft cottoned blanket.

She heard water pouring and discovered an oval arched entrance carved out, leading into another tree trunk towards her five o'clock. She entered and discovered a circular-shaped bath carved out of wood and filled with water. It was still so strange because the water didn't ripple whilst the cool breeze waved through the rooms. There were no taps, nor were they any pipes, which made Juliana wonder were all the water came from.

Nevertheless, she entered the bath and leaned back slowly. The water cuddled her and kept her warm. She shut her green eyes and hoped that her adventure would be more peaceful, only to be interrupted by Quinton shaking her back to her reality.

'Wake up, baby!' Quinton shouted. 'You are having a bad dream!'

Juliana awoke and found herself confused and dazed back to her reality. The world she'd begun to love was taken away from her and so was Arabella. She woke up fully clothed and annoyed.

'Why did you wake me up? Juliana asked.

'You were yelling out my name in your sleep!' Quinton replied. 'Was I wrong to wake you, love?'

'No!' she replied. 'I guess not!' She sulked and realized that Arabella wasn't by her side.

'Baby, are you okay?' Quinton asked. 'What's wrong?'

'We had a child! She was so beautiful, love!' Juliana whispered as she sat up and folded her skinny arms around her knees. 'You would have loved her so much!'

'You are not making sense, my love!' Quinton said. 'Tell me about your dream and don't leave out any details!'

His frown was plastered with a smile as he lay beside his lover. He listened carefully as Juliana spoke, and her words left him completely amused. She knew that she sounded absolutely crazy and remained uncertain of his reaction. Her eyes widened as her face glowed from a painted bliss of excitement. She opened up and told her lover about her hopes of having a child. From afar, they looked beautiful to watch, a couple of lovers whispering sweet dreams to each other. It was heartfelt and slow, the gentle touch, the warm kisses causing goosebumps.

Quinton kissed Juliana on her forehead and hugged her tightly because her sadness was beginning to consume her and she inevitably knew that nothing was ever going to be the same ever again.

A few days passed. It was the weekend. Juliana had begun to withdraw from reality, hoping to land in her subconscious world to be with her baby again. She expressed her deepest desire to Quinton that late afternoon after their late lunch.

'Let's go and make a baby, my love!' Juliana whispered.

Quinton had always wanted Juliana to bear his children, but their timing was wrong. A lot had occurred within his life, and he wasn't prepared to a father as of yet. The idea had dwelled within as he turned the tap on and watched the water fill up inside the sink.

'Do you want a baby, my love?' Quinton asked in a low tone. 'Because of that dream you'd had? Or because you want to be the mother to my children?'

'I want you to give me a child, babe,' Juliana whispered and Quinton turned around.

He looked into her green eyes, and for the first time ever, the world within her eyes told a different story. She'd matured and had grown into someone so extraordinary. He remained uncertain about her proposal as he switched the tap off. Juliana's skinny arms lengthen inside his white collared shirt.

'Stop it!' Quinton stated and laughed out loud.

'I won't stop and until you agree!' Juliana said and scratched his chest with her nails inside his shirt.

'Someday, my love, someday!' Quinton replied then altered her right hand from his waist with his right hand and kissed the softness of her lightly toned hand. 'Go to bed, Julie. I will be with you just now!' he whispered and turned around to kiss her on her lips.

She made her way upstairs whilst Quinton tidied up. He entered his bedroom minutes later and found his lover sleeping so peacefully underneath his duvets. His bedroom became her new sentry, for she did not want to leave. The moonlight shined inside of it, and the energy prevailed differently from what he was used to. The dark pain diluted into his body slowly started to disappear, and his heart was mildly content with current events. He lay by her side and closed his eyes after kissing her lips constantly.

Quinton shut his eyes and slept, drifting away from reality within his mind, blinking to the bright sun in his sight. He awoke in a completely mysterious place. There were a lot of trees surrounding him. He noticed enlarged red roses waving in the distance. They were smiling. They had round green eyes. It completely baffled his mind as he stood up from the green grass. The dream that Juliana had was synchronised with his imagination, and he was also lost in a mystical world. It was dark in the forest as he walked towards it and discovered tree houses established within the thick trunks and thick branches. He looked up and walked onto a staircase that rotated upwards around a thick dark brown tree trunk. The red chimes sounded mellow tunes in the background, and at the same time, he could also still hear Juliana's heart beating in the background. The sound of her heart grew slightly louder as he stepped on the wooden staircase and moved upwards. He discovered a communal world, yet something was terribly wrong. He could feel the tension in the cold air as the dusky sun clustered into the morning.

Heavy winds rushed through the empty alleys and forced his path towards another staircase. He looked towards the empty complex and noticed dried bloodstains on the wooden floors then realised that he was covered with leaves around his private area. It began to feel natural to him as Juliana's heart started beating even louder as he stepped onto a wooden balcony. A part of him knew where he was going as he started to smell Juliana's scent drift through the wooden corridors. It was quietly awkward as he moved past closed doors and entered a dark hollow passage that led to wooden stairs carved out through a thick hollow trunk.

The leaves awoke from snoring and shook off their sparkles of dust repeatedly. Quinton found that visual absolutely bizarre as he walked into the hollow branch and discovered a tree house at the top of the stairs. A door emerged from within the trunk. There were two wooden spears levitating in mid-air as Quinton stepped onto the final wooden step, and he knew that they were guarding something important. The wooden spears moved apart slowly, and he pushed the heavy door.

The sound of Juliana's heart beating started to throb inside his head, and he knew that he found his lover again. She was somewhere within his mystical world, and he was immediately fond of the world they created subconsciously. The house was absolutely different to what he was used to, and he stepped onto the first wooden block gently. The rest of them aligned and directed him towards the only door at the top of the hollow room. The lanterns switched off as the sun shined in through the kitchen window frame, and he felt a sense of comfort relish in his heart as he opened the only door. The sound of her heart was beating slowly in the background, and there she was covered in a large smooth flexible leaf. The sun shined bright from the bedroom window frame as Quinton sat on the wooden bed frame. He smiled and was astonished by the beauty radiating from Juliana's skin. Her thin dark eyebrows and eyelashes remained beautiful as Quinton stroked her right brow. Her brunette hair waved away from her face as she woke up in a delightful mood.

'See, I told you!' Juliana said. 'I wasn't being crazy!'

'I didn't think that you were crazy. Just little dramatic, that's all!' Quinton replied and laughed.

Arabella cried as she awoke too, and her sound alerted him.

'What's that?' Quinton asked as he unwrapped a large leaf by Juliana's left side.

Arabella stretched out her arms as she yawned. Her genetics resembled Juliana's in every single way possible, and her small nose turned pinkish from the cold breeze. Her small lips were incredible beautiful in light pink as she yawned again. Quinton felt absolutely in love, paralysed in an endless moment. He looked into her green eyes as he picked her up. He fell in love with what they had subconsciously created.

'She is so beautiful!' he said as Juliana hopped onto her knees and moved clumsily closer towards them both.

The leaf unveiled as she moved on top of it, and she witnessed a picture-perfect moment as she looked up again. A visual like no other projected into her green eyes as looked as Quinton holding Arabella tightly. The sun shined brightly onto their unborn baby as Quinton turned on the bed towards the hollow. Her hands gracefully touched Quinton's shoulders as she came closer and wrapped her long legs around him.

'Come with me!' Juliana whispered into Quinton's right ear. 'I want to show you something!'

'What do you want to show me?' Quinton asked as they both stood up.

'I want to show you something!' Juliana said in excitement. 'Just follow me!'

They left the tree house, walked downstairs, and the atmosphere was completely different to what Quinton had seen in the early hours of the morning. Everything was back to normal. There was a handful of people sweeping off all the dried leaves from the alleys and over the edges. Everything appeared differently from the top as they looked downwards and discovered the colossal magic hovering in their world. It cleaned the tree house village. The blinding sun shone brightly through tree leaves, and a layer golden sparkles levitated in mid-air, sticking onto everyone's moist skin as they walked through the complex.

Quinton closed his brown eyes and inhaled the fresh air around, and as his lungs expanded whilst his eyes were closed, a terrible projection was cast into his mind. It was completely dark around as he stood at the same position, and sounds of wolves groaning and grunting echoed from the bottom area. A pitch-black horse with lava eyes moved through the communal area in slow motion, and its darkening mist puffed from its nose and from the rest of its body as it moved in a circular motion. It sniffed through the communal area and entered open doors as it searched.

Quinton was completely astonished by his new ability to see the past without actually being there. He opened his eyes again to an atmosphere completely differently to what he'd just seen.

'I saw a horse!' he said and looked at Juliana who seemed shaken tremendously by her lover's words.

'Julie,' he stated, 'what's wrong?'

'Something happened last night!' she whispered. 'Something so horrible, love!'

She paused and completely withdrew from the moment as flashbacks rushed into her mind. The dark visuals of mist wolves running through the alleys, the sounds of their claws scrapping the wooden floors, and the smell of fire burning parts of the tree house village petrified her. She explained the story whilst he looked and observed everything around her.

'So they won't come during the day?' he asked and kissed Arabella on her forehead.

'I don't think so, but we must reinforce before the sun sets, my love!' Juliana replied and headed towards the staircase by the alley.

'Come, there is more!' she said as she turned her body whilst holding on to the wooden railing. 'We have created a beautiful world, my love. I want to show it to you!'

Her hair swung side to side as she stepped onto the staircase, and Quinton realised that her firm arse had begun to excite him. Green leaves hovered over his body and covered him whole. He smiled and acknowledged the pleasance of magic surrounding him because he knew that he wouldn't be as embarrassed as he thought he would be.

Larissa saw them from another balcony as they were about to leave the tree houses.

'Mother!' Larissa called out from a distance. 'Come with me!'

Quinton was still undeniably confused about the children they'd spiritually created as he also followed his child Larissa towards the darkness. He started to hear people chanting loudly in the distance and war cries echoed through the dark alley. They moved closer and a sense of obligation relished through Quinton's heart. Golden sparks landed gently onto Juliana's shoulder as she moved towards a blinding yellow light, and the sun began to peep through the green leaves from the top angles. They entered a hollow amphitheatre, and their arrival seemed long awaited. The massive population chanted loudly, and the atmosphere turned rowdily pleasant to both Juliana and Quinton. They both felt a sense of reign pour into their souls as they stood before a crowd that applauded them. A monarchy had arisen in the mystical world, and masses were gathering in the hollow tree from different entrances to see if the rumours were true about Quinton's appearance.

The hollow room echoed with words coming from different angles, and joy was restored fully to their world. A moment of authority had lapsed into Quinton's mind as he looked around and felt power blog onto his sight. He felt like he was finally home and finally knew his existence mattered most to his people. Their presence to the congregation was overwhelming, and everyone inside the hollow tree felt safer than ever because a king and queen had finally risen from their reality and into their mystical world. The loud voices chanting gave both Quinton and

Juliana goosebumps, and they finally acknowledged the large crowd by waving frequently. Wings flapped from every single person in the room, and their different colours extracted colourful dust towards the stage.

'Take a walk with me, my love!' Quinton said and made a thorough exit.

Larissa took Arabella in her arms and departed with two guards holding wooden spears in their hands towards the tree house at the top.

The tree houses looked magnificently beautiful to Quinton's and Juliana's eyes as they discovered every single passage throughout. Every piece of wood from the planks covering the tree houses to the natural wet branches shined in metallic light brown.

'We must get married today!' Quinton whispered into Juliana's right ear.

Those were the words that every single girl would have liked to have heard. A smile glowed from her face as she looked into his brown eyes. He lowered underneath her and got onto his left knee.

'Will you marry me?' he asked and looked up into her green eyes.

A moment of silence seemed to approve of their domain, and there was nobody else in sight. The wind blew a breeze through the passage, and Quinton waited for answer as she looked up the empty blue sky. It all felt magical to her as she inhaled the fresh air and looked at all the golden powder floating in mid-air. Birds flew in different directions, and they chirped consistently as they landed onto their thatched nests. The chirping echoed loudly throughout the atmosphere whilst the red chimes sounded melodies. It seemed highly convenient to Juliana, for she was a foolish romantic. She listened to the sounds around her collaborate and create a tune so sweet for the moment, and thus she looked down at that moment and waited for her heart to agree. It throbbed slowly as she smiled at him, and he so was momentarily mesmerised by her beauty. The sun shone so brightly on her, and she remained still whilst his brown eyes remained glued on to her beautiful face. The chirping bird sounds were so loud inside of Juliana's head as she smiled goofily like a fool.

'Yes, I will marry you!' she whispered. 'I will marry you!' she whispered again. 'I will definitely marry you!' she repeated loudly for their world to hear. Ironic, nobody heard anything and seemed like her words were drifting away with the slow breeze, so she screamed out to the top of her lungs, 'I will marry you, my lover!'

He stood up straight with assurance and lifted Juliana upwards in happiness. Everything felt slow for a while as they kissed to the harmony in atmosphere. Their commitment towards one other was definitely an act of faith towards their eternal of love. They were finally bonded physically, emotionally, and spiritually through their own terms, and they knew that nobody in their real world would ever break their bond. Nothing else mattered for a while, and they found themselves lost in complete transition.

Their mystical world was behind them, and they finally found themselves all alone in between abandoned clustered thin-branched trees surrounded by maroon thorn bushes, and large red rose petals spread wide in different directions to cover up the scenery. The soft grass smoothened their moods, and the sound of birds and chimes created mellow sounds. The green leaves unveiled below, exposing everything. They made love and synchronised their thoughts for the future into one motion.

The walk back to the tree houses turned mellow to the sound of the red chimes hanging on the weak branches. Rays of sunshine peeped through the green leaves, yet darkness covered the pathway in certain areas. Green leaves were melded back onto their waists, and their privacy was restored. They acknowledged that they were in love with each other and felt completely adorned by their new merger of marriage as they strolled through the forest. The large roses were toning down and falling asleep as Quinton and Juliana walked past them. Birds had stopped chirping within the tree nest, and the lights were beginning to shine from their nests with beautiful colours in different combinations. Some lit up red, sky blue, bright yellow, earthly green, and orange. The winds had waivered slower, and the branches were more composed as Quinton guided Juliana towards the wooden staircase. He remained gentle and chivalrous throughout and insisted that she watched her every step. She absolutely admired his gesture and felt lucky to have an amazing man from a different place. It was merely ironic to say, but she had stated in the past that Quinton was a diamond in the dirt. Everything about him was compelling and convincing. It was evident that he wasn't selling any brands to her and that he was indeed a lover sowed from genuine material.

They were astonished by their latest creations as they stepped into the community complex. There were more muscular men in white wings, ready to assemble for an apparent war. It seemed as though they were approaching another devastating conflict. Thus, Quinton remained at the bottom with his new army whilst Juliana made her way back to their tree house to be with Arabella and Larissa. Halfway through her walk upwards, she immediately realised that Quinton meant so much to him that she ran all the way back down and kissed him goodbye in hopes that he'd survive the darkness' brutality.

He appreciated Juliana's concern, but he felt a sense of victory approaching him. It was a matter of delegation and responsibility crusting in his mind. Thus, he ordered his men to different sections of the tree houses. Men were positioned in passages and alleys. Some flew around and upwards to the top of the branches to check if any invasions were about to commence. The community slowly but surely parked away their belongings in the complex area and hid from what could indeed be the biggest war they'd ever encountered. Windows were shut with wooden planks tightly, and doors were closed by many of those that felt vulnerable to the mist.

The birds within their nests were still lit brightly, for it was still peaceful within the atmosphere. Quinton stood at the bottom of the tree houses with a long wooden spear in his left hand, waiting for the darkness to approach, but nothing happened. It was quiet throughout the forest, and all they could hear were red roses snoring in the distance.

The sky was covered in stars, plastered with twinkling stars. They shone brightly over the forest. The weather was mildly warm. Quinton inhaled the fresh air brushing through the forest trees. The soldiers amongst him remained patient, almost as if they were trained for combat. They remained disciplined and quiet. The main tree house at the top was guarded with army guards everywhere, flocking in different directions, protecting Juliana and her child. She was uncertain of the events that would occur and feared that Quinton wouldn't make it out alive. Therefore, she prayed for his return, and this was the first time she'd ever allowed herself to connect to a higher spiritual power. She wasn't quite sure if her prayer would ever be answered, but she prayed anyway whilst holding on to Arabella tightly, who'd fallen asleep peacefully in her mother's arms.

The lighting peeping from the kitchen wooden holes vanished within seconds, and it was completely dark outside. Only Quinton and his army could see the change in the weather. The wind grew stronger, and it began cooler. Everyone exhaled out steam from their mouths as the cold crept into their domain, yet still they waited with bags of golden powder and wooden spears in their hands. Quinton could sense that at any moment, an evil so unexplainable or describable would relive itself into his life again. A part of him had always expected evil to crawl back, and his timing of that very thought was accurate as he looked up and watched heavy layers of dark clouds cast over the dark forest. The moist smell of rain came with the dark clouds, and he knew that a terrifying nightmare had finally arrived to destroy the pleasantness in their dream.

A monster so familiar to him walked out of the forest, and it was followed by a misted horse and packs of misted wolves howling. He remembered the figure so clearly as it appeared in the distance. It was holding a sharp-bladed dagger, and its metal shined brightly within the darkness. The horse's and wolves' eyes glowed in bright yellow as the dark army aligned itself for miles surrounding the thick tree branches. Quinton had prepared his men and placed them in strategic places throughout. Some hid within the leaf branches with bows and arrows, ready to attack the dark army. The weather wasn't on their side, and Quinton knew the oncoming storm would make it extremely difficult for his men to fly, for their wings weren't accustomed to heavy rains.

This evil was after Arabella, and Quinton absolutely knew that his child was meant to be born into their real world, a world advocated by demons crawling through the woodworks and advising people to commit sin through unrighteous laws. At the same time, he realised that Juliana was meant to bear his child, regardless of bad timing. This child represented a sense of hope to them, and the mystical world was a dimension of their own imagination created to filter them away from the harassing reality, a place they could momentarily escape to and allow themselves to fall in love without being judged by anybody.

All these thoughts rained into Quinton's mind as he looked around and saw birds flocking away. Their magical light glowing from their bodies switched off, and they flew away from their nests. He could hear their wings flapping away loudly as they vanished from the foreseeable terror. Their small hearts throbbed extremely fast inside their chests as they disappeared away from the dark clouds. The tree house branches were the only visible structures vaguely showing from a distance.

A reeking smell clouded the surface, and a wrath of awaking evil dove down like a fish and flooded the forest with havoc. Roses rotted, and the green stems dried into a dark brown colour. The red pedals detached slowly and turned pitch-black before touching the green grass that had also started to lose colour. It was slowly turning pale right before everyone's eyes. Men amongst Quinton took deeper breaths as they also witnessed the wrath of evil, gnashing through their beautiful forest. Most green leaves dropped dead to the ground as the reeking smell flowed through the empty passages.

It was still so quiet as the mist hovered at the bottom. An army of dark soldiers holding daggers emerged from within the mist and also on the outskirt balconies of the tree house village, reeking of a smell of dirt and wave of fear like rippling waters splashing into the cold current. There was a familiar hunched figure in the middle of the front lines, huffing repeatedly and staring directly at Quinton, and Quinton absolutely knew that he would have to face his nightmare on this cold night.

'It won't bother me again!' he thought to himself.

A pack of howling misty wolves emerged from the crowd. Their lava saliva dripped onto the ground, and a fire sparked. Their howling echoes petrified those hidden inside the tree houses, and the echo flustered Quinton's mind as he looked around and saw that most of his men were uncertain of their outcome. He closed his brown eyes and tried to grip the little bravery he had stored somewhere within his lean body. His soul turned rattled and uneasy as he held his wooden spear tightly with hopes that everything would work out his way. He quickly realised that they were already seized and none of their wooden spears would lead them into victory. They needed material and needed protection. Therefore, he imagined it the same way he used to imagine his imaginary friends as a child. His eyelids remained sealed, yet something shone brightly through them. Their bodies shimmered of sparking golden powder which had levitated from their small bags. The golden particles sparkled brighter than usual, moulding itself onto their skin and turning into armour and body protection. Their wooden spears turned into golden metal spears, and silver shields appeared from nowhere. Their bodies and wings were covered with shimmering gold. The alleys shone gold. Confidence and courage was restored within their hearts.

Juliana's prayer was answered, and the outcome of it was miraculously coincidental. Their good magic did nothing but anger the dark army on the opposite side. The misty horse huffed in aggregation as the misty wolves howled from all angles. The men beside Quinton chanted loudly towards the dark army whilst Quinton remained quiet and still with his brown eyes fixed towards the large hunched-back figure as its wretched wings spread widely. The sound of an old clock ticking slowly amplified inside his head as he waited in anticipation and hoped for victory as an outcome. His mind flashed back to the events of Little Venice in Colmar, France, and the spectacular site of Juliana dressed in a nightgown standing by the balcony whilst the hotel see-through curtains grazed over her smooth skin. That memory appeared larger inside his mind as he stood still by his men, listening to the ticking sound inside his mind. There was another flashback of the sun setting in the background as Juliana remained still by that balcony of his home, looking at the rooftops of many homes which seemed so peaceful to him. He felt drawn closer to that memory, yet he seemed so far from it as he tried to move towards it. A part of him had forgotten that he was about to participate in a battle, for that memory projecting within was all he looked forward to. Ironically through the mist of things, he could see peace, and as he stepped closer towards the memory, it vanished right before his eyes.

The battle had begun.

Quinton remembered his mother's words: 'Evil is not patient, nor is it kind. Its only purpose is to destroy anything that looks remotely beautiful, for it is obliviously ugly. It's envious towards love because it does not know how to love'. Every second that the clock ticked loudly inside of Quinton's mind whilst he waited patiently for a sign from above only imbedded more hate in the evil. The misty horse huffed and galloped. It raced forward ahead of the wolf pack. Its rider appeared to be a shadow dripping lava from its eyes. The horse's strides were long. Its muscles contracted as its metal shoes dug into the dry grass and left brown burn patches as it galloped towards the golden shine. The wolves howled loudly as they followed.

Quinton felt the epitome of all the problems gather into one motion. They were tormenting and chanting towards him, and everything he ever had been scared of in the past was directly heading towards him in slow motion. He looked at every angle in front of him and watched their mist turn into blinding smoke. The blinding smell of black smoke and its terror seemed so amplified to his eyes. Their lava eyes glowed of horror as they moved closer. Their teeth were sharp as they groaned, and their mouths dripped lava. They were hungry and ruthless, stomping through the dried grass, and as Quinton focused on the momentum of the horse, staring as it transformed in a shadow, he remembered a story his grandfather once told him when he was a child. The moral of the story was 'darkness only lives inside an old man's soul if he lacks the strength to restore his peace within his mind, the same way his peace had been stored away within his heart during his youth,' and at that moment, Quinton prepared for impact as he realised that he could not run away from his problems. He was growing older and needed to find peace before his darkness could destroy him. His last view before impact was his grandfather walking away from him into the distant bright light, and as his grandfather waved, the horse breached the golden bright line in his sphere and attacked. As its rider struck out its sword, he remembered the car accident that he'd been in with his deceased friends. His mind capitulated as the horse's dark impact withdrew life from him.

He began to see the past event that had occurred. It was even slower than before as he turned his head to the left side and watched the bright light ahead. He dove back and remembered the accident as it happened. Benjamin had steered right towards a right lane at the red traffic light and the beauty of the night city street lights that Quinton loved so much momentarily gathered and darkened turning into a black hole, sucking the life out of the three individuals in that car. That impact of the darkness spun the black Mercedes Benz into a 180-degree angle. Quinton looked up at shattered windscreen in his concussed mind frame; he could see the road that led him to that exact moment whilst his face bled on the right side. He felt himself zone backwards from that car accident at that moment and remembered Elaine's smile as she gave him half of her burning cigarette. Her smile painted an image so close to the love permanently stored within both Benjamin and Quinton's hearts. His subconscious mind frame was beginning to put the pieces of the puzzle together.

'Oh fuck!' Benjamin said as he felt indecisive at that moment whilst turning towards the right lane and hoping that his acceleration would advocate them towards safety.

His last words mumbled out, 'I'm so, sooo, so sorry!' after the cars had crashed.

After that impact, Quinton could see flashbacks of Benjamin holding on to his beautiful girl as she closed her eyes next to him whilst bleeding through her mouth. She died crying next to him, begging him for life because she too wanted to live more than anything. This one life that most people take for granted was pledged for insurance, yet that application toward insurance to a higher spiritual power failed as Quinton watched his friends die in front of him. Benjamin's face was bruised in dark blue as he bled internally. Quinton remembered the blue flashing lights from his peripheral vision. The thought of him lying there alone replicated to current events.

He opened his brown eyes and watched the smoke waiver above him and coughed, yet he didn't feel defeated by it. It was only the first obstacle in his way to finding peace within himself. He stood up with his eyes open and watched his men fighting the evil that had entered their domain.

It felt like an endless battle as sweat dripped from his forehead. He pierced into a black wolf that dove towards him. The ratio of his men to the wolves was even as he helped fight in combat. Within minutes, the tree houses were under attack, and evil had managed to enter the tree house village complex area. The misty horse was way ahead of the rest. It knew where it was heading too, for Arabella's scent was amplified.

Juliana waited inside their bedroom whilst holding her unborn child tightly and also listening to the evil sounds echo in the background. Lightning struck closely to the tree house, and Arabella began to weep. The distance from the bottom staircase on the ground to the top of the main tree house was at least one hundred metres, yet Quinton could hear his unborn child crying. He removed himself from battle at that point and made his way up. The hunched figure followed him and killed everything in its way. Quinton wasn't concerned about his monsters moving closer towards him. He was concerned for Juliana and Arabella's safety, for he knew that love can overcome any obstacle.

There was blood dripping everywhere, and wooden staircases were imprinted with dark red stains. By the time Quinton reached the blue front door, he discovered that their tree house was already invaded and filled with panic. He raced up the levitating wooden stairs. The misted horse had been killed by the army guards with their golden metal spears inside the only bedroom at the top, and Juliana was by the closed window frame, stroking Arabella's smooth soft hair in the dark. Heavy footsteps alerted him and his army guards within the bedroom. He felt a scare so astonishing to him that he felt his heart throbbing so loud inside his chest as they all turned around and faced the opened door. They all held on to the metal spears tightly yet remained uncertain as the wooden planks on the floor shook tremendously to every heavy step coming closer towards them.

The crowd outside began to cheer, and their tones lit up a victory throughout the dark atmosphere. The hunched-back figure stood still to the sounds of defeat, wondering through its indecisive mentality. It did not move closer to the levitating wooden steps, and its steady black heart started to fill up with hate. It stood cowardly whilst its dry dirt dripped onto the wooden floor. It had finally realised that it could not overcome the bright golden barrier of love glowing from that one door, and as Quinton stood in front of Juliana and Arabella alongside two army guards, everything started to make complete sense inside his mind. He'd always been afraid to let go of his monsters, and in most cases, he believed that he needed them to survive through most events because they were necessary evils, that they were a defensive mechanism to equip him for the dangerous world he lived. It was all in his imagination and, finally as he stood up, prepared to die for the love he believed in.

All the chains that were binding him from his true potential metaphorically broke off from his ankles and wrists. He finally understood the true meaning of mental freedom. Yet he still understood that the real world was a place where all humans were slaves to the system, working to pay for their freedom instead of understanding that they were all born free to begin with. Humans obeyed rules and regulations because obeying an authorised authority is all they ever knew. The concept of love had set him free because even though they would wake up to their reality on this very morning, their dreams and hopes for better days seemed clearer.

The rain showered over the tree house village, and the dark clouds evaporated into nothing. Rays of bright sunshine rose from the far hills, and peace restored itself. Quinton's darkest nightmare vanished into thin air. The monsters within the tree house village vanished away. Evil had been defeated from their hearts, and they were finally content with love. However, he knew it wasn't the last time he'd see those monsters, for he knew they would come back and to try regain the territory of his heart.

Chapter Twelve

Rose's Petals

The sky was gloomy with grey puffs of clouds everywhere. The smell of fresh green grass and fresh tulips gave Quinton and Juliana a sense of hope for a new life to be made. They made their way to their veranda and had breakfast. She smiled at him as she waited for his reaction because his face remained expressionless and indescribable for a minute. They were back to their reality and supposedly knew that they'd brought back a gift with them from a higher power, a gift which was meant to be destroyed by the evil lingering on dark outskirts of their hearts. Their outlook on life was more positive than when they'd first closed their heavy eyes. An idea ran through his mind as he walked through his empty hallway on the first storey of his household and a greater image of himself projected from the side frame mirrors. He walked taller than ever, and his heart strengthened inside his chest. Even through all the troubling issues that the world had thrown at him, he felt peaceful within himself.

Juliana made her way to the pool house in the backyard and sat alone quietly on wooden outdoor pool chair whilst everyone else woke up in the living room. She planted her light-toned feet onto an old colourful rug underneath her chair with mere thoughts of smoking Dunhill cigarettes, and at that point, as she slowly picked up that dark blue box of cigarettes, she felt discouraged. It wasn't evident that she would bear children anytime soon, but the idea of Arabella left her feeling differently. She wanted to be healthier and allow her body to become a carrier for the baby she wanted.

The two lovers had had friends over from the previous day. Everyone had gathered in the living room, servicing breakfast for themselves. Emily Lith had stayed over the night with Anthony and they'd shared intimate relations. Her heart was guarding a secret with a lot of unscripted information that only Quinton knew about. Through her brown eyes, Juliana Rose was momentarily the most beautiful woman she'd ever seen. She wondered what she'd to Juliana as she stood by the living room, looking at Juliana outside through the open wooden window. Nature framed itself around Juliana as her green eyes remained glued towards a bunch of delicate beautiful red roses planted by the green grass. The beautiful red texture on the petals reminded her of the dream she'd had a few days, and at the same time, she could feel someone's eyes burn the back of her head. She turned around and looked towards the open windows at the living room section and noticed Emily looking at her. The moment persisted awkwardly as Quinton stepped onto the veranda and kissed Juliana on her forehead as she looked upwards. She gripped on to Quinton's pillared forearms as they looked at the clear distance. She slowly kissed his right inner arm as he placed his chin on top of her head, and as her pinkish lips touched his smooth skin, Juliana couldn't quite shake the feeling that Emily was attracted to her, and rightfully so, she got notification from her lover after asking.

The day passed, and people slowly started to clear out of the Barker household after an afternoon of watching episodes on the telly. Quinton felt slightly empty, for his home was empty without his family. The hallway projected memories of his sisters' loud laughs and his father's Cuban cigar smell as he closed his eyes, but as he opened them, the images of his sisters hopping around in the passage vanished away with the wind blowing through the opened balcony door. He began to miss his father so dearly and felt a hollow void punch through his heart as he stepped onto the veranda outside to smoke a cigarette by the pool area. A lot ran through his mind as the wine sunk through his bloodstream, and as the day passed, it got dark. So did his thoughts of drowning in his desires of a three-way with Juliana Rose and Emily Lith. They'd grown comfortable with that idea and had allowed it to marinate within after he'd mentioned it after everyone had left.

Quinton made love to both women and lay beside them within the Barker pool house's only bedroom. He smiled as he observed the similarities of both women and stroked their hair strands with his hands, admiring their looks. He closed his brown eyes, hoping that he would fall asleep as easily as they did.

The week started the next day. Quinton wasn't particularly prepared for his Monday blues. He'd received another call from an investigation group that morning. It was a public holiday, and like most holidays, he'd hoped for peace and tranquillity, but that wasn't the case because he was summoned by a gentleman on the phone. His heart however was whelmed with a sense of joy, and his muscles were revived from the intimacy he'd had with Juliana and Emily. Quinton noticed that his excessive baggage of problems and unnecessary nerves had temporarily vanished from his life as he walked around the house after answering the home telephone. Smuggles jogged besides him as he moved around and relived memories paging through an old family album. Juliana stayed coiled comfortably in a blue sheet by the balcony, tapping her burning cigarette onto an ashtray, exhaling smoke from her mouth, drowning in guilt every single time she smoked. It must have been her spiritual awakening, her fellow guardian angels telling her she'd be having a child soon. She needed to stop indulging in bad habits.

Soon afterwards, Quinton found Juliana dwelling by the balcony. They passionately kissed and made their way along the balcony. Quinton sat beside Juliana, and he felt compelled to stay as he looked at the beautiful view of the Diamond City. He inhaled the last bit of the burning cigarette and squashed the burning bud into the ashtray.

His heart was content with the mere thought of Juliana being safe in his home. They were stronger than ever despite the misleading feelings they'd individually had from Emily Lith. Juliana had no knowledge of Quinton's misleading feelings, which kept cropping up randomly over the past day. Thus, he felt uneasy about Emily leaving that Sunday morning. She'd woken up earlier than both Juliana and Quinton as she left to mark herself present at home before her parents awoke for their church service. A piece of Quinton's heart gradually wanted Emily to stay, but he knew of the conflict that would arise from it. Therefore, he let her go.

Quinton drove into the main road and followed the directions that he'd received via his Viber application, and a long lonely hour passed into the third quarter of the day as he proceeded to an unknown location within the country. He remained sceptical because he wasn't sure where he'd end up, and all he knew was that it was important for him to be there alone; therefore, he also turned on his GPS settings on his Blackberry for safety purposes. He drove as rural children played on the gravel road with a plastic ball, kicking it around and making noise on the left side of the road, and the village was remotely quiet at the end of the long gravel road. It was too quiet, and that immediately arose suspension within Quinton's mind as he branched off towards a shallow valley. The area was clogged with dry thorn trees with grey trunks on the roadside as he drove past and turned right into a sandy road. Within the near distance, Quinton could see an abandoned wooden barnyard painted in fading maroon, an old sky blue tractor plotted on the left side of the barnyard without an engine and without workable wheels. He immediately felt a sense of déjà vu, for he'd subconsciously been there before.

The warm breeze stroked the top layer of the dried thatched grass as Quinton stepped out of from the red Grand Cherokee. He could sense an unwelcoming feeling as it gushed through his heart, and the vile atmosphere wasn't pleasant at all. There were no birds chirping or flying around, and yet there were so many empty nests by the only thorn tree on the right side of the field. He began to wonder if he'd followed the directions correctly as he turned around to search for signal on his

Blackberry. The battery signal bars were low, and the network bars were disruptively moving about as he moved closer towards the open wooden door. He looked at the rusty hinges attached to the maroon wooden door and felt the history of the place gush through his soul.

The barnyard was owned by a late old man who had died in his late seventies, and it was said by many that his ghost still lingered within the barnyard during the late nights. It was haunted, and nobody ever wanted to purchase Patrick's farm after it was auctioned by the government because rumours winded through everyone's ears after he'd died mysteriously. Within the late stages of the first millennium, Patrick, an old man, farmed for a living. He mostly farmed corn and potatoes throughout the wide field with his rural village associates, and he believed that he'd make his first fortunes before passing away. The farm bred life into the atmosphere. The yellow corn within the fields had brought life to the farm, and its green stems made the scenery lively. It was always so warm around, and he would give watermelons to the children of the village after long productive months. His blood ran through every single root within the ground, and his heart brought peace within the area. Everyone supposedly loved him and helped him with his farming, yet at the back of his mind, he knew that jealousy lingered underneath the shaded bushes and the trees aligned on the hilltops.

As days went by towards December—a month before the second millennium—Old Patrick was on the outskirts of his farm in the early hours of the morning riding his old horse, and he looked at his broken-down sky blue tractor. He knew that his equipment could still serve its purpose. Therefore, he grabbed his tool box from the maroon barnyard and started working on the engine. Little did he know that he would encounter an enemy he'd made in his past. His enemy's vengeance had begun when he was thirty-seven years younger, for he was part of the old South African defensive force that was assembled during the apartheid era. Patrick was an old man with a vile history he'd never wished for but had it nevertheless because he had to keep up with the times. At the time, they were all brainwashed to believe that people from other race groups were inferior. Yet a part of him knew that all people were all equal before the eyes of God, but he could not run away from the evil that controlled the country. He was a lieutenant general in his army base and had always followed the directions that was given by the old regime because he feared that they would also execute him if necessary.

On the 28 January 1961, the radio intercom alerted his station base of havoc occurring within a township nearby, and his crew were first responders to the township which were also known as homelands at the time. Tensions had already escalated from the Sharpeville massacre incident that had occurred the year before, and the people of the majority population within the country had finally resorted to building an armed struggle. Patrick was part of it all, the secrets sealed by the apartheid government. He'd seen the blood of a lot people from different races being spilt through the streets over many townships by his command.

His last enemy's vengeance started from the day they drove an army vehicle through the streets of a township, killing many innocent people in their path and searching for leaders of a rapidly growing arms struggle. They raided a household at the right corner of the street as people scattered away from the violence and dodged AK-47 bullets. Patrick raided that small shanty house with his crew of soldiers, and they found a member of the MK arms struggle trying to hide his family of four boys, one girl, and his beautiful wife within the main bedroom closets. The youngest boy, John, had hidden away from the rest in a box in the first bedroom parallel to the main bedroom seconds before the house raid began, and he witnessed his family being executed. Loud shots echoed through the small house and into his ears. His heart throbbed intensely as he heard his siblings and parents screaming, begging for mercy before the soldiers emptied their magazines into their bodies.

That day defined Patrick's growing enemy for the rest of his life as he grew up and fought against the old government, searching for that one leader that had his family executed. Patrick had seen the small eyes peeping through a small opening box in the first bedroom but hoped that his good deed towards that matter would go unpunished.

The reconciliation commission events took place after the country's first democratic elections, but attending those events never brought peace to John because deep down within his heart, he wanted revenge and he wanted to find Patrick more than anything.

Patrick never wanted to believe that his past would come back to haunt him one day until that one late afternoon by his wooden maroon barnyard in a different country. He'd tipped his tool case onto the green grass by the sky blue tractor after unscrewing the engine bolts. He could hear footsteps approaching from the back as he unbent and tried to stand up straight. John's shadow hovered over him as leaned back on the sky blue tractor to the sight of a 9-millimetre pistol pointing at him. They looked into each other's eyes as the wind blew, and it was quiet within the area, but they could both hear the chaos and gunshots from that specific day when John's home was raided. Patrick noticed the resemblance in the brown eyes of the man that stood before him, and he was speechless. Ironically, he did not want to die violently. He hoped that the child within the brown box would've found peace within the world like he'd tried to, but it was quite evident that his days on earth were at an end as he looked into John's eyes. Patrick saw nothing but pain as he looked into them.

The old man pleaded for his life as John pulled the gun trigger twice and killed an old man he's searched for his entire life, and yet his heart wasn't fulfilled. Patrick's last words plunged into the land, and his soul sowed through the cornfield as his body fell onto the green grass then bled to death. John disappeared after that hot summer day in Botswana with Patrick's body to bury it.

Long years passed, and the villagers could still sense Old Patrick's spirit gladding their hearts. They all knew of his goodness regardless of his shady past, and they'd all tried to maintain his farm after he'd passed away, but none of them could sustain the roots that he'd grown. He was the heartbeat of the corn and potato fields around, and the atmosphere within the area was never the same again as his ghost waivered through the long lonely night, unrested and rattled.

As Quinton entered the barnyard, he found a man tied up to a light brown wooden chair. History was vaguely repeating itself, and Quinton could sense the spiritual radiance within the barnyard as he rushed towards the helpless man. The man's wrists and ankles were bruised from the red rope binding him to the chair, and his mouth was covered in duct tape. He couldn't see anything because his eyes were covered with a black cloth. Quinton immediately unbound him and tried to rescue him until he realised that it was his uncle Steve. His uncle muttered through the duct tape, and his tears leaked from his swollen bruised eyelids. He'd been brutally beaten. His cream white suit had bloodstains and dirt all over it.

Quinton looked down at his helpless uncle and felt a third person's spirit lingering aside.

'I had the honour of meeting your father a week ago, and he asked me to do him a favour!' he said. 'He asked me to invite you to this barnyard after finding Steve!' he stated.

The stranger's body was plump and short like a greedy fat pig with an agenda to eat everything in sight. Quinton immediately realised why he was summoned as his eyes followed the stranger's hand gesture towards a dusty table within one of the three stables. There was a silver pistol imprinted with glowing danger. Its metal shone brightly, and it significantly glowed brighter towards Quinton's brown eyes. The scenery was deemed dark and clustered with dust. Small rays of light shone through the wreaked maroon wooden planks. Quinton knew that he'd stumbled towards death as he tripped whilst walking towards the dusty table. His hatred towards his only uncle prevailed in his brown eyes as he picked the pistol and walked back. Quinton did not know what would happen, but the feeling of having power over another human being was overwhelming as he pointed the silver pistol towards Steve's bald head.

Steve closed his bruised eyelids, and tears raced down his plumy cheeks. His whole life flashed before his brown eyes, and for the first time in his life, he wasn't sure of the outcome as he felt the silver shine reflect onto his head.

'You have to understand,' the stranger said, 'the only way your father will be released from prison is when Steve vanishes forever because the charges won't stick if the main suspect is nowhere to be found. The lawyers will do their part!'

Those vile words sunk into Quinton's mind as he looked at his helpless uncle and heard the wild misted horse galloping in his mind.

Nobody else could hear the sounds of late Patrick's last moment except for Quinton as he listened to the vivid gunshot echo in the background of his mind. His heart throbbed intensely as he placed his finger onto the metal trigger, and the havoc of many people dying to violence in the past flamed a brutal picture within his mind. He closed his eyes as the stranger spoke and metaphorically felt victims' blood wash over his face. The sorrow within him embarked on a journey to the harsh past as he stood still on the dirty gravel roads, watching people scatter away from silver bullets. A bomb exploded towards his left, and a warehouse waivered into flames as its metal sheets scattered away.

Quinton opened his eyelids and felt differently about his motives. He wasn't bred to kill, and he knew that this one convenient moment for his family would impact him for the rest of his life as his finger slowly brushed against the metal trigger. His heart and mind triggered with uncertainty, and he stepped away from death's hoax. The darkness was beginning to compel him again as he looked at his helpless uncle. Horse sounds within his mind grew louder as he blinked continuously. Quinton stepped away as the stranger spoke, but the horse chuckles remained so loud within him that he could not hear anything the stranger said. He wandered to the end of the barnyard and opened another old wooden door for a whiff of fresh air then stumbled to an unexpected view.

There was an abandoned old white cottage glued closely to the hillside and imprinted underneath amarula tree branches. Concrete rocks patched widely from the barnyard and tracked all the way to the old white cottage. The side skirts were clustered with tall thatches of dry brown grass. Quinton stepped onto concrete rocks and moved away from the tensioned scenario in the barnyard. A part of him wanted to run away from it all, but walking away seemed more sensible. It was awfully quiet around the cottage as he moved closer whilst avoiding the ripe and rotten amarula fruits on the concrete ground. He stepped onto the wooden steps, and the dry white paint on the wooden steps beside his feet brushed off with the wind.

'Hello, anyone there?' he asked but felt hostility breach his body as two cracked window beside the open door frame spat out layers of thin dust towards him. It was unexplainable as he tried to think of the science behind the mystical energy flowing through the area.

He closed his eyelids, and the area came alive right before him. It was all a pleasant mirage as he opened his eyelids and watched the old white cottage momentarily breed life into itself. Everything shined new. Glass particles trended, mending themselves back into shape and attaching themselves back into the window frames. Quinton could smell the wet white paint on the wall planks, and the past railed through his mind. The area smelt fresh, and Quinton could see some villagers planting seeds within the empty fields whilst most of them watered the rows behind. Their children played hopscotch underneath the amarula trees and ate the sweet ripe fruits from the provided brown basket placed by an exposed tree root. Quinton could always picture the future at times but also wondered about the passive things that had occurred in the past as he stood on the porch by the door.

The misted horse galloping within his mind earlier appeared from back of cottage. It appeared different as it emerged brown. It had its handler, the old man Patrick. His face was unshaven with grey hair, and he looked utterly miserable as he tied the horse saddle next to the pillar of the porch. He sat on the porch stool and lit his smoke pipe as he rocked his chair whilst staring at the barnyard.

The villagers within the empty field began to clear out as the sun glazed off the small valley towards the west, and the younger children followed the elderly villagers towards the barnyard and vanished into thin air. As Patrick inhaled the smoke within his pipe, he looked downwards at his ring finger and fiddled with his wedding ring that he'd had on years after his late wife passed on.

'My heart remains unrested years I have been murdered!' he said, and Quinton turned shocked as he realised that Patrick was looking at him. 'My late wife has found peace within her heart, and I guess that's why I cannot find her!' he stated. 'I wanted to have made great fortunes before dying, but that wasn't the case!' He shrugged slowly after inhaling smoke.

'I hope that you do not kill him,' Patrick stated, 'because your heart will never rest once you have killed!' He rocked backward and forward.

'I know this fact because I have killed a lot of innocent people. I wish I hadn't done so, but I did!'

Quinton looked towards the barnyard, and it looked beautiful shining from the maroon paint. He thought of other options as he sat next to Patrick and watched the old horse bite into the shining silver metal container and swallow its ripe apple fruits. A musky thought of death caused an imbalance within him, but he knew that his father would rot in prison if he did nothing about Steve's disappearance.

'You have to make an executive decision!' Marcus would say whilst drinking American bourbon in his study, and Quinton sat there digesting his father's words and wondering what Beth would do for her husband with her Christian morals. The thought of Juliana finding out that her lover has been turned into a killer would devastate their relationship, and as he thought more of the other ways to process, he realised that he was talking to ghost. It momentarily occurred to him that it wasn't normal to see dead people as he looked at Patrick rocking in his chair.

'Do you think that you will ever find peace?' Quinton asked as he lit a cigarette from his left pocket and watched the last bit of bright rays disappear over the clustered valley.

'I don't know!' Patrick said as Quinton's phone rang continuously.

Quinton picked it from his right pocket and answered it.

'Baby, I'm bored! Where are you?' Juliana asked and exhaled in boredom. She fiddled with her golden cross as she wondered around the Barker household, switching lights on and carrying a wine glass filled with Chardonnay wine in her right hand. Quinton paused for a while, and the conversation imminently turned slightly awkward as he looked around.

'Um, I'm coming home soon!' Quinton stuttered. 'I'm with my mom,' he said for a more assuring lie.

Juliana placed a pot under the kitchen sink and poured water into it. 'Well, I'm start cooking for you!' she said. 'Come home soon!'

'Oh yes, Anthony has left. He said that he couldn't wait and had to return to South Africa to see his parents off!' she added, and as she hung up her phone and placed it onto the kitchen counter, Beth drove into the driveway slowly.

She'd just returned from South Africa and seemed highly exhausted as she entered the main entrance whilst calling out for her son. Instead Juliana answered as she poured the Chardonnay wine into the sink.

'Oh, hello, Juliana!' Beth said. 'Where is my son?' she asked.

'He said that he was with you, but clearly he just lied to me!' Juliana stated as she poured uncooked macaroni into the boiling pot.

'Okay, I will be upstairs if you need me. Let him know that I am looking for him!' Beth replied.

'We could bond maybe?' Juliana asked and smiled.

'I thought you would never ask!' Beth smiled back and opened the fridge. She poured herself some Chardonnay wine and offered Juliana a glass too.

'Here you go!' she said and handed Juliana a filled wine glass.

They had endless conversations about glamour and the latest fashion trends, drinking away as the sun settled down into dusk, and they both wondered where Quinton was on this unusual night.

Crickets sounded in the background as Quinton stood up next to the burning lamp hanging by the porch entrance, and he felt drawn to the darkness in the background. He looked at the silver pistol as he picked up, and he remained uncertain as he walked away towards wooden steps. He looked at Patrick as everything around him vanished away and the scenery turned old again right before Quinton's eyes, and Patrick vanished away in the end. The old man's chair rocked forward and backward, which initially puzzled Quinton even more. He walked away from the old cottage and used the early full moon light as guidance back to the barnyard door. Steve had blacked out to the brutal beating he'd received whilst Quinton was by the old cottage. The stranger lurked from within the darkness with a burning cigarette in his right hand, and his patience had worn out.

'I have a beautiful wife to get to!' Quinton said. 'We need finish this job!' he stated as Quinton pointed the silver pistol at his uncle's bald head.

The moonlight shined through holes in the metal roof, and the light shined onto the silver metal. Quinton looked at the shine for a split second as it reflected into his brown eyes, and he knew that he wasn't capable of murder. Therefore, he unarmed himself and placed the silver pistol back onto the dusty table.

'You can do whatever my father told you to do, but I will play no part in it' Quinton said as he looked at the stranger in the distance, ashing his cigarette and blowing out smoke from his mouth.

'Goodbye, Steve!' Quinton whispered and walked away. 'We will pretend like I was never here!' Quinton said as he glanced at the stranger and dismissed the topic at hand.

He closed the maroon wooden door slowly and felt the rusty hinges scratch the little humanity he had left within his heart. Slowly but surely the old clock from his student apartment in London clocked inside his mind as Steve awoke inside the barnyard.

Quinton opened his car door and felt a terribly shock as two loud gunshots echoed in the air. A few teardrops raced down his face as he entered the car and pushed the engine start button on. He reversed backwards and drove away without brightening the car lights, knowing that his uncle was dead or at least he thought so.

Quinton entered through the front gate of his home slowly and wept in sorrow as his car engine idled by the garage door. He looked through his panorama sunroof and tried to see the good in his part of ending another human being's life, but all he could momentarily see was the full moon shining back at him. It was awfully quiet as his mind flashed back all events in the past of his uncle, and he felt guilt within his gut to the memories of his uncle laughing out loud in joy.

'Boo!' Juliana shouted as she crept from outside with excitement.

She slowly realised that Quinton's heart was troubled and imbedded with horror as she opened the car door. He did not notice her presence as she spoke to him, for his mind was miles away. She placed her warm hands around his warm body as he wept like a small child. His tears soaked her white T-shirt as she hugged him closely and placed her wine glass in the can holder.

'What's wrong?' she asked, whispering whilst rubbing his back softly.

He knew that this one secret would have to go with him to his grave and thus kept quiet about the matter at hand as he continued crying.

'Come!' she said as she pressed the engine button off and grabbed his car keys from the passenger seat.

He sniffed as he wiped the tears from his face and entered through the front door quietly. Juliana poured the rest of his wine into a potted plant because she realised that she needed to be attentive towards her lover. The plasma screen was on, and Juliana had been watching fashion television alone. Quinton lay quietly onto the brown suede couch and slid off his shoes onto the wooden floor. His angle was tilted clockwise as he observed skinny women walking on the catwalk in their designer clothing. He did not want to speak, and Juliana understood as she brought him a glass of cold water and a warmed-up meal for him. Quinton had completely lost his appetite as he lay quietly and closed his baggy eyes. Juliana joined him and lay behind him quietly whilst holding on to his left hand and kissing the back of his neck.

He was completely petrified of the outcome and his heart throbbed intensely as visuals of his bruised uncle swept passed his mind every second. Juliana felt so synchronised to him. Therefore, she could feel the pain that he was feeling in his heart. His mood had affected hers, and their hearts were aching badly. She switched on the cool air conditioning system to reduce the heat within the room.

They slept on the couch, and both railed back into their mystical tree house village. Juliana opened her eyelids within their world, but Quinton was nowhere to been seen. It had lapsed onto her judgement that he was hiding something from her, and she wanted to know the truth behind his recent salty tears. Her unborn child was clustered away from her, and that rattled her heart as she panicked towards the tree houses, yelling out for somebody. It was quiet in between her echo and the red chime melodies. The empty passages reeked of sadness as she wandered everywhere, calling out for Quinton and Arabella but sensing that she was alone.

Quinton hadn't opened up to her. Therefore, his heart had momentarily closed and barricaded heavy barriers towards Juliana's heart. He was lost in another world as she wandered up to the their tree house to look from her unborn child but couldn't find Arabella as she uncovered the heavy melded leaves in their bedroom, and tears amounted heavily from her eyelids as she looked out the open window frame as the sun peeked. She could not understand the concept of it all, nor did she understand if she was in a musky dream or an elusive nightmare observed during the day.

Quinton also opened his eyelids, and their world was completely dark. He was lost in a different time zone, and the sky above was painted grey without any shining stars. Juliana's heart throbbed fast as she wept quietly to the loneliness, and Quinton could hear her crying as he wandered through the tree house passages. The red chimes within his world weren't moving at all, yet the wind blew in different directions. It was completely bizarre as he looked around the complex and found nobody within it. It had occurred to him that maybe every single child he had created with Juliana before had vanished away because Arabella was finally on the way. He was expecting Juliana to bear a child soon, and maybe this was the case. Her heart beat grew louder within his mind as he walked up the staircases and entered their tree house. He realised that there weren't any birds resting in their nests with their glowing lights on, and he stumbled in the darkness through the door whilst calling out for Juliana.

She turned around and waited from him in the bedroom, hoping to see his shadow lead him in through the bedroom door. And as he walked up the levitating wooden stairs, he entered an empty bedroom but could still hear Juliana calling out for him. She looked at the open bedroom door and called out again, but Quinton wasn't there to be seen. He looked at the open window frame in the darkness, and he couldn't see Juliana as he called out her name. Their hearts throbbed differently to each other, but they knew that they were in the same room. Their names echoed through the thick hollow rooms in the tree house as they yelled out for each other. They stood still and felt the vibrant feeling of their voices rush through their souls in the same bedroom. Juliana's sweet soft sound drew Quinton closer, but it felt like her voice was drifting away as he moved towards the open window. She felt his presence as he stood next to her, but neither one of them could see nor touch each other.

'I know you are here!' she said. 'I wish you would just open up to me already!'

Her words slurred slowly into his ears as he closed his eyes and listened to the softness in her tone. He wanted to express himself and open up, but the darkness had completely consumed his heart, for he knew that his uncle's death was the epitome of his high barriers, and as he opened his eyelids to the darkness in the bedroom, he felt Juliana's heart radiating away from him. Her voice lowered until it muted before him.

'Julie!' he said and waited for a reply, but nobody replied.

She called out for his name repeatedly as the sound of his heart drifted away from her as she kept quiet in hopes of hearing him again; she felt a kick within her stomach. The internal pain caused her to scream out for his name as she kneeled on the wooden floor. Her nose turned pink as she wept from the lack of his support, and he felt helpless because he could not see her nor feel her presence. All he could see was the darkness approaching him in waves of terror, and he fell backwards in agony. He felt nostalgic and sad as he could call out for Juliana again with the hope that her name would advocate and shield him away from his colossal monsters. This wasn't the case as he kneeled on the wooden floor and felt goosebumps crop through his upper body as a wide hand touched his left shoulder.

'Let her go!' it said as its reeking smell whiffed through Quinton's nostrils.

Quinton turned his head and felt the terrifying nightmare unveil before his brown eyes. It was the hunchback figure that he'd always subconsciously feared.

'Are you here to kill me?' Quinton asked as he stood up to face his fear.

'Not all, we have a lot of things to do!' it said as he looked into Quinton's brown eyes. His lava eyes dripped, and flames caught on the wooden floor within the tree house. 'My name is Luther, son of the wondrous world!' he stated as he lifted its muscular greasy hands towards the wooden plank ceiling. 'I'm here to help you!' said Luther as the wind grew stronger around them. 'Wake up now,' Luther said, 'and your dreams will come to life!'

Quinton looked around for a while, and his soul levitated in front of his brown eyes. Luther's lava eyes turned gold as Quinton looked into them. He knew that it was all a facade, but his heart wanted the gold shining through Luther's eyes as he raised his left hand forward. His mind was momentarily hypnotized as he walked away towards the open bedroom door. He looked back as he followed Luther down the wooden stairs. He knew that Juliana would never trust him again. She sat against the wooden planks and cried herself to sleep in the tree house bedroom whilst Arabella grew within her stomach.

Quinton awoke to the early hours of the morning and felt drawn away from Juliana even though she was right next to him. He wondered what their dream meant as he looked towards the wooden ceiling in the living room. Her body was warmer and feverish from the cool air in the living room, and her face was dripping in sweat.

'Baby!' he whispered and kissed her forehead softly. He could taste the salty excreted liquid from her pores as he melded his lips into his mouth. She opened her green eyes, and the glow within them had disappeared into the early dark morning as she shivered. Quinton moved closer and hugged her as they lay by each other, but he felt something separating him away from her. He tried to hold on to the miraculous magic they formed with their hearts as he held on tightly, yet she felt differently and wasn't willing to show any affection towards him as her body heated slowly to the change in weather outside. She sneezed repeatedly as Quinton tried to be more attentive towards her, but her heart wasn't beating as equivocally as it used to, for she knew that their relationship was in trouble. Thoughts turned into assumptions as she looked at him, and she concluded that he was blatantly cheating. A lie scripted in his brown eyes as he looked away and avoided the tension in the air.

'Where were you last night?' she asked. 'Do not lie to me!'

Quinton fixed his brown eyes towards the ceiling as light unveiled from outside. The curtains lit in bright maroon as he looked towards Juliana and felt the dark within manifesting. Images of his uncle ran deeply in his memory as he stood up and opened the sliding door to smoke a cigarette.

Beth woke up from the master bedroom and walked slowly toward the hollow passage in a delightful mood until she opened the main balcony doors and saw Quinton inhaling the dirty nicotine into his lungs. She did not say anything at that moment and understood her son's troubles as he inhaled the cigarette by the veranda.

'When you are done killing yourself, refresh and meet me by the car!' she said. 'We are going to see your father this morning!'

Quinton choked on the smoke as his mother spoke and felt ashamed, for he'd disappointed her. Everything he was doing evoked disgrace, and he couldn't feel a balance within himself as he carried on smoking as if he had heard anything she'd said.

'Well, are you going to stand there and carry on?' Beth asked as she looked at his son falling victim to the legalized bad substance.

His mind shook in fear at the thought of his list of sins. He looked into the distance and exhaled out grey smoke whilst smudging the cigarette bud into the glass ashtray, and he knew that nothing will ever be the same again.

After two hours of driving away from the Diamond City and entering a different location towards the western districts, Quinton looked out the window as they entered a small. They drove to the outskirts and entered a gravel road, leading to a remote prison. The thick fence surrounding the compound lengthened high with barbed wire everywhere, and it felt like Quinton was entering the cornerstone of his reality. It seemed like hell on earth as he looked at German shepherds barking at the car. He sensed that the dogs knew of his treasury, and as he sunk into his passenger chair with guilt piping through his heart, it throbbed intensely as he closed his brown eyes. Guards walked around the car with black AK-47 guns and searched the car for anything illegal whilst asking Beth for her visitation purpose. She looked at her son and wondered what was troubling him so much that he couldn't gain composure. His face dripped of sweat as she parked the car by the signing-in office.

'Get a hold of yourself. Your father hates weakness!' she said as she opened the car door. 'Well, are you coming or not?' she asked and closed the door softly.

Quinton looked at his mother and wondered if she'd still be as supportive towards Marcus if she knew the real man she'd married. It had occurred to him that she was blinded by her love for the finest things in life, that she would blatantly turn her back on reality whilst using her spiritual beliefs as a defensive mechanism.

Quinton and Beth entered the visitation section after signing in with their identification cards, and the walls were painted in musky grey, portraying depression with its dull colour. The metal bars were painted white, and the atmosphere smelt of dirt combined with heated rubber from the guards' black shoes. No smiles glowed within the clustered room, and misery existed within everyone's souls. Quinton sat beside Beth and waited for Marcus to be presented from the other side. They sat quietly and could hear chains coming closer from the other room.

A dominant spirit hovered within the room as the grey door opened up on the opposite end of the room, and Marcus walked through it with handcuffs tightly binding his wrists together. He'd lost weight prior to the horrible prison conditions, and his skin was darkly pale. His eyes were ruby red and baggy from lack of sleep. He sat on the opposite side and smiled at his family as Beth's tears raced down her face and spoilt her eye lace make-up. She closed her eyelids and wiped her cheeks with a tissue from within her suit pocket. Marcus spoke to Beth as minutes passed, but he never once looked at Quinton, which initially made him a coward for asking his son to perform such a treacherous act. For the first time ever, Quinton could see a lie within Marcus' eyes. It was quite clear as Quinton glanced around at other prisoners and reached an epiphany that Marcus wasn't as innocent as he claimed to be.

'Are you okay?' Marcus said as he noticed his son's gloomy looks,

'I'm good, just observing your home!' Quinton stated as he looked into his father's eyes and saw a yellowish colour within them. *Nothing seems clear anymore* were the words projecting at that back of his mind as his father spoke more.

He could see Steve's resemblance more clearly on Marcus' face as he observed and realised that they could indeed be the same at heart. Marcus seemed to be craftier about his business deals more than Steve, and Quinton sat there, wondering if he'd ever find a way out of it all. His golden moment for the finer things in life slowly evaporated from his mind as he realised that he was indeed a product made from a deep sadness.

The loopholes within his mind started to fill up as the past unfolded in front of his brown eyes, and he knew that he would never find peace within his soul again. He realised that his heart would ever be robbed of any happiness if he was to keep any secrets from Juliana Rose, and as he thought of a way to open up his lover, he realised that it wasn't really his information to share. Their relationship would be strained forever because of this information, and Quinton wondered if Juliana would weather the storm with him if he came clean to the police. As much as he was an optimistic person, he knew of the reality and understood that Juliana would leave him. It wouldn't have been right for him to string her along anyway, and because he loved her so much, he would sink her along with him. Quinton concluded as he thought of Juliana Rose's genuine love that she should never know of his wrongdoings. He looked downwards at both his hands as Marcus turned his focus to Beth, and he could imaginatively see Steve's dark red blood dripping from his pink palms as his parents spoke in the background. He hadn't pulled the triggered and thus wondered why he felt personally guilty for his uncle's murder, and at that point, he felt evil reigning more in his heart as his heart throbbed slowly.

Chapter Thirteen

Blood Pipes Flowing towards Uncertainty

After a few weeks of legal proceedings, a final verdict came in the end to release Marcus Barker from prison, and the government unfroze his company's assets. It was stated that he wasn't responsible for his younger brother's deeds, but he received two years of probation for supposedly acting carelessly in ensuring his company's integrity. It never did make sense to Quinton as he read the verdict. The company had lost a lot of clients throughout and mainly lost its credibility towards fulfilling their commitments. It all started to feel normal again as everyone in the household proceeded with their daily activities, but Quinton kept his distance from his parents for good reasons. He felt differently about them and didn't idolize them anymore due to his part in supposedly ending his uncle's life. As a child, he'd viewed his parents like superheroes, such as Superman and Wonder Woman, but that ideology changed as he grew up and realised that his parents were just human like everyone else. They were bags of flesh structured with skeleton bones.

'Just human,' he thought to himself the day he realised that his parents also made mistakes. He was almost in disbelief when everything negative about them aligned into a series of events whilst growing up. The temper tantrums coming from his father and the lies that his mother would usually make to him were the deep-rooted elements that had built him into the man he was today.

Marissa Rose called Juliana around eleven o'clock in the morning, concerned about her daughter's future commitments and appealed for them to bond more. They'd grown estranged after Andrew's funeral, and Juliana had always pretended like everything was fine around Quinton, but most of time, she cried herself to sleep in Kimberly's room which initially had turned into her room after a while. She'd stopped sleeping in Quinton's bedroom after Marcus' release and mainly felt that Quinton was acting differently towards everything. Their dreams weren't synchronised anymore, and she wondered if he still loved her like he used to. Initially she played a part in the whole scenario by shielding her heart away from him. She sensed that she couldn't trust him, and on this day, she tried to find the truth by snooping around his bedroom, searching for any information on his Blackberry and invading his privacy by logging on to his social media accounts. It occurred to her that her theory was misled because she knew all his passwords, and as she sat quietly thinking of other theories, she felt an explosion within her stomach. Therefore, she rushed towards the bathroom door and entered. Her head ached on her way to the toilet. She gripped her brunette hair away from her mouth and puked. Her heart throbbed extremely fast as she sat by the toilet seat a few seconds later and realised that her menstrual cycle was late.

'Oh man!' she whispered as she tilted her head towards her knees.

Her reality racked on to her unstable mindset as she closed her eyes and hoped that it was not true. She wondered what Quinton's reaction would be towards her being pregnant, and with her sixth sense, she felt something growing within her body as she looked into the toilet and felt another wave of vomit coming out of her stomach towards her mouth. The pain was excruciating as she placed her right hand on her flat stomach and felt a gully cramp near her pelvis. The idea of Arabella and her beauty brushed positivity into Juliana's mind as she picked up her phone and wondered who she'd call. She scrolled through her contacts and felt uncertain as she reached Quinton's contact details. The idea behind calling him on his phone from downstairs was to keep everything discrete. She brushed her thumb upwards onto the touchscreen as she entered Kimberly's bedroom, and she called her mother back.

Juliana took a deep breath as the dial tone commenced in her left ear and wondered what she'd say to her mother as she looked at the calendar on the wall. She was at least six days late and felt noxious to the smell of the flourishing flowers coming through the balcony from the garden at the bottom.

'Marissa Rose's phone, please leave a message, and I will get back to you!' And a beep sound commenced after.

'Hey, Mom, please call me back!' she said and dropped the phone in anxiety.

Her breaths grew shorter by the minute as she struggled to grasp for air, yelling out for Quinton. He turned around in the living room and muted the plasma screen with the remote, unsure of what he'd heard.

'Julie!' he shouted.

'Quinton!' she shouted and panicked by the bathroom sink.

Juliana took deeper breaths, staring at herself in the mirror. She felt drowsy. Quinton rushed into Kimberly's bedroom as Juliana collapsed onto the black tiles in the bathroom. Her right hand unclenched, and water streamed in between her fingers as she blinked continuously facing her moist hand. The premature thought of being pregnant felt pleasant in the past, but she realised that a baby wasn't an accessory or a pair of Louis Vuitton heels that she'd wear for a few months and pack away. Their timing was initially all wrong, and their reality was finally taking a severance course. Quinton lifted Juliana off the tile floor and placed her onto the bed within seconds. He was lost for words as he looked at Juliana unconscious and felt her steady pulse on her neck. He yelled out for assistance, and the household help rushed in from the ground floor. It was very unusual for Juliana to collapse. Thus, Quinton became highly concerned for her well-being as he stepped away from the bedside.

'Get her water!' Wendy, the help, said as she sat on the bed and placed her right hand onto Juliana's sweaty forehead.

Quinton rushed towards the bathroom and filled a red plastic cup with cold water and rushed back and handing it to Wendy, the household help who seemed experienced in handing matters of this nature. She'd been reinstated after Marcus' release and had grown to love Quinton's family since their humble beginnings. Juliana choked on the small amount of water entering her mouth as Wendy wiped Juliana's forehead with a clean kitchen cloth from her pink apron.

'She is dehydrated!' Wendy whispered as she looked at Quinton's pale facial expression. 'Drink some water,' she urged Juliana who'd seemed figuratively paralysed by the thought of having a child.

'Quinton, please take me to a pharmacy!' Juliana mentioned as she sat up straight. 'Just need to buy something!' she said and placed her soft feet onto the wooden floor.

Quinton rushed towards his bedroom to grab his car keys and found himself puzzled about Juliana's request to visit the local pharmacy.

'Get clean first?' Wendy suggested as she looked at them both in their pyjamas.

'Okay, we will!' Juliana replied. 'Thank you so much, Wendy!' she said and attempted to smile.

Her beautiful smile hid her pain away although droplets of it lingered on her eyes. Quinton switched on the water tap within the shower booth. Juliana slowly walked towards him. She was terrified, and he could see her sadness looming within her green eyes as she stepped into his space with her arms open. She was extremely tired of arguing and fighting with him. The only way to shut him up was to hold on to him and allow her silence to advocate for her peace. His heart still throbbed indifferently as she placed her head onto his chest and felt the love that she'd so longed for. She did not want to move, and the sound of warm water raining within the shower booth drilled her into confusion as her heart throbbed loudly for him.

'I've missed you!' she said.

'I've missed you too, babe!' Quinton replied and placed his lips onto her forehead.

'I wasn't talking to you, Quinton!' she stated. 'I was talking to your heart, baby!' she mentioned.

Juliana looked into Quinton's eyes and felt hesitant about revealing the truth. She remained quiet as Quinton led her into the shower booth, anxiously waiting to purchase a pregnancy test from the closest pharmacy to be more assured of her status. Quinton became more affectionate and more attentive towards Juliana as he stood next to her. They held on to each other tightly as the warm water rained onto their bodies. They made love.

A part of him knew this could be the last bit of their happiness because everything about their reality had concluded differently due to current events. Quinton was keeping secrets from Juliana, and she was beginning to do the same. Her mother had booked a flight back to Johannesburg, South Africa. She kept that information hidden from Quinton as she closed her green eyes and she placed her head onto his chest.

Her stomach cramped again. She touched her belly with her right hand. A seed had cropped up within her stomach, and the thought of being pregnant suddenly plunged Juliana into sickness as her fever increased. Quinton could hear a baby crying in the distance as the moment turned utterly quiet. He couldn't hear the water droppings in the shower booth but could only hear the sweet cries of a newborn baby. His arms remained clenched around Juliana and everything started to add up as he brushed Juliana's wet hair away from her forehead with his left hand. He could see the unscripted truth projecting in her green eyes as she looked up at him.

'Are you pregnant, love?' he asked and waited as she scrolled through her mind for an answer.

'I don't know!' she replied. 'I'm so scared! Hold me!' she sighed, closing her eyes and placing her head back onto his wet chest again.

His pulse rate increased rapidly as her answer rattled his mind. They knew that they'd been careless throughout and wondered if they'd made a mistake. The signs towards this moment had unveiled toward them in their previous dreams, and they knew of the inevitable but also realised that they weren't ready for the responsibly. Juliana shook continuously and felt a chill creep up her spinal cord.

'I'm taking you to the hospital, baby!' Quinton said as he switched the water handle off and picked up Juliana as she shivered more.

Their bodies dripped with water onto the black tiles in the bathroom and onto the wooden floor as he carried her into Kimberly's bedroom. They dried off, gently applied lotion, and dressed comfortably within minutes. Juliana tucked her brunette hair into the pouch of her red hoodie and sat on a bench downstairs by the main entrance, waiting for Quinton to find his car keys in his bedroom. She closed her eyes as her body increased in heat. Her pores secreted, and the excess amount of sweat dripped onto her dark blue jeans as she looked down at her dark blue Toms on her feet. She felt constricted by her tight jeans and drowsy by her change in body temperature. Her nose turned slightly pink as she sneezed repeatedly, and something about the atmosphere within Quinton's household tangled her mind into a knot. She was confused and did not understand her sudden sickness as she looked at Quinton fidgeting with his car keys as he walked down the wooden stairs, wearing a dark blue polo golf shirt, mustard chinos, and light brown loafers on his feet, and a silver watch shining brightly throughout. His presence radiated a sense of hostility even whilst he pretended that everything was fine. The monsters within his mind were growing large, and he knew that his existence was trailing towards nothing significantly pleasant. He stepped off the last wooden step and kissed Juliana on her forehead.

For the first ever, his touch felt averagely normal to her. She stood up before him and hugged tightly with hope that her uncertainty would vanish away from her heart. The person she'd fallen in love with was deeply caged away within his body. Therefore, she tried to squeeze the affectionate person out of him. He always remained so gentle towards her and opened the front door for her. She held on to his hand and walked with him towards the passenger door with a baffled mind state, wondering what secrets were hidden within his big heart. It wasn't normal for Quinton to keep anything from her, but like all men who know the delicacy of their lovers, he also knew that revealing every information can lead to a disastrous ending.

That heavy anchor of information stored within his mind was slowly sinking him away from her, and they could both feel the effects of the water clogging their hearts away from love. She closed her green eyes as she reclined the passenger seat backwards, and her mind slowly drifted away from reality and into her dreams.

Quinton did not speak much as he drove away from his household, and dark thoughts of his dead uncle gradually passed within his mind from time to time, but he suddenly got used to the idea of his uncle's blood metaphorically dripping from his hands. He would imaginatively see the bloodstains imprinted on his clothing, and every single time, he would try to wipe his hands against his clothing, looking at his reflection in the mirror, but he also felt evoked towards insanity as he'd search himself for clarity. His mind could not make out what was real anymore, for his dreams and nightmares gradually became plain and aligned with his reality. He knew not to speak of such matters to Juliana, and their partnership was strained because of his secret.

Minutes passed as his silver watch ticked loudly in the car. He drove towards the nearest private hospital, and it was quiet within his car, but his mind remained loud with Steve's cry. He looked at the red traffic lights and felt like a cow being led into a kraal. The idea of balance and supposedly somebody else influencing his daily decisions bothered him as he thought of the system made to keep humans under control. His mind inflated, and he became stubborn towards human conventions. He didn't want to listen to anybody anymore because nobody seemed credible now, and as he turned left towards the hospital, Juliana's Blackberry started ringing in the cup holder.

She awoke and squinted at the touchscreen whilst brushing her brunette hair backwards with her left hand. They glanced at each other with uncertainty as Quinton parked in the empty parking lot. Juliana wondered what she'd say to her mother as she looked at Quinton for advice, but he was just as speechless as she was. Her left thumb swiped halfway through his clear touchscreen, and she paused until the phone call went to voicemail.

'Let it ride, baby!' Quinton said and opened the car door.

She turned nervous as she opened the passenger door and realised that she was walking towards a dark uncertain future. Quinton looked at Juliana and could sense hostility coming his way as she folded her arms and kept quiet as she stepped through the front hospital sliding doors. The medicine smell from the indoor pharmacy closest to the cafeteria in the near distance entered through her nostrils, making her noxiously sick, and she sat on a light brown couch away from the reception whilst Quinton asked for assistance. The scenery projected brightly towards her green eyes as she looked downwards at the sunlight reflection on the tiles underneath her feet.

'Come!' Quinton whispered, and he held on to her slippery, sweaty right hand in her red hoodie pocket.

Her instinct willed her upwards as she held on to him tightly, and they walked away, but a part of her wasn't sure of him anymore. They entered a depressive state on their way to the consultation section and tried to subconsciously prepare for the worst news, which initially was supposed to be their best news. Their minds couldn't quite wrap around the supposedly extraordinary gift coming their way, and their hearts were stumbling towards the beautiful gesture coming from above as they stepped into another waiting room.

The tiles were cool, and the atmosphere around was hollow. Trolley wheels rolled slowly in the background and grazed over every squared tile. Telephones rang around them, and all sounds manifested into an echo and rattled Juliana's mind as she waited quietly. She placed her head onto Quinton's thighs and closed her eyelids with hopes that she was being paranoid about her pregnancy.

In that state, Quinton's brown eyes remained glued towards a large round silver clock with a dark blue metallic background layer, and he thought of the imbalance a child could cause to their future and also wondered if it was selfish to have such thoughts trailing within him.

An old man walked out of the first door and was gently assisted by a nurse in light blue outfit. She guided him towards the exit and watched him walk alone though the empty passage.

'Are you sure I shouldn't help you?' she asked, and her sweet tone rushed into Quinton's ears. He looked away as he realised that the nurse looked like Layla.

Her eyes shone of bronze, and she kneeled by Juliana who was momentarily floating in and out of consciousness.

'Are you okay, darling?' she asked and looked at Quinton for an answer.

'She is sick!' he replied. 'We don't know the cause!' he added and stroked Juliana's hair away from her forehead.

'Well, come in!' the nurse said and stood up straight.

Her name tag proclaimed a rare name, and her persona immediately drew Quinton in. He immediately realised that he was drawn to strangers that resembled the people he already knew, and this attraction wasn't sexual at all but definitely heart filling because his heart throbbed purely for Layla. This ethos made him realise that he had a wandering eye for other women, and that bothered him because he wasn't always that way. He was losing his morals to the comfort he had in his immortal desires and his mid-twenties were initially his stagnation for mistakes to occur because it seemed as if though a lot of people around him weren't bothered by the experimenting. The single room had an office table, two wooden chairs on the visitation side, and on the opposite end was a hospital stretcher and light blue curtains around it. Juliana sat on the hospital stretcher and took off her red hoodie.

'Sir, I need you to step out for a minute!' Amelia, the nurse, stated, and Quinton seemed uneasy about the request.

'It's okay, baby. I will be out in a while!' Juliana said as she brushed her straight brunette hair backwards and smiled.

Quinton sat on the sideline on a bench and wondered what he'd say it to his parents as he looked around the hospital and a memory so far gone within his memory bank rushed towards him, unveiling fast from the past. He remembered himself walking through the same passage in his little red sneakers as a child, walking behind his older sister as she dragged a dark brown teddy bear behind her. They seemed so lost after escaping from their aunts at the reception, and they marched searching for their parents who were in the delivery room. It was the moment Beth was giving birth to Kimberly, and Quinton could remember walking behind Malinda, wondering where babies came from. They looked at the white walls, and everything seemed different as they discovered large light brown doors flapping in different directions at the end of the curved passage. There were a lot of grey wheelchairs compressed and stacked in a storage room on the right side, and Quinton could remember the first unpleasant feeling of deemed darkness rushing towards him from the storage room. The thought of evil rattled his little mind then, and he held on to his sister's teddy bear's hand as they walked together towards the light brown doors.

Quinton stood up from the bench and walked towards his memory and felt an uneasy wave of evil brushing at him again as he moved towards the light blue flapping door, which were light brown before. The light brown doors around him in the past had turned light blue, but the hospital structure was the same. He turned right and faced the additional dark curtained hospital room, which had been renovated from a storage room, and could see the yellow eyes glowing within the room.

Luther had found him again. The younger version of Quinton stood still by the light brown doors with Malinda and heard Kimberly crying out loud from inside the delivery rooms, and the present version of him could hear Arabella's loud cries within his mind as he remained still, trying to subconsciously dismiss the dark cloud hovering over his head.

'Your child will destroy everything!' Luther whispered into Quinton's right ear, and his presence was invincible as Quinton looked towards the hospital room.

It occurred to him that he'd imbedded darkness into his life, and he did not know how to get rid of it. The visual memory vanished right before his brown eyes, and all he could hear was Arabella crying out loud inside his mind whilst he walked back to the waiting room.

Juliana walked out of the hospital consultation room with Amelia, and they seemed uncertain of the Juliana's sickness. She had a prescription paper in her left hand and a red hoodie in her right arm. Quinton looked downwards at her beautifully shaped body and analysed her flat stomach as she fixed her white belt around her hips and fixed her red bra strings on her shoulders.

'Thanks so much, Amelia!' Juliana said and smiled as she faced Amelia.

'You are so welcome!' Amelia replied. 'Keep her safe, Quinton!' she said.

'I will!' Quinton responded and seemed sceptical of their happiness. Juliana seemed so much better than before, but her silence kept Quinton anxious.

'She is such an amazing person!' Juliana stated as they walked towards the pharmacy section. 'She and I should hang soon!' she added and passed the prescription list to Quinton.

He glanced down the list and saw 'pregnancy test' at the bottom. 'Pregnancy test?' he asked.

'Yes, baby, but we must remain calm!' she replied with maturity. 'I'll sit by the cafeteria, love. Please get those for me!' she whispered and moved closer for a kiss on her lips.

There was still life in their romance as her lips touched his. The feeling of love radiated and bloomed on their bodies as their lips touched once more. She closed her eyelids and held on to that mesmerising vulnerable feeling as Quinton walked away from her. Her phone vibrated inside her jean pocket and rang seconds after.

'Hey, Mom' she answered.

'Your voicemail seemed urgent. What is wrong?' Marissa asked.

'Have a fever, and umm, well, I think . . .' Juliana paused and sat on red plastic chair and placed her items onto the smartly carved-out wooden table. 'I think that I'm pregnant, Mom!' she added and grinned with uncertainty of her mother's reaction.

It turned quiet for a while as Juliana and Marissa thought of their next words to each other. Her mother sat on to her bedspread in her bedroom in Johannesburg, facing her late husband's photo, and she felt as though a knife had pierced her heart.

'Mother?' Juliana said and waited for a response, but no words were expressed from her mother for a while.

Marissa's breaths grew louder over the phone as she stood up from her bed and walked towards her balcony with disappointment plastered all over face.

'Well, I'm not sure yet!' Juliana stated. 'I'm so sorry. I will find out and let you know!' she stated and hoped for a response. Instead, her mother hung up the phone, and the *beep* sound shattered both their hearts into a dozen pieces.

Salty tears raced from Juliana's green eyes face as she looked downwards and realised that she missed her mother so much and needed her more than ever. Her mind clinched onto the memories of her youth, and she felt incredibly nostalgic as she thought of how lonely her mother must be without her daughter or her late husband.

Quinton noticed Juliana on a downward spiral, and he knew that he was to be blamed for the sudden sadness. There was a deep-rooted sadness within her soul which added more pain to her sorrow every single time she was upset, and as her tears raced down her cheeks, she felt a deeper longing that Quinton couldn't fill anymore. He knew this factor as he brought all the essential products from the pharmacy with him, and he was momentarily embarrassed of the negativity silently growing within him about his supposed unborn child. He discovered Juliana's tears dripping onto the floor as she placed her face in between her thighs.

'You did this!' she said as he kneeled down and hugged her tightly, hoping to scrape away her oncoming depression and advocate the goodness within him.

'Let's go find out first, baby. I will always be with you, always!' he said and rubbed her back whilst his right cheek was stuck on to her right cheek.

His words breached her right ear drum and the word 'always' stuck on to her mind at that moment. She stood up with her mind somewhat reassured, but her heart had deeply sunk into his vortex as they walked out through the front hospital sliding door. The humid weather brushed their faces as they prepared for the inevitable, they and individually walked towards Quinton's Grand Cherokee. She entered his port of uncertainty as he started his car and drove away. His watch winded slowly as it ticked to their moment of truth, and they kept quiet throughout their trip back to Quinton's home, wondering if a murky future was unfolding right before their naked eyes.

'I'm so scared!' Juliana stated and clinched onto her red hoodie, waiting for Quinton's words of wisdom.

His mind had drifted back to the dark cloud hovering over his head, and at the same time, his watch ticked so loudly into his ears. His mind was close to eruption, and she immediately noticed small frown lines cloud his forehead. Therefore, she held on to his left hand tightly by the cup holder.

'We'll be fine!' he replied and thought of the goals he hadn't achieved whilst looking back at the time he'd spent in his home country.

He felt Steve's image plaster onto his face and immediately felt like an underachiever with little virtues, using his parents' fortune for comfort. Quinton had gotten used to the idea of getting a severance package every once in a while and knew that he'd actually have to work if Juliana was pregnant.

The Barkers were false, painting a pretext of happiness, pretending like everything was fine whilst evil grew within their souls. Beth had made her way home from her law firm as the sun wandered towards the western world, and she was in a magnificently good mood until she noticed her son's pale face in the living room whilst Juliana was lying on Kimberly's bed upstairs. Quinton and Juliana had agreed to hold off the pregnancy notification until the house was soundless that evening. Marcus was back in his study, and it seemed as though he'd not changed much after his months in prison, and it was quite evident that he was back to plotting against his competitors as the smell of cigars waivered through the empty passages.

'Are you okay?' Beth asked her son and closed the maroon curtains in the living room.

'I'm fine!' he replied and looked at the plasma screen, pretending to focus on CNN.

His mother stated and asked, 'Juliana is leaving soon. Don't you think that we should have a special dinner before she goes?'

'Beg your pardon?' Quinton said in confusion.

'I spoke to Marissa on the phone, and she said that she'd already bought a plane ticket for Juliana!' Beth said. 'Juliana didn't say anything to you?' she asked and moved towards the main entrance.

'No, she didn't!' he replied and felt the world crumbling around him. He couldn't quite grasp the elements working against him as he sat up straight and picked up his light brown loafers from the wooden floor.

'Well, I thought that you knew, hence that facial expression of yours!' she added and walked away. Her heel points poked onto the tile floor as she entered the kitchen and poured herself a glass of white Chardonnay wine.

Quinton stood up in the living room and walked towards the wooden stairs, speechless and heartbroken because he did not want Juliana to leave. It was blatantly selfish as he realised that he was becoming possessive of her. Maybe he was holding on to his last bit of pleasant humanity stored somewhere within her body, or maybe he was scared of what he'd become without her being there to support him. He looked at the open main balcony doors and remembered the New Year's Eve party that his parents had thrown awhile back, and he immediately saw Juliana standing there in her blue evening dress smiling beautifully at him. Everything seemed so different then as he smiled back and watched the image vanish right before his brown eyes to the cool breeze blowing in from the world. He walked through the hollow passage destroyed by their recent revelation, and he feared for the truth.

Kimberly's bedroom door was open, and he entered gracefully, hoping to see his lover sleeping peacefully, but instead the white duvet sheets were untouched. The bedroom balcony sliding door was open, and Juliana had been seated there on the couch with her legs folded. Her mind was miles away as Quinton called out her name, and she felt distorted by her foreseen future. He moved the curtains in front him with his left hand, entered through the balcony sliding door, and found Juliana cuddled alone in her little bubble.

'It's time!' he said, but she could not hear him.

She thought about her music for the first time in a very long time and realised that she'd given up a career for love without any insurance. At that moment, she realised that sadness was indeed her muse and immediately felt compelled to sing again. Her own voice rose within her mind, and she could remember the first time she'd ever met Quinton at the music festival. His presence had preserved a view of man who was lost in the world, willing to find out if life had anything else to offer besides misery, the same misery that she'd had. Initially, she started to see that love is a cosmetic star that brought about unpredictability and uncertified happiness through their dark skies.

They could feel themselves falling from above as they walked into Kimberly's bedroom, and they felt the hard surface floor cripple their minds as they entered the bathroom. Quinton switched on the bathroom light whilst Juliana unwrapped the brown pharmacy packet and took out the pregnancy test box. She looked at Quinton as she walked towards the toilet, and he looked back whilst seated on the edge of the bathtub. Quinton took the pregnancy box from her right hand and silently read the self-explanatory instructions. Juliana seemed nervous as she placed the pink and white pregnancy stick between her legs. She closed her green eyes as she pissed onto the tip end of the pregnancy stick, and her heart throbbed intensely fast inside her chest, beating against her black lungs and increasing her nicotine cravings.

They waited for the truth after Juliana had wiped the pregnancy stick with toilet paper. She placed the pregnancy stick onto the bathtub edge and looked at Quinton whilst his brown eyes remained glued to the white blank space on the pregnancy stick. He turned extremely quiet whilst she spoke to soothe the mood, and her voice slowly started to decrease as he zoomed in towards their moment of truth. He grew impatient and therefore stood up and held on to the pregnancy stick with his left hand, stepping on the black tiles and trying to dismiss the darkness within him from speaking out. Juliana kept quiet as she zipped her jeans and washed her hands by the basin. She waited to see if he was a real man or just an imposter claiming to be real.

Nothing else mattered at that moment as they stood before the wall mirror and waited. Juliana's nerves pounded within her skin as the white blank space on the pregnant stick turned positive.

'Well, I guess there is the baby we so wanted!' Quinton said sarcastically and hoped that that positive sign would turn negative after some time but nothing changed. He wondered what he'd say to his parents as Juliana placed her skinny warm arms around his body and placed her soft hands onto his upper back.

'I'm so scared!' she whispered and placed her head onto his chest, facing his dark bedroom on the right side of bathroom.

She felt crippled within, and all she wanted to do was sleep by him and worry about everything else later. His mind juggled all options, and he thought of the blessing from above and how it would cause an imbalance to their lives. He slowly inhaled the cool air coming from his youngest sister's bedroom and felt flustered.

'Come, let's go to bed!' Juliana said and held out her left hand as she walked towards his bedroom.

He looked at her soft hand and knew that he had to rise up to the occasion and be a real man. It was all confusing because they weren't from the same region, and that initially caused a lot of tension between them as they lay by each other quietly and tried to rest, but their futures seemed uneasy as they closed their eyes and hoped for the best.

'We will be okay. I promise!' he stated and kissed her forehead as she snuggled up beside him.

'Quinton, I'm leaving soon!' she said.

'I know!' he replied and covered Juliana's body with his cream white duvet.

'I'm sorry I didn't tell you before!' she whispered.

'It's okay. We will find a way!' he whispered back and kissed her soft lips.

'We always find a way!' she added.

Her love essentially inspired him to be better, but the bomb shell that had just been dropped made other alternatives elusive.

They awoke the next morning hoping that the previous day was nothing but a bad dream. It seemed normal as the sun glazed through the maroon curtain sides whilst birds chirped on a thorn tree nearby. Juliana looked towards the ceiling, picked up her Blackberry from the wooden floor, and looked at it in disbelief as she noticed eleven missed calls and an additional email from her mother.

The email read:

> I have changed your air ticket to tomorrow night at 20:30.
> I hope that you are on that flight back home. I miss you,
> and I hope that you know what you are doing. I pray for you
> always and hope that you understand that I'm your mother,
> and I will love you unconditionally.
>
> Yours sincerely,
> Marissa Rose

Juliana read the email again, and her eyes became wet as she realised that she was still pregnant. Everything about this moment was surreal, and she wondered what she would do next with her life as she sat up straight. She gave Quinton her Blackberry to read the email, and he felt dented within his heart by the words on her touchscreen.

'Please don't go!' he pleaded and planted his face deeply into his pillow, feeling dispersed by her upcoming departure. 'Does your mother know?' he asked.

'Yeah, she knows, and that's why she wants me home so quickly!' Juliana responded and stood up slowly, making her way to the shower whilst Quinton switched on his laptop by his study table.

He tacked his sport magazines into one pile and opened the maroon curtains by the bedside for first time that week. He joined his lover within the shower. Juliana closed her eyes as Quinton held on to her tightly whilst the warm water rained down. Her mind was troubled with havoc as winds blew misery within, and she did not know where they'd reach their child. Essentially, Juliana's mindset was gravitating towards the northern hemisphere simply because that's where she'd grown up, but she also wondered what Quinton would say about this matter. They stood together but their hearts were moving away from each other. She could not feel the vibrancy in his heartbeat anymore, and his mind was lost in a different time. He looked back at his youth and felt tormented by his lack of success.

Quinton placed his right hand onto Juliana's flat stomach.

'We will be okay!' he said twice and kissed her wet forehead and brushed away her wet brunette hair away from her face with both hands.

She wanted to run away from him at that moment, for everything around her was so confusing. He was still so passionate yet lacked honestly in most cases. His answers throughout were initially vague, and she hated what he was becoming. Their relationship was strained because they didn't communicate as much as they used to, and as the warm water rained onto them, they realised that they were in a toxic relationship that would probably end in disaster. She feared for their outcome as she stepped away and felt a deep hole open inside her chest, wondering if she could ever find herself alone and without him.

His thoughts trended similarly as he picked up as a yellow sponge from the soap hanger and gestured to wash her back with aroma shower therapy gel. She turned around, and he placed his warm left hand onto her left shoulder whilst he placed the yellow sponge onto her lower back and washed her thoroughly. She felt captured by his gentle hands, and it was extremely difficult for her to ignore the power he had over her body.

'I'm all yours!' he whispered into her right ear, and she longed to hear words like those coming out of his mouth.

'I know you are. I'm yours too!' she responded.

They were trying to hold on to what they had, but the universe was acting so defensively towards them. She closed her eyes as he kissed the left side of her neck and dropped the yellow soapy sponge onto the wet floor. They attempted to make love but felt different after recent events.

'Stop!' she said and gasped for air. 'We can't do this anymore!' she whispered in agony.

Their inner wounds opened up at that point as those words lashed into Quinton's ears. 'Okay, I will stop!' he replied and held on to her body tightly.

'Not this, everything!' she said. 'I can't do this anymore!' she added and slid off. 'We need to stop this!' she said and looked down.

She was tired of disappointing herself and believing that love was the best resort. Initially, they knew the love that kept the human race highly spirited but also found out that being in love was a completely different scenario and mostly heart draining. She needed to shell herself away from him before it became too late, and the thought of staying with him led her to believe that she would lose herself inside their relationship. Thus, she walked out and entered Kimberly's bedroom alone and closed the door behind her.

Juliana walking away shattered him, and he couldn't quite understand her motives for doing so, especially with the situation they were in. The visual of his future with her immediately turned blurry within his mind, and he did not know what to say to her.

He wore a silky white T-shirt and searched for a pair of dark blue jeans in his wardrobe. His mind scrolled through all options as he thought of the way forward. He wore his pair of light blue jeans and placed a red snapback cap on his head. He needed time to think alone. Therefore, he looked for his car keys around his bedroom whilst wearing his white sock, fitting his feet into his high-top dark blue sneakers.

Every sensitive touch gushed out from Juliana and rushed towards him, imprinting her fingers onto his back as he walked past Kimberly's bedroom without saying anything to her. He'd always wondered what it would feel like to walk away from the relationship he had with Juliana, and at first it felt normal as he walked out the front door, but as he walked towards his car, it felt like he was walking up a steep mountain. It became extremely hard to take in her recent words as those same words stabbed him repeatedly in his heart, and as he looked up for pride, his heart shrunk into peanut size.

He reversed his car and called his friends as he drove away from his home. Most of his friends all had to leave for their next semester within a few days, and saying goodbye in an old-fashioned manner seemed highly appropriate.

Chapter Fourteen

Drifting Apart

Sandstorms circulated wildly around the Diamond City. The main roads were congested with the traffic of public transportation vehicles everywhere. Nothing seemed clear anymore as the dust blew towards Quinton's car during rush hour. He felt momentarily lost without Juliana as he thought more of her. Hazard lights within traffic were lighted in different sections whilst multiple sandstorms blew from residential areas onto the main roads and into to commercial areas.

Quinton looked around and wondered whether the country was blessed, for it had amazing potential and good developments rising or whether it was cursed by a deep-rooted sadness relishing through the dusty atmosphere and causing people to act so unpleasantly towards each other. His wise friend had said to him earlier, 'Envy and hate is accustomed to what's essentially ugly because of its inability to grasp the beauty of love, for love knows how to blossom even in the darkest places in the world. It's patient and grounded. It brings stability. It is needed because it's always in a position to lead your heart towards peace.' Quinton understood those words clearly as a lot people looked at him in an unfriendly manner whilst he moved through the traffic jam, listening to the latest hip-hop artist's albums from his iPad connected by Bluetooth to the car system. His nerves were eased by the alcohol that he'd consumed at William's house, and he was glad that he'd met up with most of his friends to say goodbye to them.

An epiphany had reached him minutes after he'd walked past Juliana earlier that all good things indeed come to an end. Those words were sinking through his skull into his brain slowly, causing a ripple effect through his body and into his heart. A tear dripped from his left heavy eyelid, and he realised that his heart was still big as it throbbed loudly within him. It was growing bigger than ever regardless of how small he thought it was. Quinton was shocked by everything working against him.

'How did we get here? And how do I fix it?' he asked himself whilst paranoia reigned over him and he realised that he was losing someone so important to him.

'Love can be also crazy and overwhelming if one isn't taught how to handle it properly,' his friend had said earlier too.

All these words and feelings racing towards him were destroying him as he realised that he hadn't learned how to love purely. He gripped the leather steering wheel tightly, trying to hold back his tears by looking upwards but they raced downwards even faster than usual. The dust outside represented more than just his place of origin, but it also represented an ongoing struggle for him to see the truth of unclear pictures, the truthful reality that he did not want to see whilst the traffic started moving again. His mind had been clouded by Steve's death that he couldn't see that Juliana wasn't meant to return to him because her heart belonged to her music and his heart belonged to his world. They were products made to influence the world by the goodness in their hearts. His heart was manufactured to be vacant towards others, but he didn't want to be selfless towards anybody. He wanted to be selfish with everything, including Juliana's love, and to be completely consumed by everything she had to offer to the world. Initially she was his world, but she didn't want live in him anymore. That aspect bothered him so much as he drove through the front gate and into his home driveway whilst wet tears streamed from his brown eyes. Quinton and Juliana were supposed to have been two strangers passing by each other instead of them pledging long-term legions to each other.

Juliana was beginning to see that her path wasn't aligned with her lover's path anymore. Therefore, she wanted to run away from him now but still felt so consumed by his love. She felt crippled by recent events and felt evoked from her independence the second she sat on the dinner table that Beth had set up. The kitchen and main entrance smelt of sweet-and-sour chicken stew, a whiff of boiling pasta, and fried onions. Supper wasn't ready yet, and Beth wondered why Juliana wasn't in the mood for some Chardonnay as she offered a full glass.

'What is wrong, love?' Beth asked as she placed both glasses onto the dining table and sat on a chair.

'Nothing, I'm okay!' she said, lying to herself and Beth.

'You are just like my son, Juliana!' Beth stated. 'I'm a lawyer. I know when someone is hiding something!' she added.

'Well, I'm leaving!' Juliana said and started crying.

'Yes, carry on!' Beth said, encouraging Juliana to realize all her baggage, placing her left hand onto Juliana's back. 'It's okay. I told your mother that I will always be here to listen to you!'

Juliana took a moment to think about her next words carefully whilst glancing at Quinton's family portrait in between two arch entrances, one leading to the kitchen and the other leading to the main entrance. Two drops of salty tears dripped onto the table as she wiped her pinkish cheeks with the serviettes next to the silver cutlery.

'Please excuse me!' Juliana said and walked away.

She tried to outrun her problems as she rushed upstairs to be alone in Kimberly's bedroom but felt invaded by a knock on the door.

'Please just leave me alone. I will be out soon!' she said and sniffed.

'May I come in?' Quinton asked after poking his head past the slightly opened bedroom door.

'Go away!' Juliana replied and covered herself with the cream white duvet.

'I'm not going anywhere until we've fixed this!' he said and closed the bedroom door behind him, moving towards the bed slowly.

'What are we fixing?' she asked whilst weeping.

Juliana uncovered herself and sat up straight. Her eyelids were moist, polished in pink, and she looked devastated whilst sniffing more. Her mind spiralled whilst she spoke, and she felt completely drowsy. She was having another anxiety attack as Quinton sat by her and gently placed his arms around her.

'I shouldn't have come back!' she added.

Her words buried his confidence, and yet he couldn't quite let go of her body. They kept quiet as the wind rushed through the open balcony door. Quinton stood up, switched off the bedroom light by the bathroom door, and entered the bed with Juliana. Quinton's parents were downstairs, having dinner in the dining room and celebrating their victory against their odds. Beth giggled through her flash of memories and increased the volume on the surround system with a remote control, singing along to a mellow classic song from the past, and whilst she did so, Juliana's mind drifted to visuals of her beloved mother.

Juliana wept more underneath the duvet covers. Every guitar string flicked within the song flicked the cords within her heart as her tears streamed. It was all coming down on her. She broke down.

The lyrics came from the open windows downstairs onto the wild winds outside, through the cool atmosphere, and entered through the balcony sliding door. It was so loud within the household. Quinton and Juliana couldn't think of anything at that moment but to enjoy their little time together. She rested her head onto her left shoulder as the song played. They were so exhausted from fighting against each other. It only felt right for them to keep quiet and to allow the song to finish off. Goosebumps cropped up on her skin as the wind blew in and scattered the inner white curtains in different directions.

'Should I sleep by you?' Quinton asked whilst massaging her back gently.

She felt highly nostalgic, depressed, and gutted by the decision she'd made to leave him. Being together one last time brought back their memory in Little Venice as they lay by each other. Quinton slid off his shoes and moved closer towards Juliana in Kimberly's bed. Their memories unchained within their minds ran free and wild through the plain white ceiling above them. A projection of the time well spent and those memories unfolded right before their naked eyes. They could see everything they'd done and how happy they were. It all seemed so simple in the beginning, a smile for a smile, a kind gesture for a kind gesture, profound intimacy and pure selfless love projecting brightly through their darkest and saddest ending, so they believed. No words could accommodate or bring closure to the despair blustering through their hearts at that moment. Juliana placed her right hand onto his chest and felt his heart chanting for closure as it throbbed within his chest. She'd never known of it to be that loudly vibrate, and this made it extremely difficult for her to shy away from the love they still had for each other. His heart punched repeatedly against his lungs as loud as he closed his eyes. It punched continuously for attention almost as if it knew that she was being avoidant towards him. His sadness duplicated and plastered onto her face as she lay quietly by him. It wasn't in their nature to be this depressed, and they evidently knew having sex wouldn't cure the deep-rooted disease that kept cropping up every single time they were faced with problems.

'Never call a problem a problem. Rather, call it a challenge. That way, you know that you can overcome it' Marcus would say whenever advising Quinton on a particular situation.

Quinton kept quiet whilst Beth played more music from the surround system downstairs, and he waited patiently for Juliana to say something much meaningful to his ear, but she also kept quiet.

'Do you believe in fate?' she asked, the same way he'd asked her the first time. Quinton wasn't so sure of his answer. A lot had happened since then, but he searched for a thought within his mind to uproot an answer yet still gave the same answer that she'd given before.

'It depends on one's path!' he replied. They laughed out loud for a few seconds and reclined back into their depressive state. Her departure had turned into a memorial service, and they couldn't quite understand all the emotions that had gathered into the bedroom.

'These pregnancy tests aren't accurate. I think that we should try again in the morning!' Quinton stated and lifted his phone upwards to a ringing tone. It was Emily Lith.

'Why is she calling you?' Juliana asked and frowned.

'I don't know. Ask her!' Quinton replied and handed Juliana his Blackberry.

'Emily!' Juliana answered.

'Oh hey, a little bird told me that you are leaving tomorrow!' Emily stated. 'I'm with some friends. Come over!' she added.

'Okay, we will come over just now!' Juliana replied and hung up immediately. 'Why would she call you!?' Juliana asked.

'Well, for that reason, I guess!' Quinton sighed and sat up straight.

'I'm not disloyal to you like you think I am!' he said.

'I don't think that you are disloyal. You just keep things from me!' she said.

Quinton looked towards the bathroom lighting and avoided that conversation by standing up.

'Let's go hang with your lover!' he said and laughed.

'She is your lover too!' Juliana said and stood up with uncertainty.

'Then why are you mad that she called?' he asked.

Juliana turned quiet to the question. 'You have always had a way with words, baby!' she replied. 'She mustn't try fuck you whilst I'm away!' she said.

'So does this mean that we are still together?' he asked as they both stumbled through the awkwardness.

Juliana accidentally kicked her black luggage bag and tripped over another right by the bedside as Quinton switched on the bedroom light.

'I love you!' he said. 'You are so clumsy, it's adorable!' he added words and laughed at the same time.

The lights were back on, and her spirit was slightly uplifted as she wore her dark blue palms and brushed her brunette hair backwards with a pink comb next to the bedroom mirror. She was an absolute mess. Her cheeks were moist, her eyes were red from crying before, and her nose was pink from sniffing.

'We need to be logical and face the truth soon though!' she said and walked towards the bathroom to wash her face as Quinton walked into his bedroom and changed into a tight-fitted black T-shirt.

They felt the voids within their hearts enlarging again whilst ignoring everything that was already scripted within their next chapter. The wind wavered away until it turned cool outside. Grey clouds above drizzled out cool drops of agony onto them as they walked towards the front gate to Emily Lith's household on the same road. Nothing constructive was said in between their vague chats, and the tension hovering within their radius boiled their uneasy minds into frustration. Quinton wondered what he'd say to Juliana to keep her from leaving, and she wondered what she'd say to him to make him understand that her love for him ran so deeply that she'd even sacrifice their relationship if it resulted in them growing up. She looked towards the right and watched him speak as they walked, wondering he if knew of his greatness yet. His words drew her closer and closer. His presence was adorning every single time, but she also felt that he didn't belong to her and thus didn't want to be possessive of him anymore. Her decision to leave him whipped her heart senselessly with more pain.

'The world is sadistic, I suppose,' she thought to herself, and she wore the bravest face she'd ever worn in her entire life as walked on the tarred road, underneath thick tree branches. Her salty tears peeped over the edge of her eyelids. She feared that she'd cry at any moment whilst he kept speaking. He looked at her as she pretended to be composed.

'Stop!' he commanded and reached out for her love with both hands.

She hesitated from the friction of his hands touching her forearms and stepped away from him immediately as she realised that she would always feel drawn to him.

'Stop pretending like everything is fine. There is a possible chance that I'm carrying a baby right now!' she said. 'What's going to happen?' she asked. 'Am I going to stay here, and we live happily ever after?'

All these questions entering through his ears lured him into his darkest side. His brown eyes painted twenty-two years of harvested pain, existing from the time he could remember teaching himself how to ride a bicycle alone. He could not bring himself to lose her, for she was supposedly the light at the end of his tunnel.

'We have to make it work!' he shouted, knowing that he'd lose composure. His red blood boiled within his body as he spoke, sounding illusive and mad.

'Please don't shout at me!' she pleaded in a low tone, hoping he'd see what he was becoming.

But he didn't stop shouting at her. His mind was weighing an imbalanced life consisting of love, obtaining money, and grasping real power over other people. Juliana could see her nightmare rising out of his brown eyes whilst his mouth moved. It seemed so quiet for a few seconds, and everything felt slow as she evaluated his facial expression. Her heart grew more placated by the idea of running away from him forever. 'He can't possibly be the man I fell in love with,' her subconscious whispered.

She slowly reached out for his face with her right hand, feeling sorry for him. Her light-toned right hand mediated for peace as its warmness touched his cool left cheek, and all the demons causing havoc and wars within his heart ran and hid cowardly to the darkest parts of his soul. He couldn't quite understand what he was becoming. Their unborn child cried out loud within his mind as her hand gently imprinted onto the back of his neck.

'I'm sorry!' he said. 'I'm so sorry!' he sighed and searched for forgiveness in her green eyes.

Her face glowed from an unknown reason. She was definitely ageing with more beauty as every second passed, and her maturity level was beginning to exceed his. The frustration kept building inside of him as they walked. He couldn't say anything right anymore, for anything he'd say would lead to an argument.

'These things happen, Quinton!' she said and rang the intercom in front of the Lith residence.

The yard was wide with green grass everywhere. A grey brick road curved right with street lamps on both sides, leading all the way to a grey mansion established around a few trees. Emily's family mansion glowed bright from the wall lights around the edges. It smelt earthly and moist around the yard. The sounds of folk and indie music rushed towards Juliana's ears as Emily answered the intercom.

'Have a problem opening the gate!' she said.

'I'm coming!' She hung up the intercom and switched off the camera monitor by the doorway in her home.

'We are drowning!' Juliana said whilst trying to overcome her exhaustion.

Their faces projected misery towards Emily who was in a delightful mood yet felt partly curious to know their mysterious trial. She pressed onto a dark green oval gate remote with her left hand and waited for her favourite couple to enter.

'Actually, take all that negative energy and leave it here!' Emily said, smiling like child in a candy shop.

Her brown eyes lit up Juliana's mood as they all hugged each other. Quinton remained mostly quiet behind Emily and Juliana as they all walked to the grey mansion. The sounds of folk music blasted from the household windows as Quinton listened more whilst trying to block out the sounds of loud crickets in the green grass. Emily's dark blue M6 was the only car parked in front of one of the four dark grey garage doors. She opened the only grey door in between the garage area and the mansion. Something about the entrance reminded Quinton of a vague dream he'd had in the past of a little girl running towards him happily. It seemed quite bizarre as Emily's German shepherds moved towards them and sniffed Juliana's ankle. One of the dogs sniffing was a replica of the one he'd dreamed about. Nothing made sense as Quinton walked through the grey door and heard a childish laughter commencing through his ears, but there was no child running towards him. It all persisted to be unclear as he looked around and hoped for more signs to unveil before his brown eyes, but nothing else happened.

'Never knew you had German shepherds!' Quinton said.

'Eh, just a recent thing!' Emily replied. 'My dad got them a few days before I returned!' she added.

They all entered the courtyard and saw a dozen people seated on white garden chairs underneath her colourful umbrella. The surrounding grey walls were poked with larger circular light brown wooden window frames everywhere. Her house was very transparent from within and absolutely lovely to the common eye. There were so many light brown wooden door frames leading to different areas of the house. The inside was brightly lighted and absolutely beautiful to observe. Emily introduced Quinton and Juliana to her friends. The ratio of men to women was evenly accurate with a diverse balance to the scenery.

The playlist of mainstream folk music was delightful to Juliana's ears. She sat down on a black leather couch and covered her legs with Emily's dark red cotton blanket. It was a bit nippy outside, but she found complete comfort within her mind as two hours passed. It wasn't easy coming to terms with the fact that she was pregnant as the pregnancy stick had stated. She started contemplating about her blurry future whilst drinking mango juice and zoning out to everything mentioned.

Emily's southern hospitality showed a different side of her that Quinton knew nothing about. She seemed kind and generous to her visitors, offering them snacks and food she'd made that afternoon. Juliana hadn't quite realised how hungry she was until she feasted on a plate of beef lasagne and garlic bread. She remained seated and planted by Quinton on the black leather couch, but they felt so far away from each other. She didn't even want to hold on to his left hand. What began as a sweet partnership had turned into a sour merger with time. The sweet taste of the saliva on Juliana's tongue had turned bitter once Quinton French kissed her. He did not understand how their magical chemistry was all the sudden turning into a pit of shit. Her intention was to be avoidant towards every awkward glance coming from him for everyone's best interest around. They were fighting in a war without weapons. It essentially felt pointless because neither one of them could win. Their energy gloomed the atmosphere, and everyone turned bleak from it.

'I think we should go!' Juliana whispered into Quinton's left ear. 'Our conflict is clouding the area!'

'I agree!' Quinton replied. 'But we need to speak!'

'About what exactly?' she asked and felt strained by his words.

It seemed as if he couldn't say anything right to smoothen the frustration streaming through their veins. It began to rain as they stood up from the black leather couch.

'Emily, may you please drop us off?' Quinton asked and felt the cool breeze rush towards him.

'Yeah, sure!' Emily replied and entered through the living room sliding door to grab her car keys from an oval basket placed in the middle of the dark brown shiny dining room table. Lightning struck in the distance and caused an unpleasant torturous pain to Quinton's heart as Juliana walked away from him. His mind had exhausted all short-sighted options, and he didn't know how to control the outcome of the situation. It rained heavily as they all entered Emily's car. The interior smelt fragrantly new and elegant.

No words were exchanged throughout their short trip to the Barker household.

'Here we are, guys!' Emily said as she indicated right towards the black front gate.

'Thank you so much for dropping us off!' Juliana stated and rushed out from the passenger door after hugging Emily and saying goodbye.

Quinton opened the gate with a dark green remote from the backseat. He inhaled the fresh air and remained there, floating in a pool of sadness whilst Juliana ran towards the house. The driveway was wet and slippery from the green algae on the edges.

'Thanks so much, Emily!' Quinton said. 'We will chat soon!'

'Okay, love!' Emily replied and shifted the automatic gear stick into reverse.

He opened the left backseat door and walked out slowly, acting unfazed by the heavy rain drops washing over his face. The strong wind brushed against him, drifting him towards the right. Tree brunches waved wildly as he walked past the front gate. He did not look up as the thunder struck closely at first, but he could see Juliana from a distance, trying to stand up on the driveway as the thunder struck again. She stood up slowly with an injury on her right ankle. Quinton rushed towards her as she tried to limp forward.

'I'm here for you!' he said and picked her up. 'Are you okay?' he asked, filled with compassion in his brown eyes.

He kissed her soft wet lips repeatedly almost as if he was knocking at the heavy door guarding her heart away from him. She nodded slowly with her eyes closed and hid her face within his chest. They were soaked and wet as Quinton entered the house, carrying Juliana in his arms.

The house seemed strangely quiet. There was still a smell of dinner lingering from the kitchen entrance, and most of the lights around were off except for the lights upstairs next to the balcony sliding door. The hallway crept of cold chills as Quinton moved towards Kimberly's bedroom. He kneed onto his Kimberly's bed slowly and placed Juliana onto the bedspread gently.

'I'll always be here to carry you—remember that,' he whispered.

Quinton's love for Juliana was intensely consuming and impeccably confusing to say the least. Juliana frowned with the pain aching from her ankle as it swelled a little. It was slightly sprained and bruised pink.

'It fuckin' hurts!' Juliana sighed and placed her right hand on her swollen right ankle.

'Hold on!' Quinton said. 'I'll be back in a bit!' He rushed towards the bathroom doors and into his bedroom.

Juliana covered herself with the cream white duvet and left her right leg exposed to the bathroom light. Quinton returned and switched on the bedroom light by the bathroom entrance. He noticed the scar on her left thigh shaded by the cream white duvet. It reminded him of a dream he'd had on his trip to London whereby he a light brown horse was drinking from a clear crystal, and he certainly knew that Juliana was the loyal horse, but he also wondered why she wanted absolutely nothing to do with him.

'I can do it myself!' she said and reached out for the black medical aid kit on the bed.

'You get on my nerves when you get like this,' Quinton said. He kneeled and gently wiped her pinkish right ankle clean with a warm grey facecloth. 'Do you not understand how much I love you?' he added whilst wrapping her bruised ankle with a transact patch and covering it with a white bandage. 'What must I say to make it better? What should I do?' he asked and brushed her wet brunette hair away from her forehead with his right hand.

She looked absolutely beautiful as ever.

'A painting framed for any moment!' he whispered. 'Whether I'm in pain or scared of something, I can always look at you to bring me peace!'

She blinked in shame and looked down, realising that she still was trapped within his good heart. Her aching pain temporarily disappeared whilst her moist skin consumed his affectionate touch.

'Look at me!' he commanded. 'What do you see?' he asked and parked his lips onto hers for a few seconds. 'What do you see?' he asked again and sat by her side.

'I see a world covered in secrets!' she said. 'Open up to me, and tell me what you are keeping from me!'

'I can't tell you because it's not secret to begin with!' he said.

'So there is a secret?' she asked and moved away from him.

'Yes, there is!' he replied and paused for a while. All words within his mind jagged up and down as he wondered what he'd say next to Juliana. 'I . . .' he said, trying to paint a lighter picture of what had occurred under his supervision.

'Yes!' She gestured. 'Go on!' She placed her soft hands onto his jaws. 'You are so strong. I wish you could see that!' she whispered whilst looking directly into his brown eyes.

'I can't tell you!' he said, pleading for her to understand by looking directly into her green eyes.

'Well, I need you to leave me alone then!' she stated bravely yet remained uncertain of his reply as she lay underneath the cream white duvet. 'You have been drawn into a world filled with preconceived idea of wealth and a trail of pain that follows with it!' she said. 'I will not be shaded into your pain anymore!' she said and wept quietly.

He stood up and walked towards the bathroom door then stood still with his eyes closed by the brown door frame, wondering what he'd say to make her understand that he hadn't changed into this lost cause she could momentarily see. His throat remained clogged with voile secrets. He knew that he couldn't say anything right anymore thus switched Kimberly's bedroom light off and closed the door behind him.

It rained heavily throughout the late hours of the night and into the dark cloudy morning. The power within the household had gone off from midnight thunder showers and multiple lightning strikes in the Diamond City.

All the empty passages within the house were emotionally vacant. There was no life within the house. The thick passage walls had a lot of African cultural paintings, which echoed out a tribal sound of drums and laces beams. The early awakening was slightly dreadful, and Quinton felt as like he'd had slept much. His face was moulded with heavy bags underneath his red eyes. He couldn't quite remember anything he'd dreamed about and couldn't quite figure out why his body was so strained. It felt awfully strange to have awoken away from Juliana, especially because it was her last night. He lay flat onto his back underneath his maroon duvet covers whilst consuming the thought of being alone.

A whiff of cold air rushed through the small opened wooden window frame, disturbing his train of thought and derailing him out of comfort. He closed the window tightly, walked through the bathroom door onto the cold black tiles, and felt weary to the thought of seeing his lover again.

The bedroom door hinges rattled Juliana a little with fright. She was a bit jumpy from her insomnia. She hadn't moved a lot throughout the morning mainly because she was paralysed with thoughts of a newborn baby. The thought of motherhood kept her mind mildly incoherent on the bed with her legs folded. She glanced at her pink lighter and the box of cigarettes in her open toiletry bag whilst Quinton spoke to her from a distance. He moved closer with diminishing hope that he could close up the hole opening up inside her heart with warm hug.

'I haven't slept much!' she said, sounding exhausted yet calm despite recent events.

'I can see!' he replied and cuddled her warm body.

Her soft lips were still drawn to his moist lips, leading to a profound kiss. The rain had washed away the heat outside, and the garden smelt fresh with lily and lavender flowers. Her face looked pale and pink on the edges of her nose and ears. Her steady pulse rate rippled a love frequency into Quinton's heart. He hugged her tightly yet felt absolutely powerless and miserably human as he realised that he couldn't interfere with the course of nature nor with the will of God. He imprinted an invisible love mark on her right freckled shoulder by parking his lips on her soft skin.

'I'm going to make you breakfast!' he suggested. 'Don't move!'

A dry smile cropped from her pale face, which fractured his heart even more, not that he knew it at the time. She decided at that moment to bury her heart into a deep grave within her mind, pleading to demolish away her weakness for him.

Beth and Marcus had left whilst Quinton was asleep, which seemed equivalently bizarre to Juliana because she noticed Marcus packing a lot of dark blue luggage bags into a black Range Rover. Everyone within the family had a black chest of dark secrets hidden within them, and it only seemed right for them to avoid each other at all times. Quinton couldn't quite frame old memories together that consisted of all his family members in one picture. He stepped onto the dark wooden steps, heading to the kitchen and found a handwritten letter pressed underneath an empty water glass on the outdoor table by the courtyard entrance.

Dear Son,

We are on our way to South Africa, and I thought about refraining from telling you the truth, but you deserve to know because it concerns you too. Your father has inherited a rare cancer—the same cancer that took your grandfather away when you were just a toddler. For the past two years, we have been going to specialist surgery experts in Johannesburg, Gauteng, and it seems that they cannot remove the lump within him. We have an appointment tomorrow. We left today to go and meet with our elderly family members to ask them for advice and to ask them to pray with us.

We thought about taking Juliana with us, but I know you wouldn't have been pleasant about that. Therefore, we didn't ask so that you and she may have some alone time.

Hopefully the Lord is in our favour and that your father heals with time. We will call you after surgery for an update. Keep blessed.

Love,
Beth

Quinton immediately folded the letter in half and placed it back underneath the empty glass. He felt suppressed deeply into a lake of depression whilst trying to paddle his heart afloat, and he remained quiet by the kitchen entrance, yet still his mind moved in different directions like a beacon placed in water, hoping that he wouldn't drown in sadness. The world sickened him. He didn't want to grasp the importance of his father's health as he entered the kitchen and threw all negative thoughts to the back of his mind, hoping to ignore everything bad working against him.

He acted a simple script he'd written within his mind upstairs and simply made Juliana breakfast. The dark brown wooden bedside tray had a red bowl of cornflakes cereal and strawberry yoghurt in a white bowl, two tablespoons, and fruit salad in the second white bowl filled with fresh paw paw slices, sliced bananas, diced pineapples, and sliced red apples. He also had a small red jug filled with fresh warm milk and a small red sugar container. His gesture seemed utterly sweet as he carried the bedside tray upstairs and placed it above Juliana's legs.

Her right ankle was still slightly bruised, but she'd grown accustomed to the pain. She didn't notice Quinton's kind gesture, for her mind was miles away, and her green eyes were drawn to the outside world through the open balcony sliding door. Her mind flashed to red chime melody sounds arising from a previous dream, and she could see Arabella giggling out loud within her arms. The joy of innocence rushed towards her heart as she looked into Arabella's small green eyes once more. She found herself completely lost within their precious synchronised dream again. The sounds of birds chirping from all directions outside the tree house alerted peace within her soul. Her thoughts were consuming, and she felt extremely drawn to this moment that hadn't occurred in reality. There was something so profound about their unborn child, and Quinton could also hear the sweet joy of innocence gushing through his ears from thin air. It all became too much for him to handle at that specific moment, but for some odd reason, his tear ducts were completely drained dry. He couldn't weep anymore, and he was definitely becoming strange to sensitivity. The universe was draining out his weak emotions whilst he stood still on the wooden floor, trying to equilibrate his problems.

Juliana's stomach grumbled and teleported her vivid mind back to reality.

'You have always been so kind!' she said and picked up a silver tablespoon from the bedside tray with her left hand. 'Thanks you so much!' she added and ate the strawberry yoghurt from the white bowl.

Quinton sat by her feet and massaged her right ankle gently and adjusted to his thoughts. He gently pressed his thumbs onto her right swollen ankle and exhaled the fresh air coming from outside with his eyes closed. His heart was gripped with terror, for he feared losing his father and Juliana at the same time.

'I'll come down after I've sorted myself out, okay?' he suggested, and she nodded whilst eating her fruit salad.

They looked into each other's eyes for a few seconds and wondered what they'd say to each other to make everything sound better. Juliana had decided to stay home and guzzle mango juice whilst Quinton made a short trip to the nearest shopping mall within a middle class suburb area to purchase more pregnancy tests from a pharmacy. Everything around him seemed normal, but the world within him was crumbling into bits. His nerves were exploding, and his skin was burning from the heat. It was still cloudy outside, a little warmer than usual, but he felt like he was wrapped in foil paper and placed inside an oven. He couldn't hear anything, nor could he hear anyone speaking in the background as he walked past a lot of busy restaurants. His primary focus was to find out whether Juliana was really pregnant or not.

It wasn't long until he returned back home and found Juliana packing her clothes into her luggage bags whilst slightly limping in Kimberly's bedroom. They weren't speaking to each other much as a short period of time passed. Quinton sat on Kimberly's bed, and Juliana entered the bathroom alone.

All three pregnancy test sticks proclaimed positive as Quinton looked at them by the bathroom sink in between the two bedroom doors. He looked at the wall mirror, and slowly the image before his eyes aged. His hair turned grey on different areas of his head whilst his skin turned dry on his cheeks, and a few wrinkles cropped from his forehead within the mirror. He saw his whole life pass by him, and he felt like stuck within one frame.

'Okay! That's that!' he said and walked into Kimberly's bedroom.

Juliana started packing her clothes into her luggage bags even faster as though she was running out of time. She'd hoped for negative results, but it was quite evident that she was pregnant.

'Don't come near me!' she said.

'And why not?' he asked with his arms open.

'Because I don't want to be with you anymore!' she replied, hoping to push him away with harsh words. It was momentarily working, and she definitely despised herself for saying those words out loud to him. Her intention was to seem heartless. She wanted to drive him away so that her departure would be more simplified to her heart.

Quinton walked away and stood by the bedroom door, facing the hollow passage.

'You should not say things you can never take back!' he said whilst looking at the curtains blowing in different directions by the main balcony sliding door.

He walked downstairs, and the written letters within the letter he'd read earlier dangled in front of his brown eyes, causing him to worry even more. The thought of his father dying rippled through his heart, causing it to break a little as he lay on the suede couch and closed his brown eyes.

It seemed darker outside as Quinton awoke to the alarm on his phone and saw Juliana rolling her luggage bags towards the main entrance with the help's help. The time was ticking so slowly from his silver watch, and yet everything had escalated too fast. His world was burning into aches right before his brown eyes as he looked around whilst his peace levitated away from his soul. He didn't know which way to go or what to say. The only thing he could do was accept that Juliana no longer loved him anymore.

'Everything else will fall into place with time,' he thought to himself whilst carrying Juliana's luggage bags to his car.

She limped away from the main entrance after hugging the help goodbye then sat quietly in the left backseat and surfed the Internet throughout the short trip to the international airport. There were tuneful sounds playing out from the car surround system, and sweet guitar strings from the song kept Quinton dazed in another dimension within his imagination as he parked in a busy clustered parking lot closest to the airport entrance. He looked in the rear-view mirror whilst daydreaming back to the time Juliana was cartwheeling across the soft grass in her white summer dress in France. The image before his brown eyes was completely different to the visual inside his mind.

Juliana looked miserable and deflected into a depressive burble. Her smile was translucent, and the emerald in her green eyes painted pain into Quinton's heart as he lowered the volume knob with his left hand. Salty tears lingered in her eyelids whilst she inhaled slowly and tried to keep composed.

'Please do not say anything!' she pleaded and closed her eyes. Tears dripped onto her black letterman jacket. 'You have honestly been the best thing that's ever happened to me!' she said and cried out loud.

Her words came out in agony, and she couldn't quite express herself accordingly whilst she cried. Quinton couldn't take it anymore and thus opened the driver's door and made his way behind the car and opened the left back door.

'No, no, come closer!' he said as she hesitated and moved away from him. She definitely seemed scared to be drawn back into his arms. 'Please!' he pleaded, which sounded disgustingly shameful and pathetic as bits of his heart deteriorated away.

Everything about their relationship was damaging the goodness within him, and he could feel the anger within his crooked heart boiling into rage. He immediately stepped away and felt his brown eyes strain and turn red from pain. A few tears leaked slowly from his eyelids. He quickly brushed the weakness away from his cheeks once he realised that he was daunted by his past of recklessness.

'Come!' he said. 'We must go!'

He found a silver luggage trolley parallel to his car and loaded Juliana's luggage bags onto it. She stretched her ankles and rotated them anticlockwise before stepping out of the left back door. They didn't say anything to each other whilst Juliana walked behind Quinton. He pushed the trolley towards the airport entrance and felt gloomed by reality as the large sliding doors opened in different directions.

It had turned dark outside, and the street lights were amber, glowing with misery and inflicting depression into Quinton's soul whilst he smoked a cigarette outside by the parking lot. Juliana sat alone inside the airport departure section. Her intention to be heartless had backfired and melted her heart into a pothole of regret. There were ten minutes left until she'd have to check into the boarding section. She wondered what would happen in her life after leaving Botswana in such a cold manner.

'Am I making the right decision?' the soft British voice within her mind asked.

She looked at the glass wall and saw an aeroplane departing slowly on the wide tar road towards the north. The lights on its white metal wings flicked into red as it turned and faced the south side. Her green eyes zoned out towards it as time wound towards her departure, and she wondered if Quinton could come back to her even after the way she'd acted towards him. The plane on the tar road took off within fifteen minutes. Juliana stood and waited in line by herself, wondering if she'd destroyed the last bit of hope that Quinton had in their relationship.

There she was by the check-in point with five minutes to spare. She placed her luggage bags into the baggage scanner and handed in her airplane ticket, along with her British passport to the flight attendant.

Quinton looked around for signs everywhere by the parking lot, but the sky was dark without the stars he adored so much. He wondered if falling in love with Juliana was a feeling enchanted from fate or a mistake drawn coincidentally by two people who craved each other in a lustful manner but had also falsely led themselves to believe that they had found true love. A lot of thoughts ran like wild dogs and spiralled in his heart to make his mind indecisive.

Time ticked towards the future whilst she waited by the check-in point whilst his mind was reminded of the past and clinched onto her miraculous smile. Her laughter reigned over his heart whilst he exhaled smoke from his lungs and stepped onto the burning cigarette with his light brown right loafer. He looked up once more and felt impeached by the dark sky opening up slowly. The half moon shone bright onto airport. He felt obligated and drawn closer to Juliana for some unknown reason.

'Maybe that's the light at the end of the tunnel!' he thought to himself, but he didn't quite understand what that meant at the moment. He just knew that nobody in his world could make him as happy and miserable at the same time like Juliana could. It felt quite extraordinary for his heart to beat so fast from just one thought of Juliana. He rushed back to the departure section, but Juliana was gone when he arrived. She'd grown tired of waiting for him, but a part of her wanted to stay back with him.

'Juliana!' he shouted out repeatedly from the booking section, next to two police officers. They wouldn't allow him to pass through without his passport and a booking pass.

Juliana could hear his voice in the distance, and every second time he called out her name, more tears raced down her cheeks. She remained seated whilst her name echoed and bounced off the airport walls.

'Sir, we are going to have to ask you to lower your voice!' one police officer suggested.

Quinton grew frustrated and impatient. 'Please let me go through!' he pleaded but got dismissed entirely.

'Sir, please step away from the yellow line!' the other police officer said and moved closer towards Quinton whilst he shouted out for Juliana.

The vibration of his bass rattled Juliana's heart into fear. She sniffed and cried alone whilst waiting to board the airplane that would take her away from her pain. Quinton stepped away and looked at the plasma screen towards his left and noticed Juliana's flight being booked. He'd run out of time, but the silver watch on left wrist ticked more and made it evident that the world was still moving on whether he liked it or not. He looked towards the glass wall and watched Juliana step onto the elevator staircase and into the airplane. She could not see him because the glass wall only allowed visual from his side. He swallowed the bitter saliva within his mouth and accepted that he'd lost Juliana's love forever. He exhaled and walked away from the glass wall in regret. There were so many words he still wanted to express to Juliana. She was the mother to their unborn child, and she was carrying a gift wrapped with love within her stomach. That thought itself left him baffled. He tried to write a plot on a white page within his mind and to address the way forward, but the page remained blank. The pen inside his mind wrote in ghost ink.

'I love you, Juliana Rose!' his inner voice said, hoping for those letters to appear in blood red on the blank page within his mind, but nothing happened.

His mind was battling with his heart, and it seemed as if his organs were fighting in an endless war. He needed to end this ongoing occurrence and to adapt to a different way of life before his desire for true love could destroy him.

Chapter Fifteen

Dawned By Responsibility

Two months had passed by extremely slowly. A season of dry beige autumn leaves, leafless branches, and wild winds had perished away into the past. A wonderful season had flourished into the beautiful country, Botswana. Quinton had come to terms with his father's sickness. All the surgery appointments that had commenced after weren't successful. Thus, Quinton agreed to step into his father's shoes to manage the family companies. All moments and investments made by his parents had led him to this exact moment. He looked around his father's office and knew that he was supposed to end up on this very spot, regardless of the goals he had. It seemed as though he'd accepted the strings that he'd tied him to his foreseen wealth. He did not know how to escape the web of multiple obligations and felt trapped in a corner.

'The universe always seems to find a way to humble us all,' Quinton thought to himself whilst partly reading paper documents on the wooden table and thinking of his father's health condition in the office.

Juliana's stomach had stretched beautifully. Her weight gain wasn't much because of the tall length of her body. The foetus within had fully formed its internal organs. It was about 8.5 centimetres long. Marissa remained supportive throughout and communicated with Beth about Juliana's well-being. Quinton's parents weren't surprised to hear the good news of Juliana's pregnancy. The thought of an innocent soul brought joy to them, and they hoped for some prosperity through this. Juliana attended regular routine check-ups and tests with Marissa in Johannesburg, South Africa. She absolutely loved the foetus' heartbeat playing from the doptone instrument. At first, the sound of a small irregular heartbeat beating faster than usual was overwhelming to her ears, but as weeks lapsed, she began to admire what she and Quinton had created. Marissa and Juliana had fallen in love with the thought of having another child running around in their garden. This gift from above had brought them closer to each other. It was exactly what they needed. The genuine smiles, baking lessons, movie marathons, long shopping sprees, and heart-to-heart conversations mended their broken hearts. Juliana was beginning to love the South African diverse culture. She couldn't quite understand her mother speaking in Zulu, but the sound of another African language gushing through her ears brought joy to her heart. A part of her found comfort through her pain, and she'd grown stronger.

Quinton called every day since her departure from the international airport on the outskirts of the city, but Juliana never once answered his calls. It was completely heartbreaking because she knew absolutely nothing of the pain he carried every day. Despite her efforts to avoid him, she felt guilty about ignoring him completely. Therefore, she'd send him pictures of the growing foetus to his office email address. And he would sit in his new office afterhours, drowning in paperwork, signing maintenance cheques, analysing chart sheets, and trying to avoid Juliana's emails. It wasn't in their nature to be so avoidant towards each other, but they didn't know what to say to each other anymore. Quinton's life seemed to be more and more predictable as time passed. His weeks were scheduled for work and sleep. The pressure of having everything led him into frustration because he couldn't quite understand the ethos of his path. His bloodstream consisted of nicotine and alcohol, which mostly blinded him more towards lustful occasions, but he reframed himself from being concluded into the typical stereotype of a black man who'd abandoned his pregnant partner. The situation was much more complex, and he knew that he could only help by momentarily working and saving up for his unborn child. It felt like the right thing to do instead of living off his parents' wealth and pretending like he'd worked hard for his trust fund.

Quinton craved Juliana's incredibly soothing warmth in between her legs every single night whilst back in his townhouse apartment. His British pug, Smuggles, brought him temporary joy. His oldest sister had decided to leave Smuggles with him to try to get him to channel his emotions out, but her efforts had failed. He'd become accustomed to wearing a mask of deception, which covered his true pain. It seemed as if his heart was lost in a different time zone. He didn't want to move on. Thus, he never once stopped calling her every day, but sadly again, she never once answered. She was scared of the words he would use to draw her back in, and she was terrified of letting him know that she still loved him.

He awoke midday to a beautiful sunny Saturday. He'd carried a burden of having illusive nightmares during the day of his father passing away. Every inch of his body wanted to gravitate toward the south to be with his lover once more. He couldn't quite navigate his mind away from everything happening around him, for it all seemed as boring as the colour beige despite his recent views on the world—the many beautiful and colourful butterflies flying around and the growth of many plants brought him some of sort of hope. A sprinkle of faith from his mother led him to believe that everything could be fixed. The suburb area sidewalks and backyards of many homes looked amazing from the dark green trees scattered in different places.

He walked around his apartment and cleaned up the lounge whilst Kimberly was sleeping on the couch. She'd returned from boarding school in South Africa for a midterm break. Her persona was somewhat different from the norm. She had a nose piercing on her left side, smuggled red lipstick on her mouth, last night's make-up on, a black cocktail dress on, and a pair of black Jimmy Choo heels by the couch. There was a smell of J'dore Dior perfume lingering on her light brown skin combined with the smell of cigarettes on her natural long black hair. Whiffs of vodka reeked from her clothing. She was hanging like a wet blanket on a clothing line. Quinton looked at his youngest sister, and he began to see the same qualities that his mother had.

Kimberly had two dimples on her cheeks whenever she'd make a facial expression. Her eyebrows were thin and dark. Every single feature on her face seemed replicated from Beth's genetics. Kimberly looked so beautiful despite all the make-up she'd had on. The wild party lifestyle had turned her into a slight trumpet. She loved the late nights and the street lights that she and her friend would pass whilst her friend drove from one club to another. Her soul was untamed by family conventions.

'Kim, wake up!' Quinton said and ripped the light brown couch from underneath her body. She opened her light brown eyes and dazed towards the white ceiling whilst Smuggles nibbled on a dry bone by the kitchen entrance.

'What is the time?' Kimberly asked and sat up straight then noticed that her iPhone 5 was off.

'It's almost close to one o'clock, hey!' he said and opened the balcony sliding door. 'What time did you get here?' he asked whilst opening the dark maroon curtains.

There were light brown boxes piled in a corner. Some filled with clothes and others filled with sentimental things like Juliana's pictures in small wooden frames, her old high school hoodie imprinted with her scent, a necklace she'd wear on semi-special occasions. Quinton couldn't address his pain and thus kept everything that reminded him of Juliana in the corner of his mind, mostly hiding away his pain in those light brown boxes and hoping for peace within his mind.

'Kim, I need a favour from you!' he said and walked towards the kitchen to prepare breakfast. He felt slightly claustrophobic and trapped within a box containing a deep-rooted depression. 'I'm leaving for today, and I will be back on Tuesday!' he said. 'Monday and Tuesday are public holidays, okay. Therefore, I need you to house-sit my apartment for me and not tell anyone that I've left!'

Quinton's request for discretion led Kimberly to believe that he was trying to run away from something or run to something. She wasn't sure what his intentions were, but the thought of him being devious left her restless.

'I want to come with you. That way, I can meet Juliana,' she said.

Kimberly's absence throughout Quinton's relationship with Juliana made her pave a way for questions—the type of questions that left her brother's mind into a paralyzed state.

'What is she like?' Kimberley asked whilst in Quinton's bathroom, wiping off her make-up by the mirror and brushing her teeth with a new toothbrush from the pantry section in the kitchen.

'She is amazing!' he replied whilst zoned out into the plain white wall. He was falling in love with a picture he could imaginatively see on the wall. The image started to paint in different colours from the left side of the lounge and towards the bedroom door on the right side. It was a wall painting of Juliana by a clear stream. She was facing a stream that flowed towards the right. There were beautiful wet rocks on the edges of the river. Circular yellow strokes of sunlight graced her light-toned body perfectly whilst she remained still like a statue. The green grass looked so amazingly textured underneath her feet. Her skin tone was textured in beige, mostly mixed with peach to show the lightness of her skin.

'She is beautiful!' he said and closed his brown eyes to find a way out of his vivid imagination.

Kimberly entered the kitchen wearing her brother's light blue tracksuit pant and a light white T-shirt with the caption 'I own your mind' written in red.

'So you must get her back!' she said and opened the strawberry yoghurt container then searched for cutlery in the kitchen drawers. 'You can go, and I will babysit Smuggles and your apartment!' she added.

'No parties though!' Quinton stated and looked at his youngest sister for confirmation.

'Okay, fine. I promise I won't throw a party!' she said. 'First, you must shave. You look harried and worn out!' she said and laughed out loud. Her head ached heavily whilst she opened her mouth to swallow strawberry yoghurt from a plastic spoon. 'Oh yes, my birthday is on Thursday which means that you actually have to be back for that!' she said. 'By the way, why haven't you unpacked your boxes yet?' she asked. 'It's unlike you to have your paintings stacked in one place!'

Kimberly spoke a lot about love, trying to voice out her option about something she knew nothing of. She didn't notice the pain she was causing whilst she asked him questions of Juliana and meddled in her brother's previous affairs.

'Let's watch *The Lord of the Rings* trilogy after I've booked my plane ticket for tonight,' he suggested whilst frying bacon on a red pan on the electric stove.

'I'm going back to bed, Quinton. My head is throbbing!' she said and closed her eyes for a while. Her head felt heavy, and her eyes were strained red.

Quinton willed his doubtful mind towards having hope, and he believed again that he could rekindle a flame with Juliana. He couldn't quite imagine another day without her anymore, and he finally wanted to be open about his part in Steve's disappearance, hoping that the darkness within his soul would vanish forever. A part of him remained uneasy about revealing his darkest secret to Juliana. He sat quietly by the balcony, eating breakfast and contemplating the way forward. His life was on a dusty crossroad as he thought more on the world around him, and he couldn't see clearly the road that would best fix his happiness. Love and peace were the only aspect that's mattered to him most, and the thought of his unborn child being fatherless lured him one step closer to Johannesburg, South Africa.

He started packing his luggage bags in his bedroom whilst Kimberly slept peacefully on his bed. He momentarily concluded to take just enough clothing for the long weekend, but his subconscious was railing him towards packing for a longer period. He wasn't sure of anything anymore, and showing his love again to Juliana terrified him, almost scaring him away from packing. 'You just have to be brave,' Juliana's voice came in his ears. His thoughts had created an elusive succubus of Juliana that was controlling and influencing his decisions. It seemed as though she was right beside him whilst he kept packing and booking for an online plane ticket at the same time. He called to confirm his booking whilst seated on the wooden floor with his legs crossed.

'Hello, yes, I've called to confirm a booking,' he said and blinked repeatedly whilst facing the open balcony door in his bedroom. 'I've booked for the eight o'clock one!' he continued, unintentionally thinking of Juliana again with his eyes closed.

His left hand fidgeted with a zip on the luggage on his left side, then at that moment, he could feel Juliana's love behind him, and her warm arms wrapped around his waist.

'Come home to me!' her voice whispered and lured him away. 'Come back to me!' she continued and laid her head onto his upper back whilst her illusive light-toned hands clinched onto his chest after hugging him.

'Sir!' a male voice echoed from his phone whilst he inhaled fresh air coming from outside, taking in every warm touch radiating Juliana's illusive scent.

'I need you back home!' she whispered into his left ear and bit it slowly. Her long brunette hair strands brushed over his left shoulder and onto his left chest whilst he inhaled a whiff of Juliana's perfume gushing from her wrists.

'Sir, hello!' the voice echoed again and caught Quinton's attention, causing Juliana's illusion to evaporate into thin air.

'Please make sure that you come to our office to pay before 4:00 p.m.!' the service correspondent stated.

'Awesome, thank you!' Quinton said whilst trying to grasp what had just happened to him.

'Anything else, sir?' the gentleman asked.

'No, that's all!' Quinton replied and hung up.

His heart was tormenting him and racing fast within his chest, knocking against his brain and pleading at him to leave immediately. He felt the second hand of his clock clapping his face as it wound clockwise, and he aggressively moved his hands to proceed faster than scheduled. He packed faster and zipped his bags whilst breathing intensely and tried to hold back overdue tears. He missed Juliana so much and wanted to rest by her side again even if it was just for a few nights. His world crushed and burned into ashes once more as tears dripped down from his bottom jaw. He felt secluded more than ever from the Diamond City, and everything around didn't shine as brightly anymore. Having money and materialistic possessions seemed to have also turned into an illusion because everything around seemed to deprive him of true happiness. He wondered what he was supposed to do to find a balancing equilibrium to his challenges, but at the same time, all those thoughts galloped like wild horses within his mind, and this experience itself gripped and chained his heart to the south where Juliana's fruits seemed more ripe and sweet to his tongue as every second passed.

The red kitchen clock had wound to five o'clock in the afternoon as Quinton entered through the front door after running a couple of errands for Marcus, paying for his plane ticket to Johannesburg, South Africa, and checking on the security staff at the family warehouse office block. Everything was going according to plan, but he couldn't shake his impatience anymore and thus piled his luggage bags by the front door and scrolled through multiple channels in the living room whilst he waited for his cab driver.

He couldn't ignore the small American black suede box he'd stacked into a safety box a month ago within his clothing wardrobe then wondered if it was right time to propose to Juliana. Nothing was clear, but diving into the deep end of their musky liquid love seemed more logical than giving up. He pressed onto the numbers 3, 3, 8, 2 on the grey safety box keypad attached to the white wall within the wardrobe and watched the grey steel door unveil a moment of his supposed clarity. He picked up the black suede box he'd hidden from himself with his right hand, and his time stopped for a while whilst he opened it with both hands to see the crystal-clear shining rock within. The diamond rock shone brightly, and sun light rays reflected off his eyes as he closed the wardrobe door and wandered into the living room once more then immediately stirred his mind with assurance that marrying Juliana would lead him to a greater path of glory and that her love was destiny calling, and he was ready to answer.

His Blackberry rang right as his butt cheeks landed on the couch, and everything he'd ever learned, experienced, and observed about love led him to this very moment as he answered his Blackberry.

'Yeah, I'm coming down now!' he said to the cab driver then hung up.

He knew that he could not turn his back on his lover anymore and thus picked up his luggage bag and placed it by an elevator at the end of the passage.

'Kimberly, I'm off, hey. Don't forget to feed Smuggles, hey!' Quinton said and picked up his second luggage bag and wore his light brown loafers then shut the door behind him.

His mind raced extremely fast through the streets of Gaborone to the main road that led to the international airport whilst he walked towards the elevator still distilled with impatience. He stood by and watched the wooden elevator doors open.

'You are making the right choice,' Juliana's voice said as Quinton placed both luggage bags into the elevator. The dark blue carpet floor felt so soft to his right foot as he removed his right loafer and picked up an old sentimental coin that belonged Juliana. He began to notice that everything around him signalled right to Juliana and thus he believed that he was making the right decision.

Within fifty minutes after boarding a plane from the international airport to the airport in Johannesburg, South Africa, Quinton had arrived safely. He could smell wet paint from the reconstruction of the pathways leading to the terminal areas. It had rained heavily during the day, and the cold front had commenced from the cool grounds. The amber lights around the airport and on the highways painted a beautiful picture, yet all Quinton could think about was proposing to Juliana whilst travelling to Sandton in a luxurious cab. He arrived at the Rose residence and removed his luggage bags from the trunk after greeting the security guards at the main entrance of the residence.

Quinton realised that arriving unannounced at ten o'clock in the evening wasn't ideally appropriate anymore. The thought of entering an uncertain situation slowly felt dreadful as he walked along the driveway whilst pulling his roller luggage bags towards the Rose residence. All the lights were lit brightly everywhere within the household. All windows around, from the far left end to the far right, were uncovered. The household main entrance was wide open, but Quinton did not feel welcomed by silence screaming loud in his ears. He knocked on the door with his left hand and placed both luggage bags by the entrance then looked left into a large mirror frame on the wall. It was the only piece of furniture piece still in its place. Every other piece of furniture in the living room on the north-east side of the entrance was covered in blue plastic, and there was a lot of light brown boxes piled together in the kitchen as Quinton looked to his right.

'Hello!' he shouted out which seemed inappropriate as his voice echoed and bounced off the empty walls in the house.

'Yes, come in!' Marissa replied in the living room.

She was sealing a box with clear tape and writing a label onto it with a black permanent marker whilst seated on a red carpet. Juliana stood still in the storage room, unsure of whether to exit and greet or to hide. She switched off the storage room light whilst Marissa and Quinton spoke in the living room. Marissa noticed the light switch off and understood what she had to say.

'Well, I'm glad you are here, but Juliana has left already!' she said, intentionally lying to keep Quinton from hurting her only child. 'She is halfway down to Cape Town. Her cousin Samantha is driving because we have decided to move there!' she stated, but none of it made much sense to Quinton as he looked around and noticed Juliana's pink watch on top of a box next to the kitchen entrance behind him.

Marissa feared losing her daughter again and therefore rippled more lies.

'I need to see her!' he said whilst trying to cope with the distance growing between him and Juliana as every second ticked away.

He didn't want to understand, and whilst he spoke and pleaded for the truth, the foetus within Juliana kicked repeatedly whilst she stood by the door, almost as if it knew that its father was around. Juliana groaned in pain but kept quiet whilst in shock, stationed by the door frame and wondered what to do next. She placed her left hand onto her chest as her heart throbbed fast, and it imaginatively tried to dive out of her chest and hoop towards him.

'I think you need to let her go!' Marissa suggested and then stood up straight in front of Quinton. It was quite evident that Juliana had poisoned her mother to believe that Quinton was treacherous and deceiving. 'Just go home and recuperate. Allow growth to restore you!' Marissa said. 'Then you can come and see my daughter. Only after you have allowed yourself to grow!' she added.

Quinton picked up his phone from his right black jean pocket and called Juliana. He wanted to hear her voice again, but the event in motion quickly turned awkward as her phone rang loudly in the kitchen.

'I guess her phone isn't that smart, hey. It forgot to leave for Cape Town!' he said sarcastically and wandered into the kitchen then found a glass half full of mango juice next to Juliana's Blackberry and her black guitar.

'She isn't here. She is gone!' Marissa said. 'Let her go!'

Quinton strolled towards the entrance whilst yelling out for Juliana then swerved towards a hallway on the left side, passing the dark storage room underneath, and made his way up a flight of stairs to the bedrooms to find Juliana. Marissa hid Juliana by closing the storage door completely and locking it afterwards.

'I'm calling the police if you don't leave immediately!' Marissa shouted out from the bottom of the staircase whilst Quinton stood by the doorframe of the guest bedroom and reminisced a misty past.

It all seemed blurry within his mind as he looked around the guest bedroom he'd slept in before. He opened the small black suede box and placed it by the wooden window frame then walked away whilst coming to a conclusion that Juliana didn't love him anymore. He needed to end this ongoing occurrence of errors and accept that his life was meant to be based around wealth and greed—the only things that could mask his sadistic life.

'May you please tell her that I love her so much?' he said and picked up his luggage bags then walked away from the household and stood outside by the main gate, contemplating his next move.

Marissa wiped off Quinton's details from Juliana's phone and unlocked the storage room wooden door to discover her only daughter soaked in tears.

'I love him!' Juliana stuttered and sniffed at the same time whilst moving to the kitchen to find her Blackberry.

'Juliana Elizabeth Rose, put that phone down immediately!' Marissa shouted.

'I need to be with him right now!' she sighed and slowly placed her Blackberry onto the kitchen counter.

'He is nothing but a nightmare clothed beautifully like a Sunday daydream!' Marissa said and manipulated Juliana. She knew that it was the only way for her daughter would find strength through the mist of her despicable weakness.

Quinton lit a cigarette by the security booth and inhaled every drag faster than usual.

'Roger, may you please call a cab for me!' Quinton requested to the security guard after reading his name tag on his left chest pocket. 'Thank you!' he said then sat on top of his luggage bag and rested his right hand on the other luggage bag, wondering if it was good idea to leave the wedding ring by window frame without notifying anybody.

He seemed indecisive and uncollected to the thought of love. It was driving him mad to the brink of disaster. His nerves boiled within his bloodstream, and he made a conscious decision to call Emily Lith, the only person that could sell him a dream compiled with false love and false intentions. He needed a vibrant woman to be attentive to his needs. Thus, he listened to the dial tone commencing from his Blackberry and waited patiently.

'Emily, hello!' she answered and giggled,

'You are the right person to call. I want to see you!' Quinton responded and laughed out loud.

'Quinton? Is that you?' she asked and smiled.

'Yeah, where are you right now?' he asked then realised that he was acting wrongfully by requesting for Emily's attention.

'I'm in my apartment, too exhaust to do anything right now!' she replied. 'Why'd you ask?'

'I'm around your district. Meet me somewhere!' he suggested and noticed a red cab turn inwards onto the main entrance. Its wheels squashed on the scattered moist jacaranda flowers on the pavement.

'Well, come to my apartment first!' she suggested.

'That makes sense. That way, I can leave my luggage bags in a safe place!' he stated.

'Okay, great. I will text you the direction to my apartment complex!' she said and hung up immediately.

Quinton looked around and subconsciously knew that he'd never see this place again, especially because the Rose family was moving down south to the Western Cape but also knew that he couldn't let Juliana leave without him stating his true intentions. He then wondered what his true intentions were after showing the cab driver directions to Emily's apartment.

Juliana stepped outside by her mother's bedroom balcony and sat on a dark brown fireside chair and placed her juice glass onto a 1930s chrome-and-ebonised wood coffee table then picked up her black guitar and started stroking the right strings. She hadn't sang in a while and wondered if the right words would stream out of her aching heart. The pain she was carrying was turning itself into her strongest niche, and her foetus loved the sound of the guitar notes. It kicked gently as she stringed a few notes together, and whilst she did so, her mother discovered the wedding ring in the guest room whilst sweeping the beige oak floorboards. Marissa stepped onto the guest room balcony and watched her daughter channel all emotions into beautiful music from a distance then made a conscious decision to place the small black suede box into her dark blue tracksuit pants and keep it away from Juliana. Her main objective was to keep Juliana out of harm's way and guide them both away from a world of pain.

Cape Town seemed like a safe haven to Marissa and a place she could help bring up Juliana's child. She listened more to Juliana sing softly and the magic gushing out of the guitar. and it brought tears to her brown eyes.

Juliana looked towards the north-east past the large apple tree in the backyard and directly at the city. Her vision was momentarily blurry due to tears lingering on her eyelids, but she could see something so beautiful. There were so many amber street lights in the distance glowing brightly, and they magically gravitated upwards from their spots and collaborated into one glowing ball in the dark sky. She smiled whilst more tears raced down her cheeks then cried more in confusion. Her music was the light at the end of her tunnel, and she could see clearly through her tears of joy. She'd escaped from an emotional jail cell, and her happiness liberated her heart from her depression. Juliana knew that she'd not overcome all obstacles in the world in one moment, but finding true love within her heart first could help her grow and find prosperity through anything else.

She looked downwards as her foetus kicked happiness within her stomach, and then she smiled as she rubbed her stomach gently with her right hand and placed her black guitar on the coffee table with her left hand.

'Don't worry. He will find his way back to us one day!' she whispered downwards then kissed her left hand and placed it gently on her stomach.

Within a few seconds, she found more inspiration and picked up her black guitar again then sang out loud as if she was the only person around.

Marissa walked into her bedroom and slowly approached Juliana then placed a white box filled with tissues on the coffee table next to the juice glass and kneeled behind the fireside chair and hugged her daughter tightly.

'We will be fine!' she whispered into Juliana's left ear.

Her daughter nodded emotionally and wept more to the feeling of her mother's genuine warmth.

'I know!' Juliana responded and then stored away her passionate love for Quinton deep within her heart then laughed out loud. 'You know,' Juliana said.

'Yes!' Marissa replied and laughed out loud then sat on another fireside chair beside Juliana. She looked into her daughter's beautiful green eyes and concluded to refrain from showing her daughter the engagement ring in her pocket. 'It's for her own good,' Marissa convinced herself whilst wiping Juliana's moist cheeks with tissues from the white tissue box. 'Let's go to bed, Julie!' Marissa suggested.

'Okay, I'm coming!' Juliana responded. 'Give me five minutes!'

Her mother walked towards the bathroom whilst she picked up her Blackberry and wrote a text message. At first, she did not know what to write, but within a few minutes as her mind drifted away into the past, her fingertips started to pour out suspended words from her thoughts and onto her touchscreen.

Quinton received a message a few seconds behind since his phone switched off due to low battery. He'd tried to read it but got interrupted by Emily's pleasant voice. She seemed happier than ever as she hugged Quinton tightly. A whiff of vodka lashed through his nostrils from her mouth as she spoke and lured him into her parents' luxurious apartment with hand gestures. It was convenient for her to stay there because it was rent- and hassle-free for a grad student.

'Those bags look heavy! Are you running away?' she asked and smiled.

Quinton placed his luggage bags next to the door. 'You have an amazing place!' he said and looked around with a glance of exhaustion.

Her apartment had a welcoming glow, a lot of glass and aluminium doors from the kitchen on the left and a spacious balcony that linked to the living room on the right. A spacious lounge linked to the balcony and a separate passage led to three bedrooms, a master suite staircase at the end of passage. The walls were beautifully plastered with navy blue paper. Quinton wondered what would happened if he ended up in Emily's bedsheets. He seemed indecisive. She could see weakness within his brown eyes as he unintentionally glanced down and scanned her body upwards as if she was a barcode. Her light-toned legs were exposed through her black gown and her red lingerie scripted her intentions. Her plan to seduce him was momentarily working.

'Are you hungry?' she asked. 'I've made you something to eat in the kitchen, and there are also delicious leftovers!'

'Yeah, just realised how hungry I am!' he said. 'Oh yes, where can I charge my phone?' he asked and unzipped the front pocket of his luggage bag whilst Emily walked towards the kitchen and flaunted her body like a lingerie model on a catwalk, swerving her amazing curves.

'This way!' she said and switched on the kitchen-balcony lights next to beige fur curtains. 'Just plug your charger here by the microwave and take a seat outside. I will bring you something warm to eat, okay?' she said whilst he plugged his charger onto the wall adapter and inserted a charge pin into his phone, then as he smiled, a whip of lightning outside struck the dark sky, and it began to drizzle.

'Oh well, you can just eat inside then!' she suggested. 'Just take your bags upstairs and get comfortable, then come downstairs and eat this up!' she said. Her sexual innuendos tenderised his aching heart and soothed it into a false love trap. 'Oh, please take your shoes off before you step onto the carpet in the passage. It's new,' she said. 'And one more thing, would you like some red wine with your meal?' she asked whilst pouring herself a mixture of vodka and Sprite into a glass.

'Yes please, and thank you so much for the hospitality!' he responded then slid his light brown loafers off his feet and carried his luggage bags up the master suite staircase.

He looked around and discovered a cream white castle armchair and a castle footstool facing a wide window on the left corner. There was a small blanket on top of the castle footstool and a few different-shaded green pillows on the castle armchair. Towards the right wall, in between the closet door closest to the bedroom entrance and the bathroom door on the opposite end was an odd chest of drawers painted white. It was beautifully designed and textured with old wood.

He felt more at ease as he stepped into the shower booth and rinsed off his troubles. His quest for comfort had drawn him into a downfall spiral of lust as he stepped back into the bedroom. He'd entered a moment of impact, a moment that had an ability to change his whole persona, and he wasn't quite sure how to carry him and thus felt haled in pressure. He wore dark grey and dark blue square-patterned pyjama pants and a white shirt made out of cotton then placed a golden rosary in his right pocket. It was a gift Beth had given to him awhile back, and for some reason, he believed that having some sort of spiritual sentiment would advocate for the goodness within him whilst he intentionally did the opposite.

The atmosphere downstairs was completely different from before. The lights were dimmed, and candles of different colours were lit everywhere. A few red candles burned brightly on the floor surface far away from the couches. It looked absolutely romantic and heart feeling to see someone else pay so much more attention to his needs, and yet everything about that moment seemed highly immoral.

'I've made you some *pomme dauphinoise*!' Emily said. 'Come sit next to me! Oh yes, poured a glass for you!' she said and leaned backwards on the couch then slid her slippers off her feet. She'd set the glass table and placed the dining cutlery in a decorative manner then switched the television channel source to USB mode and scrolled for soothing music. There were different genres of music folders, but she decided to click on an indie playlist to ease off the tension on his shoulders. It began to pour heavily outside and onto the clear glass and aluminium doors.

'Come closer. I won't bite!' she whispered through the loud lightning strikes outside then wrapped her legs around him as he picked up his wine glass. 'You seem so far away. Talk to me, Quinton!' she said and pressed her chin onto his left shoulder.

He swallowed soft bits of potatoes and drank more wine. He felt incarcerated by a blend of being in love and being heartbroken by the same person at the same time and then wondered if it was such a good idea to be with Emily at that particular moment. She seemed overly kind and seductive. All these thoughts kept him muted for a few seconds.

'I know why you came to Johannesburg!' she said. 'You are here to see Juliana, aren't you?' she asked. 'It's okay. You can say it. I won't be offended!' she whispered and closed her eyes. His cologne scent swung her heart into a flimsy state whilst she inhaled slowly.

'Yes, I am here for her, but she is leaving tomorrow!' he replied and took another sip from the wine glass.

'Well, forgive me for being blunt, but I'm going to pound your pain away, then you can run back to her tomorrow morning!' she whispered slowly in his left ear.

Quinton looked into Emily's brown eyes and searched for a sign to seclude him from thinking of Juliana, and all he could see were Emily's eyes burning with lust. He felt like he was betraying himself to a moment of weakness.

'It's okay. I know you love her so much, and I know of the responsibly that consumes you. You deserve to be happy and have a smile on your face!' she said.

Her persuasive words were enough to lure him closer and eventually over the cliff edge of his sanity. His mind scanned over his decision whilst he passionately French kissed Emily. He realised that he was so far gone that he wouldn't even know which way to go if he was to try to backtrack his way to his innocence and purity. Emily placed her hands softly onto his back as he plunged himself closer towards an uncertain wet vortex. She loved the pleasurable pain, and the feeling of Quinton's teeth grazing against her skin stimulated waves of lust within her knickers, wetting her petals and causing her to act unladylike.

'I missed this!' she whispered and hoped for a reply, but his mind was railing towards a perpetual state.

He was fighting an endless battle of ongoing inflicted pain and his desecrating affection for real love.

'Just shut up!' he whispered.

Quinton slowly unwrapped and ravelled on to a foreseen chapter into his life. He noticed something strange within her light brown eyes—a fickle teardrop carrying her burdened sadness advocated for her to be loved wholeheartedly again.

'Are you okay? Should we stop?' he asked and leaned backwards with his knees pressed onto the couch and her back thighs pressed against his thighs.

'No, I'm fine!' she replied and smiled like a fool whilst her light brown eyes scripted a different story of pain.

She had a preconceived idea of true love mounted around materialistic things, and she'd always vowed to never allow herself to be used unless it involved trade, but for the first time ever, she was beginning to love Quinton wholeheartedly without expecting anything back. The realisation of real love tormented her heart and impacted her brown eyes to extract a stream of tears. She stood up and offered her right hand.

'Come with me!' she suggested. 'Let's go and make each other feel better!'

Quinton stood up and realised that he was sedated and confused into a daze.

'What's in the wine?' he asked and stumbled backwards onto a single couch.

Emily kneed the glass table corner with her left leg and stumbled onto him in a drunken manner then kissed him roughly on his lips. The right side of his bottom lip leaked a drop of blood as she nibbled gently with her teeth.

'It's okay!' she whispered into his right ear.

He looked around and saw the walls on his right caving inwards towards him. The lightning strikes outside became closer and more enhanced. Everything appeared brighter and magnified.

'It's okay. You are okay!' she whispered again in between her kisses and then wormed her tongue into his mouth.

He felt a sense of muscularity over him and thus stood up immediately and walked towards the passage then looked back before proceeding forward. He noticed how fast his heart throbbed at that very moment. Every heartbeat was synchronised with his eyesight, zooming in and out repeatedly as every second ticked away. Emily moved towards him slowly and reached out with her left hand. She held on to his right hand tightly and guided him towards the master suite staircase at the end of the passage. He looked down at his feet and noticed the wooden floorboards cave inwards. His mind was gassed with paranoia whilst he stood still by the staircase and felt like he was drowning into the floor.

'Come with me!' she said and moved upwards.

Her words echoed loudly within his head whilst he lifted his right foot upwards onto the staircase and hallucinated, watching the glass staircase shatter into pieces. He knew that he was hallucinating, and maybe his subconscious was guarding him from entering into a world of deception. Nevertheless, he ignored everything and made his way upstairs into the master suite bedroom after a struggle then noticed that it was slightly darker then he'd expected. There were curtains opened by the clear glass windows.

'Come and find me!' she whispered and giggled.

Quinton moved closer towards the bed and gently crawled onto the bed as Emily pedalled backwards into the light. He crawled towards her and allowed his heart to feel affection from another person besides Juliana. Even though he wasn't pleased with his daze, the moment was different from what he was used to. Maybe a night inside another woman would do him justice and maybe bring him closure. He wasn't sure which thoughts best suited him whilst he slid off his pyjama pants and threw them onto the floor whilst the world within him shook in tremor for a few minutes.

'Make it stop!' he shouted in paranoia whilst his mind spun like a car wheel rolling down a steep rocky hill.

'Quinton, look at me. Come down!' she said and gripped his face with both hands. She was drunk in lust. Her words slurred more as she spoke, and those words echoed loudly within his mind again whilst his eyes wandered into different sections of the bedroom.

'Let me take control. Just lie down!' she whispered.

They made love.

Emily cuddled Quinton from his right side and spoke, but he couldn't quite ignore the dents on his heart. Despite his recent revelation of everything about himself, he immediately understood that he had to let Juliana go because he wasn't the real man for her anymore and also understood that she deserved a real man who wouldn't be drawn into average human conventions, a man that wouldn't be bounded by the idea of progressing through greed. He became accustomed to the idea of letting go. He shut his heavy brown eyes and rested quietly whilst his heartbeat slowly settled down.

Fresh cool air breezed from the air conditioner on the wall as he opened his eyes and discovered that he was alone on the bed. His lower body was covered in a cream white bed sheet, and despite his exhaustion, he felt slightly exonerated and relieved. The sun had reached its midday peak, and everything around seemed normal. He sat up slowly and dangled his feet by the bedside. The duvet sheets were piled behind the castle armchair, and a lot of pillows were on the floor too. He stood up slowly, wore a pair of tight red briefs, from his luggage bag, and stretched by bathroom door then walked towards the staircase on his right side, trying to recall every single minute of what had happened within the early hours of the morning. It was all hazy within his mind, but he soon realised that he needed to see Juliana as he started to remember seeing her on the wet glass window. He rushed towards the kitchen to find his Blackberry and discovered fifteen missed calls from his mother and an unread email.

After calling Beth repeatedly, her number immediately turned to voicemail. Thus, he opened the only email notification from Juliana Rose.

> Forgive my mother; she was only trying to protect me from being hurt again.
>
> We have already boarded the South African airline to Cape Town, Western Cape.
>
> Our items will arrive a day after with some other local delivery.
>
> I do not know if we will ever meet again. I'm not sure of anything anymore.
>
> We are having a child together. I will contact you when I'm close to delivering this child because I want you to be a part of her or his life. We owe this child the best care and the best environment.
>
> I do understand the life that you are accustomed to. Therefore, I do not pass judgement towards you, nor do I resent you for being yourself.
>
> I'm sorry that I hid from you last night.
>
> I'm scared of the words you may use to lure me back towards the north.

I need to find myself again.

I hope that our paths cross again someday. It would be remarkable and heart filling to feel this feeling one day, and I for one cannot wait until that day adorns my life again.

I do not know where my path will take me, but a part of you will always be with me.

You have been amazing and incredible in your own way.

I can remember your compassion, your charm, your outspoken personality, and most of all, the sound of your heart beating loud like an African drum. You have taught me a lot about myself. I've seen the best parts of myself when you are around. I've learnt how to love purely without expecting anything in return, and it's all because of you. Your path is paved with thorns and pain, but I know that you will overcome it because you were born to be great. You are a star glowing during the day. The sun may shine onto your skin and try to deprive you from standing taller, but you are my king like I am your queen. Our blood drips of burning gold. We wear white clothing because our souls hover on the lake of purity. We are not perfect though because we are also humanly stitched.

Follow your heart and find the path of glory to your own salvation. Allow yourself to work on your mistakes. Find peace and comfort in this world of sin. You were born to rule your own kingdom and to overcome anything negative.

Rise up and reach your full potential.

Being average isn't a calling but a proclamation made by those that want you to desecrate the African dry soil. Your body may turn thirsty from time to time from the heat, but your mind must forever remain moist in knowledge and wisdom because through that, you will be free from all troubles spiralling within your mind.

I know that you'll nurse yourself to greatness and become such an extraordinary figure to the world.

Remember, we are all born to be kings and queens of our own empires.

Find freedom from those that are wretched and keep your family close.

I will always love you. You own my heart, body, and mind, but right now, I have to be by myself and to find independence because I'm a ruler too.

This message is a reminder of our love, a notification to remind you that anything is possible and that our love will only grow strong as times passes.

Love,
Juliana Elizabeth Rose

Quinton firmly placed his phone onto the kitchen counter and left the kitchen to the balcony. Every second passed by, and he felt the distance between himself and Juliana defeat any chance of hope he had towards finding peace again. He could imaginatively see his heart being squeezed of its last drop of blood as a tear leaked from his right eyelid. Emily walked through the front door in a jolly mood as he wiped away his tears from his face with his left hand.

'Hey you!' she said and placed her handbag onto the couch facing the plasma screen. 'So I'm sorry I didn't wake you up. You seemed so tired!' she said whilst placing her car keys into a dark brown African-decorated bowl filled with dry fragrant leaves and straightened a long dark blue rug next to the chest of drawers parallel to the couch. 'Would you like something to eat?' she asked and stood by the kitchen-balcony entrance.

Quinton kept quiet and searched for strength within him.

'I'm guessing she left already?' she asked. 'It's okay. I'm here for you!' she whispered and placed her arms around him from behind then kissed his back softly.

There was a tattoo scripture on the middle of his back which read

'The world will only be peaceful
once every single human being on this planet
has learned how to love purely with their
hearts and without expectation to gain wealth from it.'

Emily read it and felt drawn in by every single letter. She didn't know much about Quinton but felt fascinated by the mystery he presented.

'When did you get this tattoo?' she asked. 'I haven't seen it before!' she said.

Quinton looked towards the busy world on the left side, and he could finally see the path he had to take.

Emily read out every word again whilst Quinton listened carefully. Those were the words that Juliana had said once before. He started to reflect on that memory and could see Juliana lying right beside him, tilting her head upwards to face him. Her dark brown curly hair strands hid her extraordinary beauty away, and all he could see was her cute pink nose and her beautiful round green eyes. Her green eyes remained fixed towards his brown eyes. She spoke out those very same words slowly in her mesmerising British accent, and Quinton felt temporarily reunited with his only lover.

'I've just got it recently!' he said to Emily.

He needed to keep himself distracted from thinking of Juliana. Thus, he walked towards the living room and switched on the plasma screen with a black remote. There weren't many interesting channel selections as he scrolled through most channels.

'More wine?' Emily asked and laughed out loud.

'You're funny!' he replied and smiled. 'I just need time to come to terms with everything happening around me!' he stated and stepped into the kitchen whilst Emily poured herself a glass of red wine.

'The only we can get by every day is through soothing out our nerves. Life is so difficult, even for those that fortunate enough to have money!' she said and took a small sip from her wine glass. 'There is so much pain everywhere. We can't all avoid it, but I think we can all accept it for what it is!'

'And what's that?' Quinton asked and realised how beautiful Emily looked in a plain white summer dress as she hopped onto the kitchen counter next to the refrigerator and slid off her cream white palms from her feet.

'An indirect blessing!' she said, but that answer left Quinton in limbo.

He understood what that meant, but he couldn't bear the thought of Juliana leaving him to be a blessing. Emily's small toenails were painted red. She immediately realised that Quinton was looking at her feet. Therefore, she curved her toes inwards.

'Stop looking at my feet!' she said.

'And why not?' he asked.

'Because!' she responded.

'Because what?' he asked again then looked upwards. 'Something is different about you today!' he stated and walked towards her.

Her brown eyes remained fixed to his upper body muscles.

'You are so weird!' she said and felt slightly intimidated.

He stepped into her sphere whilst she opened her legs and allowed him in then slowly shut her eyes as he lifted his right hand slowly and placed it onto her left cheek.

'You look so beautiful, but I can tell something is wrong!' he whispered as she placed her arms around him tightly.

'Nothing is wrong!' she replied.

'Since when do you drink like this!' he asked and placed his warm left hand onto the back of her neck then massaged it softly.

'We are both damaged goods, Quinton. We are so messed up and sad. We can't be placed back on the shelf even if we wanted!' she whispered and clenched on to that moment by wrapping her legs around his waist.

'So I'm going to ask you again, would you like some wine?' she asked.

'Okay, I'll drink with you!' he replied, taking caution of Emily's sudden sadness.

She hopped off the kitchen counter and opened the refrigerator.

'We will share the glass. Come!' she said and picked up the wine bottle with her left hand then slowly shut the refrigerator door with her right hand. 'Come with me!' she suggested and walked towards the living room, hoping that he'd follow immediately.

He remained still and watched her walk away, wondering what story she had hidden within her heart.

'Are you coming?' she asked.

'Close the kitchen curtains and I'll get the living room ones!'

'Sure thing!' he said and did as commanded.

It quickly turned darker within the living room. There was a slow warm breeze blowing into the living room from time to time. Sounds of vehicles and hooting entered from the balcony. The plasma screen volume was low, and all they could hear in between the news anchors debating about Western foreign issues and related third-world issues, and the street sounds was a storm of anxiety and loneliness spiralling around the two of them on the couch.

'I'm glad you came. I've been so alone!' she said in a low tone. 'I feel crazy when I'm alone!' she added and took a large sip from the wine glass and placed it onto the glass table. 'I feel like my monsters want to break through the walls when I sit here alone drunk of wine on most nights!' she mentioned, and as she spoke, a revelation unfolded.

Quinton understood her completely because he felt the same way. He also took a small sip from the wine glass and placed it back onto the glass table. There was still a wine stain on the carpet floor from the previous night, and his gold rosary was still underneath the left side couch.

'Tell me something. Why are we like this?' he asked.

'Too much money I guess!' she replied and giggled.

'It's not the money! Has to be something else,' he said whilst trying his best to erase the pain he was feeling inside his chest.

Emily leaned backwards and gestured for Quinton to do the same. Their nerves soothed, and they finally found comfort within their pain. It seemed more and more appropriate for them to be with each other at that very moment.

'I'm sorry for drugging you last night. I wanted you to feel something stronger!' she said and placed her right hand onto his left chest.

She wasn't used to the sound of his heartbeat, but the feeling of it throbbing brought her some sort of temporary joy. Quinton leaned forward and filled the wine glass up to the brim then took a larger sip from the wine glass and handed it to Emily.

'Thank you!' she said. 'You can't be half naked and I'm fully clothed!' she said and stood up quickly, dazed and slightly unbalanced, then removed her white summer dress and threw it into the right side couch.

'It's actually so hot!' she added.

'It's actually way too hot!' he replied then took a second to collect his emotions and his thoughts back from wandering into a different dimension.

'Everything has been so difficult lately. I don't even want to go back home!' Quinton said and leaned forward again then held on to the wine glass gently.

'You don't have to go home. Stay with me for a while!' Emily suggested, but Quinton knew he couldn't avoid the reality of the path.

'I can't stay here for too long. I must accept that we weren't born to find real love and head back home to drown in paperwork!' he replied and leaned backwards again then placed his right arm around Emily's neck.

She held on to his right with her right hand then kissed it softly. Her fingernails were also painted red. They were soft, warm, moist, and gentle.

'You take life way too seriously lately!' she stated the obvious. 'Let's do something fun and reckless!' she said and smiled.

He could see her brown eyes script a tale of danger as she looked at him, and she could see uncertainty inside his brown eyes. They were each imbalanced by the idea of being foolish, yet regardless of that, he wasn't accustomed to acting in such a wicked manner anymore and thus wondered why she still acted immaturely towards the feeling of pain. He couldn't quite grasp the thought of taking drugs with the heavy responsibly he had.

'No, nothing reckless!' he replied, but a large of part of his mind wanted to run away to the mind-controlling substances.

She pulled out a box of cigarettes from the side of the couch and leaned forwards to pick up a metallic black lighter from the glass table.

'At least a head rush, right?' she said and bit on to the cigarette bud with her straight white teeth. 'Do the honour for me!' she said and passed the lighter with her right hand.

Quinton sparked the lighter with his left thumb, and the flame burned brightly between them. She moved forward slowly, and the cigarette tobacco burned as she inhaled the smoke. He looked into her brown eyes as she exhaled the grey smoke towards the balcony entrance then felt compelled to do the exact same thing, knowing that he would at least be one step closer to death. The feeling of a head rush mesmerised him whilst indulging on red wine. Emily wormed her tongue into his mouth, and the feeling of her bittersweet warm tongue brushing against his tongue stimulated a lot of organs within him.

'Let's not ruin the moment. Just relax with me!' he whispered to her, even though he knew that having sex with another person besides Juliana wouldn't mend his heart because it was still broken.

Juliana's departure had left him indecisive, and he wondered which way to proceed with his actions. He immediately realised that every second away from her was essentially the universe's way of testing his character, and he did not want to fail anymore.

A few hours clocked over their endurance of bonding and laughter, and it became slightly clear to Quinton that his mindset on life was mainly based on the purity of those two elements. He felt slightly guilty for laughing and drinking lavishly with no worry whatsoever. Emily had allowed herself to open up more, which enabled Quinton to discover a different a world she had hidden within her heart. Her apartment had a tall dark brown shelf next to the plasma screen, filled with romance novels, political-based novels, and marketing books mostly untouched and placed there for decoration. The top shelf consisted of her father's African and African-American jazz collection.

'Got a record player?' he asked and picked up the wine glass from the same glass table and took a small sip.

'It's in one of the guest rooms!' she replied and sat up straight. 'I'll go get it!'

'Awesome! I'll get the food!' he said, then they individually walked in different directions.

He opened the refrigerator and took out mini burgers from a small see-through plastic container and a large ruby-red container filled with small cooked spicy chicken wings.

'It's a bit heavy!' Emily shouted from the second bedroom.

'Okay, I'm coming!' he replied then placed the food into a small oval plate, placing it into a microwave for a few minutes.

There were a lot of emotions sprinting recklessly and carelessly within Quinton's heart. At a point, he felt like he would break into a million pieces whilst all those emotions terrorized and caused havoc within his mind as he discovered that he missed Juliana so much more than words could describe. Despite all those emotions clogging his heart, he essentially realised that he needed to unwind and temporarily clinch onto a glimmer of happiness even if it meant drinking more wine and acting calmly to the fact that he'd just lost the person he purely loved the most.

'It's fine. I've got it!' he said and picked up the record player.

It wasn't as cliché and old as he thought it would be because it wasn't dusty at all. Matter of fact, it looked new.

They walked into the living room together, and as he placed the record player onto the glass table, he felt darkness hovering over him. It knew that he wasn't at his weakest, and it also knew that he was vulnerable.

'Get the food!' he said, and she gladly agreed with a smile on her face.

She didn't feel the wrath of loneliness whipping her body into sadness. A part of her gradually allowed her heart to feel love again. She stood by the microwave and wandered into the grey parts of her mind, drifting past everything that had caused damaged to her heart. It occurred to her in the past that everything about her previous relationships revolved around emotional abuse. She was used to emotional terrorists using the will of love to obtain anything they wanted from her, which made her a sceptical person because she was tired of being plucked like turkey before Thanksgiving.

'Should I bring vodka and cranberry juice?' she asked as she placed the food on the glass table.

'Yeah, sure, why not!' he replied and sat quietly on the couch closest to the balcony glass aluminium doors for a few seconds then rushed upstairs to refresh himself.

It wasn't long until he was finished. His phone rang as he walked into the living room again, but he did not hear it because Emily had made a conscious decision to turn it upside down to mute it from him. She didn't want anyone to disturb her moment with a lost soul such as Quinton himself.

'Quinton, we have Polish vodka, and we also have Russian vodka. Pick?' she said and lifted both bottles with both hands from the small wine cellar in the small pantry by the corner of the kitchen.

'What's the difference?' he asked with smooch on his face.

She kept quiet and thought carefully about that question then laughed out because she realised that she didn't know anything about the different types of vodkas, except to indulge on it like an old successful drunk.

Quinton plugged the record player's black cable onto an adapter.

'I give up!' she said and smiled, feeling safe again once she reached Quinton again and sat beside him.

'I've got some records of my own, you know, some folk music!' she said whilst stroking the top of his head softly and slowly.

'Yeah!' he replied sceptically whilst looking at the jazz record collection on the glass table. 'I'm not really a jazz fan. Bring the folk music!' he said and nibbled on the mildly spicy chicken wings and sat back on the couch whilst Emily walked in through the passage and hid inside the first bathroom right along the passage.

She wept, and he could hear it loud and clear. He gently knocked on the door and twisted the knob clockwise. The wind from the open glass window brushed against him as he entered and closed the bathroom door slowly, anxiously waiting to hear the truth hidden within her heart.

'Please open up to me!' he said, discovering that Emily was just as heartbroken as he was.

There was a temporary stain of sadness printed onto their faces. She looked at him as he walked closer to the bed and felt clogged by old memories of different men walking in and out of her life.

'I'm tired of being used!' she whispered as he sat right next to her and felt plastered with shame.

'I don't get it. Then why did we make love yesterday?' he asked.

She shrugged her shoulders and searched for a deeper reply within her mind. 'We were having fun, I guess!' she said and giggled through her pain.

He sat down and crawled up into a ball, placing his head in between his knees. She took a look at him and found herself captured by the tattoo on the middle of his back as soon as his left hand touched her right hand. She wasn't sure what to make of his affection, but despite that mere thought, she also knew that he was just as troubled as she was.

'I'm sorry. I'm still trying to find myself within all the chaos!' he stated.

'It's okay. We will be fine,' she assured him.

He stood up and walked away without hesitation, contemplating his wretched behaviour and wondering back to the past days when he wasn't so dented. His phone rang loud as he stepped into the living room from the passage. He rushed towards the kitchen with high hopes for a call from Juliana Rose, but instead it was his mother.

'Hello!' he answered.

'Hey, so Kimberly tells me that you're away!' Beth stated. 'Well, anyway Juliana called me numerous times because she didn't have your current number!'

'What did she say to you?' he asked and stepped towards the balcony, curious to find out if Juliana was okay.

'Nothing much, she just wanted to know how everyone was doing!' she replied and exhaled. Her car alarm went off in the background whilst she spoke to her son. 'You must come home soon!' she said and walked into Kimberly's bedroom then pressed her car keys.

'Why did your car go off?' Quinton asked and walked into the living room and subconsciously picked up a record and removed it from its cover. The disk looked like a large plastic plate with circular deep tracks on it. 'I bought her an engagement ring, Mother!' he said, whilst Beth remained speechless on the other end of the call.

'And?' she asked after a while and walked into the living room downstairs then picked up a full glass of white wine from wooden floor right next to the brown suede couch. 'Carry on!' she said and had a small sip. 'Did she say yes?' she asked and hoped for a positive reply.

His silence stated otherwise whilst he stepped outside to the balcony again and his face melted into grief.

'No, she doesn't know, I think!' he replied.

'I think you should stop everything and evaluate how you want your life to go!' she interrupted whilst strolling around the backyard pool in a silky dark blue gown. 'By the way, what do you mean 'I think'?' she asked, and he explained everything regarding that matter.

Minutes passed slowly, and he broke into a million pieces whilst speaking to his mother. Her tears streamed down her cheeks whilst he spoke about the love he had for Juliana.

'You will recover!' she said and planted her legs into the warm pool. 'Come home soon!' she added and looked upwards towards the dusk sunset. 'Right now, focus on being the best father that child will ever have,' she said, remembering the biggest secret she was hiding from her only son.

The thought of that very secret uncloaking rattled her mind whilst she took another sip from her wine glass.

'Come home and we will talk!' she suggested and watched Marcus switch on the kitchen lights. She wondered if he'd ever forgive her if she unveiled the truth.

'Okay, Mother, chat soon!' Quinton replied and hung up his Blackberry. He realised that Emily was right behind him as he turned around.

'You bought her a ring?' she asked in shock. 'Why would you do that?' she asked another question, which drove Quinton to the brink of devastation. Every single word coming out of her mouth pierced his heart with sharp nails, and he felt stuck in a rut, wondering which words to use.

'What do you want to hear, Emily?' he asked. 'That I loved her so much to the point where I feel so damaged without her!' he said. 'What do you want to hear?' he asked again. 'Huh?'

She sat on the middle couch and kept quiet, trying to understand the love that Quinton had for Juliana.

'What makes you think she wants to be married?' she asked.

Her questions was valid, and he did not know how to answer it, except to trail on the sideline of her questioning by being avoidant and pretending that her questions didn't have an impact on his mindset.

'Just sit down and take in every second slowly!' she said. 'Gather your thoughts!'

He rested his back on the couch whilst folk music played from the record player, and he began to see previous precious memories of his love for Juliana more magnified and amplified on the white ceiling. Her laughter grew louder within his mind as he lay there, thinking of how beautiful she was with her miraculous smile, her beautiful round green eyes which at times glowed in emerald, her straight white teeth, her deep dimple, and her light skin tone. Juliana had turned into a mirage inside Quinton's dry, thirsty imagination, and he couldn't deny the plastered pain over his face.

A stream of long-awaited tears streamed from the opposite ends of his eyelids, and he felt so exhausted merely from fighting for real love. Nothing else mattered to him though, and he knew it, regardless of his untamed manner. 'It was all for real love,' he thought to himself whilst images of Juliana swept passed him from the left side and on to the right side like a quick slideshow. Sadness clouded his mind, and he felt the memories of Juliana beginning to disappear away from him.

He could hear and feel the vibrancy of her heart throbbing loudly against his left ear drum whenever he'd place his head onto her chest. Goosebumps cropped onto his skin as his mind recalled the way her soft warm hands would softly scratch against his chest. Quinton shut his brown eyes whilst the music played, and he could feel all the emotions that he'd ever felt galloping like wild horses on an empty field of love. He felt angry for allowing himself to feel love then grew sadden by its ability to break him down then smiled to the pleasures of it. It was all consuming and confusing as the sound of Juliana's cry alliterated, and chanted loudly within his mind. He wondered if he was going crazy and becoming obsessed with the one person he couldn't be with anymore. She was so far away from him, and he knew that he couldn't run away from the reality of his life due to work obligations and other responsibilities. He wandered through every single thought and frame-grabbing image without any intention of stopping then realised that he liked the pain he was feeling. Something about his pain drew him closer to the brink of death. It occurred to him that he was finally imaginatively walking into a moment of clarity, or he thought it was. He was accustomed to the pain of being heartbroken. A part of him could see the beauty of death lingering above him as he lay quietly and wondered what it would feel like to be set free from the world. He'd established that he was also being cowardly at the same time for having such thoughts because he'd soon be a father to their child.

'You will see her again!' Emily said. 'It's not the end of the world!'

Emily did not understand it was the end of Quinton's world. He couldn't see the future painted brightly without Juliana in it. An idea popped up inside his mind and plunged him towards pursuing love again. He wanted to leave everything behind to be with Juliana Rose but found himself faced with a tragic dilemma between that and his normal life.

Chapter Sixteen

Motherland

The Rose family had settled into their new apartment on the coastline of Camps Bay in Cape Town, Western Cape, South Africa. The warm temperature was inconsistent because of the random small rainy forecasts and cool winds blowing in different directions. Juliana had fallen in love with the sloppy city. The atmosphere was incredibly magical and fascinating to her green eyes. She could feel the soul of the city rushing through her body and paralysing any doubts she had about relocating. Her smile glowed brightly as she looked downwards from her bedroom balcony. She could see seagulls flying together over the cool water above the vibrant beach. There were so many people camped by the beach side, and her whole perception of life was altered within one second. She felt limitless and unbounded by her past, regardless of her pregnancy.

The foetus within her stomach kicked happiness whilst she indulged on a glass of fresh mango juice. Her mother called her name out, but she couldn't hear anything but the sounds of people laughing on the walkway and the sounds of waves crashing in the ocean. The salty seawater smell cast her monsters away, and she finally found real peace within her heart. The sun was setting, and the cool breeze rushing through her balcony brought her some sort of distracting closure from thinking of Quinton.

'Julia!' Marissa said. 'Come downstairs, baby. Food is ready!'

Their house was incredibly amazing and glowed beautifully from a distance, situated amongst long-branched trees. The area was eco-friendly and clean. Everything about the new environment brought great joy to the Rose family. All interior designing work was designed Marissa's younger sister who'd started her own interior designing company about a year ago within the city called Inner Firelanee Co. Juliana's bedroom consisted of a king-size bed and nothing else. It was still empty and large with space which inspired her to paint. She loved the idea of her bedroom being empty because it embraced the idea of a new beginning. She'd just finished refreshing from a warm shower and had dressed into a medium-size white T-shirt, loose white linen pyjama pants, dark red slippers that Quinton had bought for her, and light red silky gown. She looked absolutely beautiful and flourished like a yellow lily flower blossoming after a rainy season. Her curly brunette hair was slightly wet, and her moist curls gave her an exotic feature.

Her mother's bedroom was situated right next to hers, and there was another spare bedroom on the opposite side of the passage. They'd wondered what they would turn the bedroom into. There were clear thoughts of turning it into a toddler's playroom and blurry thoughts of turning it into an art room, a place they could both go and paint. They were both extremely talented painters and extraordinary gifted musicians. The ability to create a song, a painting or sculpt anything was part of their DNA.

Juliana stepped onto the wooden floor in the passage and felt serenity as she walked towards the wooden staircase ahead. There was a mesmerising smell of fresh duck being roasted in the kitchen, a smell of fresh fish sauce dressing, a whiff of boiled mixed and chopped vegetables, and potato chips being fired in a small pot. Juliana walked straight into a wooden walkway bridge, which led to another passage that led to a lounge area and mini bar section. She looked towards the right side and discovered a visual like no other. The beautiful amber street lights glowed brightly through the glass wall in front of her, and the buildings on the outskirts of her peripheral vision lit the fireworks within her soul. She finally knew what genuine happiness felt like, and yet she felt slightly guilty whilst dawning to the fact that she'd left Quinton behind. A part of her wished that he could see the same picture she was looking at at that very moment. She wondered if he'd ever find happiness the same way she did, and as she reached the ground floor, she found her mother clutching on to something within her white apron. Juliana wondered what Marissa kept hidden away from her, and an epiphany clocked onto her timeline as she realised her mother was hiding something important.

'Let me head upstairs to refresh quickly. You can start without me!' Marissa said with a hint of nervousness in her tone.

A moment of truth unfolded as her phone slipped from her moist hands, and as she tried to pick it up, the engagement box accidentally slipped from the apron pocket and onto the wooden floor.

Juliana felt absolutely horrible as she opened her green eyes widely and realised what she really meant to Quinton.

Marissa picked it up and walked away to the staircase.

'What is that?' Juliana asked and followed her mother.

'Let it be, Juliana. It's nothing!' Marissa replied then felt Juliana's left hand grip her left arm.

They argued.

'He doesn't love you!' Marissa shouted and placed the black engagement box back into her large apron pocket.

Juliana reached out and placed her right hand into the large pocket. Her mother realised the magnitude of what the engagement ring could do. It had a possessive power that could alter her daughter's heart. It had the ability to change the course of their destiny and bring about instability to their happiness. Marissa knew that her daughter would give up a lifetime of happiness to be miserable and in love with Quinton. Juliana knew that deeply within her heart, she'd sacrifice the beautiful scenery of the motherland to burn harshly under the burning sun in the semi-desert as long as she was with her only lover again. She'd go anywhere with him.

'You know I'd move to the moon if he lived there!' Juliana said, realising that she'd made a terrible mistake by leaving.

It all seemed too much to take it as she felt the butterfly effect of losing love. Her temporary happiness vanished into thin air while her foetus kicked within and caused discomfort. She grinned in pain whilst they both clenched the engagement box in her right hand. Marissa did not notice the pain all over Juliana's face because she was merely focused on taking the engagement box away from her daughter. Juliana placed her soft left hand onto her small plumping stomach whilst her right hand remained glued to the engagement box then tried to move backwards, forgetting that she was on a staircase. Her left ankle got imbalanced. She slid off her and fell.

'Let him go!' Marissa repeated and ripped the engagement box away from Juliana's right hand.

The loud sound of Marissa's words echoed into her Juliana's ears repeatedly as she fell downwards and turned unconscious as her head hit the wooden floor, drifting her mind into another dimension.

Her mother screamed out to the top of her lungs whilst panicking and shaking. Juliana could hear church bells ringing slowly above her in between the silence. She awoke in an unfamiliar place. Her body ached in pain as she sat up straight from a long bench. She looked around and found herself in an old rectangular church hall poked with cracked arched windows. The walls were made out of limestones, which were attached together with grey concrete. She sneezed twice from the dusty particles in the air, then a wave of fresh air brushed against the arched wooden doors and rattled her mind. Another wave of fresh air pushed the doors, leaving the main entrance open behind her. She looked back and stood up slowly, and she could see a short layer of green grass ahead. The water was crystal clear from far with small ripples in between. Its beauty restored hope into Juliana's heart as she discovered an incredibly large lake ahead. She realised that she was barefooted as she looked down at her light-toned feet and felt the soft fabric on her sky blue summer dress with her left fingertips. Her body was slim which caused a lot of panic and confusion inside her mind for a few seconds until see looked up and noticed a child running by the side of the lake in cheerful mood. A tall figure appeared from behind the child, and that visual itself mesmerised Juliana into a delightful mood. At first, she didn't notice the tall figure behind her child but soon discovered that it was Quinton.

There was a storage cabin painted in blinding white behind her projected family. She smiled whilst stepping down from the concrete steps and onto the soft grass to join them. Her young daughter looked so beautiful and elegant in a long peach summer dress and white palms on her small feet. Juliana knew that it was her daughter, Arabella, because of the identical resembles. Arabella was just as breathtaking as her mother. Their beauty brought great joy to Quinton's heart as he picked up his daughter and laughed out loud. The only difference between Juliana and her daughter was that Arabella had light brown eyes and her curly hair stands were black instead. Juliana was pleased to see her only lover smiling without a care in the world. It seemed as though their troubles were behind them.

The scenery looked extremely bright to her green eyes. She moved closer with caution, wondering if everything around her was real or just an illusion. Arabella's laugh grew louder whilst Quinton tickled her. For the first time in a long time, she could see radiance of love flowing from Quinton whilst he also laughed out loud. He was wearing an Indian cotton white shirt with rolled-up sleeves to his elbows, a gold rosary with small golden beads around his neck, a silver watch on his left wrist, a pair of rolled-up dark blue jeans. His soft feet were moist from the soft green grass. He smiled and looked at Juliana, the same way he did when he met her for the first time within that red and white tent.

'You guys look so beautiful together!' she said whilst they kept laughing.

Quinton bent downwards and placed Arabella back into the green grass to allow his daughter to run and explore around.

There was so much fire burning inside their child's heart, and they knew that they'd created an extraordinary being. Their daughter's laughter destroyed any structures barricading love away from their hearts, and they both smiled to the purity she possessed. Arabella ran towards her mother who kneeled onto the soft green grass to hug her daughter, but instead Arabella ran right through her as if she was an elusive hologram. It caused confusion within her mind as she turned around and called out her daughter's name, but Arabella did not turn around. Instead, she ran towards the right side of the church and cartwheeled on the slope and fell. She seemed as clumsy as her mother, and Quinton admired the beauty of that very moment.

'Quinton!' Juliana said and turned around.

Her heart twitched as Quinton walked through her body, and within that split second, his smile turned into a frown, which initially painted sadness into her face. She could hear his thoughts projecting out loud by the sound of his voice.

'One step at a time!'

'One step at a time!'

'What am I doing?'

'Directions!'

'Directions!'

'Directions!'

'I need help!'

'I miss Juliana!'

'I miss Juliana!'

'So lost in the world!'

'Come on, get a hold of yourself. You have a daughter!'

'Why am I panicking?'

'Repeat these three words to yourself. I. Am. Okay!'

'I am okay,' he whispered yet remained unsure of his words and unsure of himself.

Quinton stepped away from Juliana and repeated those very words then inhaled the fresh air slowly and felt a heavy load of anxiety drop off his shoulders. Quinton walked towards Arabella slowly, and Juliana felt her heart drifting away from her chest as he walked towards the church entrance.

'Don't go too far!' he shouted and looked back at the steady lake then felt cloaked into redemption whilst admiring the view in front of him.

There were hills aligning straight for a few kilometres and curving inwards beside the lake, and at the end of the lake was an opening.

Quinton looked straight at it and knew that he could overcome all the obstacles, basking in redemption.

'Honey!' Juliana called out and moved closer, finally finding herself trapped between the glare of beautiful existence and the reality of her life.

She watched love walk away from her heart and alter her mind into a propelling state. Her emotions wound clockwise and enabled her to realise that fate wasn't in her side. Nothing about her recent happiness would stabilise permanent comfort, and she finally knew where her heart belonged. It wasn't scripted with the universe's commandments, but Juliana knew that her love for Quinton could defeat all odds of reality.

'Honey!' she cried out and felt saddened to the visual in front of her, lowly esteemed by the glow of love flossing right before her green eyes.

'Please!' she pleaded. 'I can't lose you both!' she said to herself.

Time slowed down and soaked her mind in sorrow as Quinton opened his car door and allowed Arabella to enter it. They drove away on a gravel road towards their gloomy future, and Juliana stood there whilst tears streamed down her face. She felt a false sense of freedom tranquilise her body back to reality which made her feel merely alive and free as she opened her green eyes. A part of that freedom brought guilt and plastering pain into her life, which made her feel alone again trapped in a hole.

She awoke with tears streaming down the side of her cheeks. The bright lights above her head were overwhelming to her consciousness and inaccurately leading her into believing that Arabella was gone. This moment caused panic within a few seconds after listening to the sounds around her. There was loud beating sound of her heart in between alliteration sounds of the ambulance syringe.

'What's going on?' she asked and tried to sat up straight on the hospital stretcher.

'It's okay. You are okay!' a female paramedic said. 'I'm just running some protocol tests!'

Marissa could not bear to look at her daughter, for she feared for Juliana. No words were shared between the two. Juliana looked at the paramedic whilst the ambulance swerved through different lanes.

'You kept that away from me?' she asked and felt driven away from that trust she had.

There was no reply for a few seconds whilst Marissa thought of a way to explain her motives but realised that her words would be invalid to her daughter's ears. Juliana looked to the ambulance roof and wondered if she had lost Arabella, which caused her a slight anxiety attack.

'Is my baby okay?' Juliana asked whilst breathing heavily.

'Juliana, just relax. Your baby is fine!' Marissa responded whilst seated by the edge of the back doors with a seatbelt strapped around her upper body.

'Ma'am, her pulse rate is too high!' the female paramedic said to Marissa and injected Juliana left arm with.

Juliana seemed highly irrational and unstable, driven into madness by her recent dream. All she could see whilst falling in and out of consciousness were images of Arabella running around and giggling whilst cartwheeling away on the soft green grass by the old church.

Within minutes of that incident occurring, Quinton awoke from a blackout and felt his heart twitch irregularly to the effects of smoking numerous cigarettes whilst lying quietly by himself on the left side couch whilst Emily tweeted away on her phone in the kitchen.

They'd completely forgotten about the food on the glass table. It had turned cold and dry. He looked around whilst music played loudly from the record player and listened to his thoughts. He could hear bells ringing in the background of the song. He scrolled through his phone and swung through pictures of Juliana then deleted all those after viewing them. The pain of losing her wouldn't go away, and the way he felt about her made Emily slightly subconsciously jealous because she'd never seen love so genuine and profound. He didn't remember the dream trend he'd just had but immediately felt soothed into despair, tormented by heartbreak, whilst he metaphorically bled through the silence.

'I think you should call her!' Emily said and sat right beside him.

'And say what?' Quinton asked and sat up straight, feeling drowsy and dehydrated from consuming a mixture of beverages.

He nibbled on the cold food whilst speaking to Emily who seemed ill mannered, but he didn't care much about anything anymore.

'I don't know, but isn't that what love is about?' she asked and looked into his brown eyes.

'Just calling for no reason at all!'

Emily expressed herself more on the topic of love and placed her arms around his shoulders. He began to realise what he meant to her, which led him into confusion, and he found himself in a very complex situation, a matter of love to his heart versus a matter of lust to his body. He couldn't quite figure out which aspect mattered the most at that very moment. All he wanted to do was call Juliana and listen to her speak, to hear her breathing through the phone, and to feel close to her again. He dialled Juliana's number, and her phone rang for a while on her bedroom window frame, but nobody answered.

Two hours had passed inside the intensive care unit. Juliana Rose was finally conscious enough to be consulted with accurate information. She'd fostered the idea of keeping her unborn child away from anyone that had the power to yield their world into darkness, subconsciously realising even the slight will of allowing herself to show love resulted towards unnecessary pain. Her mind weighed all options of a way to proceed forward with a lie about having a miscarriage. She needed this idea to collaborate out of someone else's' mouth then had an epiphany that her mother was the only person who had the will to be dishonest with her.

Her mother's mindset was also gravitating towards the same idea whilst wondering around the waiting area. They'd not spoken since. Marissa had never seen her daughter acting out in that matter and knew that she had to get rid of her daughter's adoration wrapped with genuine love for her lover. She realised that the only way to sink her daughter's thoughts of running back was to meddle with their affair and to pull their strings apart forever. She picked up her phone and called the father's unborn baby.

Quinton's phone rang whilst Juliana entered into the waiting area on a wheelchair being assisted by an old plumy woman dressed in a pink nurse outfit.

'I'm sorry for fighting with you!' Juliana said, and Marissa dropped the phone call to attend to her child.

'It's okay!' Marissa replied. 'I'm going to fix everything, and everything will be okay!'

They looked at each other for a few seconds, and they could see words projected and bypassing each other's eyes of a lie that needed to be told, or so they thought to it as a necessity.

It wasn't until the silver clock on the master suite bedroom stroked towards midnight that Quinton made his way downstairs to find his phone after awaking from deep sleep. He'd woken up after feeling chained and incarcerated by a trend of nightmares. Sleep had become his foe, for he'd always found himself fighting an endless battle with his monsters whilst dreaming. It occurred to him that something was wrong, and he could sense it as a whizz of deception pierced through his half-fulfilled life.

His phone rang and he answered. Juliana and her mother delivered the bad news. Their words sunk his heart into an all-time low, and he felt devastated. He did not say anything back, and at the end of the phone call, he hung up and pretended to be fine with the news then wandered through the guilt of his newly found freedom. He felt disgusted with himself.

There was a playlist of music playing low from the speaker in the living room, and the song levelled his mind back to the plain field of his history with Juliana. He felt driven into madness by everything around him because it all reminded him of pure love. It seemed as if love had claimed full ownership of his soul, mind, and body. He walked around the apartment, from the living room to the kitchen to the balcony, with a full wine glass in his right hand. At the same time, he contemplated his weakness to be reigned with love and wondered if showing love was his greatest strength. It seemed inevitable for him to want affection, then as his wild thoughts galloped, he finally cherished the idea of personal growth and rightful passage to freedom away from the earthly wretched intake of love. He realised that his world was corrupted by an influence of old dazzled dreams of perfection painted in white and gold or in gold and green. His colossal dreams amounted to beige disappointment, and whilst his mind dragged his heavy heart through memory lane, he felt repulsed by the way he'd been acting throughout his trip. He wanted to return home to deal with the challenges ahead of him and find some sort of closure, and he knew that he couldn't change his heart regardless of how much he tried and thus accepted the course of his fate and allowed the whips of life to enslave him back to work.

Regardless of the harsh world, his world seemed endless with the possibilities of new formalities and new conquests filled with an unravelling hope for achieving greatness. He couldn't deny the fact that he was dented by losing an unborn baby and then wondered if it was a road sign from above or some sort of proclamation directing him to see that he wasn't ready to be a father. All these thoughts circled around him and drove him to drink more and more until the world began to look beautiful through his brown eyes again. Every sip of red wine drove him farther and farther away from reality. He found himself intoxicated in the living room, lying still, vulnerable to more temptations whilst trying to find retribution and redemption. He felt like he resembled an old crippled homeless man.

His imagination wielded him away from a world he was familiar to, and he found himself being pressed onto the couch through drunk paralysis by an invisible force and felt his wrists burning on silver shackles binding him down as his heart turned rattled and aggressive, howling like werewolf. The aluminium door curtains aligning from the right end the kitchen began to move fast to a cool breeze brushing in from the opened doors, and at that moment, his stomach grumbled from hunger whilst the world crumbled around him. Everything shook tragically until he see could a beautiful femalelike structure walking towards him from the balcony outdoor table. Her glow was as bright as the sun. There were more mysterious angels, glowing and floating outside by the balcony. Only one of them landed into the balcony floor. Her sphere glowed brightly like blinding stadium light whilst the living room lighting turned extremely dark. She moved closer and lay right beside him whilst he kept falling in and out of consciousness. The living room evolved into a different scenery, and magical auroras appeared from thin air and blessed the room with pleasance. She placed her head onto his chest and placed her soft right hand onto his diaphragm, which immediately muted the pain inside his stomach.

'What's wrong?' she asked, and her voice radiated loudly into his ears and cropped up goosebumps on his skin. Her presence flushed his pain away.

His heart burned, and a spark lit within his soul as his pulse rate increased to the feeling of her warm soft right hand imprinted onto the left side of his chest. He couldn't see clearly yet was still in disbelief of the remarkable visuals above him, and as he tilted his head towards the left, he could see a blurry visual of her face and immediately knew that he was imprisoned by her angelic beauty. The bright light suppressing her smooth skin revealed and uncovered her face like a blanket. Her perfectly lengthened white-toothed smile made her blossom like a beautiful white flower unveiling itself in the beginning of a spring season, and her smile momentarily caught his attention and made memories of his harsh past disappear. It felt so miraculous to be uplifted from the disgusting rut he was in.

'I remember you!' he whispered and smiled then placed his right hand on her soft cheeks.

'You do?' she asked. 'From where exactly?' She blushed and closed her blue eyes.

'I had a dream about you once!' he replied. 'We were together in a grey mansion with a dog and a beautiful child!' And he took a moment to analyse her face.

His right hand remained glued onto her soft-textured skin by her left bottom jaw and her small left ear. Her nose was slightly short and pointy with two small nostril holes underneath. She had naturally small pink lips which glowed crystal clear to his brown eyes. Her eyebrows were black and thin, leaving him mesmerised and amused. Her body was covered in a white cloak, all the way from her neck and all the way down to her ankles. She was wearing a shiny golden ankle bracelet on her left ankle, which made her look extremely elegant and slightly desirable.

'I had to come down and see you!' she whispered. 'You aren't doing—' she said but got interrupted,

'Who are you?' he asked. 'What's your name?' he asked another question then remained still whilst inebriated.

'I'm Olivia!' she said and placed her soft left hand onto the right side of his face, which gave his body a cool chill and cleared away his intoxicated condition. 'I watch over you every day,' Olivia said, 'wondering when you will find healing!' She then blinked slowly and repeatedly whilst speaking. Her sweet tone lashed into his ears and whipped away every single bad spirit within his mind, and she smiled from the pureness she possessed inside her heart.

'What's wrong?' she said again.

'Nothing!' he replied and closed his eyelids.

'Stop lying to me. We see everything!' she stated.

'Then why are you asking me?' he asked.

'Because I want you to be honest with yourself,' she replied and exhaled from her mouth.

Her fresh breath smelt like a cool breeze of air whilst momentarily taking him away to an empty beach. He could see four footprints leaving marks of genuine love on the soft beach sand right next to the green embankment.

'What do you see?' Olivia asked.

'A beautiful place!' Quinton replied whilst wondering what Olivia was trying to show him.

'I want you to remember this place!' she said. 'Always!'

He felt the cold wave of water washing his feet, which seemed bizarre because he wasn't by the sea at all. The four footprints ahead began to disappear as the waves washed over them, and he found himself completely clueless of the sight in front of him.

'I know I've lost them!' he said then realised that Olivia had a smile on her face. 'Why are you smiling?' he asked.

'Oh, nothing at all!' she said. 'You are absolutely adorable!'

'What?' he said sceptically.

'Yes! Like a zebra!' she said and smiled.

'Beg your pardon?' he said.

'All confused with stripes. Unsure of yourself!' she said, but he wasn't listening to her speak because he was focused on the dreamy blue colour within her eyes.

'Where are you from?' he asked, and she immediately stopped speaking. 'Well?'

'I can't tell you!' she said, shutting her mouth to reframe from being honest. Regardless of that motion, her blue eyes unveiled the truth to him. He could see layers of clouds within her beautiful eyes.

'Please stop!' she said and shut her eyes, feeling shy and overly exposed. 'They were right. I shouldn't have come here!' she added and stood up. Her bright light glowed around her body again as she stepped away backwards.

'Don't go!' he said and sat up straight, feeling woozy and exhausted.

'I'm sorry!' she shouted. 'I have to return before they know that we are missing!'

Her wings spread wide from her back as stepped onto the balcony floor and levitated in mid-air for a few seconds, and within split seconds, all bright structures vanished into thin air. A loud sound of thunder rattled Quinton's comfort as he stood up and brushed the empty wine bottle off the glass table by mistake. He walked towards the aluminium doors to close them as it began to drizzle outside. All the magical auroras inside the living room began to disappear as he walked back to the couch. He remained puzzled yet felt delightful for being blessed with such a presence.

Olivia glanced down from within the grey clouds and smiled with grace. This was the first time they'd ever disobeyed the laws made by the constitution of guardian angels, a covenant of elderly guardian angels that stated that no guardian angel is allowed to interact with their human. Olivia flew through layers of heavy grey clouds and paused from above then looked downwards again. There was a small root of infatuation slowly growing inside her heart as she smiled at the beauty of connecting with an earthling. His difference made him unique and special, which began to confuse Olivia's motives. They all flew and pierced through heavy layers of cool air until the black sky above opened up slowly. She wondered if the league of elderly guardian angels would suspend her for disobeying them, and as she stepped onto the white clouds that aligned themselves downwards like steps, she heard someone calling her name.

'I'm coming!' she shouted whilst panicking within then walked past a lot of other guardian angels who scuffled around a walkway.

On the sideline of the walkway were golden doors to different sections of the first temple, partially leading to communal shops filled with endless goodies and food supplies. They also worked in a world of trading through doing good, and in order to make a purchase, an angel would have to trade a 'good deed token' for food supplies. The system they lived by kept them balanced and filled with bundles of joy. Their hearts were wrapped in pure love, and everyone around embraced the beauty of peace.

Olivia rushed through the busy walkway, and it seemed as though a lot of angels she had passed were displeased with the way she'd recently acted. She was so different from the rest, and her difference brought great discomfort because she was unpredictable. There was a golden path at the end of the walkway, and as she stepped onto the golden bricks, everything turned silent behind her, and she was completely alone. The walls were puffed clouds that changed colours depending on the individual's mood, and in this case, they were. They were stacked together all the way to the end of the path. Olivia strolled past the golden path quietly whilst smiling in joy until she could see old memories of demons chasing her through dark rainy clouds and trying to grip her golden ankle bracelet. She stepped away from a puffy cloud on her right side and disclosed her mind from thinking of the past and kept walking straight. The golden door automatically opened itself as she moved closer, and the hall she entered into was shambolic and messy. It was a sanatorium for injured angels of all kinds. There were so many angels on floating hospital beds made of clouds, and most of them looked pleased with themselves for the efforts they'd put in for defending the world from evil. There was a staircase made out of gold.

'Olivia!' an elderly angel shouted from above.

Olivia shrieked into a ball and looked terrified as she stepped onto the staircase and moved extremely slowly, wondering what the elderly matron would say to her about disobeying the law. The office above was filled with shelves of grey file books everywhere. A tall angel appeared from nowhere and looked displeased with Olivia's actions.

'How many times must I tell you you aren't allowed to communicate with the earthlings?' the mother, Alexa, said.

'I'm sorry, Mother!' Olivia replied.

'Extremely disappointed by your behaviour!' Alexa interrupted. 'Tell me what happened to the last earthling you spoke to in their dream?' Alexa asked and waited for a reply. 'Look at me when I'm talking to you!'

There was a moment of silence accompanied by sounds of thunder in the background.

'Answer me, Olivia!' she shouted, and her voice shook the room, causing grey file books and a few bottles of healing potions to scatter onto the cloudy floor.

'She ended up in a mental institution!' Olivia replied. 'I'm sorry!' she said and kept quiet.

Her mother walked towards her slowly. 'I love you, Olivia, but you act ungrateful at times!'

'I'm sorry!' Olivia replied and moved backwards.

'Don't be afraid!' Alexa whispered and placed her arms around her daughter.

They were an exact replica of each other. The only difference was the grey hair strands on Alexa's head.

'Now go and do a better job!' she said to Olivia. 'I'm sure the covenant will want to see you when you get back!'

'Yes, Mother, I will!' Olivia replied and walked away, feeling misunderstood and saddened by her mother's tone, but within seconds of returning to the main walkway, her smile erupted through her sadness, and the fire within her heart burned even brighter as she thought of her earthling. She knew it was wrong to interact with a human, but she did not feel the wrath of loneliness anymore. That was a feeling both Olivia and Quinton felt after their recent encounter. She knew what her job description was but immediately wondered what she needed to be happy, which also made her wonder if she was being selfish for having such needs.

A lot of angels flew in different directions for a second earth call, mostly flocking over households in suburb areas, above apartment blocks, and on sidewalks to prevent any monsters from rising from the depths of hell. Olivia rushed back to Emily's apartment and levitated right through the aluminium doors then found Quinton sleeping comfortably on the couch. It was quiet in between the raindrops outside on the balcony. There was a smell of jacaranda flowers waving through the area and in through the opened aluminium doors by the kitchen. He looked peaceful whilst facing the glass table and snuggled up on a long cotton couch pillow. She moved closer and lay behind him and then covered his lengthy body with her large white right wing.

'You are finally safe!' she whispered and placed her right arm around him and shut her blue eyes to create a safety cloak and to protect him from harm's way.

She'd completely zoned into him as all his memories, thoughts, and dreams were momentarily running through his mind and bypassing through her mind. She could see everything clearly, and it was clear that his mind and heart trailed towards one familiar direction, a place of tranquillity gushing with silence or perfectly aligned with sweet sounds of harmony. The thought of peace crossed his mind on several occasions throughout his dream pattern, and he involuntarily smiled whilst sleeping.

This was the first time he ever found himself happy with everything happening around him, and he could finally feel warmth covering his body like an African warrior blanket. He gently placed his left hand onto her wing without even realising because he was still sleeping then stroked her right wing softly and pulled it over his right shoulder.

She opened her blue eyes, once realising that she'd forgotten where she was for the past five minutes. It was rare for her to feel so connected. She smiled and shut her eyelids again with high hopes for profound prosperity to store itself into her earthling's soul. Her mind merged into her earthling's past history by placing her right hand onto the left side of his chest, enabling her to also feel his irregular heartbeat. She found herself opening up files within his mind, compelling information that could help her understand why his heart continuously fostered conflict that kept him secluded from a world of everlasting happiness. His past was slightly horrific and terrifying to see, but she entered nevertheless, cautiously stepping forward onto an empty dry plain field covered in red grass, filled with monsters everywhere displayed in a carnage manner, eating out his heart on the far end of the field and scrapping away the goodness of his soul in the middle. They could not see her because of her ability to cloak herself away from the evil's sight. She entered an unpleasant era of her earthling's time. His projection appeared in front of her, and it began to move slowly. Thus, she followed it back to the raw core of his misery. It stopped moving, and loud sounds of violence blew towards her ears, and she could see her earthling's family members fighting in a living room. The walls were painted in illuminating mixed striped colours of red, black, dark blue, mustard, and dark green. Quinton's age had decreased back to the age of seven. He was just a toddler at the time, peeping through a wooden door, looking at his parents displaying gestures of violence towards each other because of an agreement which had erupted from the pretext of money, and whilst this happened, his small heart slowly shrieked and crumbled into pain, causing him to be afraid of committing to the devotion of marriage.

At that very moment, it became ideal and custom to the toddler version of himself that real love didn't exist, or so he thought to himself at the time, leaving him lost like an abandoned homeless child, which was ironic because he'd then spend most of his early youth in private school boarding houses. He was clueless of righteous direction simply because he was growing up without a mentor on standby.

Within seconds, his projection enlarged and aged to his early teenage years. It was a moment of his seventh grade graduation dinner from a private preparatory school on the hills. He was wearing a white shirt, a tie striped in dark red, dark blue, and mustard colours, a pair of grey shorts, long grey socks stretching all the way to his knees, and a pair of polished black school shoes.

The anticipation of finally graduating from a junior level and proceeding to a different school for high school was slightly overwhelming to the young chap as he waited for his parents on a bench on a field in between a basketball court and an indoor hall, swinging his feet and grazing his school shoe soles against the wet. The tree branches above him waved in different angles, causing his plump baby-fat face to cloak in and out of the darkness from the moon light. There was a large sidewalk lamp twenty away from bench, and what appeared to be a dark shadow slowly turned into a male figure of a security guard patrolling the sports grounds who would soon console Quinton and advise him to stand strong.

All these memories began to merge together, and Olivia could finally see the path that had led her earthling to that very moment. She felt liberated and strong willed to unveil herself to him, knowing the consequences of interacting with an earthling, and then he awoke, feeling dehydrated and uneasy. She turned invisible and hid herself away, wondering what to do or say, wondering why it recently felt right for her to defy the law written by the covenant of elderly guardian angels, a law that maintained a balance between the world of earthlings and the world of guardian angels.

It appeared that Quinton wanted to fight his monsters alone, hence his denial for prayer and his denial for support from anyone else besides Juliana Rose. He walked towards the kitchen to have a glass of water; Olivia sat up straight on the couch and watched him fight an endless battle with himself. He was confused and lost in the darkest parts of his mind, hovering over his past like a seagull flying around in circles over large repels of nothing.

Olivia wondered if reappearing again would bring her earthling more closure or derail him into a brink of madness. She wasn't sure of a lot of things, but standing up and moving closer to the kitchen with a constitutional walk felt like the right thing to do, bearing in mind the covenant laws. Her body structure shrank to human size as she moved closer to her earthling. Quinton took a large sip of water from a crystal clear glass and looked towards the balcony door, feeling slightly compressed by the thoughts of losing Juliana's love, having the ability to foresee impossible supernatural structures and his long-term memories of his secluded youth. He closed his brown eyes, vanquished himself away from pride, and tried to pray for the first time in a while whilst successfully rattling all the monsters camping around his heart, and whilst doing so, he could feel warmth glazing over his body. All the monsters within him broke out of his back in large numbers and were crippled whilst burning on the wooden floor.

Everything seemed normal again until he opened his brown eyes and discovered Olivia standing right next to him with her warm arms around his body and her large wings spread in opposite directions to shield her earthling from harm's way. She didn't realise that he could see her until he placed his arm around her body.

'Thank you!' Quinton said, placed his chin onto her right shoulder, and unintentionally rubbed her back softly with his left hand.

'You are welcome!' Olivia responded, knowing of the consequences of interacting with him. She was slightly flattered by his ability to be gentle and grateful.

'You didn't have to come back, you know!' he said.

'I know!' she replied and smiled.

His heartbeat pulsed back to normal, and it was quiet in between the sounds of cars moving fast on the nearest freeway.

'I feel so lost!' he whispered and dwelled in the moment, hoping to find some sort of balance between his fear of falling off the wagon and his glimmer glade of persevering towards a better future, one filled with adoration and peace.

'You aren't lost anymore. I'm with you!' she whispered back and allowed herself to feel compassion for an earthling.

He immediately found himself growing strangled by his rogue persona at that very moment, leaving his mind to chant for more positivity.

'Let's get ready to go back home, okay?' she suggested and walked towards the living room.

Her wings merged with her body, and she seemed more human as she stepped in the staircase and into the master suite. They found Emily Lith sleeping comfortably on the bedspread, dreaming away of a distant land and hoping to find some sort of comfort on her path to find real love. It had occurred to Quinton whilst he started packing his clothes into his luggage bags that he felt differently about his future. It seemed slightly brighter and more appealing to look forward to. All his previous negative thoughts whirred away from his mind like an old pantry being dusted off years and years of cobwebs. He felt clean and energetic, wielded by the strength to find the best version of himself within.

The atmosphere still bloomed of darkness outside whilst he zipped his luggage bags and made his way downstairs to the passage with the first luggage bag then returned for a second trip to fetch his second luggage bag, and whilst picking up his second luggage bag, he looked at Emily on the bed and knew that he couldn't leave without saying anything.

'Emily, wake up!' he said and moved closer,

'Don't wake her up!' Olivia said, and there was a moment of silence whilst he looked towards the bedroom window towards the right and watched Olivia flocking towards other guardian angels above. His body remained restless underneath the cream white bed sheet then found himself drawn to Olivia's ability to fly away. He left Emily's apartment and never thought of returning after again.

Olivia looked downwards and smiled, pleased with herself and her earthling's strength to find a way out of his foolish atrocity. The air above felt slightly cooler. She immediately realised that she could feel weaker, more vulnerable to the world like a human being. The cold made her quiver, and she sneezed repeatedly whilst whizzing towards the bundles of grey clouds in the sky. She felt cold whilst flying through layers of white clouds, and then an epiphany dawned on her while she was on her way to the city of saints. She realised the downfall of bonding with her earthling—she was turning human in and out. Her face turned pale whilst rushing towards the entrance, and she hoped for an explanation from her mother and wondered why she was beginning to feel the effects of nature like never before. She stood onto the main entrance clouds and feared for the disciplinary hearing she'd have for interacting with her earthling. There was a church bell ringing at the top of the hill on the golden path, but it wasn't visible to anyone else. She walked up the steep hillside, and everything was muted. There was nothing behind her but layers of white clouds. It wasn't the first time she'd ever been in trouble for disobeying the laws and misbehaving to satisfy her own needs.

'Olivia!' Alexa shouted from the top of the hill. 'Hurry up!'

'Yes, Mother, I'm coming!' Olivia replied and flew towards her mother in fear.

'Brush the dust off your wings and fix yourself up!' Alexa said and showed her daughter the way onto the great hall stairs. 'You are late, and your disciplinary hearing has been moved up to now!' said Alexa as they stepped through the parliament golden doors into a great hall made out of white clouds.

The golden doors opened, and flights of stairs formed within leading to endless passages above. Olivia spread her wings and flapped away the dust from her white feathers and looked at the disappointment on her mother's face whilst prepping herself for the inevitable—to be dismissed from earthly duties. She wondered if speaking to an earthling was worth losing her job over and also wondered what she'd do if the covenant of guardian angels were to ban her from seeing him.

Alexa led them both towards a hollow passage covered in grey clouds everywhere, which gave an unpleasant feeling of fear. They encountered a four-way passage then drifted towards the right passage and walked for a few long dreadful minutes. Her mother's long white gown slimmed down and onto the clouds, stretching out for approximately two metres from her ankles. Alexa's presence radiated a source of power wielded by pure love. Her heels clicked loudly whilst her strides widened and moved in a hurry beside her daughter.

'Hurry up! We are late!' Alexa stated and held on to Olivia's right hand with her left hand. 'I hope they won't ban you from guarding that confused earthling!'

Her hand glowed from within and healed Olivia from the cold. 'See what happened when you bond with earthlings? You begin to lose your ability to be invincible from the diseases that cluster their atmosphere!' Alexa stated and opened a large silver door.

'He isn't confused, just misunderstood!' Olivia replied and kept quiet.

There was a lot of commotion and chatter within the oval room covered in grey clouds, filled with guardian angels around a large dark wooden oval table, debating the final verdicts of other misfit guardian angels. They turned around and stopped talking, mostly puzzled by Olivia's actions to bond with an earthling after being warned on several occasions.

'The Olson family, take a seat!' the largest one, Marcel, said and gestured with his right hand and pointed towards two leather interior seats on the right side of the oval table. 'Will Trevor join us today?'

'Not today, he is busy still!' Alexa replied and sat beside Olivia.

There were sixteen guardian angels seated around the Olsons. Half of them was part of the covenant of the elderly guardian angels, and the other half was just part of the jury.

'Mrs Olson, your daughter has violated a number of laws that were first made before the Black Plague!' he said on the other end of the oval table. 'These laws had to be made to keep a balance between the two worlds. The earthlings don't understand the concept of purity and the concept of loving without expecting anything in return. It is our job to make sure that they are guarded from destroying themselves!'

They all remained quiet for a second, and all sat down at the same time. Marcel opened a book covered with grey fabric material. 'Law 320 classifies that no guardian angel is allowed to reveal their appearance to an earthling!' Marcel said and stated the rest of Olivia's violations. 'Law 033 classifies that no guardian is allowed to let their guard down regardless of the circumstance!'

After he finished reading out Olivia's violations, he looked up and waited for a verdict to nest itself into his mind, feeling conflicted for the first time ever.

'A decision has to be made!' he said, and the rest nodded, agreeing to proceed forward. 'Therefore, to the jury, I will state two decisions, and afterwards, we will raise our right hands to show our votes!'

Marcel looked at Olivia sceptically for a few seconds whilst she looked downwards in shame and hoped for another chance.

'On second thought, let's recess in ten minutes!' he said, leaving everyone puzzled. 'Go on and come back in ten minutes!' he commanded.

The covenant stood up and walked out of the oval room and into a small circular room, including Alexa and Olivia.

'Olivia, wait!' Marcel said. 'Come with me!'

Alexa remained confused.

'Don't worry, Mrs Olson. She will be fine!'

Olivia's mother wandered away whilst curious about the verdict and then closed the silver door behind her. Marcel walked towards the grey wall clouds as they opened up into an arched entrance.

'Follow me!' he suggested, and Olivia walked followed.

The arched entrance disappeared behind Olivia as she moved cautiously and wondered why Marcel had requested her presence alone. They appeared to be outdoors as the clouds before them puffed into thin air. There was a waterfall ahead, streaming with cool water falling from a grand white cloud. The water was crystal clear as it splashed into a large lake. There were a lot of different animal species drinking from the same river and birds flying around with twigs inside their necks, finding empty spots on tree branches to nest new homes.

'It's a good thing you didn't tell him that he will be a father soon. That's not our information to tell. Do you hear me?' Marcel said and turned around to see if Olivia was paying attention,

'Do not get in the way of fate!' He waited for a reply but realised Olivia's infatuation. 'I don't mean to be presumptuous, but what do you see in your earthling that we don't?' he asked.

'I don't know. He is just different from the rest,' she replied. 'I can feel it!'

'You aren't supposed to feel!' he interrupted. 'You are just like your father. His heart was also wild and burned brightly like large beacon on a mountain!'

Olivia reminded shocked of Marcel's comparison whilst seeds grew from underneath the green grass and formed a wooden bench from its stem. She sat on it and wondered what to say.

'Is this world not enough for you?' he asked. 'Because the world down there is horrific, and earthlings do not learn from their mistakes!' he added. 'They love to wage war on each other and inflict pain into each other's lives. They are greedy and fat from stolen wealth. They pretend to understand the views of religion, but only use their supposed faith to apprehend others for more wealth!' he mentioned. 'They are never satisfied!' Marcel looked at Olivia and could see her resemblance of an average earthling. She wasn't satisfied with the world she lived in and believed that she needed more.

'I realised something whilst we were debating!' he said. 'Your earthling hasn't spoken about you to anyone. Why is that?' he asked.

'I don't know!' she replied.

'He seems better after you bonded with him, right?' Marcel asked and sat beside Olivia.

She smiled and nodded slowly.

'Okay, between you and I, I'm going to ask you to carry on speaking to him, but I'm going to cloak your activity away from the rest!' he whispered. 'You are going to save him from destroying himself, but the minute you start developing any more feelings, then I'm going to pull the plug from the whole operation!'

'I don't understand!' she said. 'I thought you wanted me—'

'Your earthling's heart has been damaged by others. I want you to heal him and cleanse him off any monsters before his time ends on earth!' he interrupted.

'What are you going to say to the covenant?' she asked.

'Don't worry about the covenant!' he replied in a calm manner. 'There is a way when it comes to love!' He smiled and sounded confident in his plan.

He immediately stood up and then turned chivalrous by reaching out his right arm towards Olivia. She held on to his arm as they walked back through a grey cloudy passage.

'I have a feeling he's going to need you more than ever!' he whispered as the arched entrance appeared.

They entered back into the oval room and sat quietly.

'Olivia, please call them back!' he commanded and waited for the rest of the covenant to enter, including Alexa.

They all entered and sat quietly, wondering why he'd suggested to whisper aside with Olivia.

'I have come to two options!' he said. 'The first is we suspend Olivia from her guardian duties, and the second option is we transfer her to the angels of death department in the counselling department!'

There was a moment of silence whilst Olivia and Alexa wondered what the final verdict would be.

'Please raise your right hands if you agree with the first option!' Marcel stated and counted the number of right hands in the air. 'Please lift up your right hands if you agree with the second option!' He counted again. 'This is good!' he said.

Out of sixteen working for the covenant, seven had agreed to send Olivia to the angels of death department but were outnumbered by the nine who'd agreed to suspend her from her guardian duties. The angels of death department wasn't for the fainted hearted, and it required a level of restraint from having emotions whilst working, a skill that Olivia didn't possess, and she was glad to have been suspended instead of being sent away from her family to work elsewhere. On the other hand, she was prepared to fulfil her cloaked duties to save Quinton from his monsters.

Chapter Seventeen

Quinton's Guardians

Olivia's family's history was somewhat complicated and different from most of the families above. They were accustomed to a different way mostly subsided because they were once part of the human race too. They hadn't adjusted well after their death, but with time, came their peace.

Olivia did not know what it felt like to fall in love and to experience the perks of struggling on limited resources because she'd just graduated from a local college far from where her family lived since she was born. She'd always wanted so much more out of her life than to live in the swamps with her family, but regardless of her taste for better things, her family lived in a beautiful large cottage established by an endless swamp streaming through Florida. They'd spend most of their summer holidays catching alligators and sustaining farming for a living. Their lives were somewhat humble and stable because they lived off the earth. Olivia had always wondered what it would be like to have a family of her one day whilst glancing at the genuine love that her father gave to her mother whilst back from a semester break—the way he would touch her gently and grace her body with care, kissing her cheeks from behind and tickling her in the kitchen whilst cooking together.

Trevor Olson was always such a gentleman with real value, putting his family first before himself. He was a hardworking man who owned a mechanical store, which supplied car parts to the local people, using his monthly profits to send his children to decent government schools around the area and teaching them valuable life lessons every single minute he got whilst bonding with them. His straggling manly value inspired Olivia to wait for real love, the same way her mother did.

Alexa would say, 'We met at a Woolworth grocery store. Firstly, I didn't like him because he looked too strict and that reminded me of my father, but after that day, he and I would meet randomly. His face started to brighten up more after seeing me pass by in my summer dresses, and you could say that it was almost as if the universe was trying to bring us together. I began to dream of him like foolish girl and wake up blushing on my single sided bed. But two years went by without him and I bumping into each other, and there was a large bonfire gathering at our neighbour's backyard. I was seated alone, looking at the fire, and I had completely forgotten that your father existed until he walked past a crowd of people and asked if he could sit by me!

'That was in the middle of the year 1961, around June maybe, and we got married four weeks later. The fireworks were amazing around that time. There were a lot of products coming in from the northern end of the country. Fireworks from north-western manufacturing warehouses blossomed in the dark skies.

'You know, it felt right to be married to him, and I've never regretted it because soon after that, within the next year, your twin brothers were born on the 18 September 1962. It wasn't a pleasant time to be alive because of the high racial tension and the resistance arising from the civil movements across the nation, but we managed to find some sort of peace in the swamps because not a lot of people came here and we knew that we could keep your hearts purified from evil by settling on the outskirts of danger!'

Olivia would listen to her mother blabbering about her past whilst seated back on a bench swing attached the ceiling, swinging back and enjoying the fresh swamp air. Her arms were had long veins that stretched from her wrists and all the way to her thin forearms. There was so much energy railing through them whilst she spoke, giving her daughter a lesson on the mystery of love and the wonderful feeling of being loved back. After such moments, Olivia would pledge to guard away her heart away from permissible boys and to keep herself away from any temptation, promising to keep her knees together until marriage.

Sadly their lives were short lived. In the year 1987, they died from a car accident. They were driving on the outskirts of the seaside town of Beaufort on a late afternoon when they encountered an army towing truck driving at a rapid speed. It accidentally unhinged a broken-down army truck behind, causing the army truck to swerve into a different lane which resulted in a head-on collision with the Olson family vehicle. The three of them passed immediately after impact, leaving Olivia's older twin brothers alone on planet Earth. Olivia died at the age of twenty-three without experiencing the freedom of being young and unengaged to strict human conventions, but most of all, her heart was welded in sadness because she'd never get the chance to find real love or feel anything close to it. There was a massive hole inside her chest, leaving her stitched with envy because she believed that she was robbed of the great pleasures of being an earthling. She felt that living in gradual peace whilst waiting for Judgement Day would never truly bring her happiness mainly because she was burdened with the desire to live.

There were heavy horses galloping with momentum, packed with old detoured bricks and foundational textures of a wondrous mysterious life Olivia could have lived. A heavy heart gripping gush of a sparkling will to have a second chance at life winded around her body and clocked inside her blinded mind whilst entering their home after her disciplinary hearing. She noted her strong will of enduring complications, immediately understanding her selfish innuendo inability to acquire a strangle mentality to wield such thoughts. It made her feel utterly stupid for stanching from the grace of a higher power and gravitating towards humanity because the fireworks of an oblivious universe had helped her escape the whips of a harsher reality and aided her from the incarceration of old age.

Their home was amongst other houses from the front, but all the yards were massive, covered in pasture greens for hectares. The walls were made out of limestone rocks, cut into small brick sizes. Their entrance was an arched door made from fine oak wood. Two arched windows were also framed with oak wood, except there was no glass on them. The entrance fountain had a flamingo with bright pink feathers, eating all the small fish underneath its straight thin legs, and towards the first floor, there were multiple arched entrances leading to three passages and into individual bedrooms. Their household was massive, but they always found themselves bonding outside.

Trevor would say to his lovely wife, 'The backyard field is a perfect place to be after running into trouble. You are safer there than anywhere else in the world,' stating that to subconsciously wield his lover to frame herself and preserve her extraordinary body around nature's beauty.

'Luckily you won't be leaving us!' Alexa said and sat down on a grey swing underneath an apple tree in their backyard. 'I guess you will have to work for me now!' She laughed out loud.

Olivia disliked the idea and thus interrupted, 'Its fine. I can just get a job at one of the stores on the walkway instead, maybe from the bakery!'

'Are you sure that's a good idea?' Alexa asked and planted her soft feet onto the green grass.

'Yes, I'm sure!' Olivia replied with dishonesty and felt the first glimmer of deceit.

It didn't even concern her, but her mother could see right through her recent change in behaviour. The only positive stance unveiling from Olivia was her glossing smile, gushing with happiness from spending time with an earthling. She'd never been so content with real happiness in her entire existence which made her look utterly guilty for violations she hadn't even broken yet. She ran around and gloated in happiness whilst basking in thoughts of the future, sublime déjà vu moments.

Alexa wondered at her daughter's recent change in behaviour and found her lost and tranquillised by a sweet smell of apricot pie through her nostrils whilst swinging away underneath the apple tree.

'Honey,' Trevor whispered under his breath, 'I've brought something from the bakery, something I want you to try!' He was communicating to his endless lover, and yet nobody else could hear his words travelling like little fairies amongst the winds.

Her senses were magnified and enhanced by her ability to love her husband even after such a tragic death. They were so connected from an endless earthly tribulation of struggles, knowing that nothing in both worlds could ever come between their force field of unwavering radical love.

'I'm coming!' she whispered back.

'Is Dad home!' Olivia asked, after watching her mother stand tall for a while and pause like a flamingo then immediately breaking out of her shell of content to move forward to a better moment.

Alexa's heart pumped quickly on her way to Trevor, embracing her fatal strength to be eternally entrenched by his extraordinary gift to be caring without measure. She moved swiftly and burgled through swinging on the far left end of the household by the kitchen and paused immediately to her husband's presence.

'Greetings!' she said as he turned around smiling. 'How was it?' she asked.

'Extremely raw and uncensored things are happening out there!' he replied and then opened his arms wide. 'Come to me!'

She smiled and walked towards him slowly, sensing a difference in his presence. 'Are you okay?' she sked, and opened her heart by gesturing for a warm hug. 'You smell good!' she said with her eyelids closed.

'Thank you, love!' he responded whilst grazing his chin on her right shoulder, inhaling in his lover's exquisite essence and embracing that amazing feeling of being drawn into a different magical world whilst still in the same presence.

Their love was permanently bottled with maturity and age, sweet and bitter to their pink tongues at every kiss, and heading racking at every argument.

'Your feathers are so dusty!' she whispered whilst his wings flapped slowly.

'Flew past a sandstorm on the edge of Syria trying to find a lead on the whereabouts of a demon porthole around that region!' he stated and clinched on her body, feeling her warmth radiate into him. 'Maybe I should quit working and spend my afternoons with you!' he whispered and leaned backwards to catch a glimpses of Alexa's beautiful blush.

'Your daughter had another hearing!' she said. 'I swear I don't know what to say to her anymore!' She exhaled her exhaustion with her firm cheeks blotted towards the ceiling.

'Allow her to be free, Alexa. Allow her to find comfort within her own heart. At times she is too scared to break out, and I believe she'll only find happiness then!' he stated.

'Are you encouraging her?' she asked.

'No, don't get me wrong!' he interrupted. 'I just want my daughter to be happy. Let her roam and fly free!'

'It's not up to us, Trevor!' Alexa stated.

'I know it's not up to us!' he replied. 'It's up to her!'

'To defy the laws and interact with earthlings?' she asked sceptically whilst brushing away sprinkles of dust from Trevor's shoulders with her left hand. 'You know what will happen if she continues!'

'I know, but we will always be there to guard her if it comes to that!' he responded and moved towards the kitchen doors and held on to the left one with his muscular left hand.

'Olivia!' he called out, but his daughter was nowhere to be seen.

'You know, she reminds me of you, always running around, looking for adventure!' Alexa stated,

'Isn't that why you fell in love with me?' he asked and turned around.

'True!' she replied and smiled as he moved closer.

'I forgot to do something!' he said and kissed her soft lips passionately and endorsing her heart with sweetness. She felt incredibly smitten and flattered like a young girl discovering the ethos of love.

'I've missed you!' he said. 'Let's have some apricot pie and bond. We haven't done that in so long!' He then picked a thatched nest overlaced by a smooth white cloth and walked away with the apricot pie inside of it. 'Follow me. This pie won't eat itself, my love!' he said and walked away from the kitchen.

She followed him and strolled through a passage and into another room. They lay back and rested on a couch, witnessing the beautiful glaze in the air. There were white doves flying in circles and idling around on the large empty field. Their eyes were drawn to a picture-perfect moment, enabling them to lose their appetites. They'd forgotten of their quest to indulge on the apricot pie whilst watching Olivia appear from within the whisker clouds closest to a steep hill in the background. She planted her soft feet onto the grass and walked towards the apple tree and sat quietly, slightly afraid to face her father and slightly embarrassed because she'd disgraced her family name.

'Go and talk to her!' Alexa whispered and looked up.

'But I'm so comfortable!' Trevor replied, feeling hesitant and exhausted.

'Hush and go lecture your daughter! she said and scooted him off the couch.

'Okay, I'll go!' he responded and walked away, wondering what he'd say to his daughter because he didn't care much about laws and regulations.

He wasn't embedded by the same scriptures wielding every other guardian angels, finding himself secluded inside a bubble of difference.

'Your mother tells me that you are in trouble?' he asked whilst smiling and joyed by beauty in front of him. 'What's going on?' he asked in a low tone.

'I feel judged for wanting a life!' Olivia said.

'Why would you want to go back?' he asked and sat on another swing chair beside his daughter.

'I want what you and Mom have!' she whispered, trying to avoid her mother's judgement.

'And how do you plan on getting that!' he asked whilst patting her head softy and discovering her daughter's craving to be loved by another being. 'Is that why you disobey the laws?' he asked, and she couldn't quite bring herself forth to answer and thus crumbled in tears and covered her face with her large white wings.

'I know you both think I'm stupid!' she said in between her sobbing. 'I just need to find my happiness beyond this fatal eternity!'

Her father understood where her roots of sadness had cropped from.

'And you will find your happiness. Just take the time to explore all avenues without getting into trouble!' he said, swinging slowly and trying to be more authoritative, but the thought of his daughter dwelling in a pool of sadness drove him into a wall of silence. 'Come inside the house. We must all rest soon!' he said and stood up.

'I was inside just now!' she replied and swung away, clinging on to a roguish thought—momentarily planning to run away from her beautiful sanctuary and settling elsewhere. Maybe finding shelter in a world clustered with confused earthlings, or maybe discovering some sort of closure on the hideous outskirts of the forbidden frozen mountains where lost descendants right underneath undisclosed caves of some sort.

She couldn't quite figure out what she really needed out of her endless time, but moving forward from her comfort zone seemed more and more stitched onto her throbbing heart as she walked towards her household.

'I'll head to my bedroom!' Olivia mentioned whilst unbinding herself from contemplating so much. 'Good night!'

'Good night, Olivia!' her parents replied.

Her mind remained locked away, leaving her in a wondrous land of a different place besides the one she was used to. She glided up and onto the first floor, entering her bedroom, and it was quiet. There were no signs of anything glorious to implode her life, which made her feel scolded and tricked to believing that she'd be at eternal peace, merely sounding spoilt and ungrateful for the privileges given.

All those thoughts mounted deeply inside Olivia's mind as she lay underneath a thin layer of silk sheets on an oak wood-framed bed and a soft thin mattress. Her thoughts shined brightly onto the deep voids inside her heart which were essentially reparable as she devised a plan of action, figuring out what she had to do to break free. She felt lost whilst drifting from her world and into the unknown.

It wasn't long before she found herself dazzled into a different space. She found herself slipping down into a large hole whilst falling asleep to the sounds of birds flocking in the sky. She felt clogged by her indecisive mentality, wondering which way would lead her to her own salvation. It was completely dark inside the hole, but she kept moving anyway and guiding her body away from the black greasy walls by using her hands and stepping forward with her heavy feet, scooping up heaps of grease. Her silky white dress turned greasy and dark. 'There is always light at the end of the tunnel', numerous people would say whenever squashed by the challenges of the universe, but Olivia couldn't see anything whilst moving forward in the darkness. Her bottom feathers were dipped in grease, dyed into an old blackish colour. Within seconds, she couldn't move fast and thus waited for some sort of assistance, but nobody came to aid her even after calling out, 'Hello, anyone there!' repeatedly.

It was dreadfully silent after her echo, and all she could hear were the sounds of the greasy droppings plunging onto the greasy floor. Her legs were stuck in a rut, then slowly but surely a groan arose from the distance like a thirsty beast drooling with hunger for fresh flesh. A mysterious terrifying sound grew as its paws poked into the greasy surface, leaving a trail of muck on its path towards Olivia. She couldn't see anything, but a smell of something horrific tormented her heart and altered her recent loud thoughts to fly away from her safe haven and muted them. It sniffed her dress and caused her to fall backwards and knock her head unconscious from the rocky wall beside her.

Olivia kept on diving in and out of her subconscious, blinking continuously, clipping on to a catastrophic atmosphere, and recording in visuals of humanlike creatures with crusty, achy dark grey skin using shovels to dig into a hard maroon surface, sweating out drops of agony and regret. All enslaved by subconsciously statured down suppressing dark element an invisible beating them down and crisping their souls inside.

The dark gloomy tunnels were entrenched within the darkest place of the underworld with blazes of fire on the outskirts of the pits of the biggest underground cave she'd ever seen. She was being carried away in a cage like a prisoner, hinged behind a massive Scandinavian folklore covered in dark green slime.

'Bring her here!' Grinch voices echoed from the distance, sounding lustful and poverty-stricken.

'Where did you find this one!' they asked whilst harsher, extremely vulgar words lashed out from all angles and awoke Olivia into a deeper track of an elusive nightmare.

It seemed as if the more Olivia thought of being human again, her mind would drive her vulnerable heart towards being an earthling. Heavy layers of maroon dust in the air kept her squinty throughout. Her nightmare opened her mind to the subliminal truth. Her radiant, flawless skin and beautiful black hair were covered in black grease and a layer of maroon dust to irritate her into discomfort.

'Open up now!' she screamed and caught the attention of the dark rider on top of his Scandinavian folklore. He turned his upper body and glanced backwards, puffing his large chest and laughing out loud.

'We finally have her in our domain!' he shouted and turned back around, chanting for more negative connotations and smiling to his recent success and vile glory.

'Luther, release me right now!' she yelled whilst gripping the arched cage bars.

'Greetings to you to, my love!' he replied and carried on guiding his troll onto a rockier path, heading towards a large hollow cage congested with slum houses stacked on top of each other on both sides of the rocky path.

They were made out of silver tin, but most of them were covered in black smoke aches. Crusty enslaved people poked out their faces from within the slum houses, glooming downwards onto the rocky path.

'Open the gate!' Luther shouted and hailed his beast from processing, 'Open the bloody gate!' he shouted again, sounding agitated and flawlessly wretched.

He spat a boil of yellow saliva onto the dust ground and whipped his troll on its right front leg with a heavy whip in his muscular right hand. Her carriage rattled in rust whilst moving forth. Within seconds, they'd entered into a deeper layer of doom filled with dark warriors of all shapes and sizes, grey misty wolves with lava glowing eyes, large black warthogs, and black misty horses handled by muscular humanlike figures with crusty grey skin.

Luther opened the carriage cage and gripped the back of Olivia's neck with his right hand and threw her onto the dusty surface, causing large waves of laughter from other dark warriors. He closed the cage door and dragged her away by her necklace collar into a dungeon.

'I have great plans for our earthling, love. You should not interfere, Olivia!' he said, crouched by the metal greasy bars. 'You know one day he won't have to decide which part of his conscience he needs to listen to. He and I will be best friends within the nick of time!' he whispered. 'And when that happens, I won't live here anymore, I will be back on earth for a fresh start!' He paused and puffed out. 'I must say, I didn't think it would be this easy to find you. I guess falling for an earthling can make you weak, and that weakness made your mind wander to areas you shouldn't be going, leaving you vulnerable like the rest of them!' he stated then laughed out loud and walked away.

'No one should touch her except for me!' he shouted out and led a pack of grey misty wolves back past the stack of slum houses.

Olivia looked around, shivering in a heated fever, realising that she was losing her ability to cloak away any diseases and infections from her body. She coughed and sneezed repeatedly whilst flying away and trying to find an exit from above. Her wings were heavy whilst flapping up and down, leaving her exhausted and melting her back down to a slight concussion from smashing her head on the rock. She looked upwards and could see a thumbnail moon in between the small metal bars around the hole at the top. It shined brightly in the distance and advocated for the little peace still stored within her heart until she looked at a bright bonfire in the distance and discovered vile details on the dungeon walls mostly covered in large claw marks and bloodstains marked in handprints.

The atmosphere was evidently animalistic, shading Olivia's beacon of hope. She sat down and closed her eyes, inhaling in every breath of humid filth and contemplating her misfit actions to disobey the covenant of guardian angels. She also gradually wondered what would happen to her earthling if she was to stop looking after him, knowing of his clumsy behaviour and his weak will to restrain himself from indulging provocative human conventions. Knowing the evil that hovered around and inside Luther's body, she immediately found some sort of strength to stand up and devised a plan to break free from incarceration. She held on to the metal bars for a split second and burned her hands from the heat. Her body was becoming vulnerable and weak every minute. Heavy waves of dry air clustered her lungs and caused her to lose her balance within seconds. She screamed out her earthling's name whilst fainting down on to the maroon dust and perishing into darkness.

Meanwhile, Quinton woke up on his short trip back to his home country. He attempted to have a telepathic conversation with his guardian, but Olivia did not respond. It was so quiet inside his subconscious world, and he found himself standing on an empty beach with his feet sunk deeply into the wet sand whilst cool waves of seawater brushed from the left side and onto his feet. Dark green seaweeds hooked on to his ankles as he looked downwards at his feet, and within seconds, he realised that he was stuck in a passed memory. He remembered Olivia telling him to remember the two pairs of footprints trailing upwards towards an embankment, clustered with thick bushes. This picture itself had been shoved into his memory bank, and he wondered what it meant.

For some reason, Quinton did not fear seeing his bad consciousness anymore. A part of him began to understand and embrace the darkest shelves within his mind, spaces made from his historical vile, bad relationships, which were accommodated by bad choices he'd done. It seemed inevitable for him to sin even after pleading to turn over a new leaf on numerous occasions. He realised that his guardian angel was nowhere to be seen mainly because she was drawn away to her peaceful heavenly place and not in the sunken, low dark pits within her earthling's volatile mind.

She couldn't escape from her nightmare. The only way she could break free from incarceration was to come to terms with the fact that her earthling's heart wasn't hers to begin with. Therefore, she'd be fighting an endless war. She did not want to see that factor, which essentially made her grow weaker, straining her into exhaustion. She'd completely lost the ability to clock herself away from any bad elements hovering around her earthling's body because of her close connection to him. The humid heat wore off her strength to fly away, leaving her stuck inside a dungeon in her earthling's mind.

Chapter Eighteen

Incarcerated from Peace

Olivia awoke from the dusty surface within the dungeon, and all she could hear were the swiping dreadful silent breeze strokes of discomfort brush past her dirty face. She couldn't see properly as the rusty metal bars blurred sideways. The right side of her face and her white dress were imprinted with maroon sandy particles. She sat up straight with her body aching then shuffled her bare feet backwards until her back was pinned against the dungeon walls. Her breaths started to grow fast once she realised that she was stuck within a bad dream, breaching her into paranoia and causing her to feel frightened. All the terrifying memories of her wondrous previous events spiralled within her mind and activated fear in her heart. She was scared of all the demons and the other bad supernatural things she'd fought off in the past—their loud roars, horses galloping in numbers, wolves howling towards the moon, and blood dripping everywhere made her shrink into herself. She closed her beautiful blue eyes and tried to find some sort of composure with herself whilst wondering why she couldn't break free from the bars at the top of the dungeon.

'Quinton, can you hear me?' she whispered, but he didn't reply. She wondered why he hadn't woken up yet.

His muscles were aching badly from the tragic accident he'd had a week before. His bad consciousness had managed to wield him into a coma, thus leaving him captivated inside his own mind, captivated by his own demons and locked away from reality.

'Quinton, dammit!' she yelled and smacked the dusty surface. 'Ouch!' she quietly sobbed whilst looking at her aching left hand, remembering how weak she'd become.

There was so much anxiety floating in the air as she looked around for a few minutes, willingly activating her survival instinct. She looked back down and closed her blue eyes.

'Think, Olivia, think!' she said to herself and then paused to the sound of a raindrop brushing past a metal bar through the hole at the top of the dungeon.

Another raindrop followed until it began to drizzle slowly, then thundershowers rained down. She stood up and spread her wings in different directions to wash off the black grease from her feathers. The raindrops were crystal clear. They restored hope in her heart again as she looked upwards and felt them wash away the dirt on her beautiful face. She couldn't quite fly mainly because she hadn't had anything to eat since being captured. She'd lost weight due to the horrible conditions in the dungeon, but for the first time ever, she felt strong.

'Wake up!' she said and scooped water from a rocky puddle with her hands and threw it through the rusty metal bars and into another dungeon on the far left side.

It seemed impossible to catch her earthling's attention whilst he remained glued to the dusty surface. There was nothing she could do to catch his attention because he was still unconscious.

'Great!' she said out loud. 'Just great!' She exhaled out whilst sneezing from the changing weather.

She stepped away from the cold drizzle and looked around the dungeon whilst streams of water scattered into different directions and cooled off large firepits until it was completely dark. There were still soundwaves of soft orgasms lashing within the distance, equivocally drowning Olivia in sorrow. She'd never been affected much by the evil relishing through the human race from a far distance until that very moment, looking at the cold winds blowing through the hollow passages and delivering sounds of women being suppressed against a hard place. It felt surreal and slightly overwhelming to be inside her earthling's mind, to be able to hear and see the world through his brown eyes. She'd never felt close to anybody in her entire existence until that very moment, coming to terms with her soft spot for him. Initially, she understood his persona and felt genuine compassionate for him, drawn to his self-loathing and troubled mind. She was slowly but surely growing tired of seeing him duel against the challenges of life without earning any merits and thus concluded a pledge to be beside him for eternity.

Olivia sat on the muddy surface right next to the dungeon wall and shrunk herself into a ball whilst long minutes clocked away. It had stopped drizzling, and finally the atmosphere was quiet, with an occasional raindrop falling from above and causing a loud echo. She could hear Quinton shivering in the dungeon but couldn't do anything about it.

It seemed as if he was railing through a tranquil place of the past. His mind was rewinding back to the moment he entered the front gate of his parents' home after returning. He'd thought about sleeping at his lavish loft within the city for the evening, but returning home felt right. However, it brought Quinton back to the core of his problems. He walked through the front gate.

It was windy and dark. The power had gone off within the estate mainly because it had rained heavily earlier. The pathway bricks were smeared with brown leaves made moist by the wet ground. It was quite antagonising to move towards a larger house without any sign of life in it. There were no candles lit within the house. It was complete dark within, radiating uncertainty, but regardless of his caution, he moved closer anyway and swerved right towards the entrance. He knocked repeatedly, but nobody answered. It seemed bizarre because he knew that his mother was always home every Tuesday evening regardless of any changes in her daily schedule.

'Is there anyone home?' he called out and placed his luggage bags by the main entrance, peeping at the side window frames right next to the main door.

He imprinted his face onto the glass, allowing him to snoop better, but still felt the reign of silence breaching his mind whilst rolling his eyes to different sections of the house. Out of curiosity, he drifted right with the strong wind, hopping over bushes right next to the mansion walls and thick trees planted everywhere until he found himself by the veranda doors. He stood on a large triangle-like glass piece, and it cracked into a dozen pieces. The wooden square frames on both doors were without glass, which quivered his dry skin and rippled out goosebumps as he looked at the maroon curtains moving within. He picked up his Blackberry from his left pocket and discovered a faulty network barring up and down continuously, leaving him confused. It was utterly quiet to the point where he could hear his silver watch ticking slowly whilst he scratched the back of his neck with his right hand, trying to assure himself with bravery. He gripped a the golden knob with the same hand and opened the right wooden door slowly, finally awaking his brown eyes to a broken home.

Multiples sound of his mother screaming out from violence lashed into his ears from different angles, but she wasn't around. It was almost as if his mind was railing through a past of barricaded memories, mostly ones he had selected not to remember because they were unbearable to think about. It was completely dark from time to time, but the night light coming in from main entrance side windows helped him see his way through. Towards his right was the lounge area, and he could see dried wine stains on the wooden floor and dozens of broken wine glass pieces by the arched entrance. Outside winds were becoming stronger every minute, smashing against the windows and leaving a gloomy atmosphere inside. He moved around, calling out his mother's name but instead heard his echo radiating around the household and coming back to him, reminding him that he was alone in the world.

He allowed his fast-beating heart to lead him up a flight of wooden stairs. It diverted his attention towards his parents' bedroom at the end of the right passage. He walked through the walls moulded from sadness, concluding a story of his own. All the windows on the right side of the wall were open, allowing strong winds to flick the maroon curtains in different directions. The wooden pathway to the master bedroom sparkled with glass pieces from all wooden picture frames on the floor, leading him towards a trail that unfolded a story of sorrow. Everything slowed down for a while, including a circuit of mosquitoes flying around behind him. And whilst he gripped two golden knobs and parted the wooden doors sideways, his mind shuffled through a montage slideshow of suppressive memories—an image of his youthful self inside an old wooden wardrobe filled with long summer dresses and formal coats and peeping through to see his father screaming out vulgar words and smelling of lager beer whilst slapping his mother onto the floor with his right hand. Another image blurred his view—an image of himself in the back seat of a Mercedes Benz watching his father use his muscular left hand to backhand his mother into the passenger seat and watching such precious aged wine splash onto the passenger window. He stood still and wandered to the back of his mind for past life questionnaires, wondering what would lead a man to strike a woman, especially a woman that he claims to love so much. What drove their relationship to this point?

There were a lot of unanswered questions railing through his mind at that moment as he looked towards the far left side and discovered his mother lying on top of her queen-size bed with her dark blue nightgown on. He started to remember all the dark memories that he'd prayed would disappear from his mind as a child all rushing back to him and initially helping to put all the pieces of the puzzle together, realising that he was sent to boarding schools to shield him away from a harsh lifestyle.

All windows were open, almost as if she'd blacked out during the day without closing them. Her body had melted into the puffy cream white duvets, and her muscles were watery and soft. She was intoxicated from drinking red wine for the past two days, mostly drinking because her past had come back to haunt her present. Her face was beautiful, smooth on the right, but whilst turning to face the right side of the bed, a discovery was made. The left side of her face was bruised, imprinted with dark blue fist markings around her left eye which was bloodshot red, and her large bruise mapped all the way down to the bottom of her left jawline.

'Mom!' he yelled whilst panicking and shaking her small body.

She struggled to open her eyes, and once she opened them, a stream of tears raced down opposite ends.

'What's wrong?' he asked and kneeled on the bed. 'Are you okay? Where is Dad?' he asked another question whilst she looked towards the door on the right side of the room and fixed her light brown eyes towards a chest of open drawers in the room.

There were so many layers of clothes on the wooden floor within the changing room. Her lingerie materials were hanging everywhere, and there were two empty wine bottles by the door.

'Did he do this to you?' he asked whilst she sat up straight and stood up, stumbling away from the bed and walking towards the bathroom door ahead.

He found himself torn in pieces by the damage on his mother's face, realising that he'd seen the same facial damage as a toddler. He also stumbled past an open luggage bag in the middle of the bedroom, tripping whilst following his mother to the bathroom. She used the white Italian marble tiles for lighting to see her way through and found herself trapped and caught up in an old lie. Her left eye was much more blurred which momentarily led her to acknowledge her part in bringing discomfort into their home.

'What happened downstairs?' he asked whilst she gazed into the mirror.

She zoomed into the truth, flushing her memory back to the previous Sunday evening after arriving back from church. She'd spent the whole day with church members at a country lodge, having late lunch and bonding with new members of a Catholic church. Everything changed that day because her husband had sent the whole day reminiscing of his dead brother, mainly feeling guilty because he was the one who'd ordered Steve to be killed. Marcus had made a trip to Steve's old vacant house on the outskirts of the city, a three-bedroom house with an empty sitting room, an empty kitchen and one bathroom consisting of a small single shower and one toilet. It was found close to the only large hill covering the sunset every late afternoon, a place where baboons approached in the early mornings to tilt the dustbins and empty them onto the tarred streets, a beautiful place almost forgotten for its luxurious weather conditions, its ability to maintain nature without anyone having to water the gardens. Palm tree leaves remained green, green grass remained healthy, and the birds still chirped loudly throughout. Within the house, Marcus entered whilst thinking back to the time when he was young and unengaged to adult conventions with his younger brother. They'd drive around the small city in a red Uno car which had two doors, causing havoc and acting like a bunch of degenerates from time to time. It was such a beautiful time to live, he thought to himself whilst reminiscing to the events they'd go to for entertainment. They'd take pictures and store them into their own folders or so-called photo albums instead of posting them on to the Internet like millennials do these days. His younger brother's laughter brought a smile to his face, which initially caused him to cry alone in the bathroom whilst seated on the toilet seat. The floor tiles reflected a revealing evidence, a moment of truth on the top right corner within the ceiling.

There was a square opening and a small box lingering halfway inside. He stood up and picked it from the top by stretching his arms upwards and used his fingers to move it. His body wasn't in good condition, for it ached from the third stage of cancer. Within the brown box were old photos, dusty documents of early business ideas which had failed, letters of Steve's love affairs, music cassettes, an empty White Horse whiskey bottle, a pack of playing cards inside a small rectangular blue box, and a blue engagement ring box. It seemed bizarre for a womaniser to have an engagement ring box stored away from the world. Marcus began to wonder who the engagement ring belonged to by searching through all items for clues or some sort of compelling information which could help him understand why his deceased brother had never really settled down.

It wasn't a surprise that Steve had at least a dozen letters from different women from all over the world at the time. He'd just finished travelling back from New Delhi, India, in the year 1989. It was around the same time that Marcus started dating Beth, planning their futures to start a family and to love each other until the end of time. At that moment, Marcus took a moment to appreciate his beautiful wife, glancing and flipping through all his younger brother's love letters. It turned into complete shock as his brown eyes scrolled downwards and discovered Beth's name at the end of the tenth love letter which was written on 15 November 1991, the same time that Steve was in Namibia, finishing off his bachelor degree of business administration from a local university in Windhoek.

The information scripted within the letter collaborated with the way she'd been acting around that blurry era, trying to dismiss her fiancé out of the picture for a man who was incapable of being in a committed relationship. At the time, Marcus truly believed that she was scared to have his child alone because they weren't married yet. It was such a confusing time printed with bleached blue jean pants, tropical island shirts, and vintage clothes, massive shades covering up everyone's eyebrows, cheap alcohol from neighbouring countries, cigarettes exported by those who'd travel with their diplomatic parents from abroad. Regardless, Marcus and Beth married two months later. Thus, she concluded to keep the truth away from anyone, regretting to have told Steve about it. She buried the scandal so far deep into her heart that she too almost forgot that Quinton was a bastard child made from nothing but lust, a descendent of a man who'd use his wealth to coil weak women into his cave whenever he felt the craving to fuck.

Marcus looked at the engagement ring again and discovered Beth's name imprinted within the silver rim and a beautiful Tanzanian blue diamond on the top, crusted and clamped by three silver hooks on different angles. He felt deceived and used, betrayed by a woman that didn't truly love him in the beginning. It drove him to the brink of madness whilst walking around outside the vacant house, equivocally leading his mind into anger. His boiling blood streamed through the veins on his arms and caused him to strike his driver's door with his left fist, denting the car badly and bruising his knuckles. He couldn't quite wrap his mind around the letter he'd just read, wondering why his brother would keep such valuable information hidden away.

Regardless of the questions pending within his mind, there was nothing anyone could say to excuse such deceit. He reversed his car and drove off without closing the vacant house mainly because he was equipped with mere rage, acting irresponsible and hazardous to the world. His anger rushed through his body, causing him to drive through red lights with the car hazards on, wondering what he'd say to his wife and trying to find some sort of composure within his broken heart. He found himself drifting through memory lane and resurrecting his darkest thoughts, allowing them to take root inside his mind. For the first time in a very long time, he didn't feel like he was in control of anything. His hands weren't equipped with the ability to wield the outcome to his favour. Thus, he allowed himself to be irrational by smacking the steering wheel with both hands. Tears lingered on his eyelids, causing him to drown in pain.

The front gate was open as Marcus turned right into his driveway and bumped into an empty beige clay pot on the right side, causing it to break into a garden filled with tulips and lavender flowers. He parked his car inside the garage and realised that his wife's car was parallel. There were seconds of mild recuperation whilst he waited for his mind to compile all thoughts into a reassuring motive, and whilst that occurred, loud whispers rushed through his head at that exact moment, confusing and causing him to act like a hooligan. Nothing could calm him down nor advocate peace into his soul as he entered through the garage door and into the hallway passage whilst searching for his deceitful wife, but she was nowhere to be found. He was mostly disgusted by her betrayal and her inability to be honest and therefore called out her name repeatedly whilst holding Steve's love letter with his right hand.

'I'm coming!' she shouted from the backyard within a hidden vegetable garden, clustered into a maze.

He stood by the veranda doors, looking at his beautiful wife walking towards him in her beautiful gamete dress lengthening all the way to

329

her ankles. She looked up whilst moving closer and saw pain gushing through his brown eyes.

'What are you holding?' she asked and smiled, dusting off the dirt from her hands and reaching forward to see.

He didn't reply at that moment. All he could do was give her letter back and hopefully hear her side of the story. She sat on an outdoor chair and read her old words scribbled within and immediately realised that her skeletons were beginning to crawl out of her closet. It was slightly quiet and awkward whilst birds chirped within the trees, and all she could do was cover her mouth with her left hand, mostly railed towards shook because she didn't expect her letter to be resurrected from the dead.

'Marcus!' she said, frightened of his facial expression and burying her head in shame.

He walked towards the garden as she stood up.

'I can . . . I can explain!' she stuttered whilst breathing heavily and feeling uncertain of his reaction,

'What can you possibly say?' he replied and looked back. 'I'm waiting. Well?' Marcus mentioned whilst glancing down, watching as dried leaves brushed against Beth's feet.

She thought of an answer to accommodate for her dishonesty. 'I'm sorry!' she whispered. 'I'm so sorry. I was so scared!' She held the left side of her chest with her right hand. 'I'll leave immediately!' she said and stepped away.

'You are not going anywhere!' he shouted. 'How could you do this to me!' As his voice echoed through the trees, birds flocked away from their backyard. He could feel his tear ducts extracting more tears underneath his eyeballs, straining him into sadness until he cried in embarrassment.

That unpleasant memory deflected out of the mirror and back into Beth's brown eyes whilst she blatantly addressed her indiscretions to her bastard son. Quinton couldn't quite grasp the honesty waving out with a strong whiff of wine essence from his mother's mouth whilst she looked closely at the mirror. Her honesty left him completely shocked and uncertain of himself, realising that his late uncle was indeed his biological father.

'I'm sorry I hid the truth from you!' Beth whispered and sobbed. 'But Marcus is not your father, my baby. Steve is your biological father wherever he is!'

He didn't respond but instead stepped backwards and railed off towards the passage. The information basking within his mind was overwhelming, driving him farther and farther away from his mother and back to the brink of madness. His depressive memories remained installed within his mind, reincarnating his darkness and allowing it to strive wildly within the household. Every thought wielded his desires towards the alcohol cabinet in the kitchen, and he didn't think twice about opening a grey bottle and mixing his vodka with a glass of Sprite from the refrigerator. He indulged every sip slowly, bracing himself for collision and allowing his tears to flow down his cheeks as though he'd agreed to supply the capital city with water.

For a mere second, he realised how vulnerable he was becoming and therefore bottled up his emotions and departed from his household, walking away from his problems and striving towards an old friend's residence. Her name, Nima Pedro. She was a beautifully light-toned model from the Mexico. He had high hopes of finding some sort of comfort within Nima. He was endorsed with utter embarrassment whilst trailing for Nima's love, hoping to find some sort of peace within himself.

Within fifteen minutes of contemplating his depressive state, he found himself creeping into the Pedro household in silence, trying to find a way to contact Nima without alarming her family and her pet dogs. He picked up a small grey limestone pebble from the garden and threw it right next to her wooden window frame on the first-story roof to solely catch her attention. She peeped and opened the window slowly.

'Quinton!' she whispered and squinted in surprise. 'Are you okay?' she asked.

'I'm good. May I come up?' he asked.

'Yes, of course, just wait by the study room sliding door!' she replied. 'I'll be there just now!'

Nima took a while to return to him, but he waited patiently for her by the sliding door on the far west side of the household, momentarily blocking his thoughts from consuming him back into depression. He wanted to be distracted from his taunting issues and thus fixed a faulty smile as the doorknob unhinged.

'Are you okay?' Nima asked and stepped outside in a red cotton nightgown.

'It's a bit nippy outside. Come in, babe. We will talk upstairs!' she whispered and placed her warm arms around his body. Her body smelt of fresh lavender, and a whiff of morocco oil lingered on her smooth neck.

'Take off your shoes. My parents are in the living room!' she whispered. 'We'll have to go around unless you are prepared to crawl?' she asked.

'That's fine with me. We will crawl!' he responded whilst sliding off his loafers and placing them underneath the study table.

They were in a large room filled with bookshelves filled with old novels on all four walls. There was an office table with an iMac desktop and a few sliver pens on the same table shimmering from reflected nightlight. There were multiple mirrors on golden frames on the left passage. The walls were painted dark blue, and at the end of the passage was a separate staircase which led them upstairs.

'The tricky part is crawling on the passage above the living room to my bedroom!' she whispered whilst peeping past metal rails and downwards at her parents discussing issues regarding illegal organisations in North Africa and the Middle East.

The candles burned bright underneath the passage, arising up all the shadows within the living room and imprinting them on the dark blue walls and the white ceiling. There was a massive chandelier hanging above the passage. It glowed bright on to wooden planks whilst Quinton crawled to the final destination, but its hanging crystal rocks gripped his attention and lured him into a moment of false tranquillity and drifted his mind away as he lay on his back. They were bright, shining from the moonlight outside, drawing him closer to his socially and politically aware side. He could hear Nima's parents talking about the shenanigans of politics within the African continent, speaking about how most powerful African nations had corrupt top government officials feeding themselves and denying their people rights to indulge on the wealth that belonged to everyone.

Nima's father stated in his Southern African accent, 'It's been an ongoing cycle that we can't break. It's been around like a bad disease. I look at the way that things have been handled in the past by other presidents and presidents before that. They used to make decisions for the people because they were also part of the struggle. The people used to benefit from the decisions made above, but now times have changed. Most officials have forgotten where they came from.

'A lot of those in power also came from humble backgrounds, with family members who still reside in the village areas where there are no roads, where the locals have power cuts that occur on a regular basis, little resources spent on medication, and so little is spent on medical equipment. Money goes missing, people go missing, and at the end of the day, those that have good hearts cannot overcome those that are bad simply because half the world is filled with greedy leaders who do not mind selling out their own people for profit.

'I call it twenty-first century slavery.'

'Those preaching about peace are also the ones selling the weapons to fuel a deadly war!' Nima's mother stated whilst speaking to her husband.

'It's a shame what the world has become. Preachers are using their powers to preach about money, wielding the vulnerable and controlling them by prophesying the words congregations need to hear. It hurts to see churches across the world turning into businesses instead. I fear for the human race because we are heading towards disaster!'

'Quinton, move!' Nima whispered after lying beside Quinton for a while.

'Sorry!' he whispered back and started crawling again, which felt slightly ironic because he felt mentally crippled by his mother's honesty, broken down into devastation by her dishonest past. Within seconds, they'd crossed over and through into Nima's bedroom.

'Shut the door!' she whispered. 'And take a shower. I'll be in bed, okay?'

He didn't reply but nodded instead whilst parking his dry lips onto her moist lips. She unzipped his pants.

'Wait, have you been drinking?' she asked.

'Not really!' he replied, sounding exhausted and petrified of exposing his recent discovery.

'Just go shower. I'll be here!' she said whilst exhaling out and walking towards her warm bed ahead, right next to an open window where she'd spoken to Quinton.

'Where are the towels?' he asked.

'Just go shower. I'll bring it to you!' she responded as he walked past white closet doors with mirrors attached onto them on both sides of the passage and heading towards the bathroom door at the end.

There was open area on his right side as he held on to the doorknob, discovering a beautiful large sculpture made of out clay on a chest of drawers of two skinny black women seated and facing each other with their long arms curving around an invisible globelike space and their legs stretching out and underlining the bottom of a circular bowl and curving around their bodies. It was right by a bright white wall, stationed perfectly for everyone to see. There was a silver place at the bottom of the sculpture with a caption carved within it, and he squinted whilst moving closely to read it.

'If there aren't any real men out there to defend us, then we shall defend ourselves.'

By

Nima Pedro

Nima leaned onto the last closet door on the right side of the passage whilst noticing Quinton's attention deposited on to a sculpture she'd made awhile back after coming out of a bad relationship. She realised how captivated he was by sculpture that should have no meaning to his life. His brown eyes were fixated on the caption almost as if he was pledging to defend someone and pleading to install the message into his memory bank.

'Do you like it?' she asked and moved closer to cover his body with a large beige towel.

'I don't know. I guess it makes a statement!' he replied and walked towards the bathroom door.

334

'Come and join me!' he suggested whilst opening and entering into the secluded, hidden bathroom door.

'I just showered, and I'm—' she said.

'I know!' he interrupted, sounding perceptive and longing for warm from her body or from within her body.

She couldn't quite comprehend his recent needs but only knew that she was prepared to give him anything he wanted. A part of her enjoyed giving him the attention he wanted, and he couldn't deny one true factor—the fact that he absolutely loved making love.

He remained quietly with his left hand printed on the top end of the shower booth, taunted by flashes of passive events which had occurred in the past. His mother's words grew louder within his mind as Nima cuddled gently whilst kissing his chest softly.

'Thank you!' he whispered into her left ear and rested his eyelids onto an endurable moment of closure.

'For?' she asked and looked up with a sparkle of nostalgia glowing from her light brown eyes.

'For being around, I guess, for understanding me!' he said. 'I've been a mess I know. Thank you for sticking around. You are such a champion!'

'You are welcome, love!' She giggled and placed her head back onto his chest, smiling whilst doing so and finally embracing the idea of him falling in love with her, but she didn't realise that his mind was so far gone, trailing back onto a path paved with sharp pieces which had been scrapped off his damaged heart.

He could hear his mother's recent words rushing back quickly, clogging every other thought away from his mind, and within a second, he could see Beth again looking at the mirror whilst explaining what had happened. She said, 'He wept like a broken man, unsure of his future and dangling on the cliff of no return, and once he was done weeping, his pride clouded his judgement as he dried his moist cheeks with both hands. His strides enlarged and rushed towards me like a man driven by rage. He gripped the wooden doors with his wet hands and parted them sideways, and the glass on the squared frames shattered as I stepped backwards, gliding my mind back into our dark past. That moment made me wonder why I had decided to stay with him for so long.

'He started strangling me until my lungs were on the verge on caving in, and as I fell onto the wooden floor, he asked me why I'd betrayed and lied to him, but I couldn't answer because I was grasping for freedom. My heart was beating too fast, and I wasn't strong enough to gain composure. Therefore, he grew impatient because my silence displeased him. I had no words to bring him comfort as I tried to stand up. He fielded onto me with such care, deceiving him as he wept and I began to feel his pain. There were a few seconds of closure from both sides of the ring and I thought of placing my hands on his back. He pulled backwards whilst holding my arm with his left hand, and . . .

'I could see the red pain relishing through his strained brown eyes. He looked a man that was prepared to end my life, and as he slapped the left side of my face, I could feel my pulse rate throbbing on my left cheek. It reminded me of everything I'd been through with him, and I couldn't take the abuse anymore. Therefore, I slapped him, hoping for my strength to shield me away, but I wasn't strong enough . . .

'Therefore, I wept like any vulnerable woman would do in that situation, falling off my high horse, crying out for help as my body clashed onto the hardships of life, landing into the rut of things. My bottom lip bled onto the wooden floor, and within minutes, he was gone with the wind, but I knew that my problem would linger.

'I did what any distressed person would do in this country. I drank my pain away, hoping that it would stay away. It worked for a while, but that pain will never go away because I'm looking at you right now.'

There was moment of silence clamping Quinton's mind down as a stream of warm water flowed down his body. He kept himself quiet and composed, guarding himself away from breaking next to Nima.

His mother's words continued. 'I guzzled the wine supply in the kitchen and slept!' Beth had said. 'I don't regret having you as my son. My only regret is that I wasn't brave enough to branch out on my own, and I am truly sorry for destroying your childhood because I was a coward. You deserve so much better!'

The scandal has opened up a black hole within Quinton's chest, and it was eating him up from the inside out. He could finally see the truth about himself and understood that he had been lied to for a very long time by his own flesh and blood, led to believe that he was made from pure cloth and tailored from a transparent world stitched with excellence, but that wasn't the case anymore. He reached a conclusion whilst stepping out of the shower booth, understanding that his father had always been jealous of young brother's free will, merely envious of Steve's ability to be careless and to be secluded from responsibility. Marcus' resort to domestic violence must have been a tension reliever for his miserable corporate life.

Nima rotated the shower knob off and stepped into the moonlight spot. Her smooth legs dripped off warm water, leaving a puddle around her soft feet. Her light-toned legs took his mind off the recent scandal, and after viewing the exquisite sight of the radiant woman next to him, he couldn't deny his uncle's features—the fact that he was just as dirty minded. He absolutely loved the way her sweet droplets of honey would leak onto his soft tongue whenever he'd place his face in between, giving him a rush as if he'd just had some coffee.

They were done making love within minutes, and he'd never felt so farther away from the world until that very moment, looking at the white wall in front of them. Winds had grown even stronger outside, beating against the walls and windows, rattling silver chimes by the nearest outdoor space and rattling his soul towards a different plain. He couldn't quite figure out if he was dozing off into a dream or merely driving himself away from the world he knew and into an illusive nightmare. His strained eyes were still open, drawing him closer onto an image on the white wall. It was completely dark around the room, which allowed him to see black tree trunks positioned on a downward snowy slope. He wasn't too sure what to make of this picture within the wall, but something about its difference lured him out of comfort and through the wall.

There he was still and slightly lifeless between two worlds. and as he looked back at Nima on the bed who hadn't noticed anything because she was fast asleep, he could feel his pulse rate throbbing fast, and he knew that he'd have to moving forward. Merely because of a simple primary fact—an utter truth that he was always curious to see where this path would lead him if he were to embark on it. His bare feet weren't stabbed by the cool snow on the slope, but he could feel his body temperature cooling off and settling down into the moment. His white shirt and his slim-fit black jeans could bizarrely accommodate for the weather. There were no side effects of catching a cold or having frostbite on his feet as he walked down, passing by dead tree trunks and heading towards more clustered trees. His inner palms were painted in black ash from touching the numerous tree trunks. Thus, he stopped and picked up a heap of snow to wash off his dirty hands, and as he looked back to where'd come from, the pothole had disappeared into thin air. All he could see were more dead tree trunks positioned upright on a steep hill.

'Hello!' he shouted but felt greeted by absence and a wave of his own echo.

There were no signs of human activity around him whilst he glanced at different sides of the slope, searching for another path to accommodate for his fear towards moving to the empty forest. He immediately felt a cool breeze of wind pushing him downwards towards the empty forest, collaborating with the wrath of loneliness which whipped his back and reminded him that he was enslaved by a surplus montage consisting of depressive memories. And whilst he stepped closer towards uncertainty and passing all the long black tree trunks, he could feel the absence of love reigning through his heart, reminding him that he needed the love that Juliana gave to him. All the hollow spaces within the tree trunks closed up and made him feel unwelcome in their domain.

He looked down whilst walking and could finally see footprints along his path and thus trailed and acknowledged them as his beacon of hope. The dusk sky grew impatient and turned darker whilst he moved into the depth of the forest, and as he did so, he could hear another person moving ahead of him, which made him rush farther until he could see a woman in the distance.

'Sorry, do you know where we are?' he asked, but the figure did not turn around nor acknowledge his presence.

Her body was covered in a white cotton coat, lengthening down all the way to the white palms on her feet. Everything about her body structure resembled Juliana, especially her unique curly hair strands moving to the direction of the cool breeze.

'You have not lost me, you know! You only believe so because you're afraid that I won't accept you for who you've become. I've always loved you!' Juliana said, finally revealing herself by turning around. 'I've missed you so much! You should stop deeming yourself absurd and reckless!' she said and stepped closer. 'But I know you. Your heart is amazing. You are stitched from pure love, and I know you'll overcome this challenge!'

'I've missed you so much' he mentioned and looked into her green eyes as if he'd just met her for the first time.

She looked absolutely remarkable. Her skin glowed bright and shone with crystal sparkles on every inch of her body. She was wearing a golden cross necklace around her neck and an engagement ring on her left ring finger shining brightly within the darkness. It reminded him of loyalty and reminded him of the way he used to honour her presence.

'I will always be here for you!' she whispered into his right ear whilst holding on to him tightly.

'I need you back in my life!' he whispered back, feeling nostalgic and vulnerable.

'I want to show you something!' she said whilst inhaling his essence.

'What is it?' he asked and kissed her lips softly, hoping for closure.

'Come with me!' she said and led him away towards a path on the right side, paved with grey rocks along the sides.

His feet crushed wooden twigs within the snow as they moved through the dark forest.

'You will always be safe with me!' she said. 'Allow me to show you the way!'

'Where are we going?' he asked whilst glancing ahead and discovering a burning light through a side window from a stable cottage below with greys rocks clustered around it.

'Wait. What were you doing out back there?' he asked.

'Looking for you, I'm always looking for you!' she responded. 'You are always out somewhere, always busy with something, and you never really have time to spare!'

'How'd you know where to find me?' he asked as they stepped down a path of rocks and up to the cottage entrance.

'I felt so alone whilst falling sleep, and I started thinking of the past. I know I can always find you whenever we are subconsciously thinking of each other!' she replied and turned around to face him whilst rattling a bunch of silver keys from her right pocket. 'I wasn't sure if you were thinking of me though, but I've been keeping something from you. I can't keep the truth from you anymore!'

'What have you been keeping me?' he asked whilst she scratched the locket with one of the keys.

'Just wait and see!' she said and opened the wooden front door slowly,

'Such a beautiful cottage!' he said, sounding unsure of what to observe, from the oak wood plank walls to the dark blue carpet lining all the way to a bedroom door.

There were two armchairs on top of large rug facing each other, and two metres away from the fireplace on the right side of the cottage, two dark brown chest of drawers on the left side of the passage blocked any possible entry into the lounge on the left side of the room from the front door entrance and from the passage entrance.

'Come in and close the door!' she said whilst unwrapping her white coat from her body. 'I just have one question for you. Do you still believe in us?' she asked and folded it in half then placed it onto the closest armchair. 'This is the only place where we will all be safe, hidden away from the world!' she added.

'Are we safe here?' he repeated whilst questioning.

'Yes, my baby!' she whispered.

'She is sleeping in the main bedroom!'

'So you lied to me?' he asked and shut the front door behind him.

'I'm sorry. I was told to do so by my mother because she believes that you are reckless and careless!' she responded and sat on the large rug, facing the burning wood inside the fireplace.

'I don't understand how it is that you've already given birth,' he asked whilst strolling between the two chests of drawers, entering into the lounge and noticing a familiar portrait—an unfinished painting hanging on the far right corner of the lounge.

'This is our dream, my love!' she said. 'Every time we both think of the endless possibility of being madly love, we end up drawn closer to each other no matter how far we are from each other. Our dream patterns are aligned because of Arabella. She makes us one!'

'I remember this painting,' he said.

'The same painting I discovered when I first met you!'

'You remember!' she replied. 'And what did I say about it?'

'You said that you'll finish painting it one day!' he said. 'It represents our fate, but I still can't make out what it is!'

'Yes, it does represent fate, and I'm going to finish painting it because I can finally see that you are my fate!' she said and smiled. 'Come and sit next to me. And stop worrying so much!'

He did exactly as she'd commanded, establishing that he was easily wielded the desire to be loved by his significant other. She opened her legs as he sat on the large rug and wrapped them around him tightly, placing her soft arms around his body and gently resting her chin on his left shoulder.

'I feel safe with you here!' she whispered slowly.

These were the only words he needed to hear and thus smiled in grace because he was finally at peace. He tilted his head towards the left and closed his brown eyes, embracing the peaceful environment around him. All he could hear were crackling sounds of wood blocks burning and breaking off into smaller pieces and deteriorating into ashes.

'This feels right!' he whispered.

She hummed and nodded slowly to acknowledge his words. Their heartbeats were synchronised, throbbing loudly within their chests and drawing their lips closer to each other. She parked her lips onto his left cheek, craving the taste of his sweet tongue, and as he turned his head, she glanced into his beautiful brown eyes, finally understanding her fated attraction to him. There was something so uniquely profound about his brown eyes. They presented a future filled with happiness gushing through a small period—images of her only lover picking up orphaned children and embracing them as one of his own, a caretaker with the strength to dispose of an army of nine hundred thousand men.

'You've always been so strong!' she muttered and kissed his lips so passionately, closing her green eyes and diving forward.

He gently reclined backwards and lay onto the large rug, allowing himself to be seduced by a woman he loved so much, knowing that she loved him back.

'I'm sorry for the way I have treated you!' he whispered, feeling guilty for his reckless behaviour.

'I forgave you before I'd even met you!' she said and blushed.

He could taste her essence on her soft skin. The taste of caramel mixed with an elusive sprinkle of sweet desires. Tears of joy leaked from her eyelids, and she confessed her undying love to him.

'I love you so much!' she whispered into his left ear. 'I love you so much!' she whispered again with assurance, hoping for a dialog to commerce. He understood what he needed to say next.

'I will find my way back to you, and we will be together forever!' he said whilst taking in deeper breaths. 'I promise!'

He could see a beautiful sight of one million warships packed with angels landing onto his shoreline at that moment, arriving to assist him and perish away his monsters.

Neither one of the two lovers wanted to let go. Therefore, he leaned back onto the floor, and she followed, chasing love in its rare form. Her knees were still planted onto the rug, clinched by the bottom of his rib cage. He stroked her back slowly with his right hand whilst they French kissed passionately.

Her right ear was plunged onto his left chest, resting her head on it and listening to his heartbeat. Her eyes had zoned to the fireplace. She watched burning ashes flicker from time to time. They were bonded right next to each other, reminding themselves of past trials and tribulations. He found himself drawn to the beauty of her soul whilst she spoke and giggled to memorable events. She placed her soft left hand onto his right chest, grazing and rubbing her left thumb in different directions.

'I need you to come back to me!' her ghost said, sounding cleansed and ready to move forward.

There was a moment of silence whilst he thought of running away from the world he'd been accustomed to.

'We can leave and start again, settle down in a new place!' she whispered. 'Plant our own roots maybe?' She sounded persuasive and certain of the future.

His eyes were glued to the wooden ceiling whilst he imagined the possibility of leaving everything behind.

'Sounds amazing!' he said and parked his warm lips onto her forehead. 'We will be together again!' He whispered the last words until it was completely quiet.

'Hold me!' she commanded. Thus, he did so and clamped her left leg with his legs.

'Feels better?' he asked.

'So much better!' she whispered and smiled in grace.

'This is definitely the perfect way to die!' he whispered into her left ear,

'This is the perfect way to die!' she muttered, acknowledging his words and opened her legs in different directions, giving him complete access.

They glanced at each other within that moment and smiled in satisfaction.

'I can't move!' he said, which made Juliana laugh out loud. She held on to his neck with both hands then kissed him.

'You don't have to feel alone anymore. I'm always here for you!' she muttered, grazing her teeth on the right side of his neck. 'Your home is inside of me. Remember that!' she whispered.

He nodded and held on to her tightly.

'Let's wash off and get to bed!' she suggested, placing her warm hands onto his smooth back.

'That's a good idea!' he replied and rolled over to the right. 'I wish we had done a few things differently, you know!'

'I know, but we wouldn't be who we are now if those things hadn't happened!' she replied as they stood up and walked towards bedroom door.

She opened the bedroom door slowly to avoid rattling the old door hinges.

'Try and keep it down. She's still sleeping!' Juliana said and looked back.

They covered themselves with red cotton towels which were placed on the doubled-sized bed then walked towards a baby carriage right beside their bed and the wooden wall. There was a bright lamp over the carriage. Thus, Juliana switched it on as they glanced over a pile of blankets and discovered their baby wrapped in a bundle. There she was, the pinnacle point of love wrapped in warmth. Her small hands were clenched tightly on to a white cotton blanket. Her beautiful skin tone florins he'd brightly like a daisy flower. She looked exactly like her mother except for one factor—she had black hair strands like her father.

'She's so breathtaking, don't you think?' Juliana asked and placed her warm right hand onto his upper back.

He kept quiet whilst taking in every second of that precious moment. Juliana tailed to the bathroom and switched on the lights within. The warm water ran and filled up within a circular bathtub whilst she sat aside for a while.

'Come join me!' she said whilst stripping in front of a long rectangular mirror parallel to the bathtub.

'I'm coming!' he replied.

He felt remarkably blessed to have seen such purified beauty in its natural form. His happiness breached through his heart and cracked a smile on his moist face. He immediately pledged to be a better person and walked into the bathroom and followed the path of redemption, for the love surrounding him was so consuming and heart filling. He'd accepted the bundles of adoration and finally found his path to the love of his life. It adorned him fully. His exact words throbbed loudly within his mind at that moment as he stepped into the bathtub and faced Juliana.

'Sometimes you have to deprive yourself from the things you have so you learn to deserve them again.'

His fear absolutely drowned away as she planted her head onto his chest.

'Everything will be just fine!' she said and looked deeply into his brown eyes.

She smiled with grace like she always did, embracing the idea of being in love again. They were inseparable, mostly drawn to each other by a significant moment, the same look they'd given to each other when they first met. It seemed to assure them with certainty that every challenge they'd encounter could be conquered.

'I must say, I'm afraid to be in love with you again,' she said and held on to his body tightly.

'You don't have to be afraid, for you aren't alone in that department!' he whispered into her right ear and assured her with bliss softness.

They knew they were dreaming of a different life, a world detached from other human conventions, a place where they could fall in love all over again. Her warm heart accommodated for the stress he had over the past day, and it inevitably shielded him from awaking up. He didn't want to open his eyes, for he was momentarily fine with his mind leading him to believe that Juliana was around.

'Let's go and sleep, baby!' she whispered into his right ear as he opened his eyelids. He could feel his soul drifting away from his picture-perfect moment.

Everything started to brighten up before his eyes, and his senses started to vanquish into nothing. He couldn't feel her warmth anymore, nor could he smell the Moroccan oil essence lingering on her soft skin. It seemed as if he was returning to a world he loathed so much.

He awoke to a new day, partly lost between his dream and reality and mostly lost because he'd forgotten where he'd fallen asleep. Sun rays blazed through the thin glass window beside the bed he'd slept in. The white walls brightened his mood as he sat up straight with a little positivity streaming through his veins. It was slightly nippy and cold within bedroom as he uncovered the duvet covering his body, remembering he was in Nima's bedroom.

Despite events which had occurred over the past few days, he wasn't as miserable at all mainly because he'd had a remarkable dream of his significant other. The idea of Juliana brought harmony into his heart, and his new day was uplifted into great joy. He felt glorified by the brightness projecting around. The atmosphere radiated happiness into his life once more as he fully awoke from his dreaming daze.

Nima opened the bedroom door with a beige cup of coffee in her right hand.

'You need to wake up!' she said. 'My parents have gone out for brunch!' She stepped closer to her bed. 'I'm making breakfast downstairs, babe!'

He smiled in a joyful mood.

'What is it?' she asked whilst strolling towards the passage. 'You seem chipper, without any care in the—'

'Oh, nothing major!' he interrupted. 'It must be cold outside!' he said whilst placing his soft feet onto the wooden floor.

'Yes, it is! Come have some coffee with me downstairs!' she said whilst placing her cup of coffee onto the wooden floor to wear an old university hoodie which used to belong to her mother. 'You can borrow one of my hoodies for now, but I want it back before you leave!'

'Thank you!' he replied and entered the bathroom to refresh his face.

'You seem happy. Should I take the credit?' she asked, smiling whilst blowing at her beige cup of coffee.

'Yes, you can have the credit!' he said and rinsed his mouth with mouthwash. He felt guilty yet slightly exonerated from his incarcerated sins, merely driven to change his life around and find Juliana again.

'It's actually getting cold these days!' Nima stated whilst stepping down the staircase and glancing back for interaction.

'It's definitely time to go shopping for winter clothing!' he said whilst looking at the outside world through a series of arched windows by the staircase.

'Are you ready to head home soon?' she asked.

'Not really, my mind unveiled a montage of past events!' he said. 'I don't know if I'm ready to go home just yet!'

'We'll behave like Looney Tunes for the day!' Nima mentioned.

'I'll stay an extra day for you, love!'

They walked through the house and ended up in the oval kitchen. The area was hollow and engraved with an old Italian theme—a manmade pizza oven by the far west side made of polished maroon bricks and a black kitchen counter trailing around the kitchen. There were a lot of silver kitchen appliances around. A well-built sitting area was placed in the middle of the kitchen with long wooden stools. There was a clear view of the backyard through large arched windows on the different areas of the oval wall.

'We have some coffee, juice. Take your pick, okay?'

'Maybe juice?' he asked.

'Sure, mango juice, yes?' she asked.

'Yes please!' he pleaded as she walked towards a pantry by the refrigerator. He couldn't quite mute the voice relishing through his mind, telling him to depart from the world he'd become accustomed to and find solidarity with his beautiful lover.

'Nima, do you have a charger I can use?' he asked, remembering his pleasant dream consisting of the peaceful place he'd always wanted to vanish to.

He wondered if she'd been dishonest about losing their unborn child because she was poisoned by her mother or if his dream was just a tortuous nightmare. Maybe he didn't want to believe that her miscarriage was true. His recent dream had brought him one step closer to Juliana, for he could feel her presence lingering beside him whilst he spoke.

'There is a charger in the living room where my parents were last night!' she said and poured up a glass of mango juice.

Thank you!' he said whilst holding on to the glass.

'You are so welcome!' she said and walked back to the pantry. 'I'm going to prepare some waffles for us!' she suggested.

'That would be amazing!' he said and stood up. 'Red velvet maybe?'

'Yes, I'll make them for you!' she replied and smiled.

She hoped for some sort of positivity to relish through his heavy heart to allow him to see clearly, mainly hoping he'd awake from a false mirage inside his mind. She didn't realise his heart had always been spoken for by a bird which flew away to the south coast of the African continent.

He drifted onto the blue side walls of the passage and discovered dark wooden frames. There were a few black-and-white portraits of Nima as an only child seated on a large solid oak deep buttoned linen Camden sofa by herself and smiling without a care in the world. There was another portrait of her parents seated beside her on the same couch.

'Did you find the charger?' Nima asked then looked up whilst walking into the passage. 'Don't look!' She shouted in embarrassment but found herself flattered by the way he was looking at the portraits. She did not realise he was envisioning a picture of himself with Juliana and Arabella.

'You look incredible and cute!' he said, feeling nostalgic for real love.

'Thank you!' she replied, blushing whilst walking towards the surround system. 'Oh, found it. Just charge and call your mother and let her know I've got you captive!'

He kept quiet whilst pinning the pin charger into his phone then sat by closely, wondering how'd announce his departure. He was very determined to vanish into thin air and leave his old life to wrinkle into dust. Its vile predictability had kept him depressed for far too long. Thus, he plotted because he craved and longed for his dreams to turn into reality. His dreams to ignite with Juliana kept him up at night and drove him into the early hours of his restless mornings. He knew his nostalgia was also driving him mad every single day, maybe perhaps driving him to the brink of a beautiful death, but regardless of his nostalgic thoughts growing and blossoming like purple jacaranda flowers during a hot spring season, he was determined to find prosperity.

Within minutes of his phone charging, he dialled Juliana's South African number mainly to dose her voice back into his memory bank. It rang for a few seconds, but he did not lose faith. He knew she'd answer, whether in this life or the afterlife. There was so much fire burning inside his heart whilst he waited patiently. Nevertheless, he was nervous, unsure of his next speech to convince his beautiful lover of a dream he'd had. He knew he was making an executive decision, one that would be beneficial to their futures forever. It kept ringing for a while and diverted to voicemail, which left him puzzled. He wondered if he was as delusional as he'd believed himself to be. The thought of his dream being just a dream began to scrap away his layers of hope. A part of him didn't want to conclude that his heart was frozen in the past, stuck underneath a rock somewhere deep within Juliana's world.

'Nima, just spoke to my mother, and she needs me back home!' he shouted out dishonestly whilst his feet boiled and trailed for his departure. He wanted to be with Juliana Rose so badly that he'd didn't think twice about leaving quickly.

'Wait!' Nima shouted. 'You can't just leave me like this. I have feelings too! You can't just invade my heart and walk away from me whenever it's convenient for you!'

'I'm sorry. I'm so sorry!' he replied, discovering how selfish he'd become by denying Nima the same affection and attention he'd given to his significant other.

The only thing she craved besides rough sex was for her heart to feel real love. She didn't want to be placed in the causality section and thus poured her heart out.

'Do you not love me?' she asked with tears lingering on her beautiful light brown eyes.

'I . . .' he said and turned around to face Nima. He directly used his excuse to shield the painful truth.

'Right, but not the way I've loved you, but you don't see that because you are reckless and blind. You destroy everything you touch, and you will stop at nothing until everyone around you drowns in pain like you do!' she muttered.

A cool breeze brushed against them and amplified the silence between the two, making it awkward and uncomfortable.

'It's what you do. You hurt people, and I'm done waiting for you to care,' she said.

No words could accommodate for his behaviour. Thus, he kept mute because he didn't want to dishonest anymore nor sell false dreams to Nima based on a cheap oath. He walked away,

'I'm so sorry. I just need to be with her again!' he said and felt the wrath of love wielding him away from the world he'd become accustomed to.

'Then go, but do not look back here ever again!' she shouted whilst weeping and drying her cheeks with both hands.

Her heart shattered whilst he walked away. His strides grew longer as he trailed back to his home. He wondered what he'd say to his parents, mainly contemplating what he'd say to his dying father.

'Forgive him,' Juliana's voice echoed within his mind. 'Forgive him and come back to me!'

His heart pumped out relief after listening to her voice, but he knew he had to move quickly because time wasn't on his side. Every second ticking towards the future elevated and encouraged him to rush back. He'd completely forgotten about his obligations to his family company and had completely forgotten about the responsibilities he had to uphold at his apartment.

One would say that he was possessed by the love Juliana had within her heart and in between her legs. He walked through the front gate to an unexpected setting—his yard was clean and everything looked normal. There were cars parked everywhere, sounding to a celebration, but he knew better of the sadistic cover his parents would use to cover up their issues. They'd invite people to act as barriers between them and avoid each other at all costs under the same roof.

Frankly speaking, Quinton had grown strangled to the false image presented and thus concluded to remain scarce whilst plotting to leave. He waved at the gardeners whilst they swept the green grounds and piled dried leaves in different areas. The house looked pleasant, without broken glass pieces on the wooden floor, but it reeked of misery as he walked up the wooden staircase to his bedroom.

There wasn't much to pack into his luggage packs because he'd left them from the previous night. He could feel Juliana's succubus hands imprinted onto his shoulders, almost as if she was right behind him. There were projections of Juliana at every angle in the bathroom. She was everywhere—in the bathtub blowing foam from her hands and giggling childishly. He could see her in the shower booth, leaning against the tiles whilst the water washed over her body. She owned his mind in ways he couldn't image possible until that very moment whilst entering into the shower booth and watching her succubus vanish into thin air.

'You're wasting time!' her voice whispered whilst he showered and glanced towards the brightness lashing in from the open bathroom window above the bathtub.

He could see her in the distance, calling out his name and trying to lure him away from reality again. His phone vibrated and rang in silence on his comfortable black duvet covers, but he couldn't hear it due to the sound of water drops clashing onto the tiles. His brown eyes were fixated towards the window, envisioning a beautiful dream.

Juliana left a compelling voicemail after attempting to call twice. An epiphany had lapsed into her mind as she glanced down at her stomach, realising their unborn baby deserved so much more than the world she was offering.

Inevitably they were obsessed with the idea of being together and hiding their unborn child away from the dangerous world they were in. She realised she couldn't bask through another day without him around. It was quite evident nobody could deny her the right to be loved by a man so genuine in his own way. They were determined to be with each other despite the challenges lashing onto their home front.

She lay on her bed in dark blue pyjamas and stroked her stomach slowly whilst staring at the wide ocean in the distance, wondering when she'd ever find solidarity with her amazing lover. It was a beautiful day in the city of Cape Town. There was so much life flowing through the colourful streets, giving the place so much soul. The wide beaches were packed with locals and tourists from all over the world. It projected a diverse image of peace and love which relished through Juliana's mind whilst she looked into the distance where the Indian and Atlantic Oceans met. It looked beautiful with all types of birds flying in the air. The cool breeze blew towards her balcony, but she knew it would never fill up the void in her heart. It would never satisfy her burning desire to be caressed by the only person she'd ever loved. She craved his love and everything that came with it. It was the only element of life which felt remotely real. Thus, she longed to embrace it again. She redialled his number and waited patiently as it rang.

'Don't worry. Your dad will come home soon!' she whispered to her stomach and smiled with positivity whilst glancing down at the engagement ring she'd been wearing for the past two days.

Her foetus kicked happily whilst she lay backwards onto her comfortable bed. She was uncertain of her next words whilst holding on to a mesmerizing dream.

'Hey!' he answered with relief, sounding slightly nervous at the same time. He was getting dressed into comfortable casual clothing,

'Hey you!' she replied and sat up by the edge of her bed. They kept quiet for a while, listening to each breathing slowly.

'I had an amazing dream!' they both said at the same time.

'Sorry!' she muttered.

'No, I'm sorry!' he responded.

'Go first. I'll listen!' she said as he took a few seconds to gather his wild thoughts and dreams into a compelling motion.

'I had a dream about our child. She was so alive!' he said, hoping for a positive response.

She couldn't keep the truth buried by the coast, for she knew he'd eventually find out. Therefore, she did the right thing by confessing everything. He wasn't upset, nor was he angry. Matter of fact, it brought great joy to hear Juliana expressing herself and showing raw emotions. It was all he'd ever long for—to hear her voice. She laughed and cried out due to uncontainable joy.

'I'm leaving home and coming down there to be with you!' he said which uplifted her spirits to an all-time high.

'Would you do that for me?' she asked rhetorically.

'Of course I would do that for you!' he said, checking for his Botswana passport inside his luggage bags.

'What about work?' she asked.

'What's about it?' he interrupted, sounding less fazed by the question. 'I've made a decision to leave this life behind and to start a new one with you. I hope for the best when it comes to you and I!'

She was flattered by his decision and thus blushed pink.

'I'll run away with you. I will move to the moon with you, and we can sit there until we run out of oxygen!' he said, and they laughed without a care in the world, which immediately vanquished their pain away. However, their hearts remained restless and impatient.

'Let me get ready to leave!' he said. 'I must book a plane ticket and organise for my departure from home!'

'Okay, my love!' she said. 'Hurry up and come home to me!'

'I will!' he replied. 'Just stay in bed, and the next time you wake up, I will be beside you again!' he claimed.

'Promise?' she asked.

'I promise!' he said and took a deep breath and hung up then walked out of his bedroom and on to the passage slowly.

He could hear the sound of chimes moving and people laughing outside by the backyard. However, his mind strayed to rewind to the previous night where he could imaginatively see the wooden floor sparkling with broke glass everywhere. There were so many equivalent thoughts spiralling within him whilst he looked over the main balcony and saw his distant relatives bonding with close family by the large veranda. They were all fine with the idea of pretending like everything was painted gold and shimmered with false happiness. He couldn't quite figure out what he'd say to his family and thus concluded to leave without saying goodbye. He knew it would break his mother's heart, but he'd felt the necessary measures to avoid her. He needed to dwell on the information he'd stumbled on to from the previous night so that he could come to terms with the fact that he was a bastard. That information needed to marinate in his mind before he could forgive anyone for hurting him. Therefore, he remained just as heartless as his biological father.

Chapter Nineteen

Run away from Your Pain

The burning sun was at an all-time high as the weather started to change as the bright blue sky evolved into dark grey from an avalanche of dark clouds floating in from the north. He remained slightly fazed by the changing weather whilst glooming on his wide bed, waiting for his cab driver to take him to the international airport. These were his last moments in captivity. Thus, he finally embraced his long-awaited courage to break free from the heavy shackles which had kept him incarcerated from being in love with the only person that understood him best. He could hear waves of a strong wind brushing against his bedroom window and tree branches scraping the walls outside. His eyes were strained, showing a high level of exhaustion from loitering between houses and lusting inside of Nima. He turned his head to the left and patiently waited for his Blackberry to ring on his study table beside a pile of magazines.

Time seemed to clock away slowly whilst he glanced at the silver clock between the bathroom door and the bathroom door. He wondered if his casual attire of red high-top sneakers, dark blue jeans, and a grey sweater was appropriate for travelling across the border. There were so many thoughts spinning around him whilst waiting. They were driving him insane, but one picture remained crystal clear—an image of love and peace. He didn't dwell on it much, for he knew he'd doze off into sleep and find himself stuck within a tormenting world filled with empty promises. Therefore, he sat up straight and took long deep breaths to ease off the tension weighing on his broad shoulders.

'I'm making the right decision!' he said, trying to convince himself.

He wasn't used to making such irrational decisions, but the risky endorsement of love made everything seem fine. It was the glimpse of satisfaction which had brought him to that moment, and nobody could persuade him towards another alternative. He finally believed he understood the meaning of following his destiny and that reaching out for the stars aligned within his dreams. His face shone brightly and sparkled with happiness as his Blackberry rang. He knew his valuable time was up, for his cab driver had sworn to call after he'd arrived at the front gate.

He'd used an abandoned outdoor staircase by his youngest sister's balcony. It was the same staircase he'd used in his younger years to disobey his parents and participate in peer-pressured activities. Every single person in the house was blinded by the strong wind blowing and raindrops washing off sprinkles of dust from the windows and thus couldn't see Quinton walking towards the front gate. Only his mother could see him vanish into the world. Thus, she wondered if she'd ever see him again. Her tears streamed down her cheeks whilst the red cab drove away. She kept this information to herself, for it was all she'd ever wanted—to see her son break free from the world they lived in.

Quinton sat back in the left back seat and watched his predictable future vanish away. The right window started to steam up. Thus, he wiped it clean with his right hand. No words were shared between himself and the cab driver. All his trials and tribulations flashed before his eyes whilst he glanced at every large tree they were passing through a wet window. He knew he was one step closer to relishing in real love again, for he could almost smell the Moroccan oil lingering on Juliana's soft radiant skin, his lips kissing her shoulders and his arms glued tightly around her on an average sunny day in a remote island. His thoughts were slowly gathering into one motion and preparing him to strive for his salvation. He knew he was on the righteous passage to happiness and finally believed nothing could come between him and his destiny.

Through the drums beating repeated from the soft electro music playing and lashing out from the radio, he could hear police sirens and could see blue lights flashing in the opposite lane, passing them and heading towards where they would come from.

'The world is just too hectic these days!' Samuel, the cab driver, said, sounding foreign. There was so much pain flowing with his words, addressing the xenophobic attacks and immigration issues which had escalated within different provinces of South Africa years before.

'It looks hectic, I must say!' Quinton replied, wondering if he'd made the right decision to leave without calculating the risk of losing everything in the process.

'It doesn't make sense!' Samuel said and wiped the windscreens with an old dry cloth from the glove compartment. 'There were days when their old political activists needed shelter from their old oppressive government, and our countries aided most of them, and this is how they treat us!'

'It's not everyone is the country, just those who haven't learned from the past!' Quinton said. 'Just a selected few!'

'It doesn't make sense. The Bible says, "Thou shall love thy neighbour," but they don't love their African neighbours. Where do they want the refugees to go?' Samuel asked whilst stirring the wheel.

'I have no answer for that question, brother. I wish I did!' Quinton replied.

They found themselves caught in traffic within minutes of driving onto busy highway lanes.

'Looks like an accident just happened!' Samuel said and rolled down his window to see clearly.

'Is it bad?' Quinton asked whilst scrolling through his Blackberry to reply to social notifications.

'It looks bad!' Samuel said. 'The car must have swerved off and flipped in the process, or maybe the wheels blew up!'

There were multiple people standing by whilst a grey tow truck pulled off a dark blue Mercedes Benz. It wheels were flat, and it seemed written off. The image itself looked a bit bizarre because there weren't any people within the car itself, nor was there any blood anywhere.

'Life is so unpredictable!' Quinton said and realised how selfish he'd become for leaving without saying goodbye. He felt indecisive whilst contemplating the way forward. 'Samuel, please turn around soon. Forgot my passport at home!' he said.

'Okay, we can do that!' Samuel replied and indicated to the left and intercepted the vehicle on his left.

Quinton hadn't realised he'd completely escaped a path of destruction after leaving his peaceful home. It seemed as if everything he'd escaped was slowly clinching back into his mind and holding him back from persevering to greatness. He called Juliana and hoped she'd understand his deny.

'Hello, my baby!' She said happily.

'Hey!' He replied and looked towards the steamy window.

'What's wrong?' she asked. 'Please tell me you're still coming, love.'

'I'm coming, just delayed in traffic, and I have to say goodbye to my family, but I will be there, love!' he said. 'Please be patient with me!'

'Okay, my baby!' she muttered and lay back onto her bed. 'Just be safe!'

It began to pour heavily as the cab was en route back. They decided to wait by a petrol station until the weather ceased off, but it didn't stop precipitating heavily. Maybe it was Mother Nature's way of hinting his departure, but he hadn't noticed the cautious signs projecting everywhere, like the police vehicles which had passed them earlier, the accident, and the rain pouring heavily.

'Samuel, would you like something to drink?' Quinton asked. 'I'll try and nibble on something whilst we wait!'

'Yes please, an appletiser!' he replied.

'Okay, coming back!' Quinton said and opened the back door then walked towards the café door beside the petrol attendant service point.

He waited in line after a series of doubts from picking out different items on the shelves. He wondered what he'd say to his father as his mind revealed an escapade filled with dilemmas. His mind was patronized and filled with a lot of emotions throbbing within, and at the same time, his brown eyes were glued towards a magazine shelf right next to the pay point. There was a lot of newspapers piled at the bottom with a familiar picture on the front page. It looked like a farm he'd been to before but couldn't quite recall the memory which fitted. The headline stated, 'Body found buried underneath a barnyard'.

The words before his eyes left him completely frozen. He remained quiet whilst everyone in the line moved forward to pay. He'd remembered his participation in an unspeakable act.

'The silver gun!' he thought, realising he could be framed for his biological father's murder. There were no words to bring him closure nor bring him comfort. Thus, he placed the items onto the counter and walked out of the café and back into the red cab.

'We need to leave immediately!' he said and sat in the front passenger seat.

'Okay, let's go!' Samuel agreed and drove towards the direction of Quinton's home.

'No, just get me to the airport!' he said, sounding paranoid and elusive.

Samuel spoke about mostly irrelevant topics whilst Quinton's mind drowned in guilt. He remembered Old Patrick's ghost stating the truth, 'The past always catches up to the present'. The traffic lights were red with a lot of impatient car drivers waiting to mark forth.

'Just run the red. There are no police around!' Quinton said. 'I'm a bit late!'

Samuel acted like a fool for allowing himself to be pawned towards death. They watched two bright lights heading towards their way from the left. The wrath of a higher power came towards them in momentum, and they knew they were fucked, for their lives were at risk. It seemed extremely ironic, for their car accident had occurred in the same place as Quinton's last accident. They couldn't run away, nor could they pay for their way out of that particular situation as a deep green army truck smashed into the red cab.

The pain was excruciating.

Quinton's insides burned as the impact drove him farther and farther away from reality. It gripped him away from his dreams and placed him into a coma. in a place where he'd be forced to confront his naughty monsters and vanquish them away from lingering around his soul. He could feel the bruises on his body aching with pain whilst he opened his brown eyes to an unfamiliar place. He'd entered into the cornerstone of his mind and knew he wouldn't be able to escape until he could address his past and find a way to a better future.

There was a sound of someone just as graceful and humble as himself, struggling and longing to break free from captivity just as much as he was trying to awaken to his next challenges. He was in captivity with his guardian angel, and she was just as vulnerable as he was, unable to use her powers to free them from his own world.

The dungeon walls shimmered, moist from raindrops streaming from the barred hole above. Every angle of the dungeon was revolting and made Quinton feel sick to his stomach. Therefore, he kept his brown eyes shut. He didn't want to address the challenges just yet and thus lay quietly to keep composed. There were a few drops of agony dripping on the wet floor beside his face, leaving a patch of uncertainty. He couldn't quite figure where he was until he sat up straight and saw his guardian angel jumping up and down with her wings spread in different directions. Her white wings were smudged with grease and dust. She looked up whilst chanting for positivity.

'Olivia, where are we?' he asked and slowly stood up.

'We are inside your mind!' she replied. 'So glad to have you back!'

'How did we get here?' he asked and took in every breath slowly.

The conditions within the dungeon were humid.

'I don't know, but we have to find a way out now!' she said.

'Okay, let's try gathering all our thoughts for a bit!' he suggested and rattled the rusty bars in front of him.

'I'm glad you're awake, but you don't look so well!' she said, paying full attention to her earthling as he moved around whilst holding his diaphragm with her left hand. 'Smile!' she said, sounding positive and equipped with the strength to mentally absorb everything around them.

He kept his head up, but his pale face remained without compelling emotions to motivate her back to salvation. All he could think about was his fairest lover who'd probably find out about his accident on social media if nobody his family would have the audacity to notify her.

'You really do love her, don't you?' Olivia asked, discovering her instilled ability to read her earthling's mind.

'I do miss her so much. She is everything to me!' he replied. 'She's such daisy flower. She's beautiful and remarkably light yellow. Well planted and down to earth!'

He exhaled and strolled around, searching for a gap in between the rusty bars. His recent words had brought discomfort to Olivia, which made her realise she was becoming more human every day. She grew slightly envious, from a wild seed which had been implanted deeply within her heart. It made her crave the same love that Quinton had for Juliana.

They realised they weren't alone anymore as a large figure emerged from an arched entrance by Olivia's dungeon wall. It blocked out any ray of light from passing through, and the smell was even more revolting than before. It left them completely horrified as it groaned whilst moving closer to Quinton's cage. They were beheld by dark creatures which loitered around in nights, descendants of an evil persona which managed to enter Quinton's life.

Regardless of his illuminating monsters hovering around, he knew he was the only one who could banish them away by stepping forth and becoming a better man. He was faced with a great challenge but wondered what he had to do to find some peaceful prosperity through the dust of things. His bad consciousness was fuelled by all the bad deeds and sins he'd committed over the past year. He was slightly embarrassed of his shameful past whilst waiting to face his nemesis. It moved closer and closer as he unclipped his silver watch from his wrist and buried it into the maroon soil using his bare feet. Its silver chain shackles rang loudly around his waist whilst it stepped forth.

Olivia made threats, but it didn't pay much attention. Its hands were thick, grey, and pale. It held on to its black hood and revealed its face before the bright moonlight shining from above. He could finally see what his demon looked like as it stood in front of him. Its face was dry, pale, and flat with a grey pigment. It had a deep scar trailing from its chest and all the way down to its abs. It's colour represented the small void within Quinton's heart, for his past was slightly empty without genuine love, and at that moment, he realised why he craved attention and why he needed to be loved. It turned around and walked towards the corner to pick up shackles from an old wooden table. Its back was imprinted with multiple thin scars from all the women he'd caressed in his time. It was evident his mind was dark and twisted within. His demon reeked of silence as it opened his cage and bonded his wrists with golden shackles then brutality dragged him out of the dungeon.

'Watch out for me!' he shouted, but Olivia wasn't equipped with the knowledge to understand why he'd randomly shout out words of that nature.

She looked up and felt indifferent about herself, for she couldn't fly anymore nor use her powers to barge free from incarceration. There was regret inside her heart whilst she sat down and raked the floor with her hands, having memories of her pleasant home. She'd disobeyed the covenant of guardian angels by having a greedy thought of pursuing life as a vulnerable human, which had gotten her into trouble.

'There is always a way out!' she said and scanned every single detail around her cage whilst walking around.

She noticed a larger gap in between two rusted metal bars by the top but couldn't reach it. Her inability to fly away railed her into frustration. Thus, she kicked a small puddle of water inside her cage. Large droplets flew fast and landed into the cage where Quinton had been kept captive. His silver watch immediately glimmered clear underneath the moonlight like a gemstone shining within a limestone, entitling hope. Its shiny material caught the corner of her right eye whilst she knocked onto the dungeon walls to measure the thickness between her cage and her supposed freedom. She slowly turned to the right and unlocked her earthling's words. It made complete sense, but the only problem was her distance from the watch. She searched her mind for brilliance whilst standing in the dark chamber but came up with nothing. She'd grown slightly emotional after her time in captivity. Therefore, she broke down and allowed her tears to stream down her cheeks. Her blue eyes shaded red. The vulnerable feeling tormented her heart and made her body quiver. She was starting to grow sick from the cold and thus sneezed and sniffed repeatedly. Her skin turned slightly pale as she folded into a ball by the corner and covered her body with her large wings. Her feathers kept her body warm whilst she thought of the lessons she was learning, realising how selfish she'd become for craving intimate love instead of accepting her fate.

She could still hear raindrops splashing on to the puddle in between the cages. Therefore, she stood up and walked alongside the metal bars until she could see a glimpse of light reflecting off the rippling puddle. There was a small crack within her earthling's chamber, and maybe that was his way out. She was uncertain of a lot of things at that moment, but it all started to align after a few minutes.

She spread her left wing farther than she'd ever done before by her side of the dungeon, hoping for her feather to hook on to the watch. There was a distant memory from her pleasant childhood, where she'd remembered her distant cousins creating a small cage for iguanas by using sharp titanium tools to cut through old scrappy metal pieces from an abandoned warehouse close to a ghost town. She forced herself on to the rusted bars and reached forth with her left wing. There was a loud sound of heavy footsteps from the corridor which rushed Olivia to act quickly. She could see a large shadow gaining space as time whirred away. Her left wing scraped on to the soil back and forth. There were two seconds left as she attempted to hook her feather on to the silver watch, and in the nick of time, she managed to clench on to it and curl her wing back quickly. A guarding troll passed the arched entrance with a sharp dagger on its right hand. Its face was just as pale and grey as Quinton's demon. Its watery stomach poured over its tightened dark belt as it walked past with its large bare feet. She'd clenched on to the silver watch with both hands and then waited patiently for the guarding troll to disappear.

'Okay, here we go!' she whispered whilst fidgeting with the silver watch by the corner.

She kept looking up repeatedly, for her heart gushed with paranoia. Her hands shook continuously whilst she unscrewed the silver plate underneath and took out a small lever. It shone brightly on to her blue eyes, which immediately unveiled her childhood memories. She could see the picture so clearly, almost as if she was back at her father's farm by the swamp.

There were five northern white cedar trees situated in a circle close to the swamp. She was just a small girl dressed in a long blue dress. She and her pleasant family had just arrived back from church service on a Sunday afternoon. She was running around after a butterfly on the flat green grass, exploring the environment and imagining her own friends playing beside her. It was the first time she'd ever picked up a silver quarter underneath a few dried twigs between the tree circles. Its clear shine gave her significant hope. It kept her curious because she'd never known of its real significance. It became the epitome of a silver lining in her life, a tiny item which had an ability to optimise one's mind to strive for great success. She remembered holding it and placing it directly towards the sky to block off the bright sun. Her heart was astonished with great joy as she held on to it tightly within her small right hand. She could hear her mother calling out her name repeatedly,

'Come and eat before you play!' Alexa called in command. Thus, Olivia did as told. She rushed back to the house with so much energy streaming through her thin veins.

'Mom, look what I found!' Olivia said, unfolding her small right hand upwards to her mother.

'You found a quarter!' Alexa said whilst dishing out some oxtail and rice into six plates. 'What are you going to do with it?' she asked.

'Well, I'm going to keep it!' Olivia replied. 'Maybe hide it from everyone!'

'Adorable,' Alexa said, 'just adorable. Go wash your hands!'

'Okay, Mother!' Olivia responded and rushed towards the kitchen sink.

She was filled with delight whilst she rinsed off the dirt from her hands then sat around a wooden circular table and played with her silver quarter by flicking it into the air, waiting for everyone else to join.

Her pleasant memory reminded her of the genuine love she'd always had for her parents. It kept her focused on breaking free and heading back home where she was shielded from any temptations. Her heart bled love amongst other things. It continuously yielded for affection and to be made whole. She couldn't quite explain the craving she had for affection, but she needed it.

Her strong will to see her family kept her motivated despite her left fingers bleeding from the rusted pieces. She kept cutting off small chunks of metal from the last metal bar in the corner until the metal bar could bend. It was her only chance to escape. Thus, she seized the opportunity by bending it outwards and crouching through slowly. She stood up at the arched entrance then peeped ahead to the other arched entrance which led to a communal place filled with shanty township houses stacked on top of each other. She peeped towards the left of the corridor and discovered an arched window at the end. Towards the right of the arched entrance was a flight of stairs. Thus, she rushed towards the arched window to find an escape route and discovered a completely different world.

There were black rock mountains on the outskirts shimmering wet from the rain and a narrow waterfall streaming down towards the bottom. She glanced down with her strained blue eyes whilst the wind brushed roughly against her face and blew her black hair backwards. The visual itself installed fear into her heart as she discovered the height from the bottom. She was in the middle of a long tower connected to an endless mountain. She immediately rushed towards the opposite end and climbed a flight of anticlockwise stairs. Her rattled heart throbbed loudly within her chest whilst she ran up cautiously by checking for clarity on every coast she encountered on every floor.

She slowed down as she heard the sound of metal scrapping against the floor towards the left. It was the same guarding troll patrolling with its dagger scratching the surface of the last floor of the tower. It walked towards the opposite end of the corridor then stopped as a wave of wind brushed against its back. Olivia realised it could smell her scent as more airwaves blew towards it. It turned around slowly whilst groaning and started walking back towards the oval staircase as she glued herself behind the wall. It slid its sharp dagger onto the hard surface whilst it moved closer and closer whilst she plotted an escape route. She looked up towards the staircase but knew she'd be made if she were to run upwards and thus waited for an encounter as its sharp dagger scraped towards her path.

The sound of a billion lost souls screamed loudly inside her mind whilst she took slow breaths and armed her heart with courage to defect her earthling's demons. It stood in the middle of the passage and looked towards the right at the staircase, taking in a deep breath of Olivia's scent as another airwave rushed towards his body. She unveiled herself from behind the wall and rushed towards it with long strides. It swung its left fist and aimed for her face. She ducked, swerved, and jumped onto its back then proceeded to choke-hold it. Her supernatural strength was clustered deeply within her troubled mind. Therefore, she couldn't handle the monster's strength as it gripped the back of her dress then threw her down onto the floor. It proceeded forth and swung its sharp dagger onto the floor but missed as she rolled towards the left and ran up the staircase. She'd managed to reach the end but found herself trapped by a locked door made out of dark brown wood from large forest trees. She banged onto it twice whilst the guarding troll gained momentum, and as she broke through, it gripped her right wing with its dirty left hand. It immediately pulled her backwards, and she fell down as it moved closer with its left hand clenched on to her precious right wing. Everything winded slowly as its dagger cut through the air and scraped her right thigh. She screamed out in the pain as her right thigh bled and covered the bottom of her dirty dress red. It threw away its dagger and gripped her body with its dirty hand.

A montage of helpless women being abused by ruthless men rushed through her mind whilst it held her tightly. It drove her to the brink of madness as she kicked her legs in different directions and spat into its eyes. Her fidgeting irritated it. Thus, it placed her onto its right shoulder. She immediately bit off a bit of its right ear, which made it throw her back onto the floor. Its right ear leaked blood as she glanced towards the left and spat out its rotten flesh onto the floor. She gripped its sharp dagger as it rushed and dove its sharp blade on. She was unsure of the outcome as its sharp dagger pierced through its chest and watched it roar loudly to its death. It lay heavily on top of her body as more blood dripped. It had a gloomy look in its grimy eyes whilst it lay there and died. She placed her right hand onto the left side of its hunched neck and felt its pulse rate slipping away into nothing.

There was a rippling wave of shouting prisoners below whilst she struggled to remove its revolting corpse from her body. She could hear a deadly creature hawking out loud from above as she stood up and tried to clean herself. Its cry grew louder as its echo radiated past every rock on the mountains surrounding the castle. She prepared herself from another invasive encounter whilst glancing around and discovering a small stream of cold water rushing down a steep slope and heading towards a waterfall. There was a hesitant moment which nearly lured her back into the castle until she could see a the creature evolve into a black vulture, scraping past a layer of dark clouds by the black mountain. There was no other way to go but head towards the waterfall. She climbed up the edge of the castle and jumped onto a pile of dark wet rocks. Water pierced painful chills through her skin, stabbing at her moist feet and turning her fingers numb. The black vulture dove down from above as she dove into the stream of water and allowed faith to construct an exit. Its claws clenched as it aimed towards the waterfall. She could see it rushing down as her body tumbled over and fell down the waterfall. Its claws scraped the cold stream and missed her by a split second. The cold water forced her body downwards as she tried to spread her wet wings in different directions. It dove down faster and stripped forth with one aim—to recapture Quinton's guardian. She could see a pack of wolves howling loudly from above the castle and alerting every other monster within the concrete walls and within the mountain tunnels.

The vulture opened its claws as Olivia's head partly collided with a black rock peeking out from within the steep mountain. It missed her body again as she dropped into the cold rippling water like a pin. She blinked continuously whilst drowning in the dark lake. The black vulture hovered over the lake right above the rippling water whilst her body sunk like an anchor. She was on the brink of blacking out whilst drowning. She felt helpless whilst choking and momentarily felt paralysed. Everything winded slower as her mind faded away into nothing. She could see herself passing away again. It felt better this time, for the pain wasn't as excruciating as the first time. She shut her strained blue eyes and sunk like a wrecked ship. There was a quiet moment relishing around as her heart started to beat slower and slower by the second, then her mind flashed through her previous life.

She could hear her mother calling her name repeatedly and birds chirping loud within. Her memories made her lose complete focus and spiral into an endless moment filled with despair. She believed she'd completely failed to complete her job to protect her earthling until hope sparked within her heart again.

There were a few bubbles levitating from underneath which kept her from losing faith. An individual she'd never seen before gripped her body tightly and dragged her farther down. She opened her blue eyes and could see a beautiful Indian woman pull her down to safety. The individual's flawless black hair strands rippled smoothly as she swam. Her face was moulded sharp yet feminine and soft. She had beautiful brown eyes dazing towards a destination. Her beautiful pointy nose had two small piles connected to her nostrils. The small piles were glued to her body lining by her cheeks and all the way down to her back. There were two bags containing magical blue sparks which immediately converted into breathable oxygen as she inhaled from her nose and exhaled with her mouth.

Olivia felt undeniably safe as the individual dragged her downwards and through a tunnel under the black mountain. She lost consciousness whilst the individual paddled farther through a tunnel and upwards towards an open hole above with a fire burning bright.

The beautiful Indian woman pulled her back to life by blowing air into her mouth, unclogging her lungs whilst another male individual strapped water containers tightly to each other within a carriage. Olivia kept diving in and out of consciousness whilst being carried away besides Yumna, the beautiful Indian woman she'd just met.

'Theodore, hurry up!' Yumna shouted. 'We are running out of time!'

'Brace yourself!' Theodore replied whilst whipping two black stallions to move faster.

There was a bright lamp placed between the front seats and the carriage. The ride towards another destination was unpleasant with the carriage wheels colliding with small rocks on their sandy path. Yumna stroked Olivia's black hair backwards and kept their bodies warm with her large grey wings. Olivia glanced up with shock projected in her strained blue eyes. She tried to speak, but no words came out. Her throat was burning in pain. She kept quiet.

'Shhh, just close your eyes!' Yumna whispered. 'You are finally safe!' she mentioned as Olivia obeyed and allowed her mind to drift away.

'Take the alternative route. Our trail needs to go cold!' she said. 'Our tracks must disappear!' She sounded paranoid and slightly uncertain of the outcome. It was urgent to vanish before the demons could find them. Thus, they kept moving forward inside a dark tunnel. Theodore had the ability to see within the darkness and thus directed his stallions towards the right tunnel instead of using their normal left tunnel to head back to their asylum.

'Come boys!' he said as his horses slowed down whilst passing through a large river underneath a hollow cave.

Yumna glanced towards the far right and could see a massive hole above. The moon shone bright onto the rippling water whilst she took the time to appreciate how beautiful everything could be even in the midst of such darkness surrounding them.

'I'm going to keep you safe!' she said whilst stroking Olivia's hair backwards.

They'd managed to cross over the large river and kept moving forth through another dark tunnel. Theodore looked back for a split second and realised why he'd felt the sense of urgency to fetch water unnecessarily. He could see his youngest sister's resemblance on Olivia's face which left him astonished by her beauty.

'She looks like Freda!' Theodore said whilst controlling his two horses forth.

'She does indeed!' Yumna replied and placed her soft lips onto Olivia's forehead.

The temperature declined to an all-time low as the stallions galloped faster towards the light at the end of the tunnel. A wave of cool fresh air brushed against their faces as they trailed onto a path filled with a thin layer of snow. Olivia's body began to quiver tragically as the two stallions trailed onto an uneven rocky path right beside the snowy mountain. The cold trail curved towards the left and down a narrow passage clustered with large black tree trunks and mostly wet black rocks scattered within the dark forest. Theodore whipped his horses repeatedly as they galloped wildly.

'We need to hurry up! She is shivering badly!' Yumna shouted and unfolded a large blanket made of buffalo skin then tucked the edges around Olivia's body. 'There you go, my angel!' she whispered and parked her warm lips onto Olivia's forehead, using her rare ability of changing the temperature.

Her warm lips radiated warmth from within her body and into Olivia's body. Her pale skin evolved rich as she opened her stained blue eyes. She could see a dozen water containers filled with solid ice and then discovered a cloud of black smoke erupting above and a dark smoke trail leading back to the left side of the dark forest. There was a small wooden cottage burning within as she lapsed onto a revelation that her earthling wasn't going to make it. His dreams were crumbling right before her eyes, and she felt helpless to change his destiny. She'd failed to keep him from being consumed by the evil which was also beginning to relish through his soul.

'It's okay. You are safe!' Yumna mentioned whilst Olivia glanced towards the dark sky and allowed her salty tears to flow down her pinkish cheeks.

She kept quiet and nursed her broken heart whilst it throbbed slowly.

'Close your eyes. We will be there soon!' Yumna said.

'Whe-wher-r are we . . . where are we going?' Olivia stuttered, mumbling in and out of consciousness.

'Don't tell her just yet. She's connecting!' Theodore shouted whilst controlling his black horses towards another tunnel ahead. 'That information can be extracted from her earthling by his demons. Just wait until we have made it to the next tunnel by the mountain ahead!' He shouted out whilst maintaining focus and guiding them to safety.

Yumna kept quiet as Theodore's last words swept past her ears. She began to dwell on the last precious memory of her late lover whilst glancing down at Olivia. They began to drift off into deep sleep whilst the black horses galloped through the harsh conditions. Yumna could hear Freda's heart filling laughter alliterate loudly through the cold wind whilst she held on to Olivia tightly. She allowed her senses to take in every sweet smell, soft touch, graceful sound, and pleasant sight of that special memory at their first asylum. Her smile plastered happiness into her heart whilst waking up with her black hair covering her beautiful face, then she'd glance towards the perfect sun peeping over the world as she'd become accustomed to, through an arched cave opening towards the right side of the bed. She could sense her lover's soft left hand grazed her smooth left arm and feel warm lips radiate more warmth onto her upper back.

'Come back to bed!' Freda whispered as Yumna tried to sit up straight.

'No, I must go, love!' Yumna responded and giggled childishly to the ticklish feeling.

There were sweet sounds of harmony relishing through their haven whilst they gently touched, wrestled and held on to each other, and kissed passionately. They were covered by thin sheets made from feather strings. Yumna looked up into Freda's beautiful golden glittered eye balls as she blushed at a beautifully toned woman with strong black hair, firm cheeks, a short pointy nose, and small pinkish lips. She smiled as Freda arched herself backwards to reach for a gift she'd made. Beautiful sun rays glided into their cave and shone brightly onto Freda's light-toned skin.

'I've made something for you. Close your eyes!' Freda whispered and reached into the side of her buffalo skin dress and placed it beside Yumna's face.

'Do you like it?' Freda asked and smiled whilst the bright red glare angles of the small pentagon ruby stone necklace shone into Yumna's left eye.

She turned her head and looked it for a while whilst Freda kissed the side of her right neck.

'I love it!' Yumna said and held on to it with her left hand. 'When did you make it?' she asked.

'Last night whilst you were sleeping!' Freda said.

'I can change its shape if you want me to!'

'Shape it into a heart for me. That way, I can have you closer when I wear it!' Yumna suggested.

'Okay, my love!' Freda said and placed the ruby necklace on her right hand then used her ability to change its solid shape into a smooth heart with a sharp point at the bottom.

'Perfect!' Yumna said and held on to her lover tightly then flew upwards. Her grey wings moved in different directions whilst they kissed in mid-air.

'Just remembered! I have to actually go!' Freda said whilst trying to spread her grey wings in different directions.

'No, you aren't going anywhere!' Yumna said whilst holding on tightly.

'Fine, I won't go anyway!' Freda replied.

'Let's go back to bed. I can see bags under your eyes, love!' They railed back onto their bed and felt a cool air wave of soothing fresh air rush towards them.

Their love was inebriating to the fullest, almost intoxicating at every touch and grossing out goosebumps on their bodies. They cuddled for a while until Freda lapsed onto an obligation.

'Just remembered, I made a promise to help out at the bakery!' she said and sat up by the left side of the bed.

'Its fine. I will come down and see you in a bit!' Yumna said, lay by herself, and drifted off to her darkest past whilst Freda bathed in a small waterhole within another cave.

She dwelled on her first encounter of the afterlife and reminisced about the tragic story that trailed from her previous life. She'd always been grateful for finding Freda on a green field in the middle of the valley minutes after she'd unchained herself from her father's incarceration by taking her own life simply by jumping off a passenger ship, which was returning to the coast of India. She remembered how her brutal father had metaphorically chained and attempted to drag her back to her old sadistic life to marry to a man she loathed.

Within her dark thoughts, there was a bright glimpse of light as she thought of John, the Englishman she'd fallen in love with before. She couldn't forget about him despite her great efforts to do so. He'd always linger at the back of her mind even whilst gazing at Freda from time to time. She could hear Freda humming within the other cave and water splashing in between.

'Your brother and I are going hunting later. Want to join us?' Yumna asked.

'Nope, have other things to do besides slaughter innocent animals!' Freda replied.

'You speak as if you're vegan!' Yumna said and sat up straight then laughed out loud to her lover's hypocrisy whilst emerging from the darkness and stepping into the light in her natural form with her grey wings moving slowly in different directions.

'Your body is exquisite!' Yumna complimented with a glare of lust basking on her brown eyes.

'Thanks, love!' Freda replied. 'I found something by the waterhole!'

'What is it?' Yumna asked as she kept her eyes glued towards Freda's hands and slowly watched both hands unveil a rare white Egyptian water lily.

'It's so beautiful!' Yumna stated and stared at it for a while.

'Aren't you going to wear your necklace, love?' Freda asked and tossed flower onto the bed.

'Will do so after I've bathed, love!' she said and slowly inhaled the flower's scent.

Their afterlife seemed endlessly perfect with everything they'd ever wanted which was cemented in temporary peace. They could indulge and enjoy the festivities around them, but they couldn't quite enjoy the experience to the fullest because they hadn't made it to the heavens like the rest of those that had passed on properly. They lived a slightly shady existence within their valley, smudged with a little bit of sinful flare to pass on the time until they could be judged by a higher power. There was always evil lingering and crawling within their darkness, which made them feel uneasy every day.

They weren't as safe as they believed themselves to be, and that theory arose later that afternoon. A scent of evil glided slowly into Theodore's nostril whilst hunting a few kilometres away from their valley. Its foul scent made him realise they'd hadn't escaped from the horrific war between good and bad, a hideous war which seemed more amplified simply because there weren't any human laws to protect them anymore. Theodore was accompanied by his sister's lover who'd just taken recent interest in the same activity and felt the necessary measures to bond merely because she admired the fact that he advocated for their relationship. His liberal quality made him the perfect person Yumna could speak to whenever experiencing great difficulties with her beloved. He was the only lost descendant who hadn't judged their relation. His heart was genuine towards others, and yet he wielded such great strength and power.

He could feel the wrath of a dark force rushing, blowing towards him whilst lying beside Yumna on an embankment covered in dried leaves. She remained clueless in her crouched position, ready to let her wooden arrow loose from her bow to strike at a herd of deer drinking on the opposite side of the river.

'Can you smell that?' Theodore asked Yumna who seemed confused by his question.

'The smell of wet grass?' she asked sceptically whilst whispering and aiming to kill.

'No, there is an awful smell, a burn of some sort!' he said whilst glancing towards the far left of the river and saw his black stallions starting to move in agitation. Their huff and puff alerted the deer on the opposite end, which caused them to run into the forest.

'I guess we will be eating potatoes for dinner!' Yumna said and lowered her bow.

'Something's wrong. I can sense it!' Theodore whispered to himself then stood and walked back to his horses.

'Wait. What's wrong?' Yumna asked and rushed from behind with more confusion raking her mind apart and leaving her indecisive.

'We must head back!' he said, sounding paranoid to the alarming loud screams within his mind whilst jogging back to his horses.

'Just stop and tell me what's wrong!' she yelled and gripped his left arm.

'Something is burning. Can't you smell that?' he asked and carried forth whilst she remained as still as a statue, mostly trying to inhale the airwaves of his paranoia and the breeze brushing past her face.

'I can't smell anything!' She yelled and followed Theodore on his elusive quest.

They untied their horses from a tree branch and rode off.

'We must hurry back!' he shouted.

Yumna began to wonder why Theodore insisted on using horses instead of using his wings like the rest. She trailed behind on a path paved with gravel in between a steep hill on her left peripheral view, mostly paved with green grass and black rocks, and a river streaming alongside towards her right peripheral view. Yumna felt strange from his paranoia and thus rose above and flew ahead. Theodore embarked on the trail and led his horses forth as the trail curved towards the left along with the river which would soon branch off towards the right metres ahead. He could feel the wrath of an evil gripping his heart and could see smoke hovering ahead, spiralling into the sky like a snake. The sight stunned Yumna and brought tears to her eyes as she discovered an unspeakable horror. She submitted her faith into Theodore's righteous intuition.

An avalanche of lost descendants flocked from the steep clustered valley from the left angle. They flew above Theodore and brushed past Yumna in countless numbers, their facial expression left with a whiff of fear. Theodore's horse hauled and launched him off then galloped back towards the path they'd just come from.

'We must retreat!' a lost angel yelled whilst cowardly flying away from the only home they'd all become accustomed to, vanishing into the dark forest within the distance along with countless others seeking refuge from the horror relishing behind them.

Yumna remained still, with her wings spread widely in different directions, facing a catastrophe. There were tents burning, black smoke turning the atmosphere dark, lost descendants screaming in captivity within a cage carriage pulled by a deformed troll below. Yumna looked around for a while in search for her lover but lost sight of everything as more smoke cloaked the area. She waited as the breeze shifted the smoke towards the left.

'Freda!' Yumna yelled and plunged herself towards the cage to rescue her beloved who seemed petrified and scared.

'I'll get you out. I promise!' Yumna stuttered whilst trying to dismantle the rusted chains around the metal bars by heating up the metal with her hands. 'I need you to work with me!'

'I'm scared!' Freda said, quivering in fear.

Her words alerted a demon warrior from a cave entrance above, and within a few seconds of her words drifting loudly, a long arrow made out of old scrap metal glided through the black smoke, piercing through Yumna's left wing and plunging into the middle of Freda's chest.

'Noooo!' Yumna screamed as Freda fell backwards and turned into grey stone. Her loud cry caught Theodore's attention whilst he plunged his dagger deeply into a troll's chest and jumped off its body to rush to the cage carriage.

His hope remained high as his flew towards them and heard his sister's pulse rate beating slowly within her sculpture.

'She is still alive!' he yelled, restoring hope into Yumna's heart. 'She can be brought back!' And as he attempted to break the metal bars, another arrow swiped past his head and landed into another lost angel within the cage.

'We must go. We will get her back. I promise!' He yelled, trying to persuade Yumna to unclench her hands from the bars, mostly showing the strength to lead in the final hour.

'No, we are not leaving her!' she shouted whilst weeping and rattling the burning metal with her hands.

'Look at me!' he commanded and gripped her face with both hands. 'We won't be able to save her if we don't retreat!'

His words sunk through her ears and resulted in departure. It was the last time Yumna saw her beloved, but she never once lost faith to bring Freda back. She had hope and thus used it rebuild a new asylum with the help of Theodore's leadership and the strength of a wise lost descendent by the name of Elle who had the ability to harvest other lost descendants' prayers and convert their hope into a resourceful energy to build a magical cloak which made their enemies unable to see or feel their presence within that specific valley. Their mission to gather those who'd ventured into other forests wasn't an easy task, but with great persuasion and determination, they succeeded to restore peace to their asylum.

As time passed, they became accustomed to the sounds of wolves howling whilst passing through them blindly, large snakes hissing within distant lakes and trolls patrolling hectares of flat grounds mainly looking for clues.

Chapter Twenty

Twigs and Stones

Olivia awoke from layers of buffalo skin piled up into a circular bed close to a fireplace behind her. She had absolutely no clue where she was whilst her heart pumped her body with paranoia. All she could remember were the sounds of wolves howling, visuals of her world spiralling down a waterfall, and she could feel the pain from her head knocking against the edge of rock right before drowning. She sat up straight, planting her feet onto a cold stone and placing her right hand onto her sweaty forehead for a while. There were a few whispers growing louder with the next cave, and she could see shadows passing in different directions in between the fire projecting from the next cave.

'They will come looking for her the same way they came looking for me!' Elle said whilst gathering her bundle of brunette hair from her shoulder and whipping it into a ponytail by using a thin thread of buffalo skin.

'What do you expect us to do,' Yumna asked, 'just leave her and allow them to recapture her?'

'No, I'm not saying that, but you have endangered us!' Elle mentioned. 'Although this has happened, it's good. All we have to do now is rescue her earthling because he has the encryption written on his back!'

Olivia entered their domain in her dirty white dress.

'Oh, evening dear!' Yumna said then stood up from a wooden stool carved out from an oak wood tree. She was holding a beige cup filled with warm in her right hand.

'Where am I?' Olivia asked whilst discovering a new world from the cave they were in.

She stepped towards the right and inhaled the cool breeze drifting in from the outside. It was dark, yet everything in sight remained visible from the half-moon shining from above.

'I'll get you some clothes to change into!' Yumna said whilst walking around the wooden table and vanishing into a dark arched passage parallel to the passage Olivia had just emerged from.

'It used to look better than this!' Elle said and tightened her brown dress strings on her waist then strolled towards Olivia who seemed appalled by the conditions within the cave.

'Give me your hands!' Elle suggested. 'You have been through so much, so much pain and torment!' she said and held on to Olivia's hand. Her wounds slowly healed.

'How did you do that?' Olivia asked in shock.

'Shouldn't come as a surprise that I can heal other guardian angels. You look exactly like your mother, Olivia!' Elle mentioned.

'You know my mother?' Olivia asked.

'Of course I know your mother. We were best friends until I decided to follow my earthling through its tragic journey instead of obeying the covenant!' Elle said. 'There is only so much guardian angels can do for their earthlings, but the rest is up to them!'

Olivia glanced towards the sky and saw a large creature hovering in the distance, yet it looked clueless and couldn't see nothing.

'Can it see us?' Olivia asked.

'No, it can't. I have used magic to cloak us away from the evil that lingers!' Elle said and placed her right hand on to Olivia's left shoulder.

'There isn't much you can do for your earthling now. Your body requires rest!'

'I know. It's all up to him now!' Olivia said, feeling disconnected from her earthling because of the magical cloak around them. She couldn't communicate with him nor feel his presence.

'You must be hungry!' Elle asked and turned around. 'Come, I've made meat and bean stew!'

Olivia agreed but felt guilty for escaping without her earthling. She felt disloyal for a while but also knew she wasn't in control of his fate anymore.

'Try them. They are warm!' Elle said and handed Olivia a brown bowl moulded from clay ad filled with chunks of meat and bean stew.

'Thank you so much!' Olivia replied and sat on a wooden stool, planting her feet onto a wooden handle attached to the three pillars.

'I've found some clothes you can wear!' Yumna mentioned and stepped into the light, holding a dark brown loincloth dress. 'And I've made some warm water for you.'

'Thank you so much, I'll go after I've had some stew!' Olivia said and blew on to her bowl. 'It must be hard living like this, consistently in fear for being taken away!'

'It's not easy, but it wasn't always like this. We used to live in peace before we found ourselves being attacked by evil creatures of the night, which also roam in the day, destroying the woods and slaughtering our animals for sport. This has made us realise we are indeed lost for eternity!' Elle explained. 'I've been banished from above. Therefore, I live here now!' she said and sat on a wooden stool before consoling Olivia again. 'There is nothing you can do for your earthling now but wait for him to find the strength within and break free from the chains that bind him, or otherwise, just wait for him to die!' Elle mentioned. 'It depends on whether he wants to live or not!'

It turned quiet within the cave whilst everyone contemplated what could indeed be inevitable for Olivia's earthling and a way forward. Olivia stared at the burning logs as they broke off into ashes. She found it extremely difficult to move on without her earthling and thus concluded to remain loyal to him until the very end.

'I won't leave without him!' she said and drank the stew from her bowl.

Her words momentarily rippled through Yumna's body and into her aching heart. They cropped out a fascinating stigma imprinted with adoration towards the Olivia. Her emotions were based on her nostalgic bone for her lover.

'You are right. We have to try get them back,' Yumna said.

'Them? Plural?' Olivia asked sceptically.

'Yes, them,' Elle interrupted and explained the depth of the predicament.

'I'm sorry for your loss!' Olivia mentioned and picked out a chunk of meat from the warm stew with her two fingers and bit into it. She could feel the salt burning her bottom lip as she chewed and waited for consolation from the beautiful Indian woman who'd rescued her, but instead, Yumna stood up and walked away.

'Did I say something wrong?' Olivia asked, for she was unaware of her remarkable resemblance to Freda.

'Don't you worry, child. She's just having a bad night!' Elle said and stood up. 'Well, I must go now and see if Theodore needs my assistance above!'

'Okay, thank you so much for the food!' Olivia mentioned and watched Elle walk towards an open arched entrance.

She spread her white wings apart and flew towards the left. Olivia remained quiet for a while whilst gathering her wild thoughts together from galloping around the cave. A smile cropped from her pale face as she tried to embrace her freedom, but the endorsement of it wilted her heart in sadness because she knew she hadn't completely done her duty as a guardian angel. She spread her dirty white wings and felt the deep cut she'd received whilst escaping.

'Ouch!' she said.

'I've brought some magical golden herbs for you. You can use them after cleaning up!' Yumna said and stepped into the light. 'They will help with your cuts!'

'You are so kind to me and yet you don't even know me!'

'You are right. You don't know me, so why not start from the beginning?' Yumna suggested. 'Hi, I'm Yumna, you must be?' she asked and reached forth with her right hand.

'Hi, I'm Olivia!' Olivia said, and they giggled childishly.

Yumna dazed into Olivia's watery blue eyes, and everything seemed to make sense for a while. She'd completely forgotten how tightly clenched her right hand grip was with Olivia's right hand.

'You have such a strong grip!' Olivia said.

'Oh, I'm so sorry!' Yumna replied and unglued herself from a mesmerising moment. 'Okay, I'm going to leave now!' And she did exactly that, feeling vulnerable and embarrassed from her weakness regarding beautiful women with black hair.

Olivia found the gesture slightly disturbing yet flattering for she'd never thought she would never be persuaded in that manner. Olivia immediately placed the brown bowl onto the wooden table and walked towards an arched passage with a small potion bottle filled with golden liquid and green leaves within. It sparkled brightly as she moved and lit her mind up with countless aurora and wonders. She remained puzzled and overwhelmed by Yumna's affection mainly because she wasn't sure what to make of it nor knew how to pursue it. A lot spiralled within her mind as she stepped into a steaming oval pool paved with black stone and sat on black rock by the edge. She placed the potion bottle right beside her face.

There were airwaves containing valuable information. They rushed in and entered Olivia's ears, but she couldn't grasp properly and therefore stepped out from the oval pool and made her way towards the darkness. She could hear Elle speaking to Theodore on the cliff above. They were seated on two large black rocks, staring at the half-moon and discussing the way forth regarding the high tensions growing between them and the monsters crawling within the woods.

'There is myth of scripture made a few centuries ago by a lost descendant who was also banished from above because he'd disobeyed the laws!' Elle mentioned whilst Theodore inhaled burning dry green herbs from his black smoke pipe. She paused for a while to inhale the whiff of depression brushing over them. 'Some say he made it to escape, to return to Earth as a human to mend his mistakes!'

'And where is the scripture exactly?' Theodore asked with more curiosity projecting from his blue eyes.

'It disappeared right before his eyes after he made it, many would say!' Elle mentioned. 'It later reappeared on an earthling's back in a form of a tattoo. There are two parts of the scriptures by the way. I know where the first part of it resides! Anyway I couldn't quite figure out why it would land onto the earthling's back, and then I remembered being told of the scripture's significance! It was made out of love. The lost descendant who made it initially wanted to reunite with his loved ones!'

'So it's a porthole between two worlds, I suppose?' Theodore asked, mainly confused, wondering what it would feel like to have a second chance at a new life.

'You can say that!' she replied and stood up to stretch her wings,

'I realised that Olivia's earthling loves wholeheartedly even if it destroys him. He loves the girl, and he would do anything to be with her again. That's why it ended up on his back instead of anyone else's. It chose to be on his back!'

There was a moment of clarity within Theodore's mind as Elle sat down and explained why Olivia's earthling remained incarcerated.

'The demons we are fighting also want the scripture to break free from the bondage of slavery!' she said.

'But they already have his body. Why not take it from him?' he asked.

'Yes, they do, but it won't be extracted and decoded from his body until he dies in the real world. I know this because it happened to my earthling!' she mentioned. 'It's partly the reason I was also banished, because I disobeyed and ran away with it after she died!'

'What does it say on it?' he asked, interrupting a compelling story mainly because he could recall his time on earth and how he'd wasted it by mingling with bad crowds and inevitably bringing death to his sister by driving them off a cliff after falling asleep behind the wheel.

'At first, the guardian angels I was with weren't sure what to make of the scripture as it levitated from my earthling's back and disappeared, but days later, it appeared within my white dress pocket in writing, and

I could read it!' Elle explained. 'It explained the mythology and the directions to decoding the supernatural gates, and obviously, the second part of it was missing. Hence the earthling's tattoo!'

'How do you know it's on the earthling's back?' he asked.

'Because Olivia has the same mark on her shoulder as I do, which also looks like a small black star. It appears after the scripture encodes onto its handler!' she explained further. 'Therefore, we must find him and await his fate. He will die, and we need to make sure that we have the scripture before his demons do!'

'What if he doesn't die as scheduled?' he asked, dwelling inside of the darkest parts of his mind and discovering he wasn't as different from the rest of the lost descendants.

Elle did not respond to his question because she knew her integrity would be dismantled.

'They will come looking for Olivia, and when they do, we will go and find the earthling along with those captured!' Her words began to manipulate and poison his innocent heart.

They had absolutely no clue Olivia had heard everything from within the cave below whilst standing by a small hole which appeared to be a window of some sort. She could see the forefront of a steep hill clustered with long trees moving in the breeze.

'Olivia!' Yumna called out whilst entering into the cave.

Yumna allowed herself to enter into temptation as she watched Olivia appear from the darkest part of cave and enter back into the steaming oval pool.

'I've brought the clothing you left on the table. Sorry to have walked in like this!'

Olivia kept quiet throughout whilst trying to understand the deception portrayed in front of her naked eyes.

'Olivia, is everything okay?' Yumna asked and placed the clothing beside the potion bottle.

'Something tells me you didn't find me by coincidence!' Olivia mentioned, almost prepared to confront Yumna by exploding and allowing her emotions to determine her reaction to the scenario, but within seconds, she realised how corrupt her heart was becoming.

She thought about using Yumna's weakness to achieve her objectives, prepared to lower her virtue by dismantling Yumna's heart and using it as a weapon to control. Olivia stood up within the oval pool in her natural form and stepped out at same time. Yumna turned around to refrain from acting on her intuition. The truth revealed itself right in front of Olivia's eyes, and she realised how quickly she'd been poisoned. She'd leaped from the edge of light and entered into the darkest part of her mind by asking a compelling question.

'Why are you in here right now?' she asked whilst Yumna shrunk to the touch of Olivia's warm hand.

'I must go!' Yumna insisted then stepped away from a moment compressed with false intentions,

'You aren't so different from the rest of them. Maybe you do belong here!'

Olivia remained quiet as Yumna walked in the darkness. She discovered a filthy stigma of deceit cropping out of her heart, one she didn't know existed. It was shameful, she but didn't acknowledge it so mainly because she was blinded by her undying loyalty to her earthling.

The night immediately turned long and weary for Olivia as she came to terms with the darkness relishing inside her heart. She sat on the pile of buffalo skin and nursed her wounds, merely concluding it wasn't coincidental to have been found at her weakest point. Although she'd become paranoid, a part of her couldn't help but wonder if Yumna knew of the plan made by Elle. Ironically it all seemed too scripted to be true. Thus, Olivia lay down and devised her own plan of action. She scratched out her foolish intentions of finding real love and settling down. Her idea of intimacy remained solely tempting whilst she stared towards the half-moon and hoped for a better day with regard to the safety of her earthling. She became more committed to her guardian angel obligations by convincing herself that real love didn't exist. It was the only way she could remain focused.

The atmosphere on the other end of the spectrum was quite different with Quinton's body imprinted onto the cold floor. He was facing a caged hole at the top of his dungeon, contemplating about the love of his life. The idea of holding on to Juliana kept him calm and sane, but not for long because his mind began to flash and spiral through recent events, recollecting the torture he'd endured hours before from his monsters. They were ruthless and animalistic in every way possible. He could see flashes of himself being drowned, kicked, and being questioned about a supposed scripture. The cuts on his back railed his heart into fear as he wondered what they meant by it. The idea of letting go and dying wasn't an option because even through the midst of things, whilst being tortured, his senses could still smell the black orchid essence radiating from Juliana's back. He could still feel her touch and hear her voice out loud whilst being beaten down and bleeding heavily from his mouth.

He turned towards the right within his dungeon whilst dazed from sleep deprivation and realised his guardian angel had escaped from the darkest part of his mind. It brought him some sort of relief but also gripped his neck with a metaphoric rope, lynching his heart into loneliness whilst the deafening silence strangled his strained eyes into tears. Her disappearance made it extremely difficult to remain positive and made him feel less optimistic about escaping from the hell he'd entered into. He placed his left pointing finger onto the dusty floor and drew a line slowly whilst observing every grain of sand beside his face, momentarily whisking off into more thoughts of the woman he loved so much.

'Your existence remains me of long tulip flowers growing in the back of my mind.

'They paint such a beautiful picture.

'An image of grace and harmony.

'I'm honoured to have met you and humbled to have loved you in this life and the next.

'I'm mainly grateful for the love you have given me.

'You are remarkable in every single fascinating way.

'You push me to be a better man and to do what is right all the time.

'You will always remind me of what real love looks like in its purest form.

'You are extraordinary and beautiful.

'You make the future look so beautiful.

'Almost as if I'm discovering a whole new world through a glass window on a beautiful Sunday morning.

'You are my blessing, and you are so amazing beyond measure.

'I hope to awake so I can say these words to you and tell you how much I love you,' he whispered whilst slowly scribbling through the dirt then swallowed his pride and wetted his dry throat. His brown eyes remained shut for a while, but he knew he couldn't escape from his nightmare by drifting away and waking up in reality. He was trapped in a cage like a lab rat. The hunger within his stomach grumbled and stitched his diaphragm into pain. He could feel the hunger of billions in poverty-stricken third-world countries and could hear the screams of millions crying out for attention whilst seeking out for asylum. His hallucination brought great discomfort and uprooted out the weakness within. It dug deeply into his soul, and he felt exposed and vulnerable like a newborn baby. His tears dripped onto the dirt as he wept whilst acknowledging the bad decisions he'd ever made. He was slightly afraid of accepting the truth which had initially railed him into the pits of horror and afraid of embracing the lessons he was learning.

Everything was magnified under a glass, and he knew he wouldn't escape until he'd dealt with his problems. It appeared that the touchy feeling of death wasn't new, nor was it strange to him at all. He remembered how it used to creep into his bed whenever he was alone and how it would take away a piece of his soul every single time he'd have dazed thoughts of his lover whilst drowning nostalgically. It was evident he was consistently attending his memorial every night whilst weeping for the love he craved so much. Essentially, he couldn't deny his world was gravitating on a force field of love. His efforts to break free from it were less than satisfactory, and even when he'd try forget about Juliana, he knew she owned his heart regardless of how much she believed it wasn't hers to begin with. She was the bright epitome of his dark reality and the sole owner to the fruits growing within his heart.

Within hours of contemplating a future which seemed impossible to embark, a rusted lock sealed to keep him in captivity unlocked mainly from a mere thought of his unborn child. The metal bar door opened wide, but he couldn't move due to exhaustion deep within his body.

Nevertheless, he was determined to unbind his heart from weakness and mend it gold with strength. He lay there and felt helpless for a while. His vision remained blurry as he turned his body then started to crawl, scraping his stomach onto the dusty floor and embracing the pain. He felt hungry and dehydrated but kept crawling regardless, merely clueless of where he was heading to. Nothing could stop him from rising up against the unjustified world he'd created within himself and overcoming every little obstacle barring him from finding real love. His upper back began to itch as the black ink boiled.

He lay onto his back for a while and allowed the cool surface to soothe his pain. He blinked repeatedly to remove the blur from his strained brown eyes, unsure of what to make of the grey stone statues positioned within the next room on his right. He glanced upwards towards the arched door and crawled forward and could hear their hearts throbbing so loudly within. Their eyes lured him closer. Thus, he entered into their sphere, unsure of their distinctive features basking within his deep conscious. Their pulse rate frequencies vibrated on to his body as he reached out with his right hand and touched the first statue. Its grey stone cracked all the way from its legs and up to its head. The stone exploded from its structure, and lost angels appeared from within. One of the angels revived the rest of the statues whilst Quinton lay quietly.

Every statue exploded, and angels emerged from within. They rose up from incarceration and took deep breaths at the same time. Their wings flapped in different directions, and they caused dust to hover within the dark room. Quinton coughed whilst lying down and finally accepted his last moments. He believed it was the end of his era and therefore pleaded for forgiveness. His upper body muscles ached heavily at the same time.

'I don't want to die!' he yelled and gripped the attention of those he'd just revived with pure love.

They observed the earthling within as he began to lose consciousness whilst staring towards the pitch-black space above, and as he blinked slowly, he discovered a lost descendant who had the same beautiful remarkable resemblance as Olivia. She leaned forward and held on to his cold hands as the rest of the lost descendants assisted by carrying him away. His toes scraped the cold floor whilst the lost descendants levitated in mid-air. He opened his strained eyes and glanced at every angle within the castle passages and hollow cave areas clustered with slum houses towards the right side of the path. The lost descendants held on to him tightly and guided him through the dark tunnels, and whilst doing so, he could see his world collapsing as his heart began to capitulate.

Winds blew heavily and shook the leaves off many dried tree branches beside the empty path they were embarking through. The air smelt of war and blood. It reeked foul of death, and Quinton could sense the agony from his lover. He could see Juliana crying almost as if she was beside him. The angels carried him farther and farther away from the darkest part of his mind, leaving a trail of green grass to grow behind them. They crossed over a bridge heading towards the west, and whilst doing, they could see all his demons questing on a rocky trail at the bottom of the valley which led to the north. They seemed determined to find Olivia because she was the key ingredient to reading the scripture encrypted on Quinton's back.

He remained quiet whilst levitating on his back. His mind began to drift off into a pleasant dream whilst staring at the dark sky, allowing his heart to eat at his thoughts. He could hear Juliana singing softly and could see her body emerging out. She stared up at the dusk sky whilst lying down on a hammock underneath a red cotton blanket, snuggled and coiled up.

'Come and lie beside me!' she said and turned her face to him whilst he tried to find out what the significance this was based on.

He was staring at the far end of a flowing river and discovered he was inside of Juliana's unfinished painting. His brown eyes were glued towards the glass wall metres above the waterfall cliff, and the dusk sun reflected perfectly on the water rippling towards the far end. The streaming river looked orange, and its beautiful ripples railed his heart towards peace.

'It's getting cold. Lie besides me, my lover!' she suggested and unclenched her knees and opened her legs apart.

She was wearing grey pyjamas and a silver bracelet on her right ankle. They lay beside each other and knew nothing else mattered to them. She kept quiet and dazed into his brown eyes for a while.

'Do you ever think of me at night?' she asked and guided his right hand towards her lips and gently kissed it.

'I do think of you every night before I sleep, and even in my sleep, I see you and only you!' he replied and parked his lips onto her forehead. 'You know, most of the time when we weren't speaking on the phone, I would sit by my bed and feel the pain, and whilst doing so, I would hold on to it by myself because I didn't want to upset you by telling you. I love you too much to bring you sadness. I want you to be happy even if I die soon!' he said and kissed her lips softly. 'I don't know if I'm going to wake up, and if I don't, then don't wait forever. Just move on!'

'Don't be stupid. You will wake up, and I will be there when you do!' she said. 'We will be together again!'

He submitted his heart into her nest as they snuggled within the net. She parked her lips onto the right side of his neck a while.

'What's on your mind, my baby?' she asked and placed her right hand inside his white shirt.

'I'm so hungry!' he replied as his stomach grumbled.

'Follow me then. I'll make a meal for you!' she said and rolled out towards the left then reached out with left hand.

He held on to it tightly with his left hand, but he was unsure of where they were going. They stepped out of a golden painting frame and entered deeply into his subconscious. Her costume changed and evolved into a long white summer dress. They'd entered into a dream he'd had before, except it was different this time around. The dark night deemed of uncertainty.

'Do you remember this place?' she asked. 'You once told me about it!'

'Of course I remember this place!' he replied as they stepped onto a grey concrete platform and watched the black gate open part. 'Hold on to my hand tightly and don't let go!' he pleaded, feeling certain these were his last thoughts before passing away.

'I won't!' she assured him as they strolled onto the gravel pavement slowly. 'The red roses are beautiful!'

'I'd always thought they were your favourite anyway!' he said and looked ahead. They discovered the castle he'd always dreamed about, but it was of grey stone.

'I love this castle!' she said. 'We should build one when are old!'

'I'll build anything for you!' he said as they drifted towards the left to an arched entrance beside the castle and two garage doors. He could see his phrase 'Loyalty and Honour' engraved over the arched entrance. 'Watch your step!' he said and gently showed his lover through.

She entered and stood still, imagining the endless possibilities of creating a home just as warm. The wall lights were bright. A German shepherd appeared from the kitchen door on the right side of the wall and wiggled its tail whilst sniffing Juliana's white dress.

'Come inside, my love. It won't bite you!' he said as she slowly made her way into the kitchen and started opening up all the cabinets.

'This is weird. Everything is exactly where I want it to be!' she said.

'Maybe it's because you are very influential to me and I care about your well-being. I want you to be happy—that's all!' he said. 'I care about your opinion from time to time!' He laughed out loud.

'Getting smart, aren't we?' she sceptically asked and smiled,

'I'll make you some sarmalute, okay, my love? It's a Romanian dish, mostly minced meat wrapped in cabbage'

'Okay, my baby. I'll head over to the living room quickly!' he said and walked through the vacant castle, mostly noticing how empty his life had become.

The rooms were empty; the dark wooden planks attached to the walls along with the dark wooden staircase shimmered with dust. He made his way through the passage right beside the living room and entered through a door made from oak wood. He'd always been in love with Juliana, but she never really knew the depth of it until she watched him disappear and close the door. He was afraid to show her how deeply he felt because it consumed the marrow within his bones and left him paralysed.

He spiralled down an anticlockwise staircase made from concrete and entered a narrow basement. The walls were painted beige and had electrical lights burning brightly. He looked up and stepped onto the plains of love, wetting his legs into warm water which had levelled to his knees. There were at least twenty empty wine barrels floating beside. Therefore, he moved every single one of them whilst walking through and finally consoling him because he was drowning from love. He sat on a red couch at the end of the narrow basement and planted his feet within the warm water. His heart throbbed slowly, and every pulse knocked his brain senselessly into pain.

'I don't know if she will ever know that I love her this much, but I'm drowning!' He said,

'I'm afraid to show her how deeply my love runs, it literally pours like the water streaming within her painting and I don't know how to contain it anymore. She is so amazing in every single way possible!'

There was a moment of silence after, which helped soothe his mind and apprehend his body down. His nostalgia grew and the water rose. He remained still like a corpse whilst the water crept on to his body and soaked his clothes. His real body was struggling to recover from the car accident he'd been in, and it was quite evident his was hanging by a thread. The water rose higher and touched his ears. He took his last breath and allowed himself to be consumed by Juliana's love. It was the last request he'd made to himself.

Juliana opened the oak wood door sceptically, uncertain of what she'd find, but a part of her remained hopefully whilst holding a warm Romanian dish in her hands. She stepped forth and embarked down the concrete staircase. Her heart began to throb faster as she heard sounds of water splashing against the bottom staircase. She glanced down at the water rippling against the tips of her white dress and wetting her smooth feet. There were wine barrels floating everywhere, which kept her blind from having a clear view ahead. She called out her lover's name repeatedly, but he did not respond. It caused her to panic. Therefore, she placed the dish onto the nearest step and plunged herself into the water then emerged from within. She called out again as sadness spilled from her green eyes into tears.

'Baby!' she yelled.

The sound of water splashing on to the walls and empty barrels knocking against each other drowned the only faith she had towards humanity. She poked her head into the water for a while and searched within but found nothing but darkness lingering. Her curly hair strands clothed her wet face as she wept, standing right besides an empty barrel. She placed her right hand onto it and patiently waited for peace to bring her some sort of comfort. The water temperature started to decline which made her panic more because she knew she was losing the love of her life to death.

She kept pushing more barrels out of the way. A glimpse of hope emerged within her heart and sparked faith within. Therefore, she kicked through the narrow basement and discovered a piece of furniture within the water. Her lover was right there, glued onto it. She reached in and held on to his heavy body then dragged him away. His soaked clothes weighed him down, but she kept pulling him and pleading for his life. She stepped onto the staircase and pulled his body up in a rush and tried to revive him from dying. The worst moment of his life appeared in the most unusual way. His heart throbbed slower as the cold crept through his skin. Juliana watched the water turn extremely cold and mould solid. She attempted to revive him again.

'Please wake up!' she pleaded whilst shivering and pressing her hands onto his chest.

She struggled to pull his body upwards, for his feet were stuck within the ice. The cold chills cropped out from the end of the basement and slowly formed. It evolved and moulded into a tall structure. Every particle levitated with the basement and gravitated towards the physical structure. Juliana pleaded for her lover's life as it stepped closer towards them and occurred to be something completely different from their mythology of a grim reaper. She did something neither one of them ever believed she'd do.

'Take my life instead!' she shouted whilst holding on to her lover tightly.

It stood before them and proceeded as scheduled by melting the water around Quinton's feet. His lower body lowered into a small pool, almost as if he was being dragged down.

'Take my life instead please!' she yelled and smacked his chest as a last resort.

Her words rippled through his body and cracked through the ice within the basement. He awoke and inhaled a cool breeze of fresh air into his lungs.

'I love you so much!' she cried, which railed him away from death and awoke him up in the first valley where all the lost descendants had once found refuge.

His sound reminded his heart of how strong Juliana's love was. It revealed the truth, and he knew she'd sacrifice herself to bring him back to life because she loved him so much and nothing else could come between that. He listened to the whispers of wind rushing in from an entrance within the cave where he was regaining conscious in. The bedroom was a mess, and every item of sentiment which belonged to Yumna and Freda was trashed. He could also hear a few voices waving past him repeatedly whilst lying down on the floor shivering from the cold. His body was wrapped tightly in layers of buffalo skin, and his face dripped with sweat from the fire burning metres behind his body. He struggled to break free and thus called out.

'Hello,' he said, and whilst doing so, the voices rushing from with the next cave became muted.

Footsteps grew louder as every second passed. A beautiful descendant appeared from the dark entrance, and her radiant face had an ability to tame the wildest of hearts. She leaned in and kneeled beside him then unwrapped the layer of buffalo skin from his body.

'You must be so confused. We had to wrap you up and place you here because you were shivering badly!' she mentioned whilst wiping the sweat from his feverish face with her left hand.

His warm blood streamed within her veins, uprooting great comfort, and it definitely felt like she was wiping away all his problems. He sat up straight and gazed into her beautiful blue eyes for a while then scanned downward to a remarkable piece of art hanging from her neck, clenched between her cleavages.

'It's beautiful, don't you think?' she asked. 'I made one for my lover and the other one for myself!' she said.

'You look just as beautiful as my guardian angel. Who are you?' he asked whilst brushing her black hair backwards.

393

'I'm flattered, but I'm not a guardian angel, just a lost descendant seeking refuge I'm afraid!' she replied. 'My name is Freda!'

'Well, Freda, my name is Quinton, and I am human!' he said and cracked a smile from his pale face.

'Of course you are human, and a handsome one you are!' she said and stood up slowly.

'Thank you!' he replied whilst she dusted off the dirt from her knees.

'You are welcome to join me!' she mentioned, smiling without a care in the world.

Her white teeth shone with perfection, luring him away from the thoughts he was having. He was tuned for a few minutes then remembered the reason behind his miraculous recovery from death.

'I'm so sorry, my love!' he said, feeling guilty for appreciating somebody's beauty besides his real lover whom he'd grown to love and cherish. He glanced towards the burning fire and zoned into the bright ashes breaking off within.

'Your world isn't burning down, love. You are rising up from the ashes and becoming a better man in ways you weren't when we first met!' Juliana whispered into his right ear.

He could feel her warm from behind as if she was right behind him snuggled tightly with her chin positioned on his right shoulder and her legs wrapped around his waistline.

'I will always be in your heart, and I will make sure that it beats every single day until you wake up from this nightmare!' she whispered.

'I don't know if I'm going to make it!' he whispered back, having doubts.

'Nonsense, of course you will make it. We are having a child together!' she said and kissed his neck softly.

'Don't leave. Stay with me throughout!' he pleaded.

'Don't worry. I will be with you, but do remember I'm not really here, okay?' she said. 'I don't want you to go crazy!'

'I think it is quarter past late for that!' he said as she laughed out loud. He could feel her heart beating on his back from within her busty chest.

'I'm going now. You must get up!' she whispered right before vanishing into thin air. He smiled and deemed himself absurdly in love.

'Okay, let's do this!' he said and stood up to dust himself off properly.

He looked towards the hole on his right side and discovered a few stars twinkling in the sky, which brought him hope. He made his way through the tunnel and entered another dark cave. It was trashed and reeked of misery. There were broken clay bowls and other handmade kitchen utensils on the cold surface. He kept walking, mostly stumbling from exhaustion, using his hands to guide him through the darkness and kicking past items on the cold floor. The tunnel sloped downwards and led him into a larger cave. He stood up straight and observed the environment around. There was a handful of lost descendants gathered around a bright fire burning in the middle of the cave. They were all hibernating, shrunken low into grey balls by covering themselves with their wings to absorb the warmth radiating from the fire.

'Freda!' Quinton called out whilst cautiously stepping closer to the burning flames. He was unaware of the panic he'd cause by calling out her name again. They attacked without cautious thought to wield him down.

'Stop!' Freda yelled from with a tunnel, which made all of them realise how animalistic they'd become for reacting without analysing the situation. They'd programmed themselves to defend without a conscious thought.

'We are so sorry!' one said, apologising for their paranoia. He seemed more sympathetic, wiser, and less hostile than the rest mainly because of his aged narrow face and his long white hair strands flaming in different directions. His Caucasian skin was scaled with wrinkles, endorsing him with some sort of wisdom.

'Nathaniel, put him down!' Freda's commanded to the angel who'd just apologised but still had Quinton pinned to the wall.

He gently placed Quinton back onto the ground and stepped away.

'Are you okay?' Freda asked and stepped past everyone else to smooth Quinton with comfort.

'Don't tell me you are in love with him too?' another descendant sarcastically asked.

'You don't have to be such an arsehole, Miguel!' Freda said and guided Quinton past the crowd.

'Come on, Freda, we were just playing with him!' Miguel mentioned as the other three agreed. They knew they weren't joking, and masking their faces with deception was their only way of hiding the fact that they were terrified of the evil lingering around them.

'Come sit with me!' Freda said, insisting on guarding Quinton away from their stupidity and ignorance.

'I'm not scared of them, you know!' Quinton said and turned around.

'Whoa, aren't you hard core!' Miguel mentioned, mainly envious of Freda's affection towards others besides himself.

'I'm Cindy!' the first lost descendant greeted. She smiled and reached out with her right hand. Her brown dreads wrapped in a ponytail did significant justice to show the beauty of her mixed-race skin. She was lightly toned, and her body structure seemed to remind Quinton of his significant other.

He shook his way through the small crowd, greeting another angel by the name of Victoria who seemed as mature and well suited for Nathaniel. Her aged skin had wrinkles. She seemed endlessly happy despite the fact that they were trapped in a world of chaos.

'Okay, let's all pretend like he isn't endangering our well-being with the scripture encoded on him!' Miguel mentioned as everyone else sat beside the fire and tried to ignore everything projecting from his mouth.

'What do you mean 'on him'?' Quinton asked, glancing back with curiosity railing within.

'It's not a coincidence to have ended up within this world. Have you taken the time to wonder why your back was burning up earlier?' Miguel asked which seemed to bother Freda.

'Just stop already!' she said, sounding exhausting and frustrated.

'You are all forgetting why we were captured in the first place!' he mentioned and stepped closer to the burning fire.

'Explain further!' Quinton insisted.

'You were supposed to die, but for some reason, you are still alive,' Miguel replied, which drove Quinton into conducive thoughts about the love of his life because she played a major role in ensuring his recovery,

'You are the key to opening a porthole between this world and the earth. Your guardian angel is the only one who is able to read it. You know where she is?' he asked.

'Miguel, let him settle. You will bother him with that myth in the morning!' Cindy said.

'No, it's okay!' Quinton said. 'She somehow managed to escape from the same castle we were in!'

'Then we must find her!' Cindy said. 'We must make sure nobody gets their hands on the scripture!'

'She is right. I believe we still have a purpose in this world, maybe to restore a balance here!' Victoria said.

'To what end?' Nathaniel asked. 'We'll be hiding forever if we have it within our possession!'

'I'm sure we are all thinking about using it, right?' Miguel asked, which questioned the integrity of the rest.

'That's not happening!' Freda said. 'You are always manipulating, and that's one of the reasons why I chose Yumna over you!'

'Ouch!' Cindy whispered.

'Yes, ouch,' Miguel said and walked away to nurse his wounds. He was absolutely in love with Freda, and at a point, they had a shot at love until Yumna arrived.

She appealed to Freda mostly because she was quiet and respectful unlike Miguel who'd spent his afterlife marching to his own drum and ironically believing he was God's gift to others. He wasn't humble, nor was he grateful which made him a villain most of the time.

'It's important that we find the guardian angel. The rest will follow. We will keep you safe!' Victoria said whilst facing Quinton then stood up. 'Anyway one of us needs to guard everyone tonight. I will go and do so!'

'And I will join you!' Nathaniel said which brought a smile onto Freda's face.

'Don't say anything!' Victoria said, grinning childishly and finding pleasure within the moment.

'I wasn't going to say anything!' Freda responded and clenched her knees together as the breeze swept past her body from a tunnel behind.

'We must go and rest. We will hunt in the morning and regain strength before moving again!' Marat mentioned whilst getting up to stretch alongside with the fifth quiet angel. 'Good night!'

'Goodnight to the both of you!' Freda said as they walked away and disappeared into the darkness.

'Come closer. I won't bite!' Freda said, insisting on bonding closely. She opened her right wing to accommodate for his body.

'How does he know so much about these scriptures?' Quinton asked as a blanket of feathers covered his body.

'There is another guardian angel. No one is sure where she came from, but we found her unclothed by a river once. She looked lost and scared. Days later, she began to open up about the scripture she had in her position. She explained the mythology behind it and its purpose!' Freda said. 'Miguel and I kept her secret because she trusted us with it. We promised to keep her safe, and when the demons came for her, we sacrificed ourselves to ensure her safety!'

'I don't get it. Why me?' he asked, filled with a lot of questions.

'I wasn't sure at first until you woke up. You love so deeply and care so much for this other earthling!' she mentioned and poked the fire with a long stick. 'The scripture itself was made by an angel just like us, but it possessed him right after. Some say he made it to return back to earth to be with the love of his life again!'

'What happened to him? Because surely you can't die twice!' he asked. 'Was he captured?'

'Yes, he was captured, but not in the same sense. He became different and started turning his back on everyone!' she said. 'He became his own worst nightmare and goes by the name of Luke. I assure you have heard of him, Luther?' she asked, which seemed to bother Quinton more. 'The myth states that he made a deal with the kind of the underworld to make the scripture and trade in for his new life and to have his soul back!' she mentioned.

'The things we do for love!' he said which brought a smile to her face.

'That's what I said the first time!' she replied. 'Anyway we must rest too. There will be food in the morning!'

'Lead the way!' he insisted as she stood up and walked towards the cave Quinton had awoken from. 'I'll sleep on the floor and you can take the bed!' he said, sounding gentle and chivalrous.

'Thank you, but no thanks. I have to protect you now. It's my obligation to make sure you end up back on earth!' she mentioned whilst plunging herself into the bed. 'Might as well join me!'

'Really shouldn't!' he said, feeling guilty and overwhelmed.

'Oh, get over yourself!' she interrupted and laughed out loud, which made him feel utterly stupid for declining in the first place. She unwrapped a layer of buffalo skin to accommodate for his body.

'Okay fine!' he said and moved towards the bed. He lay down and covered up as the cool breeze stroked past the bed and drifted slowly from one hole to another.

'I guess this what they mean by saying I slept next to an angel!' he said, which cracked a smile on her face.

'You have a sense of humour!' she said and clutched on to the buffalo skin.

'From time to time, yes!' he whispered and kept quiet. There were sounds of demons groaning and marching forth within the distance. 'Can you hear that?' he asked and sat up in confusion, afraid of being captured again.

'Do not worry. They are miles away. Their sounds drift through slippery tunnels within the mountains and pass right through this part of the cave!' she whispered. 'That's partly the reason why I love this part of the cave—I can hear and smell anything foul!' She lured him back down into temporary comfort but could also feel his heart throbbing faster than usual by simply placing her right hand onto his chest.

'It's okay, you are safe with me!' she assured and shifted closer to hold him.

He kept quiet and listened to the horror whipping within his mind. The sounds of trolls moving and their daggers scraping onto wet rocks left him restless. He could also hear wolves howling and sniffing for foreign scents.

'Don't think about it too much. Your heart is actually beating way too fast!' she whispered. 'Kiss me!'

'Excuse me!' he said.

'I said kiss me. It will take your mind away from the voices lurking!' she mentioned and waited for him to react.

He leaned in for a kiss. Her lips were warm and so was the temperature of her long, curvy body. He slowly French kissed her lips and began to forget about his fears. She hopped onto his body and returned the favour.

'I'm so sorry. I can't do this!' he said whilst dazed into her beautiful blue eyes. His moral compass moved repeatedly, and he knew it was beneath him to act immorally.

'I know. I'm sorry. We shouldn't have!' she said. 'I just wanted to divert your attention to something else!'

'I know and I'm thankful for it!' he said. 'But I can't run away from my fears anymore. I have to confront and overcome them!'

She lay back onto the bed and rested. He listened to every sound and took in every tormenting sound lashing at him. The visuals played in his head, and he could see the environment rooting and plants drying up as the army of evil walked passed. Helpless animals awoke from their sleep whilst hibernating and choked to their death. He could see feel the evil corrupting his soul and influencing his mind to be filth, mainly sparking his thoughts to twaddle in dirt. His mind tumbled into the root of things, railing his body to hold on to Freda tightly to restrain himself from unleashing the monster within himself. She knew of the temptation lashing towards her, but also restrained from taking advantage. He silently begged for strength to control himself without alerting anyone. Seconds passed and turned into minutes clocking within his head as he dozed off.

Chapter Twenty-One

Clarity Unfolding

Cool winds drifted through the hollow cave and awoke the lost descendants from a deep sleep a few hours later. Freda felt rejuvenated and relived, dwelling in positivity and happiness, whilst Quinton dwelled within a majestic spectrum, contemplating his future and reminiscing about old memories which seemed to bring some sort of happiness into his world.

'Morning!' she said and turned around to face him.

Quinton smiled and felt proud of himself for reframing from failing into temptation.

'Morning!' he replied and noticed how messy and bushy her black hair could be.

'Today is going to be a good day!' she mentioned whilst getting up.

'I hope so!' he said and sat up straight to observe the scenery. It was still dark outside, and the conditions seemed perfect for travelling without being spotted by anyone else.

'Get up!' Freda said and pulled of a layer of buffalo skin from his body. 'I'm sure everyone is back for hunting right about now. Therefore, I must go and help out!'

'Well, what should I do?' he asked and felt the chills creeping through his skin.

'You can join us or lie back down, maybe have another dream about making love to me and the love of your life at the same time!' she said and blushed whilst walking away.

'Wait, how do you know?' he asked and followed, mostly feeling embarrassed and exposed.

'I could see inside you mind. Not only that, but I could also hear you calling out the name Juliana whilst kissing my upper back softly!' she said. 'You need to work on shielding your thoughts. I must say, she is very beautiful!'

'Morning, my lovelies!' Freda shouted and walked towards the fire where everyone was standing beside a spit roast, cutting out chunks of meat from a warthog carcass.

'And our royal highness is in our midst!' Miguel said whilst slicing off a piece of meat from the left thigh.

'Be careful. Your jealousy is transparent again!' Cindy said which seemed to enlighten the atmosphere within the cave.

They spoke about the most irrelevant topics and laughed out loud to the memories they'd created together. Quinton sat down on a dark brown log cut from with a tree within the woods and began to miss his family. It began clear to him whilst starring at the lost descendants in front of him. Their world wasn't perfect, nor were they perfect. They were perfect for each other and loved each other without passing harsh judgement. The wielding strength of love itself bounded their hearts towards peace. They weren't bounded by average human laws, nor were they prejudiced towards each other. They'd learned to accept and appreciate each other. He sat there mesmerised by their imperfect features, from their rough pale feet, the scars on their bodies which told more stories, and their natural beauty which flourished brightly like the stars above. They brought great hope and endorsed him with peace. He was finally one with himself and mostly stronger than ever.

He took his first bite and loved the crispy taste of warthog steaming within his mouth. It was a warm bite spiced and quilted with a concept to understanding himself, mainly to appreciate his own flaws because they made him whole. They'd created and moulded him into an extraordinary being. He'd become more compassionate and caring. Juliana's absence had made his heart grow fonder. He was humbled by the long distance between and couldn't wait to wake up and rush back to her again. Nothing could convince him otherwise. His mind was formatively moulded to appreciate the love she'd present. Her affection fuelled his heart to great lengths and pushed him to be better. He finally understood the reason for her existence. She wasn't placed on earth for amusement, nor was she made to be abuse, but she existed to bring him peace and teach him how to love purely without expecting anything back. He finally understood he couldn't go anywhere without her being around mainly because her love was the hinge attached to keep his wheel of faith from falling apart.

Their flaws were aligned perfectly to bring their two hearts together, to merge as one, and to roll towards the future which inevitably presented the beauty within the world of uncertainty. He was excited to find out how deeply their love ran and thus stood up and felt optimistic about his future which looked brighter than ever.

'We must fly to the northern mountains soon, and I'm sure that's where everyone else is. There are thousands of long trees within those woods and steep slopes which makes it a perfect place to find refuge!' Nathaniel said, insisting a predictable approach.

'And why is that so?' Quinton asked and sunk his teeth deeply into the roasted piece meat he'd just carved out from a crispy warthog ear.

'Because it's easier to escape and fly away from danger. You can see the enemy coming from miles away!' Nathaniel said.

'I suggest we take the secret ice land tunnels on the east to en route towards the north just in case we are followed!' Cindy said.

'I agree!' Victoria said as everyone else nodded.

They all stood up and held on to each other's hands before bowing their heads to commence in prayer. It initially seemed bizarre to pray

403

especially given their predicament with regard to having perished from Earth and finding themselves eternally lost.

'Lord forgive us for our sins,

'We are at your mercy and ask for the strength to go on.

'We know that you have made a better plan for our existence.

'We will take the time to appreciate everything you have done for the world.

'Therefore, we thank you,' they all said which sparked a glimpse of faith into Quinton's heart.

He was astonished by their will to carry on. It was heart filling and remarkable because they hadn't lost faith in their maker. Matter of fact, they loved him even more. It was faith that kept them going.

'Let the fire burn. The smoke will lead the dragons here instead of the north, which will give us time to find everyone else, or at least it will give us time to disappear again!' Nathaniel said and pulled a multithreaded rope down within the darkness and opened up a hole above, which had been covered with stitched layers of thick buffalo skin.

'Lead the way, Cindy!' Freda said and watched the rest erupt into the clear dawn sky. 'Hold on to me tightly!' she said to Quinton whilst spreading her wings.

'Try not to drop me!' he responded, uncertain of the outcome.

'I won't. Tighten yourself!' she insisted as they held on to each other tightly. 'Are you ready?' she asked as he wrapped his legs around her waist and waited for Victoria to finish off tying his ankles together.

Freda erupted towards the sky as Quinton clenched on to her body for dear life. The adrenaline rush made him feel invisible, like nothing else could stop him from excelling towards greatness. He inhaled the fresh air rushing past his face and felt a sense of relief within his body, flourishing brightly within his heart. His insides dropped as his body uplifted and took flight. He could smell Freda's scent amongst another natural components radiating through the atmosphere. She'd levitated above layers of white clouds to enlighten him with the beautiful scenery. The clouds stretched out endlessly towards the north where he could see the peak of a few mountains shimmering brightly with snow.

'Hurry up!' Victoria shouted from the distance.

'We are coming!' Freda yelled back and took a few more seconds to observe the smile imprinted on Quinton's face. 'It's amazing, right?' she asked.

'It's beautiful?' he said and faced the east end of their world where the bright sun had begun to creep up slowly.

'Okay, we must go now!' she said. 'Time is of the essence. We should have left earlier because we have just become bait out here!'

Quinton turned his head towards the right and placed his ear onto her firm chest. He could hear her heart beating slowly, which filled his mind with curiosity because he couldn't quite figure out nor understand how it was remotely possible for their hearts to be intact even after death. Her heart throbbed loudly as if she was just as human.

The scenery captivated his brown eyes whilst being dazed by the peak of mountains, and it inevitably brought great joy, but as he turned his head towards the left whilst whizzing over clouds, he rediscovered the epitome of horror within his intuition and it gripped his heart, squeezing out the little bit of happiness floating within. His eyes drew closer towards the sight of darkness heading towards their way. It hadn't happened yet as he withdrew from his thoughts and saw nothing but puffy clouds in the distance.

'Are you hanging in there?' Freda asked whispering into his ear, and he nodded.

Freda blushed as she looked down and saw his face peacefully rested in between her chest. Thus, she placed her right hand onto the back of his head, unsure of the blissful feeling relishing through her heart. It railed her mind into guilt because she was spoken for by her beloved, Yumna.

The temperature declined as they embarked towards the east, flying fast toward the ice lands. Quinton awoke to the difference of the atmosphere, discovering the spectacular bright sun blazing brightly in the middle of the sky. He blinked repeatedly and found himself astonished by the beautiful rays of light shining onto Freda's grey wings as they flapped fast, almost painting them silver on the edges. She leaned in and consoled his heart.

'We are almost there. Just hang in there!' she whispered into his left ear.

'I want to live like this!' he whispered back, which brought a smile to her face.

She remained flattered by his comment whilst flying behind everyone else. Miguel plunged himself into the white clouds and reappeared from behind.

'You need to move faster!' Miguel shouted but glazed into Freda's ignorance. Therefore, he caught up and repeatedly the same words because he could sense something was wrong. He was gifted with the ability to sense horror and foresee eight seconds into the future.

'Okay, will move!' she shouted and shrunk her head inwards. 'He's always so jealous!' she whispered into Quinton's ear.

He kept his eyes shut because he could also feel the wrath of evil trailing from beyond, creeping towards his soul and racking off the little bit of happiness from his face.

'Don't you worry. He is always paranoid!' she whispered but flew faster anyway to bring everyone else satisfaction. Quinton glanced towards Miguel who'd struck out his wooden bow and two wooden arrows sharpened at the tips.

'Incoming!' Miguel yelled and released the two arrows into the clouds.

The arrows glided through cool clouds, and as they pierced through the sky, a large black dragon with a knight rider emerged from within the clouds. The arrows plunged deeply into the rider's shoulders. He fell off, but the dragon pursued forth. It appeared to be a large dragon with black feathers attached to it instead of black scales. Its claws were long, and Quinton could see the truth underneath its long nails. It was moulded to destroy progress, and it wielded fear into every heart.

'We are almost there, but we can't show it the route towards the north!' Freda shouted as they all formed into single formation and plunged through the clouds, heading down towards a large forest ahead.

'Head to the woods!' Nathaniel insisted and trailed behind with Miguel.

They armed themselves by striking out their daggers from their waist belts, pointing them up towards the sky mainly to show courage and strength.

The rest landed onto a trail which stretched out for miles between the secret tunnel entrances on both ends of the mountains. They ran into the dark woods to hide from danger and were led through a rocky path by Cindy. She seemed highly informed about the environment around and moved fast through the woods guiding them down a slope clustered with thick tree trunks, sliding onto a thin frozen river, which stretched farther down onto a frozen pool surrounded by more trees.

'Keep moving!' Cindy yelled, pointing farther east towards the darkness.

'Untie me!' Quinton yelled, feeling helpless.

Victoria assisted by pulling a piece of thread from behind, which caused Quinton's legs to intertwine with Freda's legs. They slowly tumbled and fell onto the frozen ice.

'Get up! We must move!' Victoria yelled and jumped over the two clumsy fools who were ironically and inevitably falling for each other without noticing.

'Go!' Quinton shouted, which prompted Freda onto her feet. 'Move!'

'Okay, I'm going!' she yelled back and ran faster through the path.

Their strides grew longer by the second until they ran past dozens of trees. They crossed over another trail, and whilst doing so, Quinton paused to the significance of a dream he'd had. He could see Juliana's ghost standing still in the middle path, facing the narrow trail.

'Baby!' he yelled at his lover's ghost, but it remained still which left him completely baffled by the visual presented before him. It evaporated into thin air as Freda gripped his right arm.

'We must move!' she shouted and pulled him away from hallucinating.

He'd lapsed on to a moment plastered with déjà vu, but it seemed slightly different as he slowed down and glanced towards the right. His dream had burned into ashes as he discovered the remaining wooden stairs and wooden pillars seeming black. He detoured towards the right path, for it felt right to chase that specific dream instead of running away.

'What are you doing?' Freda yelled, rushing back to aid him away from the horror hovering in the air. He turned around as she held on to his left hand. 'We must go!' she pleaded, but he remained unmoved by her word because he was possessed by his dream of being with Juliana again.

He stepped closer, stumbling up the stairs in disbelief of what he was witnessing before his eyes. The cottage had burned to its wooden foundation, leaving the wooden door and door frame standing in his presence. He unhinged the golden doorknob and stepped onto black ashes, ingraining his feet with dirt and painting them black. The painting Juliana had made was the only item placed on its dark wooden art stand within the first left room. It left him confused for a while because he didn't understand the concept behind his dream, nor did he understand the significance of the painting anymore given her reason—'the river of our love will always flow'. He wondered if it meant for him to hold on to a dream which seemed impossible to achieve or if meant for him to move on and allow destiny to unveil before his eyes. The idea of letting go of the only woman he'd ever loved drove him farther away from Freda's voice. He glanced up towards the sky as another black dragon, along with its demon warrior, emerged from the white clouds and hovered above the trees right beside the cottage wreckage. The demon warrior couldn't quite find passage to lower its dragon down and therefore jumped off and clamped its hook blade onto a thick tree branch then slid down onto the snow metres away from the cottage foundation.

Quinton clutched on to the painting with both hands, and within seconds, it began to deteriorate, turning into ash and into burnt grey particles. He looked down and wondered why he was holding on to the idea of love whilst it endangered his well-being. The monster groaned from the right side of the cottage foundation as it prepared to strike.

'Hey!' Freda called out to catch the monster's attention but failed.

It's stepped onto the wooden stairs, which made Quinton realise he was still afraid of his monsters. It lifted its hook blade and struck towards his direction but missed as he fell onto the cottage ashes on the wooden floor, temporarily blinding himself. It squealed like a pig as Freda gutted it from behind and allowed its body to fall right besides Quinton's body.

'You need to stop holding on to something so fragile!' she yelled and helped him gather his wild thoughts into one motion,

'Now get up and move!' she yelled again whilst he washed off the ashes on his face with the frost beside his feet.

He could see the dragon hovering above the trees whilst growling and breathing out frost to alert more.

'Thank you!' he said and stood up quickly.

'Thank me later. You need to move!' she shouted, panicking because she felt responsible for him.

He stepped away from his broken dream and embarked on a path he was destined to take. They all ran through the woods and dove into a massive rabbit hole which sloped smoothly because of the ice paving perfectly towards the bottom. They piled on top of each other within the darkness, which cause discomfort. Quinton glanced towards the darkness as Freda unpeeled herself from his body and stood up straight. Everyone else stumbled within the dark as a pair of red eyes glowed in the distance.

'What is that?' Quinton asked which caught everyone's attention. Another pair of red eyes glowed, and it caused a rippled effect within the darkness.

'Don't move!' Cindy mentioned and flicked magical dust into the air, which immediately sparked the area bright as the magical grains evolved into yellow pixies. 'Step lightly and follow me. They are aware of my scent because I've been here before with Nathaniel!' she said as they all glanced at a pack of wild rabbits which were humongous, almost the height of an average horse.

Their fur was white as snow, and their toes were as pitch-black as the darkness surrounding them. They were huddled in a circle to absorb warmth from each other.

'Doing what exactly?' Freda asked sceptically whilst sneaking farther towards the right, hoping to vanish away from the horror staring into her blue eyes.

She accidentally stepped onto a green apple used by the rabbits as food whilst hibernating from the winter. The alpha rabbit hopped forth aggressively as Freda squashed the fruit with her right ankle.

'Freda, do as you are told!' Quinton mentioned and followed.

'Oh, like you were following instructions earlier, almost had all of us captured again!' Freda replied sarcastically.

'You don't have to be such an arse!' he said. 'Come here already!'

'I'm coming. You are so demanding!' she said. 'Need to be more chivalrous, so stop acting like such a cow!'

'That doesn't even make sense!' he mentioned as she held on to his left hand.

They were assisted along the way by bright yellow pixies hovering above. Initially, some landed onto their shoulders and brushed off other earthly components on their bodies whilst they embarked through a long tunnel, which curved towards the northern mountains. They could hear a tormenting sound gaining momentum above as their tunnel intertwined underneath the trail—the sound of horses galloping wildly from their right and passing towards their left.

'Keep going!' Cindy whispered.

'Just keep moving. Nathaniel and Miguel will find their way through the tunnel!' she whispered as the yellow pixies turned into a dark blue colour. However, their glow remained yellow as it shrunk and flickered repeatedly at a consistent pace within the left side of their chests.

'The pixies must be so scared!' Freda whispered as one pixie landed onto her right palm.

'What if they don't make it back?' Quinton asked. 'Nathaniel and Miguel, that is!'

'I think we should wait for them, at least acknowledge their courage and prepare the meat we'd packed into Victoria's rucksack!' Freda mentioned as the last horse galloped away.

'Seems ideal, we will do so within a few minutes!' Victoria interrupted the suggestions lashing from different angles.

'Nathaniel insisted I take you all through the secret tunnels. We aren't safe here!' Cindy said and turned around to voice more reasoning through their indecisiveness.

'No offense, but he isn't our father. Therefore, we will wait!' Quinton interrupted and silenced everyone from speaking.

They could hear a few drops of melting ice clash on to small puddles right beside their feet.

'Well then, let's camp here and get ambushed again!' Cindy said.

'If we head to the tunnels without everyone, we will be leading all the demons to everyone!' Quinton mentioned and planted himself onto the floor. 'Anyone joining me?' he asked.

'I'll join you!' Freda said and sat beside him.

'I guess we will wait!' Victoria added and sat down. 'If you can't beat them, then join them!' she said and smiled which irritated Cindy and dismantled her visions of finding imminent peace.

All dark blue pixies began to glow bright yellow again as everyone waited patiently. Victoria unwrapped her rucksack and placed the roasted meat onto an oval bowl carved out from wood then torched a small bush of hay by clashing two rocks together repeatedly. Freda cuddled and leaned her head onto Quinton's left shoulder.

'You two are cosying up well. Shouldn't forget about Yumna!' Cindy mentioned and glanced towards the darkness and heard footsteps gaining momentum.

'I haven't forgotten about her!' Freda said, feeling guilty because she had fallen out of love with Yumna and drowning into the presence of an ordinary man.

'You shouldn't lie. It's not good to lie!' Victoria said as Freda sat up straight and unclenched her right hand from Quinton's left hand.

He could feel the void enlarging within his chest as she did so. His palm grew cold, driving his vivid mind to be squandered into thoughts of his significant other. It was inevitable for him to fall back into old habits whenever dwelling on old memories, but he subconsciously decided at that very moment to relish in the moment without guilt.

'You don't have to feel bad. Allow everything to take its course!' he said and found a reason to enjoy his existence instead of drowning his heart inside a pool filled with despair. 'It's okay to be happy!' he mentioned and held on to her soft hand. 'I'm happy right now!' he said, unsure if he'd ever wake up from his coma.

His heart began to mend itself together whilst he stared into the flames burning bright and understood that heartbreak could indeed be temporary. It wasn't as apocalyptic as he'd always made it out to be.

'If someone doesn't love you for who you are, then they don't deserve you!' he said, speaking to himself, and everyone else acknowledged his vague words.

They couldn't relate to his struggle but understood it. The pain was challenging, and he'd grown exhausted from fighting an endless battle within himself. He needed to be released from caring so deeply for the woman he loved so much because he knew it was destroying him. It was as addictive as a lethal drug being injected into his veins. He loved the incredible high it offered, but the chemicals boiling within his bloodstream endorsed him with feelings he wasn't capable of handling anymore. It drove him crazy and made him sad beyond measure. He could feel the rush within his veins causing his hands to shake repeatedly as he thought more of his significant other at that very moment. A tear raced down from his right eyelid as he mourned away the last bit of his sadness.

'Can't you hear that?' Victoria asked as two lost descendants emerged from the darkness.

'Miguel!' Cindy yelled and rushed towards the both of them without a care in the world. He'd been injured on his right thigh and thus limped forward whilst holding on to Nathaniel with both hands.

'A dragon tooth broke off on his right thigh before I could cut its neck off!' Nathaniel mentioned as Victoria analysed his filthy body for any injuries.

'I'm fine, barely scratched!' he said and threw his dagger onto the floor.

'Why is his wound bleeding so much and smudged dark blue around the edges?' Cindy asked whilst ripping off the rest of the buffalo skin strapped around his right thigh.

'I didn't notice that part before, looks poisonous!' Nathaniel responded as they all surrounded Miguel's body. 'I thought he'd heal quicker but hasn't done so!'

'His body is also heating up!' Cindy mentioned as she placed her right hand onto his forehead.

'It isn't possible!' Freda said sceptically. 'His flesh is rooting!' she said and stepped away from his body.

'This means he can . . .' she mentioned but paused for a split second. 'It means he will evaporate into nothing but a beam of light waiting for peace through eternity!' Victoria said whilst she wrapped up her rucksack for the journey ahead.

'We need to find Yumna immediately. She will know exactly what to do!' Cindy said and assisted Nathaniel by handling Miguel forward.

'What about the horses?' Quinton asked as Freda scooped water from a small puddle with her hands and splashed it onto the burning hay.

'We are unsure. We had already made through the rabbit hole before we could find out!' Miguel mentioned whilst battling through his own pain. He spat out blood repeatedly whilst hanging his head down.

'You will be okay!' Cindy said and held on to him tightly.

She'd always had a soft spot for Miguel but remained relentless about it because he was blinded by his adoration for Freda. He stumbled on to a moment of realisation as he glanced at Cindy's face and realised how much she loved him. She was worried sick, saddened by his injury, and determined to aid him back to full health. He screamed as the poisonous venom began to spread down within his lower body and scaled onto his right toes, painting them dark blue.

'Cindy, how will this other angel supposed to help with the poison?' Quinton asked whilst trailing behind Freda and gazing at the shining necklace around her neck, which symbolised her love for another.

'Because she just so happens to be the only who knows how to formulate herbals which can heal wounds quickly!' Cindy replied, and just as she did so, the tunnel magically widened into a small cave.

'Learned a few tricks from Elle!' Victoria said and kneeled onto the floor to find something as effective to soothe the pain away. 'She taught me how to enlarge tunnels once!' she said as the yellow pixies levitated higher to brighten the area.

'Neat trick!' Freda said.

'I'm so impressed!' she said and assisted everyone to rest Miguel onto the floor.

Quinton glanced towards the darkness and could see a small glimpse of light flickering within the distance. He could feel the goodness of his heart brighten up his face as Olivia emerged from the tunnel accompanied by Yumna herself. It was a miracle unclogging their minds from uncertainty and adding hope to their existence.

'Yumna!' Cindy yelled and rushed over to embrace a miracle in the works, and at the same time, Olivia rushed to her earthling and held on to him tightly.

'I knew I'd find you again!' Olivia said and kissed his cheeks repeatedly, which drilled his heart with joy.

'I'm glad we found each other again!' he said and smiled then turned to introduce his guardian angel to the rest.

They all gathered and greeted one another pleasantly. Olivia's presence drove Freda envious as she scanned the guardian angel's body. She'd railed her mind in confusion because she was uncertain about her feelings for Yumna and had misinterpreted her growing affection for the earthling right next to Nathaniel.

'What brought you here?' Cindy asked, still in disbelief for she'd reunited with a close friend.

'On our way to rescue the earthling I suppose!' Yumna mentioned and held on to Freda's cold hand but felt the difference whilst trying to clench it tightly. 'But we found him, so what now?' she asked Olivia who hadn't devised a constructive plan of action.

'Before she explains, I must tell you all something. Everything has changed after you were all captured. We rebuilt a new asylum, one safe for every lost angel within our world!' she said and explained the matter at hand, describing the new settlement within the northern mountains and how their existence flourished through the woods. She described the cloak used to disguise the normal environment from all eyes relishing with evil.

'The cloak broke minutes after Elle left with a small brigade of angels to find the earthling!' she mentioned. 'She had us all fooled!'

'What do you mean she left?' Victoria asked in disbelief, glazed in shock as everyone else clustered around.

'Where did they go?' Nathaniel asked as Yumna mixed a few herbs within a wooden bowl and attempted to make a potion just as effective as the one she'd made for Olivia.

'The cloak broke, and all hell broke loose!' Olivia mentioned. 'We were ambushed in the valley whilst everyone else was sleeping, but I managed to escape. I couldn't leave without Yumna. Therefore, I woke her up and we left!'

'At first I didn't believe her when she told me about Elle's intentions until we saw them escape towards the eastern route with dozens of others!' Yumna said and rubbed a potion onto Miguel's rotting right thigh gently with her right hand, pressing his chest down to with her left hand to keep him stabilised from waking up because of the burn within.

He yelled in pain as Cindy kneeled beside his head and held on to him tightly.

'You will be okay!' she whispered and parked her lips onto his sweaty forehead. 'You have to be strong!' she said, allowing her heart to wonder off.

A tear rained from her right eyelid as she whispered a confession, 'I love you so much!' she whispered, and as her words rushed through his ears, he opened his eyes and stared towards the blurry pixies above, discovering how stupid he'd been for taking her for granted.

'I'm so sorry!' he whispered back, and she forgave him immediately.

'Will it heal?' she asked Yumna whilst starring at the open wound.

'I'm sure it will heal, but we must find shelter soon so that you can wash his body clean and allow him to rest properly!' Yumna mentioned whilst washing off the potion from his hands on one of the many small puddles within the scenery.

Olivia clocked on to a vague thought and thus expressed it without acknowledging its repercussion.

'I can go back home and get help!' she said. 'My parents will definitely help!'

'No, they won't!' Nathaniel said. 'It's against the covenant laws to assist those lost!'

'I'm sure they can help. I'm here to help!' Olivia said, trying to find reason, but also knew Nathaniel was right.

'You are only here because you fell into temptation and found yourself lost in our world!' Nathaniel mentioned and rejected her input because he'd stereotyped her by the way she presented herself.

He believed she was spoilt rich and misunderstood the struggle endured by those lost within the plague of evil.

'I can always leave and come back!' she said. 'I'm sure something can be done!'

'Give up. Nothing can be done!' he replied and helped Miguel onto his feet. 'You can leave and never return here. Your kind won't bother. They wouldn't help us when we were in trouble. Therefore, why would they help us now?' he asked which left a gloomy silence within the hole.

'We will fight for ourselves like we've always done!' Nathaniel mentioned and picked Miguel up then started walking towards the darkness.

'Stop being so stubborn!' Victoria said and trailed behind Nathaniel, merely trying to bless him with reason. 'Where are you going!?' she asked as he turned around. 'The northern mountains are flooded with demons. We must stay together and work together!'

'We stay together, and we'll be doomed!' he yelled and caused a change of colour on the pixies above.

The area became dark blue again whilst they all argued loudly.

'Why the change of heart?' Victoria asked. 'Why now?'

'If what Yumna says is true, then we can't trust them. We are blinded by their bright wings and perfect features. We aren't like them, and we will never be like them. It's time I look after my own!' Nathaniel said and added more invalid reasons to his approach.

'We must talk!' Olivia whispered aside to her earthling as he stepped back from the conflict spiralling within the atmosphere. Freda drifted her focus towards them.

'He is right, you know—she can't be trusted!' she whispered. 'I heard of her plot to extract the scripture from your back!'

'I understand that part, but why would you want to leave me?' he asked.

'I'm not leaving you, just going to find help—that's all!' she said, and he wasn't surprised of her thoughts to depart because if it were up to him, he would have left a long time ago. 'You have to trust me!' she pleaded. 'If there was another way, then I would stay, but they don't stand a chance without the covenant's assistance behind them!'

'Sounds rich coming from you!' Freda interrupted as tension rose to an all-time high within the hole they were in.

'I'll come back for you!' Olivia said and held on to her earthling tightly. 'I promise!' she whispered into his ear.

'I trust you, but you can't leave whilst the sun is out!' he whispered back. 'We must all find refuge first before making conducive decisions about our well-being!' he said out loud and caught the attention of the deepest critic within. 'It's best that way!' he added as Nathaniel turned around to lead them through the tunnel.

'Then it's best for us to head to a remote locate, a place where Cindy and I go when the spring season comes. It's a place of peace!' Nathaniel said and found persuasive reason after the earthling's testimony. 'But first we must lie low until the sun goes down like the earthling insists. I'm sure the dusk sky is clustered with creatures of the night!' he said whilst moving through the tunnel, insisting on Victoria to create another passage farther east instead of following the original plan by heading to the northern tunnels to reunite with the rest of the other lost descendants who'd supposedly witnessed the wrath of evil.

Victoria created another alternate route towards their destination through an underground trail which paved for miles underneath the cold woods and stretched out long within the largest frozen lake. They could all see the horrors of humanity. Chemical wastes made by humans at every dark angle whilst walking underneath the lake. The visuals were disgusting and made everyone feel ashamed because they'd all contributed to the filth beside them once before. There were frozen layers of oil waste stretched right beside their path, intercepting underneath their path and passing towards the left of the frozen lake.

'Has it always looked like this?' Quinton asked as he glanced towards the right and saw a naked frozen cat, pale with its black eyes piercing at his soul. It blinked slowly as its black eyeballs glued on to his movement.

'We are passing within the lake filled with illusions. It can either show you reflect of some sort, maybe a bright future or a shameful past!' Freda mentioned whilst glancing past the illusions and staring blankly at the dusky sky. 'Or it shows you nothing! It depends what you want to see really!' she said.

Quinton glanced at the ice towards his left and could see another projection of himself trying to escape from his body. He realised he needed a break from being himself for a while and to be someone else instead whilst the image within the ice vanished before his eyes.

'It looks really beautiful during the summer!' Yumna mentioned whilst trailing behind the angel she loved the most, finding herself doddering towards an uncertain future.

'You haven't once looked at me!' she said and caught Freda's attention.

'I'm sorry!' Freda said and slowed down to walk beside her old lover. 'I'm in a weird space right now, but I'm sure I'll come back!' she said as they held each other's cold hands.

'We will be okay. My love for you will always win!' Yumna said as Freda gently rested her head onto her old lover's right shoulder and reaccepted their love as a symbol of acceptance.

They knew they were different from the rest because of their beautiful relation, and for some reason, it made their love boundless and more special because they loved each other purely and weren't bonded by what others believed to be appropriate.

'I'm shocked we have made it this far!' Quinton said as he caught up to his guardian angel.

Olivia seemed distant from the world they'd become accustomed to because she was wondering if she'd ever be allowed to return back to her earthling given her predicament. She knew the covenant would relieve her from her guardian angel duties if she were to return to her own home but also believed there weren't any other options but to try and convince her elders to release the cavalry of trained warriors to aid those who were lost.

'I'm also shocked, but I believe you would overcome your challenges!' she mentioned whilst dwelling on the punishments she'd receive after.

'Promise me you will come back!' he said, and she blankly hesitated, which gave him the answer he needed to hear. 'In that case, do not forget about me!' he mentioned and glanced up through his own illusions and stared at the dusk sky to chant for positivity.

Olivia leaned closer and whispered into his left ear, 'I will find my way back to you, but whilst I'm away, make sure you don't fall into temptation because it can destroy you. You have been put here for a reason, and it's all up to you now!'

'I understand!' he responded as she glanced towards her own misinterpretation of real love.

She finally understood the lessons she'd learned from their misguided quests for pleasure. Intimacy and real love wasn't a prize given or found easily on the plains paved with greed but given away by the universe as a gift wrapped carefully within one specific person, a human she believed she'd never meet because her time of earth had past. She accepted her misfortune by allowing the idea to pass away from her heart. The idea drifted away as she looked down whilst walking beside her earthling. She glanced towards the direction they were heading and could see an image of Theodore's face projecting on her left peripheral vision, leaving her uncertain of the future as she turned her head towards the left again. The vague visual kept her silent and confused as it dug deeply into her indecisive heart. It seemed to understand her struggle as his face smiled gracefully. She remained stunned at the revelation unfolding right before her naked eyes and therefore smiled back because he was under her skin. His piercing blue eyes had her guard down. She felt nostalgic, weakened by the visual glimmering towards her blue eyes. A part of her wanted to be held tightly and to feel affection. She believed he'd been poisoned by Elle's foul words or merely wielded away by the magic and therefore reserved her judgement until she could fully understand why he'd chosen to act disorderly.

'Don't look at the ice for too long!' Yumna mentioned. 'It will do things to you, unimaginable whims!'

'It's best to stare ahead and focus on your final destination!' Freda also mentioned whilst wondering why her brother had been weakened and blinded by a deceitful lost descendant of witchery.

However, Freda knew his loyalty wasn't as compromised as Olivia had made it out to be. She'd always been sceptical of angels from a different spectrum because of her transparent petty envy towards their strong persona which seemed to appeal to everyone else.

'It's crucial that everyone keeps quiet!' Nathaniel said as they reach the end of the frozen illusive lake.

Victoria performed another magical spell to plunge a hole through the ground wall. They all kept quiet as the hole enlarged before their presence.

'Lead the way, Nathaniel. I must ensure the closure after everyone has passed through their illusions!' Victoria mentioned as everyone walked past, entering into a small clustered space within the wet ground and awaiting for the ice to merge back.

'I hope you have all cleansed yourselves from bad spirits. You need to be one within yourselves from this moment because I know the worst will be upon us soon and we have to be ready for it!' Victoria said whilst making her way through the crowd.

She performed another magical spell to pave another underground route towards the eastern ends of their world and into the cornerstone of their waiting battle. They disappeared into the darkness and embarked on their journey.

Chapter Twenty-Two

Tree House Village

A few hours lapsed into the wary dark night as they all emerged from a hole within a dusty cave. It seemed as if they'd entered into an abandoned shrine gloomy with old candle wax within the small wall pockets at every angle. They all stared towards the left and could see a large pool reflecting linings of bright blue rays onto the grey side walls at the end of the passage and a dark brown wooden cross nailed onto the stone wall within the middle. Their bodies ached from exhaustion as they all doddered with their bare feet bleeding whilst heading towards the large pool. It shimmered brightly onto their eyes. They were extremely frail from dehydration and starving hungry for a feast to quell their pain away. Nathaniel and Cindy stepped onto a few rocks within the pool and gently pressed Miguel's body into the pool whilst the rest assigned each other different tasks.

'I'll stay here and prepare something to eat!' Victoria said, unwrapping her rucksack by untying its brown strings apart.

'We will go and scout out for any intruders in the meantime!' Yumna mentioned and followed Freda towards the left exit assisted by Olivia and Quinton.

They entered the forbidden passage paved between two steep mountain walls. It was haunted by a dreadful silence, and the surface screamed off cool chills. The area reeked dry without any signs of life throughout, almost instilling fear in their hearts as they walked towards an unknown destination.

'I'll leave after you've settled comfortably somewhere. I won't leave you like this!' Olivia said whilst trailing behind her earthling.

'I'm sure we will be fine. I have everyone here to guard me whilst you are away!' Quinton replied and felt a sharp thorn pierce through his right foot.

'It's okay to leave, Olivia. We will ensure his safety!' Yumna mentioned whilst leading them through the passage.

Freda grazed her right fingertips on the right mountain wall, and green roots arose from within. They were amused by the beauty of the growth as her fingertips left a trail of green grass behind.

'I remember they spoke of this place once!' Freda said. 'The land of growth, they called it!' she said and paused as they heard a crackling sound within the distance.

'It's incredible!' Olivia said whilst smiling to the growth flourishing beneath their feet. There were patches of green grass growing from their trail from the cave entrance to their feet.

'They said it feeds off living things and absorb them into nothing!' Freda mentioned as they moved forward and curved towards the right along with the passage itself.

They could see a full moon ahead as the passage ended by a rocky cliff.

'It's so quiet!' Quinton said, and experimented on his own by grazing his left fingers onto the steep walls.

He could feel spots of grass growing from underneath his fingers, growing as he moved forward, and an idea progressed inside of his mind as he established the fundamentals of the growth into his life. The possibilities were endless as he stopped and painted a section of the wall with his bare hands whilst embracing the beautified frame he'd made. It was miraculous as he glanced at multiple tulips flourishing bright amongst the green grass and wild red roses moving up and down slowly. He remembered the exact roses from an old dream and therefore allowed himself to be possessed by the idea of reliving that same dream again. He ran past everyone and drove his heart into free fall, punching through white clouds and plunging through the surface because he knew he wouldn't die. They all rushed behind but weren't able to save him from living his dream. The feeling of living through death rushed through his veins as he entered into the soggy ground and allowed his heart and mind to sprinkle off the dream he'd had once.

A vision he'd embraced once grew to life. He swam upwards and cropped up from within to the brilliance he'd synchronised before with his significant other. There was a large field of gigantic wild red roses snoring heavily towards the left as he stood up whilst covered in dirt. The rest levitated down slowly and stood behind him as he smiled at the beautiful tree houses he'd vividly imagined once. They could see different bright lights flashing from within the tress, and he remembered what they were—small birds sleeping peacefully within their nests. There was a beautiful vortex fixed on the full moon above, clinching onto his heavy heart and gravitating his fears away to mend him whole. He glanced towards its beauty and felt an endless possibility of changing the world. There were beautiful sounds projecting from dozens of red chimes hanging around the area.

'Are you crazy?' Freda asked whilst trying to understand Quinton's train of thought.

'No, he isn't crazy! He believes in a better world, and he isn't afraid to show it!' Olivia said and smiled gracefully. 'I believe in you!' she yelled. 'Now go ahead and dream!' she shouted as his strides grew longer towards the wooden staircase.

He made his way towards the first floor to an empty scenery, which was vacant from his desires, but regardless, he wasn't discouraged much because he'd began to hear Arabella crying out for his attention within the only tree house clustered above every other tree house.

'He dreams of having a baby?' Yumna asked Olivia as they all followed his lead up to what felt like an endless flight of circular wooden stairs and entered a clustered passage blinking brightly with more lights.

He stepped into a vast clustered passage and opened the door without hesitation and waited for all mystical wooden block to form into a staircase whilst the angels stood by the entrance and guarded.

A wave of fresh air glided through the tree hollow within the kitchen on the right side of area, and Olivia could sense her parents' presence evoking fear into her heart. She glanced up as her earthling entered deeper into his dream, and as she turned around to say goodbye, all doors sealed shut. Two lights evolved from behind as she held on to the two of the lost descendants she'd befriended. They remained confused as her parents stepped onto the wooden surface, and they seemed displeased with her actions.

'It's time to go home!' Alexa said and held out her soft hands.

Olivia understood the protocol and therefore turned around and walked towards her parents. They disappeared into thin air right in front of Yumna and Freda who seemed significantly mesmerised by the admiration projected.

'Do you think we will ever see her again?' Yumna asked and held on to her lover's hand tightly.

'I don't think so!' Freda said, holding on to Yumna's hand tightly. 'And honestly speaking, I believe her task here is done. Therefore, she doesn't need to return. I have learned a lot from her. Her heart is beyond beautiful!' she said and followed her lover's lead as they entered the earthling's dream.

The bedroom was illuminated beautifully in different bright colours. They stumbled on to a joyous moment as they saw Quinton standing by the wooden window frame, smiling at his daughter as she giggled out loud.

'She is gone!' Yumna mentioned and stepped closer.

'I know. I could feel it as soon as I entered into the bedroom!' Quinton said but remained calm regardless. He smiled at the beautiful four-and-a-half-pound replica of Juliana Rose.

He felt bonded to his significant other's beautiful heart forever and knew he won't be able to escape from it within his lifetime and therefore accepted their fate as aligned towards a bright future.

'She is beautiful!' Yumna said and gathered around to observe their beacon of hope.

'She really is beautiful!' Freda mentioned. 'May I hold her?' she asked and held out her hands.

'Please!' he insisted and handed over his pride and joy.

'Olivia told me about this other girl you are in love with!' Yumna mentioned and held on to her soft fingers out for the baby to play with. 'She told me about the depth of your relationship. Therefore, I'll make sure you get back to her!'

'We will help you get back to your home!' Freda also mentioned as they bonded with Arabella.

They felt entitled to his quest and personally responsible for his well-being. The main entrance opened up slowly, and they could hear footsteps. Quinton could feel his lover's presence right next to him. She was always there, and nobody else could feel her presence except for him. He loved it that way because it meant he could always be selfish with the happiness she presented.

'Yumna!' Nathaniel called out whilst walking towards a passage underneath the bedroom door above.

'We are coming!' Yumna responded and strolled towards the bedroom door whilst Freda remained glued to the precious baby within her arms.

'You will have a child of your own one day. I believe you will!' Quinton mentioned whilst walking away to console the rest. He stepped onto the mystical wooden as Cindy and Victoria assisted Miguel entered through the main door. His body was pale, poisoned from dark magic.

'Follow me!' he said and guided them through the passage and into an living room connected to the kitchen.

'Who did you find?' he asked curiously because they were underneath a layer of white clouds.

'We followed the patches of green grass and dove off the cliff to find such a remarkable place!' Cindy mentioned whilst gently holding on to her lover. 'But as we followed, the patches began to rot and die from underneath our feet, and right afterwards, the dry ground ate off the rest of the roots!'

'Not to worry, I'm actually growing stronger!' Quinton said whilst staring at the normality in his feet. He felt indifferent which boosted his confidence and allowed him to be extremely positive.

'Let us know when you grow weak. We will take turns at channelling ourselves to the dry soil!' Victoria suggested and assisted Cindy to gently place Miguel onto a torn couch.

She walked towards the kitchen and unfolded everything she'd prepared for them to eat.

'Are you comfortable?' Cindy asked and kissed Miguel's sweaty forehead. He nodded slowly and rested his eyes to fight through the pain within his right thigh.

'We shall rest here and move forward as soon as Miguel has recovered well!' Quinton mentioned and turned away from the wound.

'Sounds ideal, but we mustn't all dwell in sleep without guarding the area!' Nathaniel said and lounged backwards to rest his body.

'It's fine. I'll stay awake and make sure this world doesn't eat us up!' Quinton said whilst crossing over into the kitchen and discovering the pale scaling on his hands as he picked up a small chunk of roasted warthog from a wooden bowl placed on a light wooden counter underneath the moonlight.

He could hear Freda baby-talking to his giggling unborn daughter as she stepped onto the main floor and strolled into the kitchen slowly.

'It's love at first sight!' she whispered whilst adoring Arabella's beauty.

Quinton glanced towards the night sky as white clouds cleared off then rediscovered the steep mountain wall within the distance from where they'd all come from. The bottom view from his tree house was paved with green treetops towards the steep mountain wall, and he could see branches moving to the cool breeze. He glanced ahead again and could suddenly see a horse from on the top cliff with an unknown lost descendant hanging on its back.

'There is a horse!' he mentioned and paused whilst Cindy squinted and observed closely. 'And someone is crawling away from it!' he said as Freda passed his unborn daughter back to him.

'That's my brother!' she yelled in a paranoid state whilst rushing towards the main entrance.

Cindy followed after her impulsive friend as an insurance of safety whilst everyone else remained stationed in the same place. Quinton watched as Theodore dropped like a rock from the top and plunged right through the trees by the mountain wall. He remembered that feeling so clearly, of being backstabbed, falling from a high place, and landing inside an uncertain plain. Every angle had a lesson to give as he explored his mind and realised how beautiful his world could be without any temptation railing him towards disaster. He also knew every beautiful red rose picked from the ground came with a thorn and thus acknowledged the depth within the phrase and mentally prepared himself for what could inevitably be the biggest thorn heading his way. It all seemed too perfect to be true, and the beautiful waves brushing past the treetops at the bottom view made him extremely paranoid. He needed to rest his heart from the massive torment and agony pushing his soul towards fear.

'You can pass your child on to me!' Victoria said. 'I'll keep her safe for you in the meantime!' she said and held on to Arabella gently.

'I'm going for a walk to clear my troubled mind!' Quinton said whilst walking towards the main entrance and discovered his new profound trust in faith.

He stepped away from the depth of his dream and entered his core loneliness. The passages were empty with dried leaves moving as the waves of wind rushed towards him. He felt it pin into his loins as he held on to the wooden railing whilst stumbling down a flight of a circular staircase, and as he wandered towards the next flight of stairs on his left, the wild wind brushed against his body and railed him to walk towards the right passage. His mind was allowably drawing him closer towards another dream he'd had before, and he strolled towards it without hesitation, almost accepting its illusive heritage. He glanced towards the right, at the empty tree houses on the opposite passage and finally learned to appreciate everyone he'd ever met in real life because their relations, regardless of their outcome, had made him into the man he believed he was.

The passage curved towards the right and intercepted a large tree branch. He stepped into the darkness, and he strived within by walking down a circular staircase within the tree branch, succeeding to overcome his fear of the unknown, then branched off into an old dream clustered with bright yellow pixies floating next to long tree branches above. The scenery was mystical and opulently incredible from any other dream he'd had in the past. It was more amplified and incredibly beautiful to his naked eyes. He stepped onto this familiar path paved with soft green grass in between a few wet black rocks, with intentions of seeing his late grandparents seated on top of wet rocks by a river ahead. The soft texture of moist algae soothed his left fingers whilst he grazed his left hand past multiple thin tree trunks beside his path to a familiar dream. He sat down on a black rock, leaned right to wash the dirt from his fingers within the river, and patiently waited for his mind to unveil the truth once more, with high hopes for its relevant significance to bring him comfort. There were distant sounds of a large waterfall ahead. Many owls howling within the tree branches and crickets chipping rushed into his ears at that very moment. He took the moment to focus on his main desire to see love blossom brightly within the darkest parts of his mind. A glow emerged towards the opposite end of the river and evolved into a white horse. He glanced towards the right and discovered a mesmerising reflection within the water as it began to drink from within.

'She's as loyal as horse!' were the words from his late grandmother's voice projected from an old similar dream he'd had in the past synchronising into the present.

He stood up and smiled gracefully to the bright beautiful horse projecting from afar. Its horseshoes turned the water into solid ice at every step within the river, moving forward towards him. He kneeled onto his left knee as it stepped off the river and onto the soft grass right beside the wet black rock he'd sat on before. Its green eyes were glazed with his hopes of a better future, and they seemed to understand everything he was going through.

'Baby!' he whispered.

His eyes closed and were dazed from perfection as he parked his lips onto its head whilst stroking its long cream white mane with his right hand. He waited for the love of his life to appear before him, and within seconds, the beautiful horse slowly shapeshifted and evolved into Juliana Rose wearing a long cream white dress. She grinned happily as they both stood up straight and opened their eyes to observe the scenery around. Their hands were clenched on to each other, and he was mesmerised by her beauty just as much as the first time he'd ever laid his eyes on her. Her hair colour was different—blond—but her curly hair strands remained the same.

'It's time you come home!' she said and glanced at the tree branches above as they moved slowly to the cool breeze brushing past them.

'I'm not ready to come home just yet!' he mentioned, and his words endorsed her heart with sadness.

'You are growing pale again, and it's not only in this world, but in reality too!' she said. 'The doctors are uncertain of your recovery!'

'I'll make it!' he said, trying to assure her. 'I just need to address a few things here before awaking!'

'But promise to come back to me!' she asked. 'Pinkie promise!'

'Pinkie promise!' he said as they locked their right pinkie fingers together.

She held on to his body tightly and kissed his left cheek repeatedly.

'Call out for me, and I will bring you home!' she whispered into his left ear, and he nodded to acknowledge her every word. 'Is there anything else you need from me before I leave?' She asked.

'Yes, there is. Come and lie beside me once more!' he requested and also nodded to acknowledge his words.

'With pleasure!' she said and followed his lead onto the grass path.

They strolled beside the river towards a path he'd never been on before. It curved right into a den covered by algae rocks and patches of soft grass in between. He imagined the perfect place to rest beside his significant other, and the beauty of it unfolded before their eyes as they stepped down into the den. A large tunnel opened up underneath the woods, curving more and more to the left until a dome unveiled itself underneath the water. She took the lead and led him forth through the tunnel. They finally stepped onto small algae rocks and a muddy surface.

'It's so beautiful!' she said as her green eyes lit up to the visuals projecting.

Smooth wooden planks paved across the muddy surface and covered the dome with wood. Fish swam around the clear-sealed dome slowly and shone brightly in different colours, brightening up the water. A wooden bed evolved from the wooden planks below, forming into a queen-size bed in the middle of dome. Magical dust floated from behind and hovered within, creating an enforced safe room within the water.

'Be gentle with me!' she whispered, which told him to rest her body gently into the bedspread. She turned her head towards the right and watched the bedspread sheets ripple in waves slowly. 'We are forever' her heart whispered.

'I love you so much!' he whispered into her right ear, which washed her heart with mixed emotions.

A warm tear leaked from her right eyelid and raced down her right cheek.

'What's wrong?' he asked and paused then brushed away her blond curly hair strands from her forehead. She remained quiet for a few seconds whilst observing his pale face.

'I need you to wake up. I can't go another day without you!' she said as they switched roles. 'I need you to wake up right now!' she yelled.

His heart raced fast.

'We will be together again. I promise!' he said.

'Promise me!' she pleaded whilst taking deeper breaths.

'I'll wake up soon!' he said. 'You have to be patient with me!'

'I'll wait right beside you then!' she mentioned and brought his right hand closer to her soft lips.

'There is so much I still need to address in order for me to grow up!' he said, gently parking his lips onto her forehead.

'As long as you grow from this and come back to me!' she replied. 'I can't raise our unborn child all on my own!'

'You won't have too!' he assured, sounding positive about his health. 'I will regain consciousness and wake up soon!' he said but also knew he was growing weaker by the minute.

The land of growth had started to feed off his soul, and he felt so exhausted, losing his flesh as every minute passed. He couldn't move anymore and thus lay quietly without saying anything conducive.

'You are growing cold!' Juliana mentioned and sat up to pay attention to his change in condition.

His brown eyes remained glued towards his parallel world above and discovered another moment clustered with death. It felt more peaceful this time around because he couldn't hear anything for a while.

Juliana yelled his name repeatedly afterwards as she sat up and shook his arms with both hands. Her beautiful face gushed in fear as she shook his body intensely, trying to grip on to his body tightly as her soul levitated away from his subconscious and swiped back into the real world. She woke up beside his body, panicking as his body tremulously shook on the hospital bed. Juliana yelled out for help to alert the nightshift doctors nearby. Her foetus kicked repeatedly as she stood up, and whilst it did so, he could hear his unborn child's loud cry echo all the way from tree houses. He inhaled the air slowly whilst blinking repeatedly, glancing towards the right side of the bed to an unfamiliar sight.

An angel dressed with the same fashion trend as the rest of the lost descendants appeared. Her wings were dark grey, smuggling towards a faded black colour. Her cheekbones shaded her eyeballs, painting her face possessed. She was followed by an elderly lost angel hovering in mid-air. He was covered by his pitch-black wings, and his body was shrunk into a ball whilst levitating closer, holding an old wooden walking stick. His feet were long, covered in dirt, and bruised at all angles.

'Elle, it's almost time!' the elderly lost descendant mentioned as his wings widened. 'A man is at his weakest when he is sleeping or blindly making love to the woman of his dreams!' he mentioned, hovering beside his daughter.

His deep voice radiated fear into the earthling's heart whilst it throbbed tremendously fast.

'I know, Father. We must move him to a secure location and give you time to perform your magic!' Elle said. 'We must act quickly through because all forces are gaining on us!' she said whilst uplifting the earthling with her own magic.

Quinton yelled out for Juliana whilst levitating in mid-air, and she did the same, but they couldn't hear each other because they were in different worlds. His reality vanished into the dark blue water and reminded him how easily his life could be taken.

Everything clocked slower as they stepped away from the den and back onto the path within the wood heading towards the right. Tree leaves were beginning to rot away slowly as the land ate away the earthling's soul. Quinton could feel his body drying up as his throat clogged dry. His pale skin aged as he looked at his left hand on top of the bedspread and saw his reality flashing within his mind, synchronised to the electrocuting shock to his heart. His mind dove in and out of consciousness repeatedly whilst doctors electrocuted his chest to stabilise his condition. He caught a few glimpses of his significant other weeping from behind the intensive care unit door, causing their foetus to kick her stomach in pain. She fainted as he dove out of consciousness and back into his nightmare.

'We almost had him!' the elderly lost descendant said whilst trailing behind. 'But not to worry, I will bring an end to his existence soon!'

'I know you will, Father!' Elle mentioned whilst leading the earthling's body farther away from the tree houses and into dark woods covered with mist.

'You will . . . not . . . win this war!' Quinton stuttered and coughed as chills crept through his skin and weakened him more.

'The war hasn't even begun!' Elle said and stepped onto a trail of wet rocks within, luring the earthling across the river and farther away from his protective lost descendants.

'You are right. The war was long over. You have already lost!' Quinton mentioned as the elderly descendant began to perform dark magic by releasing black widow spiders from his fingers.

The black widows crawled onto the earthling's face and plunged themselves into his ears, clogging his ear drums and passing from within his mouth webs strings cover his mouth, then crawled all over his body to clock away his nakedness. He couldn't speak nor hear anything whilst they brought him to the edge of a cliff left beside the waterfall. The black spiders crawled away from his body and burned into ashes.

'I will only take a few hours to complete the potion!' the elderly lost descendant mentioned whilst wiping out herbal leaves wrapped with a large moist green leaf from within his buffalo skin pocket by his waist. 'Keep an eye out for any intruders. Our brothers and sisters are on the way!' he said and sat beside the earthling's body and flicked magical white grains of pit sand into the earthling's eyes to daze him into sleep.

Quinton slowly unclenched his guard and laid his head down onto the cliff rock. He railed away from his body in ghost form and levitated upwards from the land of growth. The tree leaves began to turn dry and beige whilst he looked around and felt strong airwaves comb through the woods, resulting in a barricade of demons rushing from the northern dry plain fields above. They halted their black horses by the edge of the mountain wall in large cavalry numbers with endless large trolls and wolves scattered in different directions under the leadership of the earthling's bad consciousness wrapped within a demon. Their energy was fuelled by all the bad deeds deceived humans had ever made on planet Earth, and their demonic ambition was strengthened by the will to escape from the hell they were in. They had absolutely no idea that their handiwork to retrieve the scripture wouldn't be compensated because everything was a lie.

The scripture couldn't be used by anybody else except for the elderly lost angel himself. He had created the illusion because that's what darkness does—it deludes the weak and takes advantage of their desires. He'd also created the scripture himself not so many centuries ago before other souls had parish into the land of growth, leaving him all alone. Many believed that his subconscious immortality was a brutal punishment from a higher power, for creating a porthole between the afterlife and the life before death.

'What about Olivia?' Elle asked. 'We need her too!'

'She will be back. Love does that to the weak!' the elderly lost descendant mentioned, whilst cooking up his potion and deceiving himself to believe love was weak. He didn't understand it, a feeling he wasn't capable of handling because of its strong magnitude and its godly will to mend bridges. 'Elle, go and find your brother, Luther, for me!' he said, mainly focused on creating a spell to destroy the earthling. 'He needs to send a few soldiers this way to guard me whilst I perform the spell. It will be my weakest point, and I can't be in the crossfire when I end the earthling's life!' he mentioned as Elle flew upwards to alert her brother.

She waved her right arm slowly, and flashes of bright light emerged from within her palm. It entailed movement. Thus, the dark army evolved into black smoke, commencing and hovering over woods. Luther plunged downwards in black smoke and landed onto the cliff, emerging out into his darkest self and evolving into monster form.

'Father, it's time for you to honour our agreement!' Luther yelled in between his huffs, kicking a pebble of the cliff with his right foot. 'You promised to release me from this world, and I have brought the last piece of the puzzle to you!'

'There, there my child!' Luke replied whilst mixing black seeds and grinding dried green herbs together within an oval wooden dish. 'Get those lost souls within the tree houses and bring them to me!' he mentioned, coughing repeatedly and spitting out.

Luther stepped onto the frozen river and crossed over onto the muddy path, heading towards the far right to the tree houses clustered above. The ice cracked and humanlike figures emerged from underneath the frozen river. Their bodies were covered in used oil washing off their grey scales, and their feet had long cracked yellow nails raking the mud as they followed Luther towards the darkness.

Luke plastered a mixture of ingredients onto the earthling's bare chest, rubbing it slowly onto the cool skin and causing Quinton's heart to beat slower by the hour. His body temperature declined to an all-time low. He could feel the wrath of a thousand winter seasons relishing through his body, causing his body to shiver and turn his skin pale.

'Father, keep his body warm. Otherwise, we will lose him too quickly!' Elle yelled from above, immediately lowering herself to assist and whisper aside. 'The only way we can extract the scripture from his body is by allowing his death to be slow. It will allow the scripture to levitate upwards slowly!' she said and gently placed her dirty feet onto the cliff. 'Keep his body warm,' Elle mentioned as four purple seeds gravitated and landed onto her right palm.

Luke sprinkled sparks of fire onto the earthling's body and watched spider web strings lit up in flames. Quinton screamed to the top of his lungs as the fire burned his skin. He stared down and saw his soul drifting away from his body. Tears raced down his pale cheeks as the glow within his body started to disappear.

'Let him burn in hell' a voice repeated within Luke's head.

'He will burn in hell just like I did,' Luke said and stood up by using his long wooden stick. 'Elle, deliver those seeds to the shrine and throw them into the pool,' he said and stepped away from the earthling's body.

He gazed up and watched the clouds scatter in different directions then drop into the woods like large heaps of sand, forming into grey fog and darkening the scenery.

'Elle, my dear, go and revive my peasants!' he yelled as his daughter flew towards the steep wall and landed onto a flat ledge. She stepped onto same plain field as the rest before her yet felt different with her motive because was haunted by Quinton's ghost. Her left fingertips left a trail of green grass cropping out from the steep left wall leading towards the shrine. Fresh air rushed past her skin as she entered the cave and became cautious of her motives. There was no turning back, and she knew of the consequence of releasing her father's cavalry. She stepped closer and glanced down at the water rippling slowly, wondering what would happen if she could stop everything from proceeding forth.

'It's okay, my dear. Drop the seeds inside!' her father's voice swept through her right ear as her eyes remained glued to the beautiful light reflecting from the moon outside.

She dropped the purple seeds onto the water and watched them glow brightly as they sunk to the bottom of the pool. Her heart compelled her mind with desires to control the army by herself. She stepped into the pool and felt her cracked ankle completely heal. The seeds slowly deteriorated and turned the water purple, and right as she felt peace, the bottom of pool opened up a four portholes. Beams of light swiped out from all four seeds, and millions of lost souls withdrew from hibernation and arrived to pay their debt to Luke. They all drifted away from the pool and evolved into ghosts then finally evolving into their natural human form as their feet touched the dusty ground. Their bodies absorbed the earthling's subconscious world and ate off his soul, causing everything within the woods to rot.

A breath of life endorsed them with hope as they walked away from shrine and marched towards the ledge to fulfil their part of the agreement. Elle watched women and men who'd already sold their souls stride towards their quest like blind soldiers fighting an endless war. She stood still whilst observing her part in unleashing them into the world and yet dwelled on an excuse of her father. The numbers grew by the minute, and she walked away from the shrine. Candles within the wall shelves lit themselves slowly as she stepped away from the exit. The earthling's soul shrunk as other souls ate from it and the trees below dried up. The visual was clear as she glanced far below and saw her old friends being escorted through the woods and onto the frozen river.

'The world can turn really cold, don't you think?' Luke asked sarcastically as Luther and the human fish-men dragged the lost descendants and threw them onto the solid river, along with Theodore and Miguel who were unconscious throughout.

Shackles cropped out from the ice and clamped on to their wrists and ankles.

'Nathaniel, we meet again!' Luke said whilst releasing black spiders from his fingertips and flicking them onto those lost descendants clamped to the solid river.

Within the nick of time, their ears and mouths were clogged with webs, disabling them from interacting nor reacting to the treachery.

'A temporary sleeping spell will do the trick' he said and flicked black powder onto their faces then turned to the trolls positioned between thin tree trunks. 'Go and prepare for battle. I will be fine here!' He mentioned.

Quinton, in his ghost form, glanced towards the bright full moon above and hoped for some sort of peace to absorb the trouble within his mind. He blinked repeatedly whilst staring above, wondering if his guardian angel would reappear again. The light appeared brighter as the moon expanded its width and shattered into a million pieces.

Those pieces sparkled whilst evolving into bright stars, flashing whilst whizzing and turning into guardian angels wearing shimmering silver armour from their wrists and all the way down to their knees. Their shins and feet were gloved in slim-fitted silver metal.

'The war has begun,' Luke said to the devil clenched to his heart then turned around to face the opposite end of the frozen river,

'Go on, my brothers and sisters! Avenge your past selves, and I will deliver you back to earth in newborn form!' he yelled and watched his cavalry of sin levitate from the treetops then whizz towards the sky to fight against guardian angels.

There were countless numbers of wolves howling and trolls patrolling within the woods and awaiting for the war to land. Luke splashed his son's upper body with a mixture of deer blood and black potion to turn his demon body into human form.

'You need to be as human as possible. It will allow me to send you through easily,' Luke mentioned whilst painting his son's body with more blood.

His daughter landed beside her brother and stared at the dark brown scales which had peeled from Luther's legs. She remained quiet whilst her feathers shredded from her wings, allowing herself to transform into a human. Her wings turned soft and melted onto the cliff rock, detaching from her back and burning into ashes.

'We must find a safe haven to complete the process and allow our magic to work properly,' Elle said and picked up the earthling's body by wielding her own magic from her fingertips.

She stepped away from the cliff and into the woods on the right side. There was a foul smell of rotten deer whiffing past her pink nose. She could see its rotten corpse covered in frost beside the rocky path she was using to find a rabbit hole. Its corpse troubled her heart because she absolutely loved harmless animals. Her family followed as they all stepped on a lot of twigs on the path and detoured towards a rabbit hole clustered within the darkness by the near left, secluding themselves from a catastrophic war approaching. They could smell death at every whiff as the smell of dead rabbit reeked within the clustered space.

'Place his body!' Luke commanded, pointing towards the cold ground with his wooden stick.

'Elle, I must your strength too to find us a scared passage between two worlds,' he mentioned whilst painting his daughter's body with deer blood. 'A new era of our lives has begun,' he said.

'Let's get it over with already!' Luther yelled as his human body adapted to the conditions around. He began to shiver as a cold breeze brushed past his body. 'I shouldn't be this weak whilst there is a war outside!' he said as his sister cloaked his body with dark shades of warmth.

'Be patient, my brother!' she said and stood beside him, clenching onto his left hand with her right hand.

'Just a while longer, and we will be out of this place, my son' Luke said and poured the last bit of blood over his head.

They stood still as Luke extracted his daughter's powers by pulling an invisible rope from within her chest and allowed it to pass into his chest. He grew stronger whilst she grew weaker by the second, and his body broke away from the bondage of old age. His children felt vulnerable as they stood beside each other in human form.

The night sky darkened whilst guardian angels fought against demons, wolves, trolls, and human fish. The woods were clustered with horror at every angle. Sharp daggers and swords clashed. Blood poured, and horrific sounds lashed out at every turn. Olivia searched for her earthling within the foggy woods whilst he stared down at the war commencing within his mind. It left her restless and horrified whilst observing the catastrophic imbalance Quinton caused and inflicted to himself. There were guardian angels flying past and through his ghost, plunging themselves into the woods to fight against all the demons which had caused havoc. His eyes remained glued towards the ledge leading to the shrine. He could see more guardian angels landing onto the passage to fight against those resurrected from within the shrine.

Lightning flashed and thunder strikes railed through the dark sky, zapping within the atmosphere in the form of perfectly aligned teeth. A vortex opened within the lightning pattern. It began to suck the earthling's life from his body. Quinton looked up within his ghost form to the visualised beauty unfolding before his naked eyes. Glimpses of bright gold burned his eyes; therefore, he kept them shut whilst moving closer to uncertainty. His heart throbbed extremely fast because he was terrified of the truth—a beautiful scripted truth of love relishing through his soul for eternity.

Quinton opened his brown eyes to an astonishing moment of strength, finding himself back inside his body within the rabbit hole, but he couldn't move because he was paralysed whilst dangling in mid-air. His chest and rib cage had been opened up by Luke who'd attempted and failed to remove the earthling's heart from within. Quinton couldn't be killed by any element of evil, nor could his heart be tempered with because it was gilded from gold. It shone brightly as its golden liquid streamed through his arteries and through his veins.

'Do it now!' Elle yelled as her father attempted to rip the golden heart from the earthling's chest but found himself blinded sided by the result.

Quinton's body slowly turned into solid gold, and his body mass increased, turning his body into a statue whilst his mind drove further away from his monsters and into his world of peace.

He could see his beautiful angel, Juliana, waiting for him along the beach on an island secluded from the rest of the world. She was standing right beside a steep embankment, waving at him with her right hand and smiling beautifully as she did when he'd first met. Her flawless skin shone brightly like a commercial farm field full of tulips during the spring season. She was wearing a long white summer dress, and its fabric glittered with peace.

'He is finally home!' Juliana said, smiling whilst opening her arms up to him. He rushed over and clenched into her body tightly then picked her body up.

They span around, laughing out loud and cherishing their moment of peace whilst the sea current washed onto his feet. She glanced down and her long curly brunette hair strands covered his face. Her lips were as soft, warm, and tasteful as a freshly baked muffin. They French kissed as the sky turned musk whilst the day turned into dusk. Quinton felt Arabella's tiny hands grip on to his right thigh. Her innocent touch startled him.

'Dad!' she said and glanced up whilst clenched on to his beige linen pants. He gently offloaded his lover and glanced down at love in its purest form.

Arabella smiled just as gracefully as her mother would, giggling to the joys of new profound youth gushing from harmony. She jumped as another sea wave washed onto her parents' feet, but failed to keep her white dress from getting wet on the tips beside her ankles.

'Thank you for this gift!' Quinton mentioned whilst picking up his daughter to observe her remarkable resemblance to Juliana.

'You are welcome, my love,' Juliana replied and stood beside her family for a while. 'Come, I want to show you something!' Juliana said as Quinton gently placed Arabella onto the moist sand.

'Arabella, lead the way, baby,' she said and gestured to her daughter. Arabella walked towards the green grass embankment towards the right and stepped onto a staircase painted beige.

'There are some people I want you to meet!' she said and held on to her husband's smooth right hand with her soft right hand.

'Where are we going?' Quinton asked whilst following love to its core.

'We are going to meet those who've pledged for your heart to be saved,' Juliana said and turned around to see her husband's reaction to the scenery unveiling itself before his eyes. 'Arabella, just wait a little bit, my lovey!' she said as her daughter paused halfway on the bridge between them and a large patch of land.

A cream white wooden double-storey beach house cropped out from a large imprinted blueprint on the sand. Its beauty flourished in the middle of the clustered jungle, painting an exquisite canvas and inspiring hope to his heart.

'I hid this place away from you because I didn't want your demons to find it and destroy it. You are finally home now, our real home!' Juliana mentioned and parked her soft lips onto his for a while.

'If you do not wake up, then I will come here and be with you, my love. If you don't make it to the real world, then I will take my own life and be with you here. We will be here with you!' she whispered into his right ear. 'You don't have to fight anymore. You can finally be free!' she mentioned and held on to him tightly. 'I will support your every decision, okay?' she said, assuring him with loyalty.

He remained quiet whilst trying to dwell on the idea of peace and weighing other factors, such as his ambition to succeed, his will to live, and his strive to change people's lives.

'Our child needs to live. Therefore, we must go back and give her a better life than the one we have. We owe her perfection,' Quinton said and looked at his daughter, admiring and cherishing his pride and joy.

A cloudless sulphur butterfly landed onto Arabella's right index finger and made her beautiful face flourish with happiness. She moved and startled the butterfly, causing it to fly towards the beach house.

'Dad, come!' Arabella yelled whilst jumping up, trying to capture the butterfly with her hands.

'I'm coming, baby!' Quinton responded and became attentive to his wife again, passionately kissing her lips and assuring her heart of his intentions to escape from his troubled mind.

'It is breathtaking, don't you think?' she asked and he nodded whilst glancing far head at the waterfall in background and birds swiping through sky, landing within jungle. They could hear canaries chirping within and the sound of waves clashing against the rocks.

'I love it, but it's not home, my love. It's an illusion, and I know we will never be truly happy here until we have enjoyed our lives to the fullest. I don't want to be haunted by regret and torment because if that happens, then I will turn into my own worst nightmare. I will turn into those demons, and I will never be at peace, for as long as other factors dwell within my mind, then I will remain restless, my love!' Quinton said as they started walking towards the beach house.

Juliana nodded, agreeing with her husband's words whilst following his leadership.

'Whatever you want, my love, I will always love you until the end of time with my restful mind, my beautiful heart, and peaceful soul!' she said as she gently placed her cool left hand onto his right shoulder.

'I will be here dwelling inside of your mind, joyfully dancing inside of your heart whilst playing your favourite song—one perfectly aligned with the rhythm of your heartbeat!' Juliana mentioned as Quinton turned right around to kiss the love of his life.

Arabella giggled whilst watching her parents demonstrate real love. She unintentionally captured the moment from a distance, subconsciously plastering it onto her walls of excellence and mentally placing the visual deeply within her heart for eternity. It would remain to her that real love did exist, and it would rail her mind towards making the right choices instead of growing up like a small percentage of scornful, scolded women who live their lives by misinterpreting the meaning of feminism and using it to disrespect men because their fathers were never around to teach them obedience, and how special a woman should be treated therefore rallying their attempts to find some sort of real affection as a blinded misguided quest. Arabella rushed over towards her beautiful canvas of love.

'Come with me, Dad!' Arabella said and attempted to pull her father who'd she began to see as the love of her life, not that she knew the significance of the lesson she'd just learned.

'Go! I'm right behind you both' Juliana said, pushing her husband forward for a while and then waited behind to observe his arrival.

Juliana smiled because she believed he'd finally found peace within his mind, and it was all she'd ever wanted for him instead of him pursuing and fighting an endless war against the real world he'd become accustomed to. His pleasant smile said it all as he stepped onto the wooden stairs in front of their home.

The sun vanished and the sky turned dark, unveiling the beautiful significance of the night. The sky was filled with bright stars clustered amongst auroras flagging slowly with the cool breeze. Quinton impounded every glimpse of harmony and peace presented before his eyes, whickering away his guard and drifting his mind back onto the vague idea of allowing himself to pass on.

Pouch lights of the beach house lit brightly as Arabella slid the sliding doors apart and entered into their home, whilst calling out, 'Grandpa!'

Arabella's words immediately alerted a red flag within Quinton's mind, for his heart had been grounded into guilt, feeling responsible for his biological father's death. He hoped for difference to prevail before his presence whilst Juliana drew the curtains aside.

'I'm in the study!' an old man yelled, coughing out whilst doing so at the end of the hollow passage far head.

Quinton sceptically turned his head to the left for clarity as Juliana quickly detoured towards the kitchen to switch off the electrical stove and place the boiling pots onto the kitchen sink.

'See, I told you that she is loyal to you,' Elizabeth, his deceased grandmother, said whilst attempting to step onto the staircase above covered by carpet décor.

'Nana, don't move. I'm on my way!' Quinton said, rushing through the hollow passage then stepping onto the wooden staircase right beside the kitchen. 'You shouldn't use the stairs alone,' he said and gently assisted her graceful grandmother. 'Hold my hand,' he suggested, but she dismissed his hands.

'Well, I'm fine, but I'm not happy with you!' Elizabeth said, sounding agitated and disappointed.

She gripped the wooden railing with her left hand and planted her left foot onto the first step. Her body appeared weaker than he remembered from his last dream of his grandparents advising him to stay with Juliana at all cost.

'You see that woman right there! She has always been your muse, your inspiration, your last breath before death, so I want you to look at her properly because you will lose her if you don't fight through this coma, and you will be here through eternity, unrested in agony, wishing you could have done certain things differently' Elizabeth said, pointing at Juliana from above.

Quinton glanced at the love of his life through an indoor framed window whilst his grandmother spoke. He realised he hadn't fulfilled his promise. He'd kept to his word, which also made him discover he'd lost integrity, making him less of man.

'She can't raise Arabella by herself, and you know this!' Elizabeth mentioned whilst Quinton's heart throbbed faster, arising his attention his cowardly mentally. 'It's fine if you aren't there. Just know that she will resent you for it and end up hating you for leaving her down there. We both know she would never end her own life to be with you, especially with Arabella on the way!' she said whilst stepping farther down. 'Now, help me down there, and go see your grandfather down the hall. I'll go to the kitchen and help your wife prepare dinner' she mentioned whilst Quinton realised the difference between appearance and reality.

Arabella rushed in from down the hall and startled Elizabeth who'd completely forgotten that her great-granddaughter was amongst them.

'I'm good here!' Elizabeth said. 'Arabella, go and help out your mother in the kitchen. I'm on my way there as well!'

'As for you,' he said to Quinton, 'I'm going to go speak to your fiancée and assure her that you'll be back. I will restore hope into her heart and make sure she doesn't have doubts about you,' she said whilst pointing at her grandson, reinstalling discipline into his world. 'Now go and speak to Prince. He's not pleased with your decor!' she mentioned as Quinton planted his right foot onto the edge of the lengthy dark blue carpet, sceptically stepping forth with his left foot to be consoled by his late grandfather.

Quinton immediately wondered why his mind had deluded his heart to temporarily submitting to the illusion of peace when a lot was still at stake. He could peripherally see his bleak past flashing through the side hall doors and the violence which had also contributed to his persona of a defined, broken young man consistently seeking out for affection. His stroll towards the doors ahead gifted him with the ability to understand his pain and the ability to overcome it by forgiving everyone who'd ever inflicted pain onto him. All the vivid large colourless art work within golden frames pinned to the walls in between the open doors projecting Quinton's dark historic past turned alive as he stood still. He observed how mysterious and beautiful art could be. Black swans paddled and dove into the pond within one frame, and shaded white and black roses planted within a farm field started to move within another frame as the breeze rushed through the passage and forced him to face the doors ahead. He stepped closer towards uncertainty as all the images beside him turned dark grey. A part of him was embarrassed, afraid of facing his late grandfather because he knew he'd disappointed the only person he'd always looked up to whilst growing up. He tried to envision a different visual in the next room as he slowly placed his hands onto two golden knobs and unhinged the doors apart.

There was an awful smell of a human corpse rotting within the room as Quinton entered and discovered his late grandfather who seemed close to meeting the same inevitable fate as before seated on a large rocky wooden chair farther right, clustered in between a pile of light brown envelops on the wooden floor and a wide table filled with dozens of open letters. His body was cloaked with a light brown linen cloth, covering him from his shoulders and all the way down to his ankle, allowing his dry feet to be exposed.

'You request so much,' Prince mentioned as he turned around to see his grandson. 'How do you expect me to send these with me every Sunday when you haven't lived up to your words?' he asked and threw another opened letter onto the table.

His face was embedded with wrinkles, and his hair had blown dry white. He slowly stood up and aided himself by gently pressing both hands onto the edge of the table, allowing him to lift his aged legs over the heap of letters clustered besides the wall and the corner of the table left beside his hip.

'Papa,' Quinton said and moved with caution, uncertain of his grandfather's next words. 'You do not look well!' Quinton stated as Prince stepped forth for a hug.

'Of course I'm not well. I haven't rested because I'm busy trying to advocate for all your sins to the court of pure justice,' Prince said and held on to his only grandson. 'I swear I have been there awfully a lot, more than anyone I know around these parts,' he mentioned then attempted to laugh but choked as a clot of phlegm clogged his throat. He coughed repeatedly as he reached for his walking stick beside the table.

'You have grown weaker than I last remembered!' Quinton said, whilst drowning in guilt.

'Yes, yes, looking out for my descendants is an exhausting job. I shouldn't be aging, but I am. Maybe it's because I've implanted my heart towards keeping you all from death, and maybe it's the reason why I'm this exhausted too because you are in great danger. However, I'm glad that you and I finally have the opportunity to talk again,' Prince mentioned and moved towards another door situated towards their right.

A cool breeze wandered through as Quinton gently opened the sliding door for his late grandfather and assisted the old man through an empty balcony situated three metres above the sand.

'I must go and make an immediate application for your safety, my son!' Prince mentioned as they stood onto a beige wooden staircase leading towards the bottom, and as they stood onto the beach sand, Prince called out, 'Massey!' repeatedly and waited.

A large black goose quacked loudly as it appeared from within the jungle and flapped its wings apart, moving closer towards its handler. There was a navy blue suede rucksack strapped to its body. Prince reached up and slowly rubbed its neck with his right hand whilst struggling to balance his weight off his left hand with the walking stick pinned into the sand.

'Walk with me,' Prince mentioned whilst steeping forth onto a sandy path trailing towards the rocky wall ahead. Quinton turned around to observe the goose again as it started to trail behind them. He glanced up at the beach house as a shadow preoccupied the bright light. Juliana stepped onto the ground level balcony and squinted whilst looking for her beloved.

'The food is ready, my love!' she yelled as her eyes found Quinton.

'I'll be there in a bit!' he shouted.

'Hurry up. We don't have much time,' Prince said whilst walking away.

'Okay, my baby, hurry back to us!' Juliana yelled back whilst Quinton stepped backwards, breaking twigs underneath his feet at every step. He turned around and jogged to catch up to his late grandfather.

'It's important that you focus on yourself first before you proceed on focusing on her. Otherwise, this dream won't exist within the next hours. Your body is in critical condition,' Prince said, whilst walking farther away from the beach house lighting and into the darkness.

Quinton followed as they both embarked through the jungle. The sand path narrowed yet remained slightly bright whilst everything else turned pitch-black. Tree leaves covered the path ahead, and it seemed as if the night starts were shrinking into nothing whilst Quinton looked up to the beauty of darkness adorning his heart. He immediately realised that dwelling within that part of his mind seemed to bring him pleasure. He'd finally grown tired of running away from the worst part of himself by learning to be at peace with his fully defined character of a scared individual walking the plains of uncertainty with the hope of achieving happiness. He stood still and racked the grains of sands underneath his feet whilst his grandfather flicked grains of golden sand from within his waist pocket. The scenery lit up brightly around them as golden sand grains slowly levitated and span around in anticlockwise motion.

'Now that you finally understand yourself and finally understand the meaning of personal growth, then you can recover properly!' Prince mentioned. 'Everything will wind anticlockwise from this moment forth, allowing you to grasp full knowledge of everything around you. It will all be more defined, and you will see clearly for what life is really about. You can always use your mind to get ahead, but the key to succeeding and finding true happiness is by learning to listen to your heart and by learning to put your needs first before anyone else's. Learn to love yourself. It will give the love of your life the opportunity to love you better when you care take of yourself first,' Prince said as the grains sparkled whilst spinning slowly.

'You do not have to run away from your demons, but instead own them and discipline them. Enslave them and claim ownership of your throne. Your queen is patiently waiting for you to stand tall and become the man I know you will be,' Prince mentioned then started to move farther down onto a slope.

Quinton followed as the golden grains moved along with them. He soon felt the irritation of mosquitos biting his left forearm.

'Take in that pain and understand the privilege you have always had. There are people within the African continent who experience malaria and experienced pain throughout their lives. Take in this experience and understand that their voids runs deeper than you can ever imagine because of the extreme poverty that lingers around them,' Prince stated and stood onto a flat rock beside a streaming river, whilst looking up at the waterfall raining down towards the left.

'Can you feel your blood being sucked?' Prince asked and turned around whilst trying to instil a deeper meaning into his grandson's mind.

'It's that feeling of something being taken away from you, and you know that there is nothing you can do but leak. That disgusting thought that everyone has when those above you take hope away from your heart by taking away your independence. It is right there taken right underneath your nose whilst you watch it happen! The world is restless with loud cries of help, and nobody is helping. You all need to come together and forgive each other for the pain you have all put yourselves through. Add peace into your lives and stop with the greed!' he mentioned as his black goose plunged itself into the water and settled besides the rock.

'Will I see you again?' Quinton asked whilst assisting Prince onto its back.

'I'm sure you will one day. It shouldn't be soon though!' Prince said and walked farther onto its scapula and sat onto his shoulders then held on to a golden chain attached to its neck brace. 'Now go back and live up to your full potential, my son!' Prince mentioned whilst storing his walking stick better his right thigh and a navy blue suede rucksack.

His black goose paddled and moved along with the stream. Quinton looked up as the sun dusked from the west, bringing a new day into his life, and finally understood what his late grandfather meant by everything unwinding, for his heart was beginning to detach itself from everything which had tormented his mind with fear.

'The minute you hear a loud cry within your mind, then you must fight with every bit of strength to dive out this place and finally enslave your demons' Prince yelled whilst streaming farther away and entering a dark cave.

An explosion within the water lifted the goose upwards through an open hole above, allowing it to fly towards the north. The bright sun slowly unveiled itself over the waterfall from above whilst it drifted towards the east. It seemed as though everything was starting to move faster as he turned around to head back to the beach house. Warm breezes brushed past him as he rushed back to his beloved whilst calling out her name. Paranoia pumped through his arteries as he called out for his child's name repeatedly, hoping for an answer, but nobody responded as he climbed the staircase and rushed through the ground-level balcony.

'Yes@' Juliana yelled and rushed towards the hallway, uncertain of her lover's sudden panic. 'What's wrong?' she asked.

'Nothing really, I always feel like I'm losing you, you know!' he mentioned and held on to her tightly, passionately kissing her lips.

'Where's Nana and Arabella?' he asked as she pulled her face away to observe the signs projecting from his sweaty face.

'You are getting cold again!' she mentioned and held his hand, guiding him up the wooden staircase and straight through a hollow passage decorated with empty golden frames in between bedroom doors. 'They went for a walk. Arabella wanted to go and feed the dolphins, so Nana took her to do so!' Juliana mentioned as Quinton turned his heavy head towards every open bedroom door whilst walking towards their main bedroom suite. 'Don't worry so much, my love!' Juliana said and turned around.

'Hold my hands' she suggested and stepped forward to park her lips onto his lips.

'Your vivid mind is always drifting away, and I just want you to be happy, my love. I want you to feel my insides,' she mentioned and guided his right hand towards her left thigh.

He gripped on to her dress as she pulled every inch of its fabric with her soft hands, gently guiding his right hands in between to please his beloved.

'You know exactly what I need to hear,' he said whilst staring at the wooden ceiling, in need of relief from frustration and inhaling large amounts of air.

Essentially they craved that addictive drug of intimacy which seemed to place them on a completely different spectrum whilst making love intensely, and it also seemed to mend their broken hearts whole from time to time. Juliana couldn't quite understand what it was about Quinton which made her feel invincible and loved like she was the only girl in the world. In all aspects, she was the only one in his world which inevitably made her feel safe from her own demons. It was all so consuming, to say the least, and she knew there was no point of return as he had his way.

He felt so connected to her at that moment as he used his right hand to brush her curly brunette hair strands from her forehead. She opened her dreamy green eyes and looked into his heavy, strained brown eyes.

'You can finally heal now,' she said and held his head close to her heart. 'It's okay to let go of your pain. It doesn't have to define you anymore. You do not have to be angry forever,' she mentioned.

He could hear her heart beating faster.

She withheld from expressing her thoughts as her inner voice stated, 'Please wake up already.'

'I miss you!' she yelled.

'I miss you too,' he responded and glanced down to discover Juliana's eyes streaming with tears. 'Hey, no, don't cry' he said.

'I need you back home now!' she mentioned, sobbing throughout as he held on to her tightly.

'I will come back. I'm trying to come back!' he said.

'Well, try harder' she yelled and smacked his upper left chest with her right palm, trying to inflict some sort of pain to back him back to life.

'You have to be patient with me. There is something I have to do still. I'm still trapped because of it, and I won't allow myself to wake up if I have not yet dealt with it properly, so please understand,' he pleaded.

Quinton glanced towards the right view and watched the sun disappear towards the west, turning the sky darker. Juliana rested beside him, trying to gasp for more air as he stared towards the ocean, gazing at the darkness approaching their beach house.

'What are you looking at?' Juliana asked and turned her head towards the left to catch a glimpse of the night arriving. 'The day went by so quickly!' she mentioned and stood up in her natural form then stepped farther away from the bed, slowly heading towards the glass wall to observe the scenery properly.

Quinton followed yet moved with hesitation, unsure of what to make of the fog hovering closer to the beach. He held on to his beautiful lover tightly, almost clenching her out of fear, staring at the empty pitch-black sky, hoping for some sort of direction to lead him to clarity. His right hand remained glued on to Juliana's right hand at that moment. His intuition slowly gravitated his left foot backwards, advocating for him to run away from the darkest part of himself.

'No, don't go anywhere,' Juliana said whilst pulling him back to discipline his own monsters eating away his soul. 'Confront your darkest fears. I will be right here with you when you do,' she mentioned as stood in front of him and allowed him to gently place his arms around her body. 'Close your eyes and listen to your heart,' she mentioned and shut her eyes, channelling her peace into his mainframe, allowing her lover to settle onto his empire state of mind.

'You do not have to run anymore, you can finally tame your monsters and put them away right here, Quinton. Listen to your heart and allow it to work with your mind. Mend yourself and come home to me,' she mentioned as he kept his eyes shut, trying to settle the score with the dark grey fog hovering before the wooden walkway ahead by the beach. 'I'll be in bed. Just stand here and enslave everything holding you back from becoming great,' she mentioned and turned around, passionately kissing his lips as if she'd never see him again. 'I will always be here,' she whispered and stepped away. She slowly swept past him and walked away from him.

'No matter what happens after this, I will always remain proud of you,' she mentioned whilst kneeling onto the bed and entering their cream white duvets to cover herself from appearing vulnerable before her lover's ruthless worst self, and he stood there by the glass wall, unashamed of appearing naked and weak to his hinged torturous personality.

There was a deafening silence amongst the fog of things whilst he waited for his worst self to appear before his presence. Time winded slower as he turned around to speak to his beloved, only to find her gone. He rushed towards their bed and uncovered the duvet then threw the sheets onto the floor, trying to dig deeply into the bed, but only to find his lover gone. A tear raced from his right eye and streamed down his right cheek as he stood up straight and walked towards the glass wall.

The dark grey fog appeared from within the golden frames around the beach house and swept past the empty hallways and narrow passages, striving faster towards the main bedroom suite to consume the last bit of his soul. He immediately turned around and faced it as it rushed towards him within impeccable force, gliding through the room in slow motion, whilst he noticed blood dripping from his right nostril and could hear the sound of people crying almost as if he was right there within the drought lands of the Middle East with millions of refugees seeking asylum from the devastating wars within his mind.

He couldn't quite grasp knowledge of the views swiping past his eyes as the fog spiralled around his body, slowly moving in towards his soul to consume him into darkness. His legs failed him as he dropped onto both knees and pleaded for mercy not only for himself but for everybody else who'd ever done anything wrong to bring out the wrath of spiritual justice. He could feel the cold fog scraping his skin, trying to grip on to the light glowing within his body. The dreadful pain of those enslaved in the twenty-first century working as slaves and in cheap factories seemed to grip on to his goodness, and he finally felt sympathy for those incarcerated from living not as freely as he did. It turned his whole perception of life around, uncloaking his dark future and reversing his fate of death, unwinding the thorns of evil from piercing into his soul.

He felt purified as he fell onto the wooden floor in his natural form, gazing towards the right glass wall and zoning out towards the jungle trees beside the beach house. The dark grey fog slowly evaporated into nothing whilst he lay by myself, shaken into a paralyzed state and trying to grasp the knowledge of his newly found freedom from running away from the person he believed he'd become once he stopped running.

Chapter Twenty-Three

Light Feathers

A stream of tears raced down Quinton's cheeks he attempted to open his bruised eyes whilst waking up from his dreadful vile nightmare, glancing up at the dark empty sky as Olivia flew him away. He felt her scapular blades gently squeezing his rib cage repeatedly and enabling fresh air to enter into his lungs. The air unclogged his heart and mind from suffocating, which inevitably allowed him to completely let go off his dreadful past. His long arms and long legs were knotted tightly to each other, allowing his guardian angel to carry him away without dropping him from above. He slowly turned head to the right and peripherally saw the woods burning in bright flames and also discovered light clouds hovering closer from the west and heading towards their place of departure. It was the dawn of a new day as the sun also appeared brighter than usual.

The unclear visual left him stunned and completely baffled, to say the least. His eyes were blood-shot red and remained blurry throughout whilst he blinked and attempted to see properly. He looked down and realised that the cut on his chest and the void within his heart was beginning to mend whole. His dry, pale skin and buffalo straps wrapped around his sensitive parts were plastered with his own bloodstains, and he could feel his body aching from the bruises cropping out of his skin. There was a sense of relief gushing through his veins as his guardian angel guided him farther away from the rotting woods filled with indifferent demons of different shapes. He'd finally escaped from the evil that controlled his darker side and the feeling of fresh air rushing and brushing against his bruised face quilted his light-feathered heart with liberty.

Olivia turned her head towards the right and made eye contact with her beloved earthling. Her black hair brushed Quinton's face as he glanced towards the empty blue sky, chanting for pure happiness as he tried to smile through the cuts within his mouth. His scripted ink tattoo evaporated from his back and swept through his insides, plunging itself into Olivia's body in the form of a glowing white seed. It defused its ability from both parties and permanently implanted itself within her massive heart, growing impeccably fast whilst it sowed her arteries with glowing threads fabricated from love. Quinton knew his monsters would never find his scripture. For as long as Olivia kept it within herself, then he would never be at risk again.

'This is my gift to you,' Quinton whispered into Olivia's left ear as her veins boiled whilst her body adapted to the change of her heart growing bigger. 'You can find real love soon, but also remember to keep me inside of your heart when you do so,' he said, and she could finally feel real love warming up her heart. 'I'm sure this will enable you to understand the magnitude of the feeling I have for Juliana. You will finally know how to love someone just as deeply!' he whispered again and allowed his guardian to grasp the idea of the finding real love.

'Thank you so much,' she whispered back to him as he began to drift off into sleep again, drifting back through Olivia's ability to synchronise her thoughts into his blank memory.

She narrowed the passage within her mind, allowing her memories to remain blocked away for a few seconds because she was unsure if it was safe for him to plunge his curious mind back to the moment when she landed within his main tree house. Her head began to ache as she stalled at his curiosity,

'It's okay. I'm strong enough to see everything now!' he said, transmitting a message from his mind and sending into onto hers without speaking.

'Are you sure?' she asked, transmitting a message back to her precious earthling.

He slowly nodded whilst allowing his mind to struggle through the narrow passage with her mind. The visual was so clear as their minds fused together. He became a part of her and could recollect everything she was feeling and also hear everything just as clearly as she could.

Quinton felt Olivia's body swiping through the sky amongst other guardian angels, flying faster towards the rotting woods to destroy the evil which had plunged its poisonous black seed within the his soul. He could see the dark grey fog clustered in between the dried brown leaves which were falling off the rotting branches. Demons took off from the dried grass and flew towards the wary sky in attempt to stop Quinton's faith from releasing him from the worst part of himself.

Olivia whiskered through the collisions above the trees and through the weak branches stacked together. She broke through the kitchen ceiling of her earthling's main tree house, yelling out for Arabella repeatedly as she quickly rushed through the kitchen entrance and towards the main entrance but quickly diverted her attention back to her earthling.

'Quinton!' she yelled repeatedly within the dark grey fog inside the tree house. She slowly turned her head towards the right, squinting as she slowly looked up at the wooden blocks levitating as a staircase towards the only bedroom door on the first floor.

'Quinton, is that you?' she asked whilst slowly levitating towards the bedroom door.

A beige mug tipped from the edge of a wooden stool besides the bed and broke into a dozen pieces on the wooden floor right as she opened the bedroom door. She discovered a shadow swiping past the hollow tree at the end of the bedroom and therefore rushed towards it. The dark shadow plunged itself into the dried leaves, which led her to dive into the trees below and land onto the fourth storey passage, where demons and angels were clashing with their swords and daggers. The floor was smudged with maroon blood everywhere as she slowly moved towards the right, trying to avoid the war occurring everywhere else. She could hear wolves howling in the distance and trolls groaning at the bottom of the communal area. There were loud sounds of feathered dragons hovering over the trees, causing all the dried leaves to fall off from the branches as winds grew stronger by the second. Olivia rushed towards the secluded passage at the end of the corridor and followed the shadow's whisper through the darkness. It waited for her to catch up and then held onto her right hand.

'Do not be alerted. I am Quinton's deceased grandfather, and at this very moment, I am also speaking to my grandson and helping him return back here, but we must move quickly because he doesn't have much time,' Prince mentioned whilst leading Olivia down a flight of clockwise wooden stairs.

'Where are we going exactly?' she whispered and sounded absurd within the darkness because Prince could merge with the darkness for the time being.

'To find him and bring an end to his torment' he whispered and swiped through the darkness. He called out, 'Pssst, over here!'

Olivia squinted towards the dark path ahead, trying to follow someone she couldn't see properly.

'Where are you?' she asked in a low tone, crouching to see ahead.

There were five humanlike structures standing on guard beside the frozen river. She crawled with caution, trying to find an alternative route to find her earthling through the fog of things.

'Do not move,' Prince advised Olivia within the dark patch between two dried trunks and an oval rock on the path.

Olivia crouched beside a large grey rock as Prince's shadow moved and crushed onto numerous twigs ahead to alert the humanlike structures which appeared to be men covered in silvery bright fish scales, but their language was different as they communicated in Silican. The leader gestured for all of them to spread out in different directions. They all moved into different directions. Olivia waited as one stepped closer towards the large grey rock.

'Pssh,' Prince whispered from behind which essentially caught the attention of the human fish. It immediately turned, which allowed Olivia the chance to strike it from behind.

She jumped into its back and plunged a sharp knife into its cervical vertebra. It dropped onto the ground as she removed her knife with her right hand, slowly wiping the blood off by using her left index and middle finger.

'Sushi is so overrated if you ask me,' she mentioned and cautiously stepped farther towards the dark path, contemplating her next move and wondering if it were wise to cross the frozen river and onto the other side. She stood still and waited for Prince to consult her further.

'No, don't leave this path!' he whispered into her ear, and farther down by the cliff, she could see seven lost descendants unconsciously clamped onto the frozen river.

She rushed farther down and hid behind a dead tree trunk then checked the coast for any other strange demons lurking around. There two trolls standing on the other end of the river, hidden within the shaded trunks ahead. They'd seen her bright clothes moving as the wind brushed past, leaving a trail of dried leaves on the path. Olivia slowly inhaled a whiff of foul rotten deer as she plodded forth, weighing her options at that very moment and waiting for insight from her earthling's deceased grandfather who seemed to have vanished into nothing. She could hear Quinton screaming out in pain within the dark forest yet felt incredibly helpless.

Olivia watched as Quinton's soul swiped upwards towards the sky, and at that very moment, she also discovered something so significant and extraordinary about the lost descendants clamped onto cool ice. They allowed their souls to replace his soul within the ground to give Quinton a chance to come back to his own body instead of remaining trapped inside of his own thoughts. Their bodies sunk through the frozen ice, and the devastated environment shot up life again. Patches of dried grass began to change back into pastures green. All the dried autumn leaves lifted up from the grounds and levitated, brushing past Olivia's body and flying back to their rightful places within their stems. The scenery changed and looked healthier than ever before.

The atmosphere appeared warmer as the sun unveiled itself from the west and the dark grey fog hovering around slowly evaporated as Olivia unveiled herself to the trolls standing on the other end of the river. She stood there as a part of the war appeared on her domain. Other guardian angels landed beside her as more demons arrived on the other end of river.

Luke flicked his fingered from within the rabbit hole and used his dark magic to create a wall from the water in the river, temporarily stopping the guardian angels from flying through to attack. After a short while of anticipating for the water wall to collapse, the wall turned into solid ice immediately as the sun lapsed past the middle of the sky and winded towards the east to set.

Darkness arose in the form of dark grey fog, whisking and worming through the woods from different directions and arising up to form more dark-shadowed structures. Olivia knew it would be impossible to see them within the darkness and thus threw sprinkles of white angel dust above to brighten the area. Her fellow guardian angels followed her leadership and also threw grains of white angel dust towards the sky, and within seconds, the last ray of sunshine vanished, leaving them surrounded by her earthling's darkness.

Olivia and a cavalry of guardians were ambushed from all angles by Quinton's darkest monsters. His shadows attacked and fought against his own faith, which led Olivia to believe that her own earthling was indeed committing suicide and needed to be saved from his worst self. She knew they were at a disadvantage with regard to using their powers because they were inside the earthling's mind. She knew the only way they could win this war was by defending themselves for a while until Quinton could address his darkest fears.

His shadowed structures struck sharp black blades towards the angels whilst they defended themselves and attempted to retreat towards a large empty green field surrounded by large red roses. Olivia hoped for the best whilst fighting alongside her parents and other guardian angels to help Quinton from his pain and to bring peace into his heart. She didn't realise it at that moment, whilst fighting for her own survival that she needed to stop fighting against him and listen to his heart.

A loud throbbing beat emerged from above and rippled through the sky which lapsed onto a conclusion. The dark shadow's black blade clashed against her sharp silver sword, which allowed her to stop and evaluate her intentions for her earthling. She paused and unguarded herself, which irritated the dark shadow. It attempted to strike again. Its blade deteriorated into dust as she kneeled onto the green grass. Its roar echoed through the field whilst she unclenched her right hand and allowed her sword to drop onto the green grass then bowed down beside her sword and demonstrated peace. It made the shadowed structures disappear as her body burned bright in light red flames. Other guardian angels kneeled beside their swords and allowed their bodies to burn bright in sky blue flames, turning the area into an absorbable energy field for the earthling to gain strength within his heart, which would inevitably allow him to return to them.

Olivia followed the rhythm of Quinton's heart through the field and back towards the woods on the right beside a hill of tree houses. She stepped onto the original path. Her every touch left a burning imprint of red flames behind on her trail towards the frozen river. She planted her feet onto the ice, and it started to melt as she stared at the wall of ice ahead. The burning energy from the field began to levitate towards the sky, and Olivia could hear her earthling screaming in pain as she moved closer to the wall, melting a hole through it as she walked into it. She could hear Quinton's heartbeat growing louder as she stepped onto the other end of the river and started to march forward towards the shaded path within the woods, burning every single demon in her way.

There was a glow of burning golden statue shimmering from within the rabbit hole. Olivia stepped closer to the sound of his loudly beating golden heart, only to find everyone who'd attempted to end Quinton's life completely covered in gold, frozen, and unable to harm his body. She stepped into the hole and moved closer towards her golden earthling's body which remained still whilst hovering in mid-air.

'It's okay. I'm here to take you home now!' she mentioned and altered her upper body downwards to kiss his forehead then lifted his body upwards and felt its hard interior melting to her warmth.

Quinton's body guided itself from danger and turned back to normal whilst Olivia carried it away from the rabbit hole. Her burning red flames were muted and ground back into her body as she walked away with his body knocked unconscious, waiting for him to address his deepest and darkest fears.

'Nobody will hurt you now,' she promised whilst walking through the hole she'd created on the frozen ice wall.

She turned around and watched the ice wall shatter and collapse before her presence, and at that moment, she knew she'd conquered the wrath of evil and had managed to bring it down to the surface where it belonged. His body shivered from a cold fever whilst she flew upwards and entered the hole she'd also created in the kitchen ceiling. She shifted towards the right and quickly made her way into the living room then gently placed his body onto the couch, kneeling before him to be more attentive to his condition.

'You have to wake up soon,' she whispered whilst using her right palm to wipe off sweat from his forehead. 'I know you will wake up, Quinton, You just have to believe love,' she mentioned and stood up as the sun unveiled itself again from the west.

Prince's shadow emerged from the kitchen and entered into the living room, shading itself within the darkest part of the living room whilst the sun rays peeped through the tree hollow in the kitchen.

'I shouldn't be here right now, but I came to tell you that he is almost ready. Therefore, be there with him when he wakes up, Olivia. I must leave and advocate for his return!' he mentioned as his shadow slowly shrunk into nothing and teleported back to his natural body in a different world.

'But wait, how will you succeed this task at hand?' Olivia asked, sounding uncertain and confused.

'At times, we must sacrifice ourselves for the goodness of love. He will wake up when he hears people screaming out loud. I will be part of those people because at the end of the day, we are all one,' he said as his voice echoed within the living room hollow.

'For the goodness of love, huh?' she said and sat beside her earthling, waiting for his arrival whilst he battled his own monsters within.

Olivia stood up and immediately armed herself as soon as she heard footsteps railing closer. She turned her head towards the main door and saw a shadow appearing from behind the door. She was unsure of whom it was. She slowly moved closer towards the main entrance and waited as the doorknob turned clockwise.

Juliana opened the main door and smiled so beautifully, embracing the light within her heart as she walked in tall in her long white summer dress. Her face glowed as the light from the kitchen hollow shone onto her face. Peace radiated from her body which inevitably brought great comfort to Olivia who'd clamped her sharp silver sword back into her scabbard.

'The doctors worked their magic and have managed to stabilize his body hours ago. They've also managed to inject his body with hydrocodone-acetaminophen oral to numb his pain,' Juliana mentioned and walked into the living room to be with her lover again. 'I dozed off in the waiting area and woke up by our safe haven by our beach house minutes before he did. I even made love to him to try increase his pulse rate, but it didn't seem to work. I had to leave there though so that he learns to stand on his own in case anything does happen to me one day. It seems as if he is still battling, but I do believe that he will overcome his fears.' Juliana said and sat beside him. 'My baby, you need to wake up now' she whispered, and she parked her soft lips onto his dried lips, gentling wiping away the sweat on his face.

Her long curly brunette strands covered his face whilst she allowed the moment to be hers, slowly shutting her eyelids and softly imprinting her love onto his lips.

'I'm going to lay next to him, okay?' Juliana mentioned and snuggled right beside her lover, gently using her left thumb to scrape off the dirt from every inch of his face.

'Your love for him is out of this world, so mesmerizing and genuinely beautiful to see really,' Olivia mentioned whilst trying to find comfort on the couch parallel to her earthling.

'I'm sure you know this already, but it wasn't easy the first time around,' Juliana said and turned her head towards the right to make eye contact with Olivia. 'But I'm always there for him, just like you, which definitely means that you love him too, and I understand that because he is such an amazing person to be around, but he isn't perfect, which makes him perfect for me.'

'I wish to find real love too!' Olivia said and smiled whilst feeling nostalgic to the bone. 'I want it to be just as unique and sweet,' she mentioned and heard more footsteps railing in towards the main door.

'Relax, Olivia. The war has been won,' Juliana said as Olivia jumped up in paranoia. 'You mustn't forget that you are in my world too, Olivia. I know Quinton so well and everything that bothers him, and I can tell you right now that you are about to be one happy angel. Everything you know about love is about to be amplified,' Juliana mentioned whilst Olivia walked towards the main door, trying to anticipate the best possible outcome whilst turning the doorknob.

Theodore walked in, smiling so gracefully to her beautiful flower flourishing to his ocean-blue eyes, which essentially made him realize that he missed Olivia so much. He'd had fully recovered after all the lost descendants had cropped out from the core of the land, leaving small shreds of their souls within the ground to keep it from rooting again.

'I'm so sorry for leaving you' he mentioned.

They held on to each other tightly which revealed how deeply their love ran. They finally unguarded their hearts and rested their own monsters aside, imminently learning to accept the illusion presented by the moment, misunderstanding the reality of it, and for that Olivia knew she'd become just as naïve as everyone else for falling in love because she knew that people always have the misfortune of creating their own deemed luck and end up misinterpreting it by calling it fate, only to find out that premature ideas of settling could've been avoided. Essentially it felt good to be just as weak as her partner because she knew that he would be there for her if she were to completely fall for him.

'I missed you so much,' Olivia mentioned whilst brushing her right cheek against his brut muscular shaved right cheek, slowly moving her face to catch a kiss.

'Great, more love-struck idiots' Miguel mentioned whilst brushing past the front door, gently patting Theodore's black hair. 'Feels good to be alive!' he mentioned, which made Theodore laugh out loud,

'Yes, brother, it does feel good to be alive!' Theodore said and stepped away from Olivia then followed Miguel into the kitchen, and whilst they confided in each other, more lost descendants railed through the entrance, entering the tree house to fuel strength into the the earthling's heart whilst he battled a war within himself. Nathaniel entered last and stood beside Olivia whilst everyone else gathered beside Quinton, waiting for him to wake up.

'The land will begin to take root again soon, and the guardians will burn this place to the ground when the trees dry up, eliminating all evil spirits hovering within the woods, and it will force Quinton to deal with his own fears.' Nathaniel said and walked towards the kitchen, glancing towards the night sky, and indirectly wondering where they'd live whilst staring at all creatures of the night groaning whilst fleeing away from guardians who'd began to clean the earthling's subconscious by throwing orange flames at feather dragons over the great mountain wall far ahead.

'Therefore, do not leave this tree house until he is conscious again. He needs to leave everything behind before moving on with his life! Smoke will appear within him in a form of dark grey fog. Therefore, don't panic when he starts coughing. That will bring his lungs cleansing for all the cigarettes he has ever smoked, and in a way, it will clean his mind from temptation and wretched mentally, aborting his mind from the worst things he'd ever done and the worst things he will contemplate to do. He must destroy the worst part of himself. Otherwise, it will haunt his soul for eternity,' he said and turned around as Victoria entered from the living room.

'I'm glad you are okay!' Victoria said and held on to Nathaniel tightly and whilst they did so, Olivia took a quick glance at Theodore who'd been staring at her the entire time.

'You all had me worried, you know!' Victoria said aloud, which caught everyone else's attention for a few seconds.

'We are survivors, my dear. Nothing can withhold us from persevering!' Cindy mentioned whilst clenching on to Miguel with such great joy,

'Maybe I shouldn't have said anything to her' Miguel said, cracking a joke whilst trying to run away,

463

'You aren't going anywhere. You are all mine!' Cindy said, smooching his right cheeks and smothering him with love.

They'd completely forgotten about Quinton for a while, chatting away in twos whilst the bright sun reappeared from the west, swiping through the blue sky in a flash and vanishing away over the eastern mountains within seconds. His body began to quiver from the heat, right beside Juliana who'd been attentive towards him throughout. She knew it was the changed in temperature commencing from the flash of sunlight and the cold darkness which had caused his body to quiver from a fever.

'Do not be alarmed. He will be fine!' Juliana said, assuring everyone else of his well-being. 'He needs to go through this!' she added whilst stroking his sweaty forehead and clutching her left leg around his body. 'His world is beginning to dry up. Let's place his body in the bath upstairs and run it with holy water. It will ease the transition and scrape off any demons lingering then turn the water within his bloodstream into lava to burn anything holding him back,' Victoria suggested whilst walking past the crowd to assist Theodore to pick up Quinton's sweaty body.

'I'll be beside him until I have to wake up' Juliana mentioned and trailed behind Theodore and Victoria.

'I must meet with my parents before they start burning the woods,' Olivia stated and walked towards the main door,

'We will come with you,' Freda suggested and followed Olivia, clenching her right hand against Yumna's right hand.

'Come with us my love!' Freda said as Yumna slowed down.

'They won't approve of us,' Yumna said, hesitating to leave because she was afraid of being judged again,

'Don't be silly. Of course they will approve. They have good hearts and do not base merit on someone's sexuality. They know that it's not their job to judge nor resent. They are where they are because they know how to love,' Freda said and turned around by the blue wooden door. 'It's okay. You do not have to be afraid anymore,' Freda said and watched her lover move closer.

Juliana stood by the bedroom door, closely observing the two lovers consoling each other of the fact that it's okay to be different, and she finally understood it all whilst embracing the difference railing towards her green eyes, understanding that love really does prevail over everything and no amount of hate poured into one's soul can cluster their hearts from overcoming the evil made by those without pure souls. She slowly stepped away from the moment as soon as Freda parked her dry lips onto Yumna's crack lips. Juliana turned and slowly proceeded forth towards the tree hollow on the opposite end and watched autumn leaves brush off the branches as the winds circulated around, leaving the forest naked and clustered with dried leaves on the walkways within the woods.

'We must leave now, but keep an eye out for him. I'm sure we will meet again one day, Juliana. We are always around,' Victoria mentioned and stepped away from the wooden oval bath, gently placing her arms around Juliana to say goodbye.

'I know I will see you again,' Juliana responded and glanced at Quinton's body within the wooden oval bath, wondering when he'd awake.

'I'll wait for Olivia downstairs before departing with the rest,' Theodore mentioned, slowly moving away in an attempt to see Olivia again, for he'd allowed himself to be clumsy for falling in love, but he also knew that she was leaving as soon as Quinton could regain conscious and thus made a decision to try convince her otherwise.

'Thank you so much for helping out,' Juliana said, acknowledging the strength that the lost descendants carried within their hearts to care even after they'd been cast away to the valley of lost angels after their death.

She allowed her pain to pour out of the wooden taps, filling the oval bath with warm water to keep Quinton warm.

'What's going on in that head of yours?' she asked whilst observing the bruises on his face, slowly scooping water with her right palm to pour onto his cuts. 'Arabella and I are waiting for you,' she whispered into his right ear and heard commotion railing downstairs.

465

Juliana held on to Quinton's right hand tightly and remained right next to him whilst everyone else plodded forward.

Olivia burst through the bedroom door with an immediately notice, yelling out whilst swiping through the sunlight flashes. 'Juliana, it's time to go!'

'He isn't ready. He needs to wake up within the woods, which will allow him to leave everything behind!' Juliana stood up and yelled back. 'But if you must go, then leave. I will stay with him until he is ready to go.'

The silence was deafening whilst Quinton's body quivered within the bath, which left Olivia and Juliana at a standstill. They tried to figure out why he hadn't gain consciousness yet whilst screams grew louder within his mind.

'Be patient with him. He is the love of my life, and I want him back home,' Juliana mentioned and sat down again. 'He needs to wake up' she said whilst cuddling his body,

'Okay, I understand. I will wait with you,' Olivia said and stood still whilst flames enlarged within the distance.

They could hear Luke's legion of lost souls screaming out as most demons burned within the woods, wolves ran, and feathered dragons flew towards the east. Their loud cries began to disturb Juliana, which made her realise that she was about to wake up in the real world. Her body slowly turned pale and cold of which she remained quiet. A tear leaked from her eyelid, for she was left helpless to bring Quinton back with her.

'Bring him home for me,' Juliana pleaded as her body started to dissolve and turn into ash within the bath.

'Promise me, Olivia! Promise me!' she yelled.

'I promise!' Olivia yelled back and walked into the bathing area and noticed Juliana's ashes hovering over the water surface, surrounding Quinton's body with fibres of love, and within seconds of Juliana's disappearance, fireballs struck down and onto the woods, mostly burning down all the feathered dragons towards the eastern mountain wall.

'Everyone is leaving, but I will stay here until you are ready to leave,' Olivia said whilst kneeling down beside the oval bath just to be closer to her earthling.

'Olivia, we must go!' Theodore yelled but felt Olivia's deafening silence relish through his curiosity whilst he stepped into the bath area and discovered her holding on to her earthling tightly.

'I'm not leaving him here,' she said and shut her eyes, allowing her mind to connect and dwell within his deeper consciousness.

'You don't have to leave him. Just bring him with us,' Theodore suggested.

'No, I want all his demons destroyed here. He has to be a newborn again. Therefore, it is also my duty to clean him before delivering him back to earth,' she mentioned. 'But if you have to go, then I will follow your scent as soon as he wakes up,' she said and turned her head towards the left to make eye connect with Theodore, assuring him of her true intention to be with him.

'If you do not follow, then I will come and look for you. I will make my way back here to find you, and if you are not here, then I will leave the valley of lost angels and make my way to heaven's gates to plead to those guarding your sacred heart to allow me to have you back. I want to be with you when this has been dealt with,' he said and leaned in for true love's sacred kiss.

Their lips slowly connected, and a bright spark emerged within their souls and brightened their skin completely, allowing their faces to glow in happiness. The kiss imminently sealed their fate, and they knew nothing would ever be the same again as the rushing throb of love impounded their hearts and merged into one.

Olivia smiled and held on to her earthling, allowing her mind to dive back into his deeper consciousness to observe his performance. She watched his body collapse onto the wooden floor in the main bedroom of the beach house.

Theodore walked away then turned around by the bedroom and glanced at his lover whilst the sun went faster than before. He found himself infatuated by her presence whilst standing there, trying to visualise an endless possibility of their future. A part of him believed that he would never see her again because she was from a different world, but the idea of trying brought him some sort of hope. He buried his heart into a heap of lies which he'd told himself about being with Olivia, and she kneeled there beside her earthling hoping for the best, not only for love, but also for her earthling's arrival.

Theodore and Olivia wondered how they'd end up together as he walked away, levitating towards everyone else waiting by the main door.

Theodore swiped through an opening above within the large hollow and brushed past dry branches. He led everyone else away from the forest fire heading towards the main tree house then slowed down and glanced back at the devastation erupting around, observing as the wild winds spiralled the fire anticlockwise around the main tree house. There were multiple guardian angels throwing balls of fire in other parts the forest, burning the dried trees down to the ground.

Olivia remained glued to her earthling whilst the heat increased and observed as the smoke clouded the scenery. She coughed repeatedly and shrunk her head into her earthling's shoulder to cover her nose from inhaling particles of ash. Quinton started to cough whilst evil spirits searched around for a safe haven, attempting to worm through his nostrils to reside inside his body or attempt to put an end to his life again. He could hear loud cries growing within his mind. Olivia opened her dreamy ocean-blue eyes and saw Quinton clamp his hands onto the edges of the wooden bath, and at that moment, she knew he'd overcome the worst part of myself and conquered a war which had endlessly dragged his heart through pain. He attempted to open his eyes as she pulled him off the oval bath and dragged him towards the bed, both coughing whilst fighting for their survival. She could hear him speak within his mind.

'I'm finally ready to go home now,' he said as she strapped his wrists and ankles around her body.

'I know, love. I've been waiting,' she replied as she crawled away from the bed, trying to avoid the smoke hovering above. 'Come! Let's go home!' she yelled and shot through the tree hollow, swiping through clouds of smoke in a flash, and as they reached the sky, the sun started to move normally, giving her full confirmation of the earthling's clarity.

A balance restored itself into Quinton's mind as Olivia's memories settled into his memory bank. His lake of wonders rippled slowly and turned steady within his mind as everything settled to the norm. His bruised eyes remained shut throughout, but he'd finally regained consciousness from his deeper consciousness, and he'd finally made peace with everything occurring, the fact that his real world could never be saved. It was doomed. He accepted the fact that he was born into a democratically facade world with systems carefully constructed to entitle the average minds with illusive hope to believe that their voices and lives mattered when in all aspects, they have no idea that they were only born to die. He thought carefully about destiny itself then finally came to a conclusion that there was a small group of people out there in the world who've devised a plan for every single human being on planet Earth. It wasn't hard to swallow for him anymore as he wandered into the back trails of his thoughts, wondering what people would do if they knew the truth of their existence. Would they riot and burn down everything to the ground if they knew that they have been pawned by their own leaders for profit? Would they accept the fact that there are people out there who have made decisions for them on how they should proceed in their daily schedules and how much money they are allowed to earn? What jobs are they allowed to have, and what type of lifestyle are they allowed to live? Quinton wasn't upset with those thoughts at all.

He merely accepted that blindness doesn't always mean that a person cannot see nor see the truth, but that their hearts have been shaded into darkness away from burning brightly and shining against all odds. He understood that the people have been robbed of their own wealth by the people they have entrusted with power. Quinton made peace with the evil seed of corruption which had sold Africa to the highest bidder, and it didn't bother his heart anymore because he finally felt detached from human conventions. His body, mind, and soul were one within his heart. He listened to his heart-throb loudly like an African drum, and he knew that he was finally a real man, and nobody could ever take that away from him.

Olivia glided over green hilltops on her quest to find everyone else. She followed Theodore's scent, flying over flat green lands and sloping valleys after slowly flapping her bright white wings past a steady wide lake stretching out towards defrosted mountains at all angles. She didn't want to leave her newfound love and thus followed his scent towards a large grey dried oak tree situated perfectly on top of a hill. Green leaves started to grow as they landed onto a flat large wooden base in the middle of the tree. Theodore's scent remained so powerful whilst she inhaled his essence, daydreaming about him which essentially made her realise that she'd become addicted to him. She needed him to appear once more and thus called out his name whilst undoing Quinton's strings off her back.

'Theodore!' she called out repeatedly.

'Are you sure they are here?' Quinton asked and sat down to rest his aching body, merely trying to address the explosions occurring inside his legs.

'They are here. He wouldn't have led me here if he didn't want me to find him,' she mentioned whilst strolling clockwise, observing green leaves as they enlarged and covered empty spaces around. 'Be patient. I will take you home just now. I must see him again,' she mentioned whilst smiling to the beautiful scenery flourishing. 'I can't leave without devising a plan to see him after this,' she mentioned, impatiently moving around, railing on to the suspicion that her parents were on their way to take her home.

'See, love feels amazing, doesn't it?' Quinton asked.

'Not really, just frustrating and consuming, to say the least,' Olivia said and smiled.

'He is around. Take the time to say goodbye,' Quinton mentioned whilst heading towards the edge of a tree branch to embrace the scenery flourishing around, glancing at birds chirping above, and following all five water streams clashing to one waterfall below, flushing down into one large hole.

Dusk slowly adorned the hour glass, and Olivia knew her parents had completed the request she made to the covenant—to destroy all elements of evil in her earthling's subconscious. All lost descendants landed onto the wooden base beside her, and they were all uncertain of their next move, unsure of where their new home would be. One thing was certain—they were all together, and nothing else mattered but that unified bond.

'I think he ready to go home now,' Nathaniel said to Victoria.

'He looks ready, Olivia. Let's send him back,' Victoria said, trying to catch Olivia's attention but knew she'd be ignored, for Olivia's mind was in different spectrum whilst holding on to Theodore.

'So when will I see you again?' Theodore asked, trying to hold every second he had with his newfound lover.

'I'm not so sure. I wish I could spend time with you,' Olivia said, staring into his deep blue eyes, wondering if it were possible to stop her guardianship work and allow herself to finally feel love. 'I will make my way back to you,' she mentioned and leaned in a for kiss,

'Are you really?' Theodore asked sceptically, uncertain of their future because he knew that love was an unsure feeling, leaving his heart naked and vulnerable.

'Yes, believe me. I will come back,' she assured him and parked her lips onto his. 'Even if it's the last thing I do, I will come back,' she said, making a promise she had no intention of keeping because knew her love for Quinton ran deeper than her infatuation for a lost descendant.

She created a trail of deceit whilst brushing past everyone on her way to confide in her earthling, feeling guilty because she'd refrained from being honest, mainly confused and scared to allow her heart to drift off into the unknown.

'You have to have the courage to love. It's a mesmerising feeling which requires strength and understanding,' Quinton mentioned whilst staring into the distance.

'You aren't upset with me for having such thoughts of leaving you?' Olivia asked and sat beside her earthling on the edge of the tree branch, dwelling inside her indecisiveness.

'Not at all, Olivia, you must find your own path after I've have returned back home,' Quinton mentioned while he sat there, observing his wounds as they all healed whole. 'I won't be mad. Stay here. It will allow me to visit you from time to time,' he said and turned his head to see if Olivia had thought about residing amongst other lost descendants.

Olivia felt strained between two options but also knew that she would be able to see her earthling often if she were to stay with the rest of the lost descendants. She knew it would be the biggest decision she'd ever make, and the fact that she'd had a glimpse and feel and taste the sweetness of love, her heart would never be the same again.

Her parents landed onto the wooden base beside the rest of the descendants and greeted every single one of them, and whilst they did so, Olivia wondered what she'd do with the scripture imprinted inside her heart, undoubtedly concluding that her life would be at risk if any demons knew of its location.

'Do not worry about that. Nathaniel and Victoria will protect you from any demons, especially if mine come looking your way,' Quinton said and glanced towards the sky as it darkened with flicks of stars scattered everywhere. His brown eyes peeled and allowed his mind to imaginatively see Juliana on his bed, back on the outskirts of Gaborone, Botswana. His heart uncloaked, and a tear leaked from his right eyelid. He'd missed her so much and wanted to be with her again.

'Olivia!' Trevor called out as Olivia jumped and rushed over to her parents. 'Come here!' he yelled, standing still farther away from everyone else, awaiting for his daughter to unveil her true intentions. He stared into her blue eyes and understood what she needed in her world. 'Is that what you really want?' he asked. 'You want to live here with them?'

'Yes, Father, I want to live here with them. They aren't so different from us,' Olivia said. 'I'm in love, and I want to live more than anything,' she mentioned, sobbing away in embarrassment because she believed she'd disappointed her father.

'No, no, no, do not cry, my love. I completely understand, but will it be fine if we came to see you once in a while?' Trevor asked and held on to his daughter from behind.

'Yes, of course you can come see me,' she said, making a firm decision to stay.

'Then you do not understand that you will lose your ability to find us above nor have the ability to perform any good magic. Your feathers won't be white, and you won't be able to protect your earthling anymore, nor will you be able to read each other's minds,' he mentioned as she stepped away,

'I understand the decision that I've made,' Olivia said, and as she turned around, her wings shaded into light grey and further dyed into dark grey.

Olivia's parents flashed off within a blink of an eye, and Olivia knew that she'd have to live with the decision she'd just made, to fall in love, leaving everything she knew behind to start a future with a lost descendant. It all became surreal whilst walking back to Quinton who'd completely zoned into the images of himself slowly waking up on the hospital bed.

'Quinton, are you ready to go home now?' Olivia asked but had no idea that she could not teleport between two worlds.

'Not to worry, I will wake up by myself. Juliana's love remains strong. Her love will bring me back' He mentioned as his body began to levitate upwards, slowly floating away from Olivia and the rest of the lost descendants crowding beneath.

'Do come back to visit!' Olivia yelled and then turned her head to glance at Theodore who'd managed to gently place his right arm around her waist.

Quinton turned and faced the oak tree beneath, observing as all the lost descendants' wings detached from their backs, including Olivia herself, leaving them powerless and back to being average humans. He understood why it was all happening and could somehow foresee the future of the spectrum below. His subconscious world would become real one day. It would become his new reality as soon as his heart fails and stops beating, and truly speaking, he could not wait until death railed towards his soul again. The idea of rediscovering this world brought much excitement into his heart, but until that day, he would remain patient and settle down on planet Earth, marry Juliana Rose, and have her beautiful ruby red rose wet at every turn.

Chapter Twenty-Four

A Lover's Hangover

Months had passed into a dreadful winter season. Most city street corners were vacant over this weekend, almost lifeless without actions, and it look like it was about to be the coldest winter ever experienced. It was the worst by far, temperatures declining all the way down to minus five degrees during all the cold nights. All tree branches around all the suburbs areas had dried up. The wind circulating around the south-east district had grown stronger over the last days, but it seemed as if everything had turned back to normal in Quinton's life. He'd successfully recovered from his horrific accident and had even managed to maintain a balance in his life after experiencing life on a different spectrum. Most importantly, he had the love of his life rest by his side, nursing his body back to health.

Juliana's stomach had grown, and it seemed as though she'd be expecting within the next month. She'd adored the idea of starting a family with the love of her life on the outskirts of the city. She wanted to settle down and become a wife to a handsome African man. Although the news rattled her mother, Marissa Rose grew to the idea and accepted her daughter's decisions to leave her all alone. It seemed as if both sides of the Barker and Rose families were admin to the wedding proposal, but neither one of them had hope towards the marriage actually succeeding given the fact that they secretly hated one other.

On this cold Saturday evening, Quinton became extremely observant to everything around him, mainly discovering how beautiful his life was about to become and how deeply his love for Juliana would soon manifest and become more magnified. He glanced at his beautiful eight-month pregnant fiancée seated opposite him on a long leather couch within his family penthouse sitting room. Her desirable body had been cloaked with a one-piece night suit, a long dark purple silk nightgown stretching all the way down to a her ankles and a pair of dark purple suede slippers covering her feet. She sat quietly, stroking her plump stomach underneath a brightly lit one-metre wooden night lamp beside the couch. Quinton remained quiet and extra observant whilst seated on a single dark brown leather couch next to another brightly lit lamp. He was wearing a new mustard turtleneck sweater, black slim-fitted chinos, and black ankle socks. The visual in front of him brought a smile to his face whilst he tried to focus on his reading session of an old Fitzgerald novel, turning another page slowly whilst glancing at his beautiful fiancée humming and singing to their unborn baby. It seemed surreal as he measured his status of a new man who'd pleaded to become better than that of his own father, deeming to do things differently and to accept the responsibility of bringing a new life into the world. He cherished the beauty of parenthood whilst seated, listening to his fiancée talk to their foetus within. Nothing else brought him greater joy than seeing Juliana flourish on her way to motherhood. She'd grown into such an extraordinary woman, gladly accepting the gift that Quinton had given to her and so willing, she was ready to return it to him. It made her stronger as a woman, and she finally felt the attachment that all mothers felt before and after giving birth.

'I can't wait until you get here, my nana,' Juliana whispered and blew a kiss towards her stomach, glowing to the thought of watching

Arabella explore around her family garden in London where she'd grown up.

'Do you want some more tea or hot chocolate this time round?' Quinton asked and stood up, walking towards the love of his love to pick up her beige tea mug, moving closer to give Juliana a kiss.

'Hot chocolate please,' Juliana mentioned and arched her back as her unborn baby kicked. 'Oh my!'

'Are you okay?' Quinton asked whilst slowly kneeling on a dark brown furred carpet right in front of Juliana.

'Yeah, although I don't think I will ever get used to her big kicks,' Juliana said and placed her warm right hand onto her plumy stomach, slowly stroking her edges to soothe herself from discomfort.

'You are doing just fine, babe,' Quinton mentioned, walking towards an installed open wooden bar right beside a closed sliding door, pressing onto an On button of the kettle.

'Just add three teaspoons of white sugar this time around,' Juliana said and turned her head towards the right to look at Quinton who'd completely zoned out towards two artificial palm trees by the balcony. 'Baby, what is on your mind?' she asked and stood up, frowning whilst moving closer, uncertain of what had driven her fiancé quiet.

'You miss her, don't you?' she asked and stood behind him, gently holding on to his warm body.

'I hope she is okay there!' he said, unsure of how to seek guidance without his own guardian angel by his side.

'I'm sure she is fine, baby,' Juliana said, attempting to be positive towards the situation at hand.

'I left her within my own world, and for the first time in a long time, I can feel its uncertainty cropping out again,' he mentioned whilst staring at wild winds whipping over the glass walls on the opposite building.

'It's not the same without Olivia, huh?' Juliana asked and placed her left ear onto his left shoulder blade, patiently listening to his heartbeat.

'I keep having unimaginable whims of what could happen to her in that world!' Quinton said. 'They do not have a system in place like we do here, and evil lingers within every cave ready to strike at those vulnerable' he mentioned and sidestepped towards the left to pour hot water into their mugs for himself and Juliana.

'But there is nothing you can do now, Quinton. You have a child on the way,' Juliana mentioned and sat onto a dark wooden stool.

'I do not having any intention of returning there, but I do hope that she is fine,' he said and railed through his own thoughts whilst the silver kettle whispered and steamed onto all the empty glass shelves on the back bar counter.

'Go and sit on the couch, baby. That stool looks so uncomfortable!' he suggested and picked up both mugs cups, gesturing for Juliana to lead them back to the couch.

'Please increase the air conditioner temperature, my love' he said and sat on top of a clean blanket which Juliana had used to cover her feet in the afternoon.

'Oh, that is horrific to see,' Juliana said after Quinton unmuted the plasma screen clamped onto the dark maroon wallpaper right beside the sealed sliding door.

'It's absolutely disgusting to see,' Quinton responded, staring at the screen and witnessing thousands of students being brutally attacked by the police in attempts to end the increase of tertiary tuitions.

'Resembles the youth revolution, portrays an error of the mid-1970s, don't you think?' Juliana asked and sat beside Quinton who had his brown eyes glued towards the events occurring within the next country.

'It's disgusting to see how animalistic governments in our own continent can become,' Quinton mentioned, diving his mind through the fifty-two-inch plasma screen, watching as his first love chanted through the windy streets of Cape Town, South Africa.

He glanced at the sliding door as winds grew stronger outside and wondered how his future could have turned out if he'd stayed in South Africa. Would he have been right there with his beautiful ex? Or would he have been part of the small selected few who expressed their racial opinions via social media or cowardly hiding behind their desktops instead of becoming part of a revolution, using hashtags to attract attention?

There was a silent moment, almost deafening to say the least. He watched the screen and saw an interview of one of the elite leaders within the region proclaiming himself as a pawned fool by making a treacherous joke to start a movement to make sure that students will fall instead.

'What a fuckin' joke,' Quinton said, lashing out towards the matter at hand. 'I look at the way an empire is established, how countless years are scarified, how tears drop from pain endured and how sweat drips on the blood soil of Africa. It's really sad to see that there are leaders out there who've been handed over power and squander its true value by plunging many years of hard work back onto the ground,' Quinton said.

'Come, lay back and rest your head, my love' Juliana mentioned. 'You do not have to worry. Your turn to make a difference will come. Be patient with failed father figures. Their mistakes bring excellence within the next generations, and I do not doubt you and your ability to lead. You will be greater and extraordinary. The world will love you like I do. They will see what I see, and honestly speaking, I am so honoured to be able to sleep next to you every night, and I cannot wait to be your wife. I will walk with you through eternity because even through death, I know that I will find you waiting for me. You are so patient and so amazing to be around,' Juliana said, stroking his short black hair backwards, trying to keep him from thinking about his own father who apparently had a few weeks to live.

Quinton had not returned to his family residence after his recovery, unsettled by the idea of reuniting with his deceitful family of liars, embezzlers, cheaters, and murders. Regardless of the family's reputation, it had appeared that Marcus had dipped his shaded heart into goodness by claiming full responsibility for Steve's death, clearing his bastard son's name from being prosecuted by the state a day after the accident had happened. One thing was clear whilst Quinton lay there beside his fiancée, listening to his unborn daughter's feet shuffle within Juliana's womb—he wanted to be a better father. It was quite clear that he'd had enough of assholes dwelling around him, pretending to look after his best interest whilst hoping to achieve some sort of payment in return from supposedly having a good heart.

Having a family seemed ideal and healthy for Quinton's soul. It brought perspective into his world, and the responsibility of taking care of Juliana and their own unborn baby made him feel like he'd accomplished greatness. His new little family changed the way he pursued his life, and finally he'd stopped drinking and had ended his off-and-on cycles of smoking cigarettes. It felt better to be clean within, for he could finally breathe properly and think clearly.

'Honey, you are dozing off, bedtime,' Juliana whispered.

'No, stay here with me,' Quinton mumbled and scooted towards the left, allowing Juliana to rest right beside him.

Juliana turned the viewing on the plasma screen, channelling to their music collection of indie, alternative, and folk music. Quinton dozed off to the beautiful melodies and rippling bell waves of a song. His thoughts unravelled and guided him towards a familiar place of peace, striding his mind onto a straight path in between steep rocky mountain walls leading towards a green field with a rare grey thorn tree in the middle. He'd implanted a memorial ground for his guardian angel as a reminder that pure love did exist in his own world. He stood before the tree and channelled his own frustration onto it, allowing it to grow long as peace restored itself into his heart again. It seemed as if his heart was still rattled by his long void of leaving Olivia behind. He couldn't find it in himself to forget because she was the only one who'd made a sacrifice to ensure his safety whilst he battled his own demons. It felt right to make a memorial ground to visit often and maybe sit there by himself, flashing through his own books of past events.

He pressed his heavy head onto one of the lengthened roots sticking out beside flacks of grass, allowing his mind to drift further into his deeper subconscious of a world he'd left behind. It was the only way he could see everything, but there was only one glitch—he wasn't able to neither participate nor interact with anyone he'd left behind. All he could do was observe the world within his mind from an angle, like a god would do. He turned himself into a wooden pigeon and plunged his mind down towards a green field, flying over hectares of green grass to the edge of a cliff. Quinton discovered a world completely different from the one he'd left behind, with hectares of deforested land below gushing with black dead roots scattered everywhere, and he could see descendants sons of lost descendants who'd turned human whipping other transfused humans—people obtained the same abilities as their animals—brutally lashing them towards wooden gates of a growing empire which was bricked with grey stone. There was no evidence of life from the twenty-foot stone wall railed all the way back the edge of the cliff.

Quinton flew down and landed on top of the stone wall, glancing down at the empire that Theodore had built for his queen, Olivia. The image gushing towards Quinton's bird's-eye view reminded him that humans can easily be seduced by power, whisking from one hand to another, possessing every ambitious man to believe that his purpose is to rule over others. He could see how easily evil could spread within his world like a plague, destroying every glimpse of pure brightness in its way, turning the smallest and purest of things from the light of day and into horrific monsters of the night. The image before Quinton's eye initially reminded him that his mind can be easily manipulated by his anger towards the people in his life. He flew over multiple villa, bakery store, shoe store, and welding store rooftops on his way to the only tower tolling over the town. He landed onto an arched window at the top and discovered a baby couch at the end of the oval wall, right next to the entrance of a staircase.

'Our child should not leave this tower until he has grown!' Theodore yelled from the bottom, sounding paranoid as Olivia stepped onto the final step, unveiling herself to the sunlight.

She gently placed her son onto the couch and turned around, slowly walking towards the arched window to observe the forest that her husband had destroyed on his quest for more power. She'd been blinded by the sun for a while whilst stepping closer to the window.

'Olivia, can you hear me!' Quinton said, unsure of whether she'd remember him.

She glanced down slowly and observed a wooden pigeon chirping repeatedly. It hopped closer, chirping loudly, unafraid of her presence as it hopped onto her right hand. She slowly lifted her right hand and looked into its eyes. Quinton looked into her strained blue eyes and saw flashes of how her life turned into shambles. She had no idea that she was looking at her earthling in the face and rightfully so. She yelled out Theodore's name.

'Witchery in the towers!' she yelled, frightened of the bird she'd held closely to her face.

Theodore dove into the room, striking out his sword, prepared to attack the wooden pigeon as it flew away and turned around halfway. Quinton glanced back and discovered how paranoid his guardian had become after forfeiting her right to resume her duties as an angel.

'Guards!' Theodore yelled, which awoke their baby boy from his sleep.

An armed guard dressed in shimmed bronze plates whipped out his wooden bow and arrow, aiming towards the bird. Quinton attempted to fly away as the first arrow missed his right wing, and as he turned around to fly back to the cliff, he felt the silver metal pierce through his back, awaking him from his dream and back to his reality.

He opened his brown eyes and starred at the muted plasma screen, almost in disbelief of what he'd seen within himself. Juliana opened her green eyes and kept quiet whilst trying to come up with a conclusion of why Quinton's mind wasn't synchronised to hers as of late.

'Are you okay?' she asked and placed her right palm onto his right shoulder. 'Come back down and rest!' she whispered whilst he stared at the outside world, observing wild winds brushing against the glass walls.

'I don't know if I will ever be okay,' he said and planted his back onto the couch.

'Sure you will. It takes time to become mentally strong, my love' she whispered and reached in to kiss his lips.

They smooched for a few minutes, but Juliana's distraction could not keep Quinton from railing his thought train towards the dream he'd just had, which initially reminded him that he wasn't in complete control of his mind. He knew that his heart still desired the finer things in life, to own an empire or some sort. Therefore, he shut his brown eyes and listened to his heart throbbing loudly, aligning its beat to his head, giving him a mild headache. He could feel the bright sun shading his face darker and could feel its sharp rays of life burning against his eyelids, advocating and taking him back to place he'd never departed from.

The silence was deafening, leading Quinton's heart into an oblivion of confusion as he opened his strained brown eyes to a striped pattern of bright red and white. He lay down alone on a red blanket on top of large block of strapped hay. His skin had turned pale, dehydrated from the alcohol he'd consumed from the night before during the hours of the music and carnival festival. He gathered his thoughts into one motion and realised that he'd blacked out after meeting Juliana Rose for the first time. All that was left around him was an empty tent, a wooden art frame and the artwork Juliana had finished painting after her solo performance. He sat up straight, blinking repeatedly, almost on the verge of weeping because everything that had happened to him before was nothing but an illusive nightmare.

It drove him mad as he sat still, trying to figure out if Juliana was real, if she'd just left without saying goodbye after her performance, or if she had left because she didn't care. Everything about this exact moment left Quinton completely baffled as he glanced up at the painting she'd made—a replica of the one he'd seen during his vivid dream patterns. Juliana's art piece initially made him wonder how deeply their love really ran, for it had enabled him to foresee a future with a woman he'd met less than ten hours ago. A tear raced down his right cheek as he stood up and planted his feet onto the dried hay grass, slowly walking towards the art piece in confusion.

'Our love will overflow. It will stream through eternity' were the words railing through Quinton's ear encrypted from Juliana's voice. He quickly turned around and found himself staring at an empty space between four blocks of hay and an empty tent ahead. The wind blew and brushed against his face, and he could sense Juliana's scent worming through his nostrils, reminding him of how strongly she owned his heart. He desired nothing else but to be with the woman of his dreams. He felt empty without her around, which drove him insane as another tear raced from his left cheek. It reminded him that nothing in the world was certain and everything he held dearly in his heart could indeed be taken away from him.

He walked away from the empty tent even more depressed than the moment when he'd entered into it, walking past open trashy green grounds with the heat basking down on his head. It made him wonder if he'd ever see the woman he'd just fallen in love with. There were flashing images of her vibrant smile gushing into his heart as he walked through the front park gates, and into a silver hunchback cab to depart back to the city he'd ran away from.

'Quinton!' Juliana yelled and threw a cup of coffee onto the floor, rushing towards the main park gates to be with the love of her life,

'Wait!' she pleaded as he entered into the cab, watching it drive away. 'Lord, install strength into my heart please,' she pleaded and hailed another cab.

'Follow that cab please,' she said to the cab driver.

Juliana's heart grew impatient, for it also needed the love that Quinton had presented, and she knew that nobody else could bring her the peace she'd encountered from the previous night. She remained quiet as her cab followed his back to the platform, fidgeting and pulling the passenger seat belt back and forth.

'That will be ten pounds,' the cab driver said whilst Juliana counted her notes in the back seat, which drove her mad as she felt his heart throbbing away. She handed the cab driver money and rushed towards the stairs on the left side of the walkway, running through the empty tunnel to catch Quinton before his departure, swiping her own train card to proceed forward through the barriers.

Quinton dwelled by the yellow line, wondering what would happen if he was to step over the line and take his own life away, driven mad by his own thoughts. He believed that he'd be able to save Olivia from the wrath of evil if he were to pass on from this world.

'Quinton!' Juliana yelled, but her words drew Quinton further away from everything, concluding himself as insane because he thought of himself as delusional.

He stepped over the yellow line and stood still, awaiting for the train to arrive, attempting to take his life away. His world trembled and shook as the train railed closer towards the platform, railing in as its lights brightened the darkness within tunnel. He dipped his right foot towards uncertainty and leaped towards his death.

Juliana reached out with both hands, pulling Quinton's right hand backwards, dragging his body onto the tile floor as the train railed in. She held on to his body tightly, for she was scared of losing someone so special. It seemed as if Quinton's suicidal attempt had caught the nearest metropolitan police officer.

'What's going on here?' the grumpy fat officer asked, reaching from an angle for his black walky-talky clipped onto his right chest strap.

'Please do not alert others. I'm with him,' Juliana pleaded and looked at the officer, sounding sincere and scared for Quinton's well-being,

'I'll take him home. I promise. I'll get the help he needs,' she suggested and helped Quinton onto his feet whilst he remained stunned by her presence, glancing at her beautiful green eyes and concluding that he was born to be with Juliana Rose.

'I saw our whole lives together, and when I woke up without you, I was devastated. I didn't want to go on without you by my side,' he said, sounding crazy and confused at this new profound feeling of love mixed with a delusional glare of darkness.

'Then that's where I will be, right here by your side,' Juliana mentioned as the officer disappeared into the corridor towards the left. 'I will not leave you,' she said, and her words entered his ear, streaming down to his heart and changing his emotions all together.

And whilst they spoke, counselling each other and trying to figure out a way forward, Quinton's phone rang.

'Hello,' Quinton answered his father's call.

'Are you well, my son?'

'I'm good, just exhausted,' Quinton said whilst Juliana held on to his body tightly, promising to never let go of the love she'd just found.

'Well, finish up your semester. I've leased a navy blue yacht down by the coast and want you to sail it with me to Mauritius for the summer holiday!' Marcus Barker mentioned.

'I would like that very much,' Quinton responded, essentially forgiving his father for the abuse inflicted to his mother, which had left Quinton with a traumatised childhood, and after dropping the phone call, he felt liberated.

Quinton finally believed that love was definitely worth fight for, and as he entered the train with the love of his weary life, fiddling with an old rupee coin that Yumna had handed to him, to give to the old homeless man as a sign of hope. He remembered the old man and how unkind he was to him before. It swamped his heart with guilt as he hoped that Ol' John would forgive him for being inhuman and unkind. Quinton essentially understood that every decision he'd make from this day forth would not only impact him but would also impact Juliana as well. Therefore, he prayed for guidance, for the first time in his entire miserable life. He chose to do right by her side, and she chose to be by his side without questioning his merit, merely understanding that love knows no boundaries.

The train doors sealed shut, and he smiled through his hangover, placing his heavy head onto the seat headrest, and she placed her head onto his chest, listening to his heart throbbing extremely fast whilst gazing at the window towards her left and as the sunlight shone through. It made her face flourish. It showed how radiantly beautiful she was. A lot was on her mind as she braced herself for an unpredictable journey.

Juliana wondered if Quinton would fully accept her if he knew what she really was. She was afraid and ashamed to tell him the truth about her existence. Therefore, she mended her light brown feathers back into her skin right as she held on to his hands tightly. She remained cautious about opening up and confiding in a human being she'd just fallen in love with and therefore pleaded to keep her secret until he was ready to see it. They knew their lives would never be the same again as the train railed into another tunnel, disappearing into darkness.

The End

CPSIA information can be obtained
at www.ICGtesting.com
Printed in the USA
LVHW08s0138100818
586431LV00001B/11/P